Come bac

Luke remembers a few things. Just not his last name. Or anyone he ever knew. He knows that he's a supersoldier, genetically enhanced and loaded up with brain implants. He recently escaped from a year-long hell of captivity, and to protect his family and friends from his tormentors, he blocked most of his memories. Now he needs them back, fast…or he and those he loves will die agonizing deaths.

Luke's dangerous plan to reconnect with his past—and stay alive in the present—has drawn his enemies' attention to the tough and sexy Dani LaSalle. He's duty bound to protect the luscious beauty from the evil pursuing them, but he can't control the scorching desire she awakens in him.

Dani's strict routine has been trashed by Luke's explosive arrival. This rock-hard slab of valiant, smoldering manhood appears out of nowhere, saves her life, spirits her away to his mountain lair, and bewilders her with tales of sadistic researchers and enhanced assassins. Is this gorgeous, problematic sex god just plain crazy—or is she? But hey. Luke can do things with his mind that are just as wild as what he can do with that body. She can't say no.

And there's no time to wonder. As their passion flares, Obsidian moves in. Luke and Dani must place their lives and their hearts on the line just to survive…

D1378005

ALSO BY SHANNON MCKENNA

IN MY SKIN

The Obsidian Files

Shannon McKenna

PRAISE FOR THE NOVELS OF SHANNON MCKENNA

"Blends an intensely terrifying psychic thriller with a
mind-blowing erotic romance."
—*Library Journal*, on *Fade To Midnight*

"Blasts readers with a highly charged, action-adventure
romance . . . extra steamy."
—*Booklist*

"Pulse-pounding . . . with searing sex and raw emotions."
—*Romantic Times*, 4 ½ stars

"Shannon McKenna makes the pulse pound."
—*Bookpage*

"Shannon McKenna introduces us to fleshed-out characters in a tailspin plot that
culminates in an explosive ending."
—*Fresh Fiction*

"An erotic romance in a suspense vehicle on overdrive. . . sizzles!"
—*RT Book Reviews*

"McKenna expertly stokes the fires of romantic tension."
—*Publishers Weekly*

"McKenna strikes gold again."
—*Publishers Weekly*

"Her books will take readers on a nonstop thrill ride and leave them begging for
more when the last pages are devoured."
–Maya Banks, *New York Times* bestselling author

"Full of turbocharged sex scenes, this action-packed novel is sure to be a

ABOUT THE OBSIDIAN FILES:

More than human...

Years ago, a group of stray teenagers were swept up into a top-secret experimental research program funded by The Obsidian Group, a shadowy cabal of super-rich global moguls. Brain stimulation, nanotech, gene modification and cybernetic implants were used to mold the runaways into lethal supersoldiers...and expand the boundaries of being human.

Obsidian's attempts were spectacularly successful—if not quite in the way the researchers had intended. Their captive test subjects rebelled, burned the Midlands Research Facility to the ground, and vanished.

Now, years later, this band of rebels live under deep cover and keep their incredible abilities secret, trusting only those in their own tight-knit group.

But the shadow of the past keeps getting longer. The Obsidian Group hasn't forgotten them—and they will never give up the chase.

The Obsidian Files are their stories...

CHAPTER 1

*D*amn. The car Luke was following jolted off the freeway and onto the exit ramp. Sooner than he was expecting.

Luke put on a burst of speed. He searched the darkness for the retreating taillights. They had vanished into the night. Didn't matter. His brain implant had connected with its onboard system several miles back.

Once he was in, that car was his bitch.

But Luke had hesitated to assume total control right away. Hadn't wanted the courier at the wheel to panic and contact his handlers. No sense pissing off vicious, powerful enemies in advance.

Bad call. Now he had to improvise. And the guy was speeding through the residential neighborhood, drifting and correcting like he was drunk or high.

Shit. Luke had big plans for Braxton's courier that didn't involve witnesses with smartphones, car accidents or traffic cops.

He followed close behind. His ASP, the augmented sensory processor implanted in his brain by Obsidian, was monitoring the fleeing car's data on a transparent screen that overlaid half of his field of vision. He could follow that car in his sleep.

Though he never actually slept. At least not how normal people did.

A sense of urgency thrummed in him. *Time check, dude. Reality exists on a twenty-four-hour grid, seven days a week. Months vary. Watch out for February.* He scrolled back in his memory.

It was exactly thirty-seven days, sixteen hours, and forty-three minutes since his escape. His ASP pegged the breakout from Braxton's cage as his personal zero hour. Reborn, after three hundred and fifty-nine days, eight hours and forty-two minutes locked in an underground, soundproof glass box, outside of time. Every second free of that hellhole was a fresh start.

But as who? As what?

Freedom didn't seem much different from captivity. He still felt like shit. Isolated, numb. Maybe that was the effect of his self-imposed brain block. He'd put up a protective wall in his head that Braxton couldn't get through with torture or drugs.

It worked. It held. But who the hell was he protecting with it?

He couldn't...fucking...*remember.*

Random things sometimes floated out of the fog. His first name, not his last. No address. No hard data on any family or friends. Nothing from his childhood. Sometimes, he got flashes of faces. Younger people, mostly. Male and female. Their worried eyes. He wondered if they really existed.

A family, an identity, a life. It was all like a mirage. Memories on the far side of his brain block shifted and moved. Elusive shadows behind frosted glass. They vanished when he tried to hang onto them.

Ironic, that he could recall every detail of the experiments Obsidian had conducted on him. Their torture was burned onto his mind.

But the memories he actually wanted were out of his reach.

Just as well. If there were people in his former life worth protecting, anyone at all that he cared about, he'd prevented Braxton and Obsidian from destroying them. He'd done the right thing. It just had a hellacious price tag, that was all.

Focus. You have a plan. Follow it.

He was a block away, closing in fast when he saw the courier's car suddenly stop. When he caught up, the driver was gone and the car door hung open. Headlights on, motor running, the car straddled the sidewalk, crushing a low hedge in front of a small house. 2425 Camden Lane.

Luke parked his black Porsche SUV and did a swift, targeted data-dive, which revealed that the house was rented to a woman named Daniela LaSalle. A nurse at the local hospital.

He checked to make sure no one was looking, and used his implant to remotely shift the courier's abandoned car into drive, sending it jouncing and rattling over the bushes and sidewalk and back onto the street again. He maneuvered it to the curb some distance down the block and killed the engine.

Blood drops stained the sidewalk. Hot blood, steaming and starkly visible to the thermal sensor in his eye implants. A trail of drops led around to the back of the house.

He heard a TV going. Lights on in living room and kitchen. LaSalle was home.

Fuck. This operation should have been smooth and secret. He had everything ready; knockout drugs, restraints, a scalpel, anesthetic, disinfectant, broad-spectrum injectable antibiotics. He didn't want to hurt the guy, but that computer chip embedded in his pectoral muscle had to be extracted tonight, one way or another. It contained the drop-off info for a shipment of Manticore gear. And Luke needed it.

Manticore Tech was Braxton's new enterprise, his latest supersoldier research lab. More advanced than the work he'd done thirteen years ago, back when Luke was an unlucky street kid, captured to be Obsidian's lab rat.

Braxton had learned from his mistakes. He'd refined and honed his craft. He'd surpassed himself. Or so he claimed, bragging into the mic of Luke's soundproof cell.

Braxton's new supersoldiers were walking, breathing supercomputers. Invincible freaks of bioengineering. By all reports, Manticore Tech had gone above and beyond Obsidian's sadistic research in the bad old days.

Because hell, things could always get worse. That was a fact Luke could cling to in an uncertain world.

The chip was crucial. That shipment contained a device Braxton had called his "wakey-wand." Cute fucking name for a dangerous brain probe, one that dissolved memory blocks.

That was his plan. Just hoping like hell that Braxton's wakey-wand would stimulate his own shredded brain. Enough to bring back memories of his vanished life.

Most likely it would just kill him. He was fine with that.

He wanted his memories back. At any cost. Without them, he was adrift to nowhere. No compelling reason to exist other than being pissed off. Wanting to punish the fuckheads.

But he didn't want to punish Daniela LaSalle. She didn't need to witness him carving the chip out of the courier's chest while the unlucky bastard fought and howled.

That would look bad. It would be tricky to justify or explain. So would trapping the guy in the transport box he'd prepared, designed to block tracking implants inside the courier's body. At least until Luke could figure out what the fuck to do with the guy. That was a blank he hadn't filled in yet.

The obvious solution, of course, was to kill him and hide his body. The ASP processor tossed that up onto his retinal screen as the optimal plan of action, after running the numbers, calculating the data, and going off the deep end. Luke sighed. Murder was not a simple one-two-three thing, not in front of goddamn witnesses, and this quiet suburban neighborhood was not a fucking battlefield. His augmented sensory processor was useful sometimes, but totally amoral. And geared specifically for warfare. It defaulted straight to blood and guts every damn time.

Sure enough, as soon as his brain implant factored in Daniela LaSalle, the ASP promptly suggested that he kill and hide her, too. So simple and clear, whereas all the other alternatives were insanely complicated. A snap of a neck, and problem solved.

Classic Obsidian, all the way. Kill, kill, kill. They lacked imagination.

Fuck that. It just wasn't his style.

Dani stared down at her bare feet, which were propped on the coffee table, and contemplated how much energy it would require to make dinner. She'd picked up extra shifts lately at the hospital and today had been her first day off in what felt like forever. She'd had ambitious plans for it. Running, stretching, laundry. Repotting that spindly Norfolk pine, a birthday present from her work colleagues. Just looking at the poor thing made her feel guilty. Cooking a big healthy pot of chili or stew, most of which she'd ladle into single portion containers and freeze.

So far, all she'd managed was to plant her exhausted ass on the couch and stream cooking shows on her laptop. Desserts to die for were up next.

The magically speeded up assembly of a pan of apple dumplings made her think of her long lost friend Naldo and his crazy sweet tooth. The guy could eat sugar all day and never gain an ounce, the lucky dog. But Nal's longing for goodies probably had more to do with his *abuela* and her fragrant kitchen back in the day. Food and love, always glued together. A subject too deep to contemplate when she was this tired.

But thinking about Naldo made her sad, so she focused her mind on the recipe.

Didn't look hard. Store bought puff pastry sliced into ribbons, wrapped around apple chunks. Drenched in butter and sugar and cinnamon. Bubbling obscenely in the oven. She smelled it in her mind. Now she was the one writhing with sugar yearning.

Damn. Didn't she have some wrinkly apples in the back of the veggie drawer?

Aw, bullshit. Nothing was as easy as those shows made it look. She didn't have any store-bought pastry dough and she sure as hell wasn't going to make it from scratch.

Get real. It was peanut butter toast for dinner. Best-case scenario, scrambled eggs.

A disembodied hand had just scooped a perfect ball of vanilla ice cream and placed it tenderly on top of the luscious dessert when the banging started.

Back door? Front door? Dani jolted up, adrenaline jangling. She held her breath, listening hard.

More banging. Scraping. From the back of the house. Like the zombie apocalypse had begun, and the zombies were at her kitchen door. *Hello. How are you. We want to eat your brains.*

Fuck. No joke. She was afraid. And she'd left her phone charging on the counter. She got to her feet, padding to the kitchen. Listening, listening.

Silence. Except for a low, distant throb from Garson Arena, five miles away. The band sold out the venue every year. A few fans got carried out on stretchers every time.

Her footsteps slowed as she reached the darkened kitchen entryway and peered at the small windows of the back door. No one appeared to be standing out there, but the motion sensor had switched on the porch light.

She moved closer. Felt a draft, though the door appeared to be closed. Her skin crawled.

Thud, boom. The door rattled and she stumbled backward, lunging for her phone and yanking it off the charger cord.

More banging. Louder. She jabbed at the keypad, relieved to hear the flat voice of the 911 operator. "What is the nature of your emergency?"

"Break-in. Happening now. I'm alone." She gave her address in a low voice, moving back a few steps. Maybe she could run out the front door.

An almost inaudible moaning sound stopped her. It didn't seem faked. It sounded like someone in pain. An accident victim or …

Dani listened for sirens. Nothing yet. Then she heard another low, grinding moan.

She eased toward the back door and peeked through the pane of glass, looking down this time. The porch light revealed a bright red smear on the steps, and then a man's sprawled legs.

Holy *shit.* Someone was lying on her porch. Someone who was wounded.

She threw the door open and crouched down. The guy was short, dark, extremely thin. He lay on his side, his hand against his shirt, which was torn wide open over his bleeding chest.

He looked up into her face. She gasped in shock. "Naldo?"

"Dani." His voice was thick and slurred.

"Oh my God. What happened to you?"

He moaned, unable to speak. She forced herself to focus. "Don't move, Naldo. Stay down." She scrambled up, dropping her phone, and ran back into the kitchen for clean tea towels, pulling open drawers. *Bang.* Not in that drawer. *Bang.* That one. She grabbed several and dashed back to find Naldo somehow dragging himself over the threshold of the open door.

"Whoa!" She seized him under the armpits and pulled him all the way inside, trying to be careful and gentle. "I got you. Let me do the work." He was so thin and scrawny. Always had been, but he was almost skeletal now.

They'd been troubled kids back in the day. Forever in the deepest of shit and never escaping the consequences. Best friends, come hell or high water, with a powerful bond.

Then, about six years ago, Naldo had vanished. She'd looked everywhere for him, worried sick. No trace of him had ever turned up.

Years had crawled by…and nothing.

"Can you talk?" she asked.

He gritted his teeth. "Y-yes." A fading whisper. "Hurts, though."

"Stay with me," she said, keeping her gaze on his unfocused eyes. Keeping him in this world. Naldo let out a cry as Dani pressed a folded tea towel against his chest wound.

Her dropped phone rang. She glanced at the screen. The 911 operator came on, calling her back. Why? She realized that the faint sound of a siren had faded away.

Fuck. The police had to be all over that arena for the big concert.

Dani reached with her free hand, tapped the screen to connect the call and activated speakerphone. She explained and gave her address again when asked. "Send an ambulance," she said. "Not for me. For a friend. He's been stabbed. Hurry." Her voice sounded tinny and small in her own ears. *He might bleed out*, she wanted to shriek.

Naldo stared up at the ceiling. His eyes looked vague and blank.

Do not die. Do not die.

Her training kept right on mechanically doing what needed to be done.

The operator said something she didn't fully hear. "*… will be there in mumblemumble minutes…*" Something like that. Naldo lifted his hand but not for long. It fell onto her bare thigh, right below her frayed shorts and slid off again, leaving a bloody handprint above her knee.

She circled her fingers around his wrist, feeling for a pulse. Irregular. Barely there. Naldo was in shock and going down fast.

His dark eyes were sunk deep into their shadowy sockets, but they had a crazy glow, and his pupils looked strange, one larger than the other. The blood dripping onto the kitchen floor made her gently turn his head to see if—

Yes. He was bleeding out of his ear. Brain trauma.

Do not die.

His face gleamed with sweat, though his skin was cool and clammy. "Dani," he croaked. "Don't have much time. Have to…tell you—"

"Later. Don't worry, I'm sticking to you like glue, buddy."

"Can't wait," he whispered feebly. "Almost gone."

"Help is on the way. I'm here. Look at me."

He did, raising his hand again like he wanted to touch her face. It spasmed into a claw that hooked his torn shirt, opening it more. Dani hissed between her teeth at the sight of the nasty slash dripping fresh blood. The tea towel she'd used was soaked. She tossed it aside and pressed a dry one against the wound.

Then she saw the scars on his sunken chest. Someone had carved the living shit out of him. But it had happened long before whatever had happened tonight.

Just looking at that ugly, snarled crosshatch of raised white marks made her sick at heart. She might never know who'd tortured him, but if she did and when she did …

He reached up, shifting the tea towel so that his fingers pushed on the side of the wound, not over it. Blood welled out, gushing down his chest.

"No!" She cried out in protest and tried to stop him, but he batted her hand away in a surge of strength.

Then something caught the light. Even smeared with blood, it gleamed as it poked out of the edge of the wound. Bright and metallic.

Naldo groped for it, gasping as the pressure of his fingers popped it out of his ravaged flesh, along with another rush of blood.

It rolled over his chest and clinked on the floor tiles. A bloody metal capsule. A bullet? Didn't look like one. Didn't look like anything she'd ever seen, in fact.

She covered the wound with the tea towel and pressed down, fighting panic. *Where was the goddamn ambulance?* She could answer that question. Picking up overgrown brats who'd overdosed on bad molly in the mosh pit at the arena. While her best friend in the world once upon a time lay here dying on her kitchen floor.

His mouth quivered, trying to form words. "J-j-juvie," he gasped out. "Listen, Dani. Juvie. It'll show you the key."

"Show me what?" She was trying to calculate how much blood he might have lost before he got to her door, and he was raving now, irrational, his mind going back to their long-ago stint in juvenile detention. "I don't want to remember that place."

"No. No. It's in your skin now." His voice had gained a little strength.

"What about my skin? You're the one who's bleeding, Naldo."

"Juvie," he panted out. "I'm sorry to put it on you. So sorry. No choice."

"It's OK." But she was totally bewildered.

"You have to help her, Dani. I tried. Didn't…couldn't…"

"Help who?"

"Ivy. Please…help Ivy."

Dani shook her head, still lost. "Who is she? Someone we met in juvie? I don't remember an Ivy."

He breathed in heavy wheezing gasps, white-rimmed eyes staring wildly. "Manticore. Watch out for them. They'll…come after you now. I put you in danger."

"Naldo, enough. The ambulance will be here soon. Whatever happened, you're safe now."

"No time left. You gotta stop them." Fluid was bubbling in his throat. He stopped to cough, wincing. "You're strong. Smart. You could try…to stop them."

His voice trailed off. His pulse fluttered. The tea towel was soggy with blood but the gaping wound wasn't pumping it out. Maybe he would live.

Of course. If her magic chant—*do not die*—actually worked. If only.

Time was running out. Naldo had the look and vibe of someone sliding past the point of no return, probably because of what was going on inside his skull, about which she could do exactly nothing, and where was that *fucking* ambulance? A distant wail grew faintly louder.

Dani grabbed a fresh tea towel with her red, sticky hand, folded it and pressed it to his chest. "Stop who? Stay with me, buddy. You're gonna be OK."

"No. I'm done," he whispered. "Too much stim. Coming apart. Sorry."

"Don't say that!" There was a frantic edge to her voice that she couldn't control. He was slipping away. She'd waited for Naldo to come back for years. Here he was at last, but mortally wounded.

What a fucking cosmic joke.

She focused on his other hand for the first time, and saw a flash of steel. His fingers clutched a small but deadly looking knife, drenched in blood.

A horrible thought came to her. "Naldo…did you cut yourself?"

His eyes flickered open. Blood trickled from his nostrils. "Had to." A faint puff of breath. "Juvie. Read it. Help Ivy. Stop them. You always wanted to stop people from…hurting. That's…what you do."

"You have to help me," she told him desperately. "Come on, Naldo! Don't do this to me! It's not fair! I just found you!"

He could no longer hear her. He was unconscious, his heartbeat barely perceptible.

All she could do was hold the towel to his chest, which no longer even seemed to rise and fall, and stare at the gray stillness stealing over his face.

Like a shadow on a tomb.

CHAPTER 2

Blue flashing light sliced through the trees as an ambulance siren wailed. Luke faded back into the foliage after he finally got a good look at Daniela LaSalle. She'd appeared briefly at the front door to yank it open for the EMTs before running back into the kitchen at the back of the house.

Until then he'd only caught brief glimpses of her. Even when he slunk through the bushes around to the back of the place to get a better look through the kitchen window. She'd been crouched down on the floor almost the whole time.

She was tall, curvy. Golden skin. Her black curly hair bounced wildly. She moved quickly. Her voice was low and strong. Stressed, but under control.

No way he could get the courier away from here now. He ignored the endless stream of increasingly violent battle plans he was getting via ASP.

A Manticore courier showing up in an emergency room would be a complicated scenario whether or not the guy survived. Which would depend on the ER trauma team's skill, and the courier's injuries, whatever they were.

He hung back in the shadows and watched the ambulance pull up, a cop car right behind it. EMTs hurried up the walk toward the front door, lugging heavy satchels.

After a few minutes, an EMT came back out. He and a guy who'd been waiting in the back of the ambulance unloaded a gurney and hustled back into the house with it.

Luke moved closer, careful to stay out of the cop's line of sight, amping up his auditory implants to listen to the rapid-fire talk and crackling radios. *Airway open. Single penetration wound. Possible hemorrhagic shock.*

Naldo, she'd called him. So LaSalle knew the guy. Had history with him. But was Naldo a first or last name? It wasn't enough info to do a dive on him.

Daniela LaSalle came out with the gurney crew, her anxious gaze focused on the man strapped to it as they lifted it into the ambulance. After a brief conversation with the driver, she jumped into a Mazda parked on the street in front of her house. Off they went, the Mazda following, as sirens started up again.

Luke waited until the ambulance turned the corner to go to his car.

No rush now. He knew exactly where it was going. Which left his attention free for a deep dive into LaSalle's life as he drove. Beyond his sensory augmentation, muscle and bone reinforcements and combat stim, the Midlands researchers had trained him to use brain implants to interface with electronics way back in the day. When he was a kid trying to survive that place.

Another year locked in another cage had honed that ability far beyond the Midlands researchers' original intentions. He'd used those long, empty hours of captivity to practice total brain control. Particularly during the times that Mark or Braxton had stun-coded him into total immobility.

When he couldn't move his body, he'd focused on teaching himself to sucker-punch those bastards with his naked brain. Because fuck them all.

Which meant that at this point, hands-free, device-free wireless hacking into databanks and rapid-scanning their contents was as easy for him as daydreaming. He barely had to think about it. He rode the data-stream wherever he needed to go.

Her social media was first, just a quick overview, saving all her data and contacts in his mental archives for more careful analysis later on. She called herself Dani, and was a Sagittarius. He lingered on a Facebook photo from a holiday party at the hospital. She liked red velvet cupcakes. She wore a low-cut black sweater and had a half-eaten red and white cupcake in her hand. She had a gap between her two front teeth. He liked it.

Two boneheaded bozos in the picture were gawking openly at her cleavage.

The DMV was next. Their half-assed encryption had more holes than Swiss cheese. He checked out her driver's license photo. The holographic overlay made her look slightly pissed off. She had a few speeding tickets on file, duly paid.

He perused a newspaper article about a local free clinic serving the community in multiple ways. Great picture of her, arms flung around her fellow volunteers. Wide grin, sexy dimples. Add that to the sweet gap between those white teeth, the direct, striking green eyes, the defiant jut to her chin. She looked tough. Tough was good. Hot. Not that Daniela LaSalle's hotness was relevant to his, uh, mission. Just to him personally.

Things got tricky once he got to the ER. He left the Porsche in the hospital parking area and went inside. Dani and the courier had gone in the ambulance bay, but he had to slip in the front entrance, somehow avoiding notice. Not that easy for a guy of his size, but he got lucky, arriving at the same time as a grizzled old man who staggered and moaned, held up under his armpits by his adult sons. He followed them right in, like part of their family. Sat near them. Kidney stones, their anxious conversation revealed. Sounded bad.

Luke gulped data while the triage nurse started the interview with the guy who had kidney stones, searching for the passcode signal to open the big doors that divided the intake area from the ER. Didn't take long to find it.

A crying woman burst in the doors screaming about her boy, who'd gotten himself fucked up at the rock concert still thumping its bass beat through the whole town.

Everyone looked her way, including the triage nurse and the security guard. His cue to ping the hacked signal to the double doors and walk right on into the ER.

The corridors inside were crowded with medical personnel, family members, staffers pushing high gurneys with patients strapped onto them, people slumped in wheelchairs. He spotted a cop leaning over a reception desk further down the hall, shooting the shit with a red-haired lady behind the desk who wore rose-print scrubs. The cop looked busy, but Luke made a quick turn off that corridor anyway.

A peek through an open door revealed an empty exam room with a white lab coat flung over the back of a chair. Luke ducked inside and grabbed it. It stretched way too tight over his shoulders and back, but if he tried not to breathe the seams might not split for a while. More eyes might slide past him without stopping.

He kept moving purposefully, reaching out with his auditory enhancements for the specific timbre of Dani LaSalle's voice. Hoping he could identify it in the noisy place.

He finally caught it and tracked the soft sound through the ER until he caught a glimpse of her sitting in a glassed-in nurse's station.

Her distress blared at him like red strobe lights. Multiple signals, small in themselves, summed up into a silent scream of grief and frustration.

The courier was dying. And she knew the guy. Cared about him intensely.

They'd taken Naldo away. Up to surgery, most likely. Nothing new in the hospital database yet about his condition. Luke double-checked to be sure.

Dani LaSalle just waited, hunched over. The gold of her skin was washed out in the brutal white glare of the hospital lights. Blood was spattered all over her, drying to a dark red. Her dark ringlets seemed to have lost some of their bounce. The in-your-face set of her jaw that he'd admired in her photos was not in evidence now. She looked shattered.

Another nurse in scrubs came into Luke's field of vision and handed Dani a cup of coffee. The nurse murmured something, patting her on the shoulder. Dani looked up at her and tried to smile. She failed. Her hands trembled as they held the paper cup.

He could roughly estimate her body temperature from a distance with thermal imaging. Too low. She needed a sweater. A lab coat. Anything.

Damn. She shouldn't be here alone. Someone should be here with her, an arm around her shoulder. Not just a busy co-worker. Someone she knew personally. A mom, a sister, a brother, a friend.

Several staffers brushed past him. The corridor was full of people. He had to keep moving.

He pushed onward and dived for more info on her family as he did another full circuit. No father listed on her birth certificate. Mother, deceased seven years ago. No siblings or relatives. Huh. So much for that.

For the next hour or so, he cycled slowly through the place like a restless shark, disappearing from time to time in bathrooms and empty examining rooms to break the rhythm but always circling back around to catch a fresh glimpse of Dani LaSalle, hunched in her chair over her untouched coffee, silently waiting. There was a bloody splotch on her bare leg, which looked shapely and strong even in the baggy sweat-pant shorts.

But he shouldn't be thinking about any of that. Not here, not now.

Then again, any guy with a pulse would, if he got a good look at Dani LaSalle. And he was real conscious of his pulse right now. He willed it to slow. *Keep focused.*

He concentrated on looking purposeful and busy as he walked, mentally sifting through the info that all the databases of the world had stored on Dani LaSalle.

Interesting stuff. Checkered past. Troubled childhood. Her mom had died of cancer while incarcerated. Damn. Obsidian would have gone nuts for this girl if they had come across her. The combination of smart, angry and completely unprotected, oh fuck, yeah. They would have eaten her up with a spoon.

He lingered over LaSalle's childhood medical history. A broken arm, a sprained wrist, dislocated shoulders more than once, broken ribs, even a broken nose, all while she was a kid living with her mom and her mom's worthless boyfriends.

It got better. High scores and accolades in nursing school, even while working part time as an LPN to supplement her scholarship. Graduated with honors as an RN two years ago. Among other things, she also did volunteer work at the free clinic he'd read about before. While studying for the Medical College Admission Tests. Woohoo. She was dead serious about a career in healthcare.

She'd taken the MCATS about a year ago and gotten an excellent score. So she dreamed of being a doctor. Huh. The woman kept herself busy.

Sealed documents from juvenile court archives showed assault charges when she was fifteen. Against a grown man. She'd whacked the guy with a cast iron skillet. Not hard enough to kill him or damage his brain, but hard enough to stop the bastard. Luke didn't need to dive to fill in the blanks as to what the fucking pig had tried to do to her.

Dani LaSalle was not to be messed with, even as a kid.

A mug shot from that incident was buried in those archives. He blew it up until it filled his entire field of vision, a big transparent overlay. She hadn't changed much since then. In the picture she wore a clingy purple tank top. Her tangled mop of curly hair was longer and wilder then.

She looked ultra pissed off. Fuming with sultry heat.

The picture winked off Luke's screen as he rounded the corner and saw the doctor approaching the nurses' station. He went inside and spoke to Dani. Young guy, tall, broad shouldered, wearing scrubs. His body language indicated that he knew her.

Luke discreetly positioned himself to see better and hear more.

"…need to talk to you privately for a moment." The doctor had that flat, careful tone. Like he was bracing himself.

So was Dani. She obviously knew that tone, and what it meant. Her mouth shook for a moment, and then she tightened it grimly, set her coffee down and went with him.

Luke followed from a distance, sauntering toward the room they had entered and lingering by the closed door, jacking his auditory enhancements to the max.

He leaned against the wall and thumbed his smartphone as he tuned into the doctor's voice. "… everything we could, but he coded at 11:20. I'm so sorry, Dani."

Coded. While Luke had been busy worrying about Dani LaSalle needing a sweater. If he'd been monitoring the hospital intake database more carefully, he would have already known that Naldo was dead. He had to watch out. Getting sloppy.

"The chest wound was relatively superficial, but there was significant blood loss, and he…"

A harrowing wail of pain from a woman on a gurney who was being rolled swiftly down the hall by two nurses obscured the doctor's voice for a moment. Luke struggled to sift through the competing sounds and tune in again as the woman's moans retreated.

"…appears to have been a brain hemorrhage. That's all I can tell you right now." Dani didn't reply.

"I'm so sorry," the guy repeated. "Are you going to be OK? Is there somebody we can call to come get you? Take you home?"

"No thanks." Dani's voice had lost its color and force. "I'm good."

Luke sidled away, keeping his head bent over the phone as the door opened. The doctor walked right past Luke and into a curtained-off alcove. Busy night.

A couple of minutes later Dani emerged, looking blank. She didn't seem to notice him, just stared around like she'd forgotten which way was out. Finally she turned and headed for the exit.

Luke let her get well ahead of him before he moved to follow, but before she could make it through the double doors a burly, balding guy stopped her. Luke amped up his ASP directional hearing once again.

"Excuse me, Ms. LaSalle? My name is Detective Rob Willis of the Munro Valley Police Department."

"Yes?" Her flat voice held a trace of assertiveness. "How can I help you, Detective?" She wasn't dressed like a nurse but she still spoke like one, Luke noticed. Even though she obviously didn't know this guy.

"May I speak with you privately?"

She paused for a long moment. "About what?" she asked slowly.

Munro gestured at a room awaiting a cleaning crew. Two chairs, IV pole, no patient, no bed. "Please. Just a moment of your time, that's all."

She was frozen for just a few seconds more, then shook herself a little and went in.

Luke slowed way down as he walked by, stopping twenty feet past the door, and started messing with his phone again.

"You told my colleague earlier this evening that the name of the deceased is Enrique Bernaldo, correct?" the detective asked.

"Yes."

"And you also stated that you hadn't seen him in several years?"

She was silent again. "That's right," she said finally. "About six years, I think."

"Ms. LaSalle, is there any chance you're mistaken about the identity of the man who died here today?"

"Excuse me?" She sounded blank with incomprehension. "Come again?" Willis just waited. "Any chance?" he repeated.

"No." Her voice gained strength. "No chance at all. Of course that was Naldo. We recognized each other. I knew him well. Why do you ask?"

"Enrique Bernaldo was found dead five years ago," the man said. "In a motel in Las Vegas. Overdose. Well known as a male prostitute and drug dealer. At the time, his body was positively identified by his aunt, Emiliana Bernaldo. His father's sister."

"Maybe that Bernaldo is a different guy," Dani said. "I don't recall an aunt in the picture. As far as I remember, Naldo was going it alone. He told me about his grandma, but she died when he was little. I know Naldo. I couldn't get that wrong."

"OK. Well, thank you for your time, Ms. LaSalle. Here's my card. Call me if you think of anything."

"He was like a brother to me." Dani's voice had begun to shake. "We talked about the past, at my house. Before he lost consciousness. He mentioned juvie. That was where we met. At juvenile detention. When we were kids."

It was clear to Luke that she was about to lose it. Even the detective noticed and lowered his voice. "Oh. I see. That's interesting," he said. He paused, waiting for more. Like he wanted to keep coaxing information out of her. Right now, when she was wrecked. Luke was about to do something stupid and attention grabbing just to distract that fat fuck when the detective saved him the trouble.

"Look, Ms. LaSalle, you can call me anytime if you'd like to talk more. Right now probably isn't the right time, given what happened and all. What I'm saying is—well, you have my card. That's my private number. Don't be afraid to use it. We can meet whenever it's convenient."

Yeah, you'd just love that, wouldn't you, buddy? Don't hold your breath.

Luke watched them emerge from the room, Willis following her this time. The guy stared avidly at Dani's ass as she walked unsteadily toward the exit. Pig.

Luke sauntered after them, keeping a cautious distance. He had to make sure that she got home safe and stayed safe. He also had to get into the basement morgue and check Naldo's body for the package, but it was too soon for that. Too much activity around here right now. Later.

He might as well make himself useful and guard LaSalle now that Naldo, that so-called friend of hers, had just gotten Dani noticed by the cruelest, most efficient killers on the fucking planet.

A parting gift before kicking the bucket. *Thanks, dude. You shouldn't have.*

Then again, Naldo's brain had been melting down. Luke guessed he should cut the poor guy some slack. Still, things could get interesting, and he was down for that. Somebody had to fend those fuckers off when they came for her. And they would come.

Hell, they were probably already on their way.

Luke got worried after a few minutes. Dani didn't go back to the parking lot for her car. She'd decided to get a cab, but apparently had no phone to call for one.

She'd raced off to the hospital without grabbing so much as a purse or a coat, and now she was standing out on that busy street in the ice-cold wind in thin, blood spattered clothes, those wild ringlets whipping around, getting in her eyes as she tried to flag down taxi after taxi. It was a busy street, and there were plenty of cabs, but they weren't stopping for her.

Screw that. He eyeballed a shiny new one stopped at the red up the street, sinking his cybernetic claws into its networked systems. When the light changed, Luke mentally nudged the cab into the correct lane. When it was close enough, he muscled it to the curb and jerked it to a noisy stop right in front of her, popping open her door for good measure.

Dani got in, leaning forward to give directions to a grizzled older man who appeared to be scared shitless by his car's strange behavior. His mouth sagged open and his eyes were bugged out. But he snapped out of it when Dani wearily closed the door and sat back, driving away with no further help from Luke.

The cabbie would probably chalk the bizarre experience up to fatigue, stress, impending dementia, temporary psychosis, car trouble. Anything he could come up with.

Then he'd just block it out. Reject the weirdness and continue on with his life.

Lucky guy, to have that option open to him.

CHAPTER 3

"So he never showed," Lewis Hale repeated, his voice hard. "No call, no word, no warning."

"No, sir." R-48, his newest operative, stared straight ahead, her beautiful face impassive. "I waited for two hours, left multiple messages, and called the emergency number we were given. When we traced the phone, we found it discarded on the side of the highway forty miles south of the designated meet site."

Hale studied R-48 thoughtfully. He'd only had her for ten days, and hadn't yet taken her measure, beyond that incredible body and flawless face. She and the other six new operatives were Level Twenties, the highest ability level that Obsidian currently developed, at least for subordinate operatives. The higher skill and power levels had been phased out over the past few years. Too many things could go wrong. And had.

It was a coup, to have successfully requisitioned seven Level Twenties. Hale's mission was vitally important to the Committee: to shut down Manticore Tech, the rival underground research lab that Braxton, that fucking traitor, had set up to compete with Obsidian.

Manticore Tech had gone too far. Hale intended to prove himself to the Committee by taking them down for good. He'd posed as a buyer and purchased one of their operatives. He wanted to study their expensive product. See what could be learned from it before the axe fell.

But it had been snatched from his hands. And someone had to pay.

R-48 was incredible to look at. Female operatives were always preselected for good looks, but R-48 stood out from the pack. She was exotically beautiful. Long blue-black hair kept in a glossy braid. Huge dark tilted eyes, luscious lips. A body that would make any man's balls ache. But that blank look on her face irritated him.

"Do you ever smile, R-48?" he asked her.

R-48 looked even blanker, if that were humanly possible. "Sir?"

"Can you smile?" he demanded.

A tiny frown creased her brow. "I'm disappointed that I couldn't successfully complete the mission, sir," she said stiffly. "Smiling seems inappropriate."

"Smile now," he commanded.

She looked hunted. Eyes darting around at her fellow operatives, all male, who stared straight ahead.

Metzer, his second-in-command, laughed under his breath. "Good one, boss," he said. "I'd like to see that, too."

R-48's mouth worked. "Sir—I—"

"Are you disobeying a direct order, R-48?"

R-48's eyes went wide, face tightening as the question triggered a programmed cascade of intense discomfort through her body. Then slowly, as if struggling to remember how, her mouth stretched into a grimace.

Hale huffed out a sigh of disgust. "Stop it," he growled. "Do you have the names and personal info for the Manticore lab personnel ready?"

"Yes, sir, I dived for them already." R-48 sank down to the computer, fingers tapping on the touchscreen with blinding speed. "The data's on your screen, and I'm calling the contact number now. One moment..." She tapped the computer. "I hacked into the Manticore system webcams last night, so I have eyes on the man fielding the call...and this one is Peter LaMonte. Located in the Singapore lab complex."

Hale consulted the data she'd put on his screen and picked up. "Hello, Peter," he said. "It's Highett. Remember me? The client who got stiffed today?"

The shocked silence on the line made him smile. "Ah...I don't..."

"I know you Manticore personnel are supposed to be anonymous, but I don't hand over a thirty-five million dollar down payment to nameless ghosts," Hale said. "I know everything about you, Peter. Where you are, where you live. Who you care about."

"But...but I can help you, Mr. Highett!" Peter LaMonte's voice had risen almost an octave. "Believe me, you haven't been stiffed! We *will* deliver!"

"Then you're aware of our difficulties with the consignment today."

"Of course, and I apologize for what happened! And it's on me to—"

"I want to speak to Dr. Braxton personally. Put me through to him."

"He's not available right now. Again, I'm sorry that the courier didn't show, but we'll make it right as soon as we—"

"I'm not that patient," Hale said. "Manticore wouldn't send out a courier without an imbedded tracker in his body. Send me the codes and I'll deal with recovery myself. I'll subtract my expenses from my final payment."

"Ah...that won't be necessary, sir." There was desperation in Peter LaMonte's voice. "We'll handle it. I don't personally have the authority to renegotiate your contract, and furthermore—"

"Give me the data," Hale repeated. "Or I will make a phone call, and you will find a nasty surprise when you get home to 150 Rose Terrace, Apartment 52, where you live with your beautiful wife, Jacinta, and your two little sons, Malcolm and Henry. Four and seven years old, am I right? My people are much closer to them right now than you are, Peter, with your fifty-minute commute through Singapore. Have I made myself clear?"

He listened to the man's panicked breathing. "Ah…our security safeguards exist for your protection, too, sir." LaMonte's voice shook. "Delivery points are randomly generated to ensure that we're both insulated from possible—"

"I don't give a fuck about your security protocols," Hale said. "I want my product and I want it now. Shall I make the call? Decide quickly. Or I'll decide for you."

"No. Please don't," LaMonte begged. "I'll get it. Just give me a moment."

"Send it to the same address we used for the drop meet info," Hale said. "You have two minutes, Peter. Get on it."

"Of course. Right away."

The room waited in dead silence as the seconds ticked by.

R-48 looked up from the screen. "He sent it, sir."

"Good job, Peter," Hale said softly into the phone. "Smart choice. Let's hope for your family's sake that we have everything we need. Have a good day."

He hung up and peered over R-48's shoulder, toying with her shiny braid. "So?"

"He's in Munro Valley, California," R-48 told him.

"On the move?"

"Stationary." She enlarged the touchscreen image with flicks of her fingers. "At the Munro Valley Hospital."

"An accident?" Metzer mused.

"Go and find out," Hale ordered Metzer. He turned to R-48. "You keep a close eye on that courier. I don't want him slipping away again."

"He's unlikely to do that, sir," she said.

"And why is that?"

She touched a tab and enlarged a diagram of the hospital campus, pointing. "That's the morgue."

Hale looked at Metzer. "Get that chip back fast."

"I'm on it," Metzer said. "Just one thing. When I come back, I'd like to, ah… celebrate." He glanced at R-48 and waggled his brow suggestively. "But you have to authorize it. You know. Since she's a Level Twenty and all."

Hale felt a twinge of annoyance. Metzer was a randy dog. R-48 was worth tens of millions. She was a Level Twenty with more field experience than all the other new operatives combined. Improved functional mods, a wider range of deep-stimmed core skills. And all the literature warned against using high-level subordinate operatives as bed companions.

It was the equivalent of using a rare, expensive electronic instrument as a sex toy. Self-indulgent, wasteful, unhygienic and potentially dangerous.

Besides, if anyone was going to use her, it should be him. Ranking squad leader.

But Rob Metzer was his number two. Junior Squad Leader, loaded up with command mods, favored son of Gerard Metzer, a powerful Obsidian Group committee member. Rob was an arrogant, self-important dickhead, but he was headed straight up the Obsidian ladder. It would be unwise to make an enemy of him.

Hale was nothing if not practical.

"Just this once," Hale said grudgingly. "But don't make a habit of it. Pick up your own meat in your own time."

Metzer grinned triumphantly. "Thanks, boss." He seized the zipper tab of R-48's tight microfiber jacket as he walked by, tugging it down until the jacket gaped over her breasts, barely covered by a snug gray microfiber camisole. "Sweet," he murmured, and looked at Hale with a grin. "We can take turns. I don't care."

"Get to it," Hale snapped. "Work before play."

Metzer swaggered out. Hale noticed R-48 pulling her jacket zipper closed as he followed. "Leave it as it is," he ordered.

She looked up, eyes wide. "Sir?"

"You heard me, R-48. Leave the jacket open."

Her hand dropped. Her lips tightened until the color left them. She didn't raise her hand again, but his skin prickled with unease.

He'd have to keep a close eye on this one.

Not exactly a chore.

Metzer put on the janitor's coveralls and kicked and nudged the man's limp body into the supply closet. The guy outweighed Metzer by at least sixty pounds, but baggy was better than too tight or too short. He just hoped he wouldn't encounter any of the other hospital cleaning staff while he was here, or they'd meet the same end as…he glanced at the laminated name badge…Juan Ortiz.

The less blood, the better. In and out.

He shoved the closet door shut against Ortiz's corpse and got his weight behind the rolling cleaning cart. He kept his head down going through the hall, but no one looked up as he rattled by. He glanced sidewise at a doctor walking past but the guy ignored him, preoccupied by his smartphone. Metzer turned the corner toward the morgue unnoticed.

He pulled the door open and heaved the cart through it. An attendant sat at the desk. He was a big, soft guy with a bald spot and a goatee, also staring at a phone.

He didn't even look up as Metzer approached.

"The other guy already cleaned in here," he said absently.

Metzer pulled out his silenced gun. The guy gasped as he caught sight of it. His smartphone hit the floor with a nasty crack. Little colored icons continued to bounce and float on the shattered screen. Some game or other. Fruit flying through the air.

Metzer showed his teeth. "It's still dirty," he said. "Needs to be cleaned again."

"D-d-don't hurt me," the guy moaned, as the gun barrel pressed into his neck.

"Shut up," Metzer whispered. "A body was brought in tonight. Young, skinny, dark hair, lots of scarring. Remember him?"

"Uh…yes. There was a guy like that."

"Take me to him right now," Metzer said. "Don't make a single fucking sound. You get anybody else in here, and I kill you both. Understand?"

"Yes," the attendant whispered.

Goatee shuffled along, wincing away from the pressure of Metzer's gun. Metzer clutched him firmly by his thinning ponytail and jerked his head sharply to the side. He sidled and stumbled, whimpering under his breath, but led him to the back of the morgue.

Metzer shoved him against the wall, trapping him in the corner behind the drawer the cringing guy had indicated. "Open it," Metzer directed. "And don't move one muscle."

Goatee pulled the drawer out. The corpse inside fit the description. Short, thin, with buzzed off dark hair, heavily scarred torso. A ragged wound on his chest right over the spot where the capsule should be. That sucked.

"This chest wound," he asked. "He came in with it? Or somebody cut him after?"

"No," the guy said, bewildered. "Nobody touched him after the trauma surgeon got done. Hygienically bagged and tagged."

Metzer pulled out the scanner, programmed to blip at the exact location of the capsule. The long bar lit up with an eerie greenish glow, illuminating the sick-looking face of the sweating morgue attendant.

Metzer ran the thing over the corpse's torso. Three times. Not a blip.

He tried the arms. A slow sweep from the dead man's shoulder to his blood-darkened fingertips. Outer arm, inner arm. Legs, thighs, and groin. He propped the corpse up, did both of its sides. Swept shoulders, back, ass. There was an object inside his skull, but that was the transponder. No way would Manticore have put a client capsule inside a courier's cranium. Nobody wanted to hack through bone to retrieve personal property.

Goatee's eyes widened, startled, when Metzer thrust his fingers into the gaping wound on the courier's chest and fished around.

Nothing in there. Just cold, dead flesh. Someone else had gotten to the capsule first. That pinch-assed dry turd Hale was going to be furious. *Shit.*

He seized Goatee's puffy throat with his meat-slimed fingers, and leaned into his face, squeezing. "Who brought in the stiff?"

The guy's eyes rolled. "I think...it was that chick who works in the ER. She came in with him. Saw her in the nurse's station earlier. They were talking about it. She had blood all over her."

"Gimme a name."

"Dani," the guy gasped out. "Her name's Dani."

"Last name?"

"Dunno," the guy said. "Swear to God. I just knew her because there was a bet on who could get close enough to read the last name on her ID. Double the money to anyone who could get her into bed. She's hot."

"Who won? Anybody?" Metzer asked, tightening his grip until his fingernails dug in and blood oozed out.

"No one." Goatee's voice was a dry thread.

Metzer grunted, eyes raking the man's heavy, sweating face. He hit a button on his phone, and waited for Hale to pick up.

"Give me some good news," Hale growled.

"Not yet. I need info," Metzer said. "Lemme talk to the new girl."

A pause. R-48's low, even voice came on the line. "Yes, sir? How can I help?"

"Get into the Munro Valley Hospital's HR database," he said. "There's a nurse. Probably in the ER. Her first name is Dani. I need a home address for her."

"One moment."

Goatee stared at the pistol barrel, fighting to draw breath through Metzer's encircling fingers, his mouth slack and trembling.

"Got her," R-48 said. "Daniela LaSalle. 2425 Camden Lane, Munro Valley."

Hale's voice blared out of the phone. "Who is this woman?"

"She's the one who brought in our stiff," Metzer told him. "No package, though. Just a big nasty slice in his chest. I need to go have a talk with her."

"Take backup," Hale said. "Four of the new crop. Put them through their paces."

"Send R-48 with them," Metzer said. "Have them meet me at Dani LaSalle's address."

Hale made a growling sound. Tough luck. The jealous old goat wanted to fuck R-48 himself.

Metzer pocketed the phone and turned to Goatee. There was a brief, awkward pause. "So," Metzer said. "Um…thanks."

The man's watery brown eyes filled with desperate hope. "Happy to help. Anytime, man. Like, whenever."

"No, not really," Metzer told him. "Just this once."

He swung the gun up and shot Goatee directly between the eyes.

The silenced pistol made a loud thump, echoing in the room like a huge bass drumbeat. Goatee toppled and fell heavily to the floor. Time to get the fuck out of here.

Metzer strode away from red-splattered morgue drawers, stepping over Goatee. He cracked open the door and looked up and down the hall. No one around to see.

Good.

CHAPTER 4

That blood wasn't going to clean itself up. But Dani couldn't seem to move. She sat on a kitchen chair, staring at the lurid smears on the sunshine yellow linoleum. She could swipe and scrub and spritz all she wanted, but from here on out, she was going to see Naldo's blood whenever she looked at her kitchen floor.

Getting home was a teary blur. She'd been in no shape to collect her car from the hospital parking to drive home. A cab finally stopped on the street outside, but she didn't remember paying the driver. She'd just stumbled out and glanced back, confused, as the cab sped off, tires squealing. Like something had scared the crap out of him.

Huh. She must look bad. Like, *Tales From The Crypt* bad.

Whenever she closed her eyes, she saw Naldo's grayish, waxen face. He'd been unconscious when the EMTs got there. After a few years as a nurse, she could sense when someone's spark was going out. So she'd known, even as she was driving toward the hospital, that Naldo was going down fast. That there was nothing she could do. Nothing anyone could have done.

Up, LaSalle. On your feet. Do something. Clean up. But her strings were cut.

She was used to seeing the aftermath of violence and cruelty. Usually she kept her emotional distance like the professional she was, but sometimes it got to her.

Like last year, taking care of Dylan. He was a skinny fourteen-year-old boy who had run afoul of his piece-of-shit uncle. Broken bones, lacerated face, cracked skull, cerebral damage. There was an army of heartless monsters out there masquerading as human beings. Preying on the vulnerable. Getting off on inflicting pain.

They made her so angry, she started wanting to deal death herself. And she was supposed to relieve pain and suffering, not inflict it.

Dylan had looked a lot like Naldo. Which really messed her up for a while.

Naldo, the little brother she never had. They had bonded at juvie. Survived over a year at the Riplinger foster home together. He was younger than her by a couple of years. Small, scrappy. Never backed down from a fight. Always ready with a smart-ass remark.

It was Naldo who first told her that she should be a doctor. She'd laughed at him at the time, but she never forgot it. She hadn't made it to med school yet, but she was a nurse because of the seed he'd planted in her brain. All because of Naldo.

You're tough enough for blood and guts, he said. *You've got the nerve for it.*

She stood up too fast and almost fell over, hanging onto the kitchen table as her blood pressure whooshed way low. A chilly, sickening rush of darkness.

She doubled over, waiting for it to pass. Tough, her ass. She didn't feel tough. Her nerves were for shit. When she straightened up, she was crying.

Damn. Crying sucked.

When she aged out of the system, she'd hoped to pull Naldo out with her, but by the time she had a job and a place of her own, it was too late. Naldo was gone. Whereabouts unknown.

His chances of survival had been slim from the start. He was physically small and pretty, and looked younger than he was. Predators and pervs would find him and use him. Drug dealers, pimps, traffickers. As time went by, finding him became less and less likely, but she kept hoping. She kept herself visible on social media mainly for him.

Here I am, buddy. Come on out of the woodwork. Anytime is fine.

She was used to waiting and hoping. She'd hardened herself to that, but not to the grim, flat finality of nothing left to wait for. Nothing left to hope for.

Dani roused herself and made it over to the laundry closet in the hall. She looked for several frozen minutes at the plastic crate full of cleaning supplies, rags and rubber gloves on the washer, wondering if she had any products that were good for mopping up blood.

The door to the hall was open. She suddenly tuned in to the racket from the living room. She'd left the laptop on, and it was still streaming a cooking show. Here she was preparing to swab up Naldo's blood while some trendy chef yapped on about bone broth. Protein, minerals and flavor! Cow juice forever! She had to make that damn thing shut up.

She stumbled out into the hall like a drunk, stepping through the passageway—

And started backward with a stifled shriek.

An enormous dark man loomed in the shadows by the door. Huge. Buzzed dark hair, vast shoulders, all bulked up with black body armor like a commando.

His eyes gleamed in the darkness with terrifying intensity. "Don't scream." His voice was deep, hoarse and scratchy. "I won't hurt you." He made a shushing gesture with his hands.

"Who the *fuck* are you?" Dani's back thudded against the wall. "What are you doing here in my house?"

"We need to talk." His voice was very calm. "Quietly."

"About what?" Her voice shook.

"Shhh. Keep it down. About Naldo."

She exploded into panicked motion, lunging for the kitchen, her phone, her door, the outside, anything to get away. He seized her from behind before she got out of the short passageway between the living room and kitchen.

She went nuts, writhing in his grip. "It was you!" she hissed. "You hurt Naldo!"

"No!" He whispered the words urgently into her ear. "No, no, no. That wasn't me."

She fought him, but there was an uncanny quality to his implacable grip. A sinking-into-quicksand feeling, as if he was using her own energy and the harder she fought, the tighter he held her.

He wound her into a shaking knot, twisting her own arms around her torso and clamping her wrists into his huge fists. Her legs were trapped between his rock-solid thighs. She strained against him, fear rising to a screaming pitch. "What the fuck do you want from me?" She forced the words through numb lips.

"For you to listen." The vibration of his deep, quiet voice against her ear sent racking shivers through her, making her legs wobbly.

She swallowed to calm the shaking. "Fine," she said. "Talk. Make it snappy."

"Don't be afraid," he urged.

Dani let out a bark of incredulous laughter. "Hah! For real?"

"I won't hurt you, Dani. I swear it."

She squeezed her eyes shut and tried not to hyperventilate. "Then why not come to the goddamned door like a normal person if all you want to do is to talk?"

"It hasn't been a normal day. You never would've let me in."

"Right! Let go of me! Asshole!"

"Shhh," he whispered again. "I came in to warn you that you're in danger."

She twisted in his grip, just enough to catch the flash of his dark gaze.

"Oh really." Her voice dripped sarcasm. "Am I. Now there's a news flash."

"Not from me," he said impatiently. "From the people who hurt Naldo."

"What do you know about Naldo? Who hurt him?" She turned to study his face again, and realization dawned. "Wait. I saw you earlier," she said slowly. "A couple times. You were in the ER. Wearing a lab coat."

"Yeah, that was me," he admitted.

"I thought you were a new resident, maybe starting an ER rotation."

"Nope, not a doctor. I was there to protect you," he told her. "I'm here now for the same reason."

"I didn't ask for your protection," she replied savagely. "Whoever the hell you are!"

"Getting around to that. Now listen. Naldo had a—" His body went still. "Shhhhh."

She froze too, waiting. Listening. "What is it?" she demanded, in a whisper. "What in the *hell* is going on?"

"They're moving in on us." He breathed the words out almost soundlessly. "Don't make a sound."

What the hell? Fear and dread overcame her.

It was too damn much. All she could do was fight. She was hardwired for it. She yanked one of her arms almost free. Tried to elbow him. Failed. "The only problem I have right now is you! Let...me...*go!*"

His hand clamped over her mouth. She pulled back and bit his hand, hard. He pulled his hand free with a hiss of pain, and she started to screech.

In a blinding instant, she was clamped against his body so tight she could hardly breathe, his hand over her mouth again. So firmly she couldn't even turn her head.

He hoisted her off her feet and kicked open the door to the laundry closet, which she'd left hanging open. Hauled her inside, pulling shut the door.

And there she was, in the darkness in her clutter of brooms, buckets and mops, jammed in between her ironing board and her washing machine with a huge, mysterious, terrifying man.

So close, he was practically plastered to her body.

Goddamnit.

Trapped. In a closet. Stupid fucking bonehead move. Luke had acted without thinking, locked in combat survival mode.

But they were surrounded, and it was the only move to make. He had to make the best of it. Keep her from making noise. Giving his presence away.

He'd gotten inside just in time. The hostiles had shown up moments afterwards. He'd seen four thermal heat signatures slinking around out there. Systematic, professional, moving smoothly into position in the overgrown foliage. No unmod would have seen or heard them. Covering every entrance. Probably listening with modified ears, just like him.

He just hoped they weren't scanning for thermals. He couldn't afford to lose the advantage of surprise, outnumbered as he was.

Now if he could just quickly, forcefully convince Dani to get down on the other side of the dryer while he went out to deal with them …

But she wouldn't. It wasn't in her nature. He needed to calm her down first. Explain that she had to do exactly what he said, this instant, if she wanted to keep breathing.

But he couldn't get the words out. At least not without scaring her so badly that she started screaming again.

Words wouldn't come. All those long months of keeping silent, refusing to speak to Mark, then Braxton. Resisting interrogation, beating and torture.

He wanted to howl his frustration, but that wouldn't help. Her heart was galloping. Stripes of yellow light from the kitchen sliced through the slats in the door and across her eyes. They were wide and brilliant, glittering with angry tears.

"Hold still," he whispered.

Her body squirmed against his, chest to thigh. She was tall and strong. Her head came all the way up to his nose. Her lush tits pressed against his body armor. The sensation made him want to ditch the damn vest. Feel all those curves for real.

Some other time. He had a job to do. And she absolutely did not deserve the shitstorm that was blowing her way.

"Dani," he whispered. "Don't scream."

He meant it as an order, but it came out rough, hoarse. Pleading.

Slowly, he lifted his hand. Her mouth was slightly open. She was panting. The pink, tender fullness of her lips made him ache down low.

A tear glittered as it flashed down over her cheek. The sight of it hurt him inside.

"Don't cry," he begged in a raw whisper. He touched his fingertip to the wet tear-track that gleamed on her smooth, beautiful cheek. Wanting to taste it.

She inhaled. Luke sensed the ear-splitting scream that was forming in her mind, and did the only thing he could think of to head it off.

He kissed her.

CHAPTER 5

Dani was so startled, she froze. What in the fucking *hell?*

His body was so hot. Hard. There was just so damn much of him. She was confused. Panic tangled with knee-weakening heat. It made her frantic.

His kiss was sensual, demanding. Masterful, but not rough. He cupped her face with his big warm hand...oh. Both hands.

Tenderly opening her mouth, thrusting his tongue in, tasting her. Not even holding her arms down anymore. He was just making mad hungry love to her mouth.

Like he'd forgotten that he needed to restrain her.

She stood still. Not slapping or punching. Just letting herself get passionately tongue-kissed in a laundry closet by a mysterious assassin. Like she just forgot that she needed to be restrained.

Like it had just...slipped her mind.

He stroked her face. Reverently. As if he couldn't believe she was real.

She felt dizzy. Disoriented. She forgot which direction gravity was supposed to pull. His hot, massive presence overwhelmed her senses. She swayed backward, off balance. Then the guy grabbed both her arms and wrapped them around his neck.

She clung to him, shaking.

Out of control. Shifting, arching, rubbing up to him. Inviting him closer, accommodating his hard bulk. He was working sexual sorcery on her there in the silent darkness, on the edge of madness, and it was working.

Her legs were opened now. Feet no longer even touching the ground. She rode his rock-solid thighs, legs twined around his, shaking with holding on so tight. No idea how she'd gotten there. It was happening so fast. No clue if she'd done it, if he'd moved her.

And now she was clenching around him. Clenching and releasing, over and over, frantically, helpless to stop. His hand cupped her ass, positioning her crotch against the hard, hot bulge of his cock, right where she needed it to be...right...*now.*

Again...again...and harder...harder, and oh...oh please...oh *God* ...

He caught her cry of shocked pleasure against his mouth as her body stiffened and wild pleasure surged rhythmically through her.

And then slowly ebbed away. Leaving her shocked...and terrified.

What the hell had just happened? She couldn't even look him in the eye. Or answer the question. Not to save her life.

He'd made her do it. Driving her to panic. Then trying to persuade her to turn to him for protection. She came back to reality, furious with herself for falling for it.

Screw it. Stress response, temporary psychosis, Stockholm Syndrome, whatever. She'd justify and rationalize later. Now she just needed to get the hell away from him.

He was as tough as an armored tank, but he had a weak spot. The one he shared with most of his fellow men, and she was wrapped all around it right now.

He was so hard. His erect cock still pressed against her. She had to shut this down.

She opened her mouth to tell him how it was gonna be—

And found his big hand clamped over it, hard. He held his fingers to his lips. Pointed at the door.

He pushed her backward into the space behind her dryer where her laundry hamper was. Pushed her head down, then her shoulders. Down, down, down. Huh? She was supposed to *kneel...?*

What the *fuck?* Did he mean for her to blow him? He had another think coming.

Click. Click. The tiny, almost inaudible sound riveted her. He pointed at the closet door handle. It was turning, very slowly. Oh *shit.*

A scream wanted to explode from her lungs. She refused to let it out.

Click. Last one. The door cracked open. The guy charged out, knocking someone against the wall. Grunts. Thuds. A choking sound.

Dani lunged past them into the kitchen, snatching her phone up off the bloody floor. She skidded out the back door and down the steps, slip-sliding in her battered flip flops and sprinted through the shaggy bushes, trying to call 911—

Someone stepped in front of her, heading her off. He grabbed her and spun her around, wrenching her arms back so sharply, pain exploded in her shoulders.

Her smartphone flew out of her hand, hit the walkway and shattered.

A big, gloved hand clamped over her mouth, pinching her nose shut, and a massive arm squeezed her throat. "Hey. Where do you think you're going?"

It was a crude, hateful voice. Not stolen-kiss-in-a-closet guy, who'd begged her to listen, who'd tried to tell her she was in danger...but she'd been too panicked to hear him.

Where was he?

His arm tightened, cutting off all her air...and she snapped. Filthy sonofabitch prick. He'd caught her on a bad day and he was going *down.*

She went nuts, flailing and kicking at his legs, his boots, but he didn't seem to feel it. She twisted, scratching and slapping.

His hold intensified on her throat, over her nose and mouth. She tried to bite him, but he wore black leather gloves. He forced her jaw shut.

Couldn't breathe. Going dark.

"…hear me, Daniela?" The voice swam in her ear, far away but weirdly calm and gentle. The heat of his breath was moist against her ear. "Answer me. Or I'll hurt you."

She felt the cold edge of a blade press against a pulsing vein in her throat. If she moved, she'd die.

The knife moved up her neck. "I'll cut off an ear to start with. Do you hear me?"

She dragged in as much air as she could get and jerked her head in assent.

"Good. Now listen. We're going inside your house to talk. My people are right over there. They'll come inside with us. Do you see them?"

She blinked tears out of her eyes as he moved her head to one side. She peered through the wavering blur.

Three dark figures, bulked up with body armor, bristling with weapons. Cold, flat eyes. Two men, one woman. Their faces looked lethal and pitiless. She nodded again.

"I'm going to raise my hand. Don't scream. If you do, they'll shoot. Your guts will be ripped apart by bullets. That beautiful smooth warm belly. I would hate that." He dragged up her bloodstained shirt and stroked her shivering flesh, over her navel and upward. "Do you understand?"

No air. Passing out. She nodded again. *Yes.*

His suffocating hand lifted. Moved down, groping and pinching as it went.

Dani rasped in a desperate wheezing breath. Not enough air. Her lungs felt locked. Her chest heaved and shuddered. Her eyes were wet and she hated that. She didn't want to let this slimebag see her cry.

He shoved her on ahead of him, making her stumble. Neck bent at an agonizing angle. Back up the stairs to the kitchen porch. Back through the wide open door and into her blood-smeared kitchen. She blinked her tears away, looking around for signs of the guy who had kissed her. Tried to keep her safe.

Had that thug killed him?

The guy shoving her slid his hand into her sweatshirt pocket, coming out with a business card. "Hmm," he said. "Detective Robert Willis. I imagine he's curious about what happened here today. Did you tell him everything?"

"What do you want?" Her voice was shaky. She barely recognized it.

She didn't even see the blow, it came so fast. Like being whacked with a board.

When she stopped seeing stars, he was smiling. A friendly smile. Young guy, blue eyes. Nothing remarkable about that face.

"You don't ask me questions, cunt," he said blandly. "That's my job. Got it?"

She nodded. Head pounding, stomach lurching.

"Where's S-22?" he demanded.

"Not responding, sir." The voice came from behind her, in the kitchen. The woman.

Blue Eyes frowned, never relenting his painful grip. "Search the place. Find him."

He dragged her through the kitchen and the corridor and into the living room, pulling her down next to him on the couch, thigh to thigh, the gun on his lap pointed right at her belly. "Now, Daniela. You know what I want. I don't even need to ask."

"Nope," she whispered. "Wrong."

He glanced at the laptop on the coffee table. The blond chef was still prattling about soup stock. The others were yanking open drawers and cupboards in the kitchen. Making noise in her bedroom.

"You like cooking, huh?" He flung a heavy arm over her shoulder, resting his hand on her chest. His fingers felt around, stroking her breast. Pinching her nipple. "I like a woman who can cook. Especially a pretty one like you."

"Can't," she croaked.

"Can't what?"

"Cook. Can't do it. I burn everything. I just like to watch them do it on TV. It's relaxing." Fuck, she was babbling. *Stop it, LaSalle. Stop. Dial it down. Short answers.*

"Do you need relaxation, Daniela?" her captor crooned. "Are you stressed?"

She shook her head violently. "I'm fine," she mumbled.

"What's that? I can't hear you."

"I'm fine," she said, more loudly.

"Good," he snapped. "OK. I'm going to ask you a few questions. If I like your answers, then everything will work out for you. If not..." He shrugged.

Her body shook. Like an earthquake was happening inside her.

The guy leaned close. "Where's the package?"

She stared back, her mind spinning with alarm and confusion. "What?"

He sank his fingers into her thigh, savagely hard. "Don't be a dumb bitch," he hissed. "And don't waste my time."

"I haven't gotten a p-package in weeks," she stammered. "I swear. I don't know what package you're talking about."

"The one in the courier. You're a nurse. He hired you to take it out, right?"

"Remove what? Nobody hired me to do anything!"

"Who are you working for?" The guy's voice retreated, faint and faraway again. The sound of her own heartbeat swelled as his hand tightened once more around her throat. Louder and louder, thudding hard. She saw his lips moving, saw the malevolent flash of his narrowed blue eyes, but couldn't hear the words.

He released the suffocating pressure, and air rushed back into her lungs.

"...just want the package, and I want it now," he was saying. "You brought him to the hospital. You were seen with him. His blood is all over you. Don't lie to me."

Her mouth worked, trying to process what the fuck he wanted. "You mean Naldo? You're looking for Naldo?"

"I don't give a shit what his name is. All I want is the package. Get it for me, or I'll cut off a thumb." He seized her thumb, bending it with brutal force, jabbing his knife against the web of skin between thumb and hand.

A sting of pain as he broke through. A trickle of blood raced down her hand and down her wrist and arm, into her sleeve. Then more blood. Weirdly hot.

"Naldo didn't have anything with him," she said desperately. "He just showed up bleeding at my door. I tried to help him, but he died. That's all."

"You didn't dig a capsule out of his chest muscle? You didn't make that cut I saw on his body in the morgue?"

Her blood suddenly chilled as the image unfolded in her mind.

A flash of metal buried in torn flesh. That bloody thing she'd seen sliding out of Naldo's chest wound. She'd forgotten all about it. Watching her old friend die before her eyes had driven that memory right out of her head.

Her attacker saw the dawning realization in her eyes. His smile widened. "Now we're getting somewhere," he murmured. "Good. Go get it for me."

"And then...you'll let me go?"

His eyes were pure ice. "I said no questions. Get it. Or I start to cut."

They stared at each other for a few seconds.

So. She was going to die, no matter what she said or did. That was very clear.

She'd have to strike quicker. Just one good stab at that smirking piece of shit before he wasted her. That was all she asked. She wanted to leave her mark on him.

Something to remember her by.

"Let me get up." She kept her voice small. Didn't dare move. "I have to find it."

"We'll go together." That vicious smile again. "I can help you look."

He yanked her arms behind her, clamping her against his powerful body. She took one shuffling step—

Gunshots. Deafening her. She felt Blue Eyes pull back and swear, losing his grip on her, while the thug by the couch crashed down onto the coffee table, collapsing it.

Dani hit the ground as more shots pounded into the wall and everything else besides. A lamp shattered. The room was dark now but for the light from the kitchen.

The sound of running feet. Another deafening gun blast. She looked up to see a third man fall heavily to his knees, clutching at the blood gushing from his groin.

Shadows moved against the walls. Shouts, yells. Crashing sounds from the kitchen.

She turned her head. Found herself inches from the collapsed coffee table, face to face with the helmeted guy who had fallen into it. One eye was wide and surprised looking.

The other was a gaping red hole.

Dani screamed soundlessly, unable to breathe—until she saw a knife sheath strapped to the dead man's boot.

She scrambled for it, crawling over the man's huge body. She seized the knife by the handle, yanking and tugging...and it came loose. A nasty looking black blade.

Fuck yeah. She had a weapon and she was going to use it.

Bursts of gunfire stuttered out, but they were down to hand-to-hand combat in there. Kicks. Blows. Rattling crashes. She glimpsed bodies flying—

"Dani! Get down!"

Yes. It was him. She knew that voice. His presence gave her a wild surge of hope.

It was too late to follow his directions. Blue Eyes had grabbed her once again, and this time, a gun barrel dug painfully into her cheek.

"I'll kill her, asshole," Blue Eyes bellowed in the direction of the kitchen.

Not a sound from the other guy. Cutting time. Dani steeled herself.

"Wanna watch me blow a hole through her head?" Blue Eyes howled.

Her chance to leave him a bloody souvenir was...right...*now*.

She stabbed the knife up into his gun hand, twisting it hard.

The gun went off, a deafening *boom*. Something huge slammed into her. All three of them crashed to the floor together. Her on the bottom, the wind knocked out of her.

The two men fought each other, right on top of her. After what seemed like forever, they finally rolled to the side, still a heaving mass of yells and grunts, blows and thuds.

Then one of the men smashed the other one's head violently against the floor.

Silence, broken only by heavy panting. Dani fought for breath, vibrating with terror as a dark figure rose up to his feet with smooth animal grace.

Not Blue Eyes. It was the other guy. Tears of relief spilled down her cheeks, but she still caught the quick flash of movement behind him. "Look out!" she yelled.

CHAPTER 6

Luke swayed backward as knives whipped past his throat and face, barely missing him. *Thunk, thunk.* They sank into the drywall behind him, vibrating.

He seized the first movable object he saw, a big potted plant, and flung it as the woman operative barreled through the entryway. The huge pot hit her on the chest and knocked her down onto the floor, spraying dirt.

She vaulted to her feet and retreated into the kitchen as he gave chase, grabbing random kitchen objects to lob at him in quick succession. He dodged them all as they circled, keeping the butcher's block between them.

Then Dani charged out and leaped onto the woman's back with a yell. *Fuck.*

The woman whipped around, bucked Dani off and threw her against the wall, smashing her through the drywall so hard, she stayed stuck there.

The operative took advantage of Luke's split second distraction to jab for his throat. He blocked her and hit back, knocking a hypodermic from her hand with a brutal blow that should have shattered her arm. Leaving him open on the side.

She darted in like a snake—and got him under the ribs.

Shit, that hurt. He ignored the burning pain as he grabbed her arm, pulling her in close. Torqueing her arm up high behind her, seizing her neck to snap it—

He met her eyes…and stopped.

What the *fuck*…?

It was like being stun-coded. His muscles were locked up. The time-warp moment seemed to last forever. He took it all in. The whites of the woman's shocked dark eyes. The smell of her combat sweat. Her open mouth. Fear, his and hers.

The spell broke. He shoved her away from him, her neck still unsnapped.

They stared at each other, breathing hard. Panicked and confused.

Not for long. Her lips curled back. A guttural shriek came out of her as she attacked. He grabbed the knife block, swung it against her head—and she went down.

For what it was worth. She was probably still alive, like the other guy. These operatives were tough. Reinforced muscle and bone, resistance to pain, fast healing. Just like his own.

He should kill them both right now, while they were unconscious and helpless. Before they killed Dani or him.

Aw, fuck it. They all had to die someday. But not today.

He sagged against the butcher's block and felt beneath his body armor. A long shard of glass stabbed deep into his side twitched painfully with every breath. Hot blood flooded down his leg. The rapid-clotting process hadn't kicked in yet. *Shit.* Bullet to the shoulder, too. Big bloody mess.

He waved away the drywall dust clouding the air. Dani coughed, struggling to extricate herself, and wrenched an arm free. She dabbed at her bloody nose with her filthy sleeve.

Luke heaved himself to his feet and staggered to her, dropping to his knees and punching the drywall until he'd broken enough of it to tug her out of the hole.

He sagged to the floor beside her, his face wet and clammy. That glass shard stuck into his guts hurt like a motherfucker.

She gasped at the sight of his bloody hand, clenched around the jagged glass.

He braced himself, grimacing. "Gotta…get this…*out.*"

"Wait!" she said urgently. "No!"

He yanked on the glass with a hoarse cry, pressing his hand down against the rush of blood that followed it. Willing it to clot.

Through the fog of pain that followed, he saw Dani rummage in a kitchen cabinet and then dash back with a roll of paper towels, flip-flops crunching over broken glass and crockery. She spun the roll to tear off a bunch, wadding them against the gaping wound.

He howled. *God,* that hurt.

"Hold that right there while I call an ambulance," she said. "Push down on it. Don't let up."

"No," he whispered. "No ambulance. Just…gimme a minute."

"You need help," she said firmly. "I'll be real quick. You just hang on, OK?"

He clasped her wrist. "Please," he whispered. "Look at me. Into my eyes. It helps."

She did. Those big green eyes, wide and worried, held his like a touchstone as the world dissolved into cold darkness and emptiness …

And then came slowly back to a murky haze of light.

Dani was done gazing soulfully into his beautiful dark eyes. The guy needed a trauma surgeon right fucking *now.*

"Can you hear me?" She kept her voice neutral. Calm.

He muttered something that could have been a yes.

"We have to get you to a hospital. That means I'm going to let go of your hand now."

"No." He dragged in a ragged breath, and shook his head. "Can't…call for help."

She tugged at her wrist. "Let go of me now," she said gently. "Let me help you." But his clasp, though not painful, was like a steel shackle. "Dani," he whispered.

It occurred to her how weird it was that he knew her name. She hadn't been wearing a name tag at the hospital.

"I'm here," was all she said. "What's your name?"

And who the hell are you? She could take a few educated guesses. With a body that fine and fighting skills like that, he had to be military. Or ex-military.

And to think she'd had the pleasure of riding all that. Before all hell broke loose.

"I'm Luke," he said.

"What's your last name?"

"Just Luke." His voice was hoarse. He was huge. Massive shoulders and arms. Wearing body armor, like her attackers, and sliced and stabbed all to hell. He'd swept in to save her like some heroic dark angel. Chiseled face, despite the swelling lump on his forehead. Gorgeous lips. Dark beard-scruff on his strong jaw.

Whoa.

Shut it off, LaSalle. She was a professional with a job to do. One that involved freely flowing blood for Christ's sake. "OK then, Just Luke," she said crisply. "What the hell just happened?" Maybe he'd forgotten about the crazy wild kissing interlude in the laundry closet. He'd taken at least one hit to the head.

"Came here…to protect you." He huffed the words out with some difficulty.

Right. You were getting into that before you kissed me. Dani shook her head, bewildered. "I don't understand. Who sent you?"

"Can't explain," he whispered. "We gotta get out of here. This instant."

"Tell me about it," she said fervently. "Straight to the hospital. First, let's get that armored vest off. So I can—"

"What?" His grip on her wrist tightened as her voice trailed off. His eyes flicked up to hers, piercing through his pain-fog. "So you can do what?"

Dani hesitated. *For starters, check the vest pockets for ID and find out exactly who the hell you really are, and fuck the educated guesses. You could be my hero. Or you could go totally buckfuck crazy on me any second.*

This would be her second 911 call of the night. She could hear the question like someone had just asked it, hanging in the air. *What is the nature of your emergency?*

She looked down at the female attacker lying still on her kitchen floor. Still unconscious, but for how long?

Yes, hi. It's me again. Same address. OK, now I have five homicidal freaks in my house who tried to kill me—but I think that at least two of them are dead. And there's a new guy bleeding out on my kitchen floor. Yeah, same floor. Not a killer, no. This one's a hero.

She'd convince the operator somehow. One thing in her favor: the hero seemed unable to get up. He pulled on her wrist to get her attention again. "So you can do what?"

"I need to check your abdomen, Luke. I have to slow down the bleeding before the ambulance—"

"No ambulance. No cops. We have to run away, Dani. Now."

He was ranting. Not good. Dani made mental notes. *Brief loss of consciousness. Uncooperative. Intermittent delusions. Possible head trauma.* Just that lump, no visible blood. Then again, his short hair was awfully thick.

"Not gonna happen, Luke. Calm down." If she could get free somehow …

But that didn't seem to be happening either.

"Gimme more paper towels," he said.

That meant he'd have to let go of her. "Good idea," she said.

She tugged. He tightened his grip. "No, Dani. Forget it. Don't call. No time for that."

Dani's calm façade finally snapped. "Be quiet and listen to me," she said. "I happen to be a nurse, if you haven't figured that out, and in my professional opinion, you're committing suicide if you don't go to the hospital right now!"

"Listen." His voice was a growl of effort. "Let me tell you what suicide looks like. The guys who attacked you? That woman? There are more. Many more. They know your name, where you live, where you work. And they'll be back. Wherever you go, they'll find you. And you will die in agony. Slowly."

"But…but I never had anything to do with—"

"No operative contact or response means reinforcements are coming. With a bigger team this time."

"Fine. So we'll tell the police that."

His ultra-focused intensity was beginning to convince her—against her better judgment. Then again, getting slammed through drywall could cause concussion. A mild one could affect her reasoning. It was as good an excuse as any.

"No," he said again. "You'll get cops killed for no reason. Dani, I'm not crazy and I'm not lying. Run with me now, or die. It's that simple."

"You'll die anyway if you don't go to a hospital!"

"No, I won't." He sounded so sure of himself. "But we have to hide tonight. If they came at us now, I wouldn't be able to defend you again. I'm too messed up."

No shit. Every medical professional had to deal with mentally ill patients in the ER and the psych ward ranting about mysterious beings known only as They and Them.

"But you're too weak to move on your own," she said stubbornly.

He finally let go of her. Got himself up onto his knees, struggling to his feet. He stood there, towering over her, panting. "Wrong," he said.

They heard the muted, repeating hum of a smartphone in vibration mode. Muffled, but they both heard the sound coming from the direction of the living room. Not hers, she suddenly remembered. Her phone was smashed to pieces on the walkway outside.

"That's coming from his jacket," Luke said. "The asshole who hurt you. That's his boss, wondering if the job's done. Wondering why there's been no update."

The vibrations stopped, after eight buzzes. So did her heart. Or so it felt.

The silence was absolute. "Convinced?" he asked. "Ready to go now?"

She stared at the woman sprawled on the floor, the wreck of her kitchen, the dark maw of her living room. The heavy, meaty stink of blood. She hesitated for a few more seconds before she answered him. "Yes."

"One thing," he said. "Bring Naldo's capsule with you."

She recoiled, seized by fresh doubt and terror. Staring at him.

He shook his head. "Don't look at me like that," he said. "I'm not like them."

"Good to hear," she said cautiously. "But whatever they wanted from me, you want it, too, right? And you saved my life so you could get it? OK. Fine. Whatever. I'm processing that. But I'm still grateful."

"Good. Now get the package." His voice was harder now. "So we can go."

They stood there, him braced against the broken wall, gazing at her with that piercing urgency in his eyes. She could feel the power in him. On her skin.

"I don't know if I should go with you," she said slowly. "What the hell is this thing? And what did Naldo have to do with it all?"

He rubbed a hand over his eyes. "Later for that." His voice was a rasp of exhaustion. "If you don't have it, let's just leave. I don't want you to get hurt. And there's no time to fuck around."

His words tipped the balance, overcoming most of her doubt. Not all of it. She reserved the right to remain sane, just in case he wasn't.

She squatted down and started sifting through the mess scattered all over the kitchen floor, starting with the area near the door. She could still see Naldo lying there, near death.

Anger surged up, energizing her to concentrate. She felt along the baseboards, ran her hand over the vinyl floor tiles. In all the commotion it had gotten kicked to hell and gone. But it had to be here.

She finally spotted it in the corner by the recycling bins.

Dani held it out to him. "Here. You earned this."

His fingers closed over it. He gazed at her without speaking. Something about looking into his eyes was like touching a live wire. She looked away, face warming.

"Thank you," he said. "You ready?"

Yeah. For a lot of things I can't have and shouldn't want.

But all she said was "Yes." She took his arm and edged past the sprawling bodies and out the front door. Then tensed, startled, as headlights flicked on outside. "What the hell?"

"My car. Remote ignition. You drive. I gotta shut down for a while. I'll tell you where to go."

She pulled open the passenger door of a shiny black Porsche SUV, trying without much success to keep him from falling into the seat like a ton of bricks.

She hurried around the front of the car and slid into the driver's seat. "Where to?"

"Highway," he said thickly. "Going north. Drive fast."

CHAPTER 7

Warehouse District, Seattle waterfront ...

Zade felt a gentle but persistent shake against his shoulder, but it was Simone's sensuous, velvety voice that reached him.

"Zade...come back. Come back to me, babe ..." Repeating it, over and over.

It was a long trip back up from the data dive. It took a while, flipping off this switch, switching on that one. He could've done it faster if necessary, but he preferred to take his time. Float up gently rather than jump up screaming, ready to destroy shit.

That never went over well with Simone.

Her name boosted him up over the top. Simone. His love, his bride. He opened his eyes to her beautiful face. Her long, thick blond braid coiled up against his chest as she bent over him. His senses opened up to take in more of her warm, sweet scent.

"Hey," was all he could croak.

"You stayed down too long," she scolded. "You promised six hour stretches, and that's still too long. I was at Asa's for ten hours, and I stopped for well over an hour at Hannah's on my way back, so you're cheating. What gives?"

Zade shook his head. He had nothing to say for himself. He'd been diving deeper and deeper into hacked databases of all kinds in his search for his brother Luke. When he was in it, it was hard to remember the promises he'd made to her. Time had no meaning in a data dive.

That was what made them dangerous.

"You need some sleep." Simone sank down on the bed next to him, putting a bulging tote bag on the bed next to his feet. "You haven't slept since we finished the kill-code scrub. Your brain needs to shut down periodically. You're still healing. And I feel like I'm talking to a goddamn wall."

"I rest. I do sentinel sleep," he protested.

"Sentinel sleep, my ass. It's not the same and you know it."

Zade sat up and ran his hand through the buzz-cut brush that covered his scalp. He still couldn't get used to such short hair. Simone had shaved off his mane when they scrubbed out the kill-code, right after their recent wild adventures, and he still didn't recognize himself in the mirror. That tight-assed military look was not his vibe.

On the up side, it made his diamond stud earring really pop.

He feasted his eyes on her. So damn pretty. A good stimulus to drag his brain back into normal mode. He'd amped up the search for his brother Luke using their new leads shortly after the code-scrub procedure. Too soon, according to Simone, but Luke couldn't wait.

Neither could he. He'd been diving for hours a day, every day. Still no results.

Every day that passed ratcheted the tension inside him higher. Simone got it, and she was supremely patient with it, but the strain was never-ending. She deserved better.

He noticed the bag she'd set by his feet. "What's that stuff?"

"Hannah and Sisko's latest passion project," she said. "I got roped into doing product testing for them. They're designing sexy spy-style tech gear for women."

"Such as?"

"Useful gadgets. You know. Stun weapons, tracking devices."

"Who are you going to track?" he asked innocently.

She tilted an eyebrow. "Back to the subject. Deep diving. Too much isn't good for you, Zade."

"I have to do it," he told her. "We tried a physical search. We combed every square inch of that whole area. If Luke had been there, we would have found him. We didn't. My job now is to keep trawling the entire fucking internet until I find a sign of him."

Simone slid off the bed and went over to the computer table by the window, where she'd left two steaming cups of coffee. She carried them back. "I know you have to find Luke," she said. "And I understand that you can't rest until you do. But you're not doing him any favors by hurting yourself. Your dives are too long. It's dangerous. And it makes you crabby."

"When was I crabby today? Yesterday doesn't count," he said, defensive.

She passed him a cup. "You've been in a nonverbal trance state for fourteen hours," she observed. "You haven't had time yet. But you'll get there. Maybe I'll go out to a movie. Without you."

She settled down next to him, fluffing pillows behind her and extending her legs, sipping her own coffee, laced with brown sugar and cream. He didn't get the preference, but liked the taste on her lips when he kissed her. Creamy sweet and sensual.

Zade figured he was only seconds away from advice he didn't feel like hearing. "Whatever, Simone. Just deal, OK? Luke saved my skin more times than I can count. I'm sorry if it stresses you out, but I can't stop."

"Don't be defensive," she said softly. "I'm not telling you to stop."

He looked her over hungrily as he drank his coffee. Usually when they were alone in the house and she was working on her research, she wore a loose draped sweater over leggings and a silky camisole, barefoot, no bra, her long blond hair hanging loose. Today she wore jeans, a waffle-weave sweatshirt and a quilted vest. Hair all braided back. Windblown wisps, rosy cheeks. She'd been doing something outdoors.

It still blew his mind that she was here with him. In his bed, his house, his life.

His wife. So beautiful and smart. Heroically badass. And she could make him combust with a single sultry glance.

"What the hell were you doing at Asa's all that time?" he demanded.

A smile twitched her lips. "Follow-up checks on Brenner, obviously."

"Obviously," he echoed.

Brenner had been part of an attack force several weeks ago, led by Mark Olund, a Midlander gone bad. The attack had almost destroyed them. But Brenner had survived, and fought back against his Obsidian programming. It nearly killed him—but not quite.

Mark and the others had all died, but Brenner hung on in a coma for weeks—until the day that he'd come out of it with a vengeance. Psychotic and screaming.

That was when Simone had performed her first ever improvised code-scrub on the poor guy's brain and brought him back somehow. Brilliant as she was.

Brenner seemed OK, from what Zade could see. These days he was working with Asa, the pain-in-the-ass brother of Noah and Hannah Gallagher, two more of Zade's fellow Midlander rebels. And Brenner gave them good info about current Obsidian research and protocols, being one of Obsidian's relatively late models. Midlanders like Zade and his band were just rough drafts in comparison to Obsidian's current cutting edge bioengineering design.

Simone followed Brenner's progress like a hawk. She felt personally responsible for his mental health and welfare, so she was often out at Asa's lair to check on him. Too often for Zade's comfort level, if he was being honest. But he tried not to be a jerk.

"Today we did some cyber-synch testing on the Obsidian weapons in Asa's cache," she told him.

"With you there?" Zade sat bolt upright, appalled. "That's dangerous! That stuff could trigger Brenner into a relapse, and there you'd be, in the crosshairs! What the fuck?"

"Brenner's not going to have a relapse," she soothed. "He's doing well. I ran tests. Solid as a rock. It was fun playing with the weapons. Plus, Brenner's teaching me new skills. His way of paying me back. He's convinced that I saved his brain. Sweet of him."

"He's right," Zade observed. "You did. What kind of new skills?"

Her smile became a teasing grin, and she hid it behind the coffee cup, still peeking at him through her sexy fan of dark eyelashes. "If you're curious, come with me," she said demurely. "You're more than welcome to do so."

He narrowed his eyes at her. "You've been spending a lot of time out there. What's that about?"

"Just keeping busy," she said airily. "Like you. Those endless dives of yours don't leave us much room for couple time. Might as well study captured Obsidian equipment, right? In fact, I've been thinking. It's a lot of driving for me every day. Maybe I can just crash out there from time to time. Asa has all those guest rooms."

True. That giant, secluded multi-level house in the woods was absolutely set up for unexpected guests. Zade launched a blazing-fast micro-dive into the house's system lists, looking under *Guest Rooms*, subhead *Nightstands*. The usual. Wi-fi and hot spot instructions. Pens and paper. Kleenex. So far, nothing ribbed or flavored.

"He wouldn't mind," Simone added.

He studied her suspiciously. She looked like she was trying not to smile. "Are you fucking with me?" he asked.

"Oh, no," she assured him. "I would never, ever do that."

"So what the hell is he teaching you?"

She rolled her eyes and sighed, smiling at him. "Fine. If you must know, I'm learning how to pilot a helicopter. And it's a blast."

Zade just stared at her. "You're doing *what?*"

"I'm getting the hang of it," she said. "Brenner's a good teacher. I'm a fast learner. When you have a minute to spare, come out with me. I'll take you out for a spin."

Holy shit. His bride was hanging out with a couple of tough guys, letting them teach her how to fly fucking helicopters. But it wasn't like he could object. He knew better, when she had that calm, cool, *what-are-you-gonna-do-about-it* look on her face.

"Wow," he said. "Good for you. Could be useful sometime. Anyhow. Back to the subject. This is my life now, babe. This is who I am until I find Luke. I'll try not to be a prick when I come up for air. But I can't stop."

She set down her coffee with a barely audible sigh. "Did you catch anything on today's dive?"

"Maybe. My ASP archives are packed with stuff to analyze. But this one was my favorite. A clue to how he might have survived." Zade leaned over and snagged the tablet on the bedside table. He wirelessly downloaded the file from the augmented sensory processor in his brain, converted the file and handed her the device. "Read that."

She studied it. "The Plagette Falls Post? Where's Plagette Falls?"

"Wyoming. Fifteen miles as the crow flies from Braxton's hellhole. Look at the date."

"One week after we got away from Braxton and Holt," she murmured. "Hmm. Interesting." She leaned over to set her coffee on the bedside table to read it, with Zade looking over her shoulder. "Local Man Claims Aliens Drive His Jeep On Canyon Road." She tapped the tablet screen. "Like it's possessed, or so he says."

"Happens to me all the time," he told her. "Snot-nosed deputy never believes it."

"Neither do I," Simone said. "Where were we?"

"Waylon Meeks," Zade said. "The guy in the Jeep. Read it to me."

"Right. OK. Plagette Falls resident Waylon Meeks was driving his Jeep Cherokee on Rathbone Creek Canyon Road when his vehicle began to swerve erratically, as if the steering wheel was controlled by someone or something outside the vehicle. The Jeep accelerated and veered toward the edge of the roadside cliff, stopping inches short of going over. Mr. Meeks exited the car, which then drove away on its own—over the cliff?"

"No." Zade pointed to the relevant line. "It left him stranded in a late winter snowstorm."

Simone continued. "'I about had a heart attack,' Mr. Meeks told reporters. 'That Jeep went nuts on me. I thought it was going to kill me, like in that old horror movie. I practically froze to death before I got a ride.' Mr. Meeks's ex-wife Beverly Stratton, of Rathbone, Wyoming, was heard to observe that Mr. Meeks is forty-eight expletive-deleted years old, which is more than old enough to know better, and he ought to lay off the tequila shots before attempting to drive. Her unsubstantiated comment notwithstanding, the Highway Patrol is on the alert for a driverless but possibly aggressive red Jeep Cherokee. If anyone sees such a car misbehaving, consider it armed and dangerous. Stay clear, and notify the authorities. And go easy on the tequila, folks.'"

Simone looked up at him, her eyes full of startled wonder. "Wow," she murmured. "You think Luke might have taken over this guy's car?"

Zade shrugged. "The timing is right. The distance is right. Assuming Meeks isn't a total nutcase or a boozehound, it would explain what happened to him. It would also explain how Luke survived barefoot and half-naked in the snow, all shot up. He's as tough as nails but even he couldn't keep that up indefinitely. And along came this character."

"Holy shit." She stared at the screen, fascinated, before she gave him back the tablet. "Luke could do that?"

"Theoretically, all of us could. We've got the right hardware and software. It's just a matter of choreographing a specific technique, you know? Like learning to juggle. There's all kinds of crazy shit we could do if we put our minds to it, but we don't. Either because we're busy with other things, or else we don't want to attract attention."

"Or because it's illegal." She shot him a meaningful look. "You know. Stealing and all that."

"Yeah, of course. Obviously."

"So, you don't think it was the tequila," she said.

He shook his head. "Could have been. Hell, Meeks could have been half-drunk or worse, but that doesn't mean he was lying. In any case, it's another lens to look through."

Simone looked thoughtful. "Did they find the car?"

"Eight days later, parked at a big box store in Bozeman. No damage, full tank of gas, keys locked inside. Sounds like something Luke would do. By the way, Meeks put the car up for sale. Won't drive it to save his life."

"I don't blame him," Simone said. "I wouldn't either."

He blew out a frustrated sigh. "But I don't get it. If it was Luke, and he's free, why let weeks go by without contacting us? It makes no sense. Whatever he's fighting, he knows we'd help. We'd do anything for him."

"I'm sure he has his reasons."

"Yeah." His voice was bleak. "Like, Obsidian caught him and killed him. Or they put him back into a fucking cage."

"I doubt it." Simone's voice was calm and neutral. "If they had debriefed him with control codes and drugs, we'd all be locked up by now. So there's that."

"Maybe so," he conceded.

She laid her hand on his shoulder. "If Luke is as tough as you say—"

"Tougher," he broke in.

"Good." She gripped his shoulder hard. "Then he's not dead. He took Waylon's Jeep and drove it off into the sunset. He can think. His ASP works. His brain's not damaged."

"Yet," he said. "It's just crazy that we came so close. We must have missed his escape by, what? Barely a day. A goddamn *day.*"

Simone took his empty coffee cup and placed it on the bedside table. Then she scooted up close, and leaned against his back, resting her head on his shoulder. A soft, gentle weight.

"Be patient," she said. "You have a new lead. Be glad for it."

"I'll be glad when I find him," Zade said flatly. "Not before."

She didn't reply. Her warmth against his back felt good. Caressing. A wisp of her blond, wavy hair had come loose, coiling on his shoulder. He reached up and stroked that soft texture, admiring the glint of gold. Inhaling her scent.

"I wish I could make you be glad," she murmured. "At gunpoint, if need be."

He let out a short laugh. "Sorry to disappoint you."

"You don't. Ever." She leaned forward to rub her cheek against his face. "I love how you care. Even when it hurts you. You never run away. That's brave."

"Or stupid," he said.

"Nope," she said. "Brave."

"Whatever." He grabbed her hand, kissed it.

She took over from there.

CHAPTER 8

"Right there," Lewis Hale said. "Stop. Back up. About three seconds." R-48 forced her mind blank. Anxiety would be visible to Hale, the team leader. His elite command mods let him assess her stress reactions just by looking at her. And his word was law.

She replayed the video as directed. It had been copied from her implanted data processor, recorded from a microscopic camera mounted in her eye. Every second of that fight in LaSalle's kitchen in Munro Valley had been captured and was being analyzed.

Her head hurt. Without her genetically altered bones and rapid healing, she would have been killed by that blow from the knife block, but its impact still pounded like a sonofabitch. Metzer had fared somewhat worse, not having as many genetic edits as she did. Command types were never as tough as subordinates like her. The process of inserting hardcore genetic edits was dangerous. The Obsidian fat cats thought twice before risking it, for themselves or for their kids.

No, all the really hazardous stuff was for slave grunts like herself.

Metzer was under observation for his concussion. Resting comfortably in bed, zonked by painkilling drugs, while she was getting debriefed and reamed by Hale.

This was the thirty-eighth viewing of this video, and Hale had finally honed in on the bad part. She'd half-hoped it might slip right past him. The glitch was subtle from the outside, just a stutter in the timing of her fight. Blink and you missed it.

Hale hadn't blinked. He might be a pig and an asshole, but he wasn't an idiot.

R-48 wiped that thought, out of caution. The chemical residue of hostile, resentful thoughts left a trail that team leaders could sense, and Hale had doubts about her already.

Fortunately, he wasn't looking at her, only at the video. Specifically, that moment in the fight where the mystery opponent choked on his kill move.

Which had been her opportunity to finish him off. She should have done it. Easily. But she hadn't. She'd glitched, and everything had gone to hell.

Hale kept running it back, playing it again and again. Each time R-48 looked into the mystery guy's eyes, the tension built to screaming intensity in every part of her body. Her head pounded harder with every second that passed.

"You froze," Hale said slowly. "What the fuck happened?"

She looked straight ahead. It was better in these cases to look blank and stupid. They didn't like thinkers. But it took energy to keep the activity in her mind shoved down that far. "I don't know, sir," she said. "There can sometimes be glitches in programming from different sources that conflict—"

"Are you fucking kidding me? In a Level Twenty? Eye contact with this combatant had a measurable effect on your fighting skill. I can see it."

"May I point out that it was a point four second delay, and the first one I've ever experienced," R-48 said. "A conclusion can't be drawn from a single isolated incident."

"Yeah? Should I wait for an even more colossal fuck-up before I intervene? Two of my Level Twenty operatives are dead. Another is injured and out of commission. Your squad commander's injured. The targets escaped. The mission failed. Shorting out at a critical combat moment is a serious issue, R-48. I'm the one who has to take the heat. It's a huge clusterfuck. One that hurts me."

"Yes, of course, sir."

Hale licked his thin, pale lips as he stared at her. He picked at a lock of her hair coming loose from her braid. Without permission to clean up from combat, she was still uncomfortably disheveled.

"Do I need to think about reconditioning you, R-48?" he asked softly, stroking the lock of hair with his thumb.

She tried to stifle a shudder. "That's not necessary, sir."

"Hmm." His eyes glittered as he let go. "The combatant at LaSalle's house must be a rogue Obsidian agent. Do a deep dive. Find out who he is."

"Of course, sir."

"I don't want to compromise your function while I'm shorthanded. It won't be easy explaining away two dead agents in one night, R-48. There will be a reckoning." He gestured toward the large data-dive tank that dominated the debrief room. "Strip down."

She was startled. "Ah…it might be more effective to wait until I—"

"Don't argue. And don't forget to say 'sir.' Get in the fucking tank. I want to know everything about that rogue agent. Cross-reference him with Daniela LaSalle. Find any connections she might have to Manticore. Don't come up until you have something I can use. And I mean that literally. I do not care if you starve to death in the tank, bitch. Or drown in data. Understand?"

"Yes, sir. I'll call a tech to thread the sensors."

"No need," he said. "I'll thread them myself."

She suppressed her revulsion just in time. Hale was notorious among the female operatives who'd had occasion to serve under him. Literally. He was famous as one of the really bad ones. Some of the top guys got off on compelling the soldiers sexually, knowing they were stimmed up so hard, they couldn't say no without intense physical and mental discomfort. And there was the threat of reconditioning. Death was better.

She stripped down to a sports bra and boy shorts.

"Take off the rest of it," Hale said. "You don't need it in the tank."

She did so. Blank face, blank mind. Not noticing the thickened sound in his voice, his heavy breathing. Not noticing his flushed face and slack mouth, the hot, buzzy look in his eyes. She wasn't there. She didn't see.

She stood there, floating elsewhere. Letting him look and look.

He had to touch her to thread the probes into the ports in her head and spinal column. His hot, sticky hands kept sliding around. He gave her ass a squeeze.

"Dive deep, R-48," he said throatily. "Real deep."

"Yes, sir."

He gave her a smack on the ass for encouragement, and she climbed into the tank and reclined on the table within it, above the water level. Slowly, Hale hooked her up to the other sensors, pinching and groping all the while.

She could have dry-dived for the info without the tank. But the sensory deprivation increased the effectiveness of a data-dive by a good percentage. And besides, Hale just liked telling her to take her clothes off. He never missed an opportunity for that.

He positioned the stimulators to make sure she didn't cut the cord out there and float away, disappearing along with untold millions of Obsidian R&D money. She'd heard that it happened sometimes, although she hadn't tried it herself.

But in a secret, barricaded part of her mind, she thought about it. When the memories trapped behind her brain blocks revealed unbearably poignant glimpses of faces, feelings. She thought about it until the stim pain came and punished her for it.

Until she had to blank it all out. Stop thinking, or else die screaming.

Freedom.

She was lowered steadily into the warm water and the pod closed, leaving her in pitch darkness. All she felt was profound relief.

She no longer had to look up at Hale's red, leering face.

CHAPTER 9

Every mile she drove into the deepening night, Dani got more pissed at herself. She was being irresponsible. Not standing her ground and insisting that this poor guy get the medical attention he needed. It went against all her better judgment.

They know your name, where you live, where you work...wherever you go, they will find you. And then you will die in agony. Slowly.

Luke's words kept echoing in her head.

Going back into that nightmare, if they were lying in wait for her like he said, was a terrifying thought. But if this guy died on her, it would be one hundred percent her fault for agreeing to run. A freeway exit for a town big enough to have a hospital was coming up. It was now or never.

She gritted her teeth and started changing lanes. *Take charge, Dani. Somebody's got to.*

The Porsche surged forward as if the gas pedal had pressed itself. She gasped and began to brake. With no success. *Shit.* This, too?

"Whoa! Luke?" she said. "Something's wrong. Your car's messed up!"

His eyes didn't even open. "Everything in my life is messed up. Just drive."

She tried again to shift into the exit lane, but she was no longer in control. The turn signal switched itself off and the SUV swerved aggressively back into the fast lane, picking up speed. An eighteen wheeler that had been gaining behind them laid angrily on its horn.

She tried to steer it back and tried again to brake. The steering wheel kept her in the same lane, and the brake pedal would not respond.

They flashed past the exit. *Whoosh ...*

"Don't worry," Luke mumbled. "Just drive. Faster."

She looked at him, openmouthed, but got nothing more from him.

And so it continued. Her hands were on the wheel, but the Porsche had its own agenda. She was pumped full of panicky adrenaline, staring wide-eyed out the windshield, hands clenched on the wheel, useless though that seemed to be. The car didn't need her.

Maybe she had a head injury she didn't remember. Or maybe a hacker was having fun with the computerized systems. The SUV was late model, with way more gizmos than her car, which no one would even want to hack.

But really? This, right now, on top of all the other stuff that had gone down tonight? It was insane. *This is only a test*, she said to herself, pressing gently on the brake.

Nope. The speedometer stayed where it was, at 70 miles per hour, like creepy cruise control. And Luke was out of it. No use asking him anything.

On and on.

Every now and then, Luke stirred without opening his eyes and mumbled some directions; get off at an exit to a different highway, take this turnoff or that turnoff. If she hesitated to do what he said, the SUV promptly took over and did it for her.

For the first hundred miles or so, she was on familiar ground. Roads she'd driven before, landmarks she recognized. Then they got off the bigger highways and onto increasingly smaller roads leading into hills, and then mountains. Narrow winding roads. No towns or farms or habitations. The onboard navigation screen was dark and would not respond to her prodding. She wished she had her smartphone with its GPS function. Not that it would make any difference knowing where they were. None of this was up to her.

And Luke was largely unconscious. Who in the *hell* was driving this thing?

After a long while, they whizzed off an exit marked by a small sign that her tired eyes didn't have time to read. Maybe it said Ass-End of Nowhere, because that's where they appeared to have ended up, on a small, poorly maintained road twisting through hills dotted with scrubby trees and bushes. No signs out here— wherever here was. No mileage markers, no lines painted on the blacktop. The winding road was edged by shallow ditches filled with gravel. She saw a sharp curve coming up right ahead.

Screw it. She lifted her hands from the wheel and waited to see what would happen.

The SUV drifted across the road, veered toward the ditch on the left and abruptly corrected, thudding and jolting out and back up onto the blacktop.

Luke lifted his head. "Ouch." He sounded irritated. "What the fuck are you doing?"

"Absolutely nothing," she replied. "Because nothing actually seems to be required of me. Blame the demon. Your car's possessed, Luke."

"Just drive the fucking thing," he said wearily.

She smacked the steering wheel. "What part of 'your car is possessed by a demon' did you not understand?"

He shifted in his seat with a hiss of discomfort. "Nah, not a demon. Just a few extra bells and whistles. Don't sweat it. We're almost there. You can rest soon."

"Bells and whistles. My ass." She lifted her foot from the accelerator, letting the car coast. Sure enough, they surged forward around the curve.

He sighed. "If you're trying to wake me up, it's working."

"Is that a fact? Well, if you're trying to freak me out, that's working, too."

"I'm trying to save your life," he muttered. "Getting you to someplace safe as soon as possible is part of the plan."

She glanced over at him. His eyes were closed again, but that meant nothing. Obviously. "There's a plan? I'd really love to hear it."

"Later."

"That's not an answer," she said through gritted teeth.

"I'm playing the wounded soldier card. Give me a fucking break."

Interesting. He sounded stronger, which was a good sign. And Dani could live with the macho attitude reboot that went along with it. "OK. Will do. Glad to know you're not slipping into a coma," she said. "That would put the cherry on top of my special night."

"I'll be fine. If I don't have to talk."

Whatever. Dani shut up and drove on through the darkness.

The road was climbing steeply again through the scrubby trees, up and out of the river canyon and then switching back and forth up a mountainside. The scrubby trees thinned out. So did the air, though the scent of pine got stronger.

After they had driven for some time along the crest of the hill they'd just climbed, he spoke again. "You're going to turn left up ahead."

"Where? I don't see it."

"Slow down."

His insistence on this fiction that she was actually driving annoyed the hell out of her. Just to mess with him, she jammed down the accelerator, and lifted her hands from the wheel.

They hurtled past the turnoff he'd indicated and lurched to a halt, wallowing in the gravel.

"What the hell?" he snapped.

"Just making a point," she said. "I don't like being jerked around."

"Now's not the time."

Dani drummed on the steering wheel, thinking it over. He had saved her life. *And then told you that wild story. Tricked you into driving his demon car. And you don't know where the fuck you are right now. Just that it's very far from everywhere.*

She would need him to get back out of here. Even aside from her professional concern for his health, that was reason enough to stop arguing with him.

She put the SUV in reverse, backed up until she could see the almost invisible driveway, and turned into it. They plunged into the overgrown bushes and trees.

The Porsche picked up speed without her doing anything, rattling and jouncing over the rutted road. The headlights revealed a nondescript building, surrounded by parked vehicles. Looked like mostly beaters. Flat tires on a few.

A garage door began to rise. He wasn't using a remote. At this point, that hardly surprised her.

Dawn was near. The night sky showed a faint glow on the horizon as they pulled into the garage. The rolling door ground down, leaving them in pitch darkness.

"Yikes," she said. "Creepy."

A light flicked on. A bright hanging lamp illuminated a crowded worktable that stretched the length of the garage.

Almost as weird as the demon car. But less dangerous. "Thanks," she murmured.

Luke shoved open the car door and tumbled out, staggering and hanging onto the fender.

She jumped out herself. "Shit! Wait for me, Luke! Was that necessary?"

"I think so," he said. "You can't carry me. I'm really heavy."

"I know, but I can help! I'm strong."

"I noticed that." His voice was wry.

She slid under his arm, taking as much of his weight as she could as they staggered through the garage and toward the interior door.

The room they entered was large and featureless, furnished with just a plastic picnic table with attached benches and a sink with a few kitchen appliances along one wall. There were heaps of boxes and equipment. No couches, chairs or lamps. Nothing personal.

It smelled cold and stale inside the place, like metal and dust and machine oil.

She guided him over to sit down on the bench and started trying to unfasten the armored vest. Luke tried to help, but she figured it out for herself quickly enough. A skill learned the hard way filling in on Saturday night ER shifts. Stabbings, gunshots, car crashes, name it.

He caught his breath as she lifted the heavy, blood-drenched vest off him. Beneath it, his shirt was stuck to his body by sweat and blood. It had dried onto the wound, which seemed to be barely oozing at this point.

"OK. We need to get this shirt cut off." Luke didn't protest, but he looked dazed and exhausted. "So where would I find scissors?" she prompted.

He nodded toward the side of the big room that evidently served as the kitchen. "Top drawer by the sink."

"How about gauze pads? Bandage tape? Rubbing alcohol? Antibiotic ointment?"

Her long list didn't faze him. "There's a hinged clear plastic box on a shelf in the bathroom. Thataway."

"Um, disposable gloves?"

He shook his head.

Oh well. But props to him for having the basics.

She found what she needed and got busy, cleaning the bloody wounds in his upper arm and side before she removed the rest of his shirt. His huge torso was covered with ridged scars. The sight gave her a chill of dread and fear.

"Like Naldo," she blurted out. "But yours are worse."

"Maybe so." He closed his eyes, dragging slow, hissing breaths through his teeth. Suffering.

"That's all you have to say?" Her voice had an edge. "What is it with you guys? What in the hell happened to you? Both of you?"

He shook his head. "Dani. Please." His voice had become a halting rasp.

"Right," she murmured. "Later."

"I swear, I'll tell you everything I can. As soon as I can."

She had to be content with that. She got back to work. Focusing on his body.

Not that she could have focused on anything else if she wanted to. Even wounded, with his breath rasping painfully in his massive chest, the guy was a mouth-watering super stud. Close proximity to him was distracting even before she got his clothes off.

And when he was half naked, the sheer breadth of his heavily muscled shoulders and chest stopped her breath.

Not good.

Concentrate, LaSalle. Do your nurse thing. Breathe. Your brain needs oxygen.

But he threw off so much heat. It made her sweat. Her face felt fiery as she dabbed on antibiotic ointment with a piece of folded gauze. She tried not to be so acutely conscious of the taut, steely belly muscles before her eyes, but he was so lean and ripped, with that dark treasure trail tapering down, sliced through here and there by the scarring.

She tried desperately not to think about the kissing interlude in her laundry closet, which now seemed like a crazy dream. It couldn't possibly have been real.

Her eyes rested on his rock-hard thighs splayed out in front of the bench, his huge quad muscles bulging against the blood-stiffened black fabric of his pants, remembering how it felt to straddle them and hang on for dear life. Her chest plastered against his bullet-proof vest while his hand cupped her ass, slowly rocking and pulsing the yearning ache between her legs against the hard, thick bulge at his crotch.

Stop it. You are working. Fuck's sake. The man just got stabbed.

Good thing he wasn't looking at her. He was hunched over, head down and shaking fingers clenched, white-knuckled, on his own knees as she finished taping the gauze over the wound at his side.

There was blood on his face, too. Or what she could see of it, with his head lowered. Sweat shone on it. Big drops standing out. She rose to her feet, alarmed by the heat radiating off his body, and reached out to feel his forehead.

He jerked sharply away, then went still. He looked up at her, eyes cautious.

"Sorry," he said gruffly. "I'm on edge. You took me by surprise."

"I was just, uh, checking," she said. "You're so hot."

He glanced up. The look on his face was almost a smile.

Her face flamed. "I mean…I just want to see if you're running a fever." *Crap.*

"I'm not," he said softly. "But go ahead."

She was so flustered, she was no longer tracking. "Huh? Go ahead and what?"

He put his hand on the gauze taped to his side. "Touch me," he said simply.

Another awkward silence while Dani's mouth worked. "Ah…"

"If you want to check my temperature, I mean." He grinned at her. The very first smile she'd seen on his otherwise grim face.

Oh, God. Dimples? It was too goddamn much. Everything they said to each other sounded like a blatant come-on to her now.

"Well. I'll just, um, find a thermometer," she mumbled, rummaging through the little plastic chest of medical supplies.

"Don't have one." His voice was thick with exhaustion. "Never needed one."

"OK, whatever." That was an argument for another day. She pulled out a piece of folded gauze and dabbed antibiotic ointment on it. "Let me take care of those scrapes on your face."

He didn't make a sound, just closed his eyes as she swabbed and dabbed. Which left her free to study every detail up close. His face had scars, too. More recent injuries on top of older ones. Bumps on his nose from being broken more than once.

"I hope you have a bed around here, because you look like you're ready to get horizontal," she told him. "And this table looks cold and hard."

"There's a bed in the other room, but you can take it," he said. "I'll sleep on the floor."

"Yeah, right. Like I would let you do that."

"You're the boss," he said.

"Hardly," she said. "I can't make you clue me in about what's going on. You just keep saying you'll tell me everything later. And I'm really hoping that *tell me everything* includes explaining those scars, and who the killer robots are, and how the demon Porsche drives itself."

"I'll do my best," he promised.

Dani harrumphed. "You're a piece of work, Luke. And we have to get you covered up." Like, right away, even though he looked great just like that. Half-naked, just neatly bandaged here and there. "Do you have a sweatshirt that zips?"

"Somewhere. Maybe." He lurched unsteadily toward the bedroom.

It was a smaller space, almost empty but for a queen-sized bed and a dresser, but the sheets looked clean and there was a thick wool blanket. She folded down the bedclothes and tried to guide him down, but gravity was too much for them both.

He fell and hit the bed hard, bouncing on it with a muffled gasp of pain.

"Shit. That was clumsy. Sorry," she said hastily, checking the bandages.

"Not your fault," he mumbled, and that was it. He was out.

She felt his pulse. Strong and steady. The nurse in her hated this slapdash patch job. He deserved better. She covered him up with the blanket, and looked around the room. Not much to see, just a bathroom on the other side of a partly open door, the one where she'd found the medical supplies. There were a couple of skimpy towels and some shaving gear. A dresser had a heap of clean, unfolded clothing on it. She rummaged through it and took the liberty of selecting an enormous T-shirt and a pair of boxer shorts for herself.

She took them into the bathroom and stopped short, horrified by what she saw in the mirror over the sink. Wild-eyed, blood streaked, hair whitened with dust. The harpy from the dark dimensions. God, how she wanted to wash.

Dani stripped down. It felt strange and vulnerable, being naked with that extremely compelling man in the next room, but he was unconscious, and the lure of hot water and soap was too strong to resist.

The spray stung the scrapes on her shoulders. She'd barely noticed them before. The shower water ran gray and pink as it swirled down the drain.

Note to self: her hand needed antibiotic gel where that asshole had sliced her. She sudsed and rinsed until the water ran clear. It took a good long while.

Fresh clothes felt so good. His boxers were loose in the waist and tight in the hips, but they weren't going to fall off. No hair grooming stuff was to be found in the bathroom of a guy with a buzz cut, so she finger-combed her tangled locks as best she could.

She emerged from the bathroom in a cloud of steam, checked on sleeping Luke before dimming the light way down, and then went to wander around.

Computers and electronic gear lined an entire long wall of the other room. Behind a closed door off the corridor was another bedroom where a chilling array of weapons were laid out on heavy-duty metal shelves. Rifles, handguns, shotguns, ammo of all types.

She stared at the highly organized arsenal, guts sinking.

Please don't let him be one of those guys who hurt people for a cause.

She backed out of that room, unnerved. Peering into the fridge, she saw beer, a bag of ground coffee and dried up remains of takeout. A couple of eggs, a near-empty tub of deli potato salad. Apparently he had even less culinary imagination than she did.

"Dani?" Luke's voice from the bedroom was low and raw. "You in there?"

"Yeah, I'm here," she called out.

His face relaxed when he saw her at the bedroom door. She was startled to see a gun in his hand. "Holy cow, Luke. Do you sleep with that thing?"

He looked down at it, apparently startled by the question. "I don't sleep much."

"That wasn't what I asked," she said.

"I keep it close, yeah," he admitted. "It was under my pillow."

"Really. Is the safety on?"

He looked, and nodded.

Dani stepped back anyway. Like that would save her from a random shot. "Guys like you get speed-tracked into the ER," she told him. "They usually leave in black bags. All zipped up."

"I get the point." Luke put the gun on the floor by the bed and gazed at her for a moment. "Come here."

She approached the bed, and perched at the foot. He shook his head, beckoning. "No, here." He patted the space between himself and the wall. "There's room. You need to rest, too."

Her face went hot. Good thing the room was dark. "Um…I'm not sure if that's the greatest idea."

"Please," he said. "Just stretch out and rest a little. You're safe here."

It was a crazy thing to do, climbing into bed with him. But it also felt like the only thing. She was exhausted.

She should be scared of him, but she wasn't. Go figure. She was too tired to think it through.

Dani clambered over him and sat up cross-legged, back to the wall. Dawn was just breaking, faintly lighting up the outline of the blackout window-blinds. The room felt quiet, secret. A hidden cave, a beast's den.

"You smell good," he whispered.

"Just your shower soap."

"Smells different on you," he said. "Sweeter. Nicer."

The shivery rush his words gave her was alarming. She headed him off. "Hold it right there," she said sternly. "No flirting. Cut that shit out right now."

"Is that what I was doing? Huh." She saw that smile flash again in the dimness. "You gonna stay with me?" he asked drowsily.

"Yes," she said.

"Good." He drifted off again, holding her hand.

At last, a good opportunity to just gawk. A nice, long, uninterrupted, inch-by-inch inventory of him. There was just enough light filtering in to make out the details. He was out-of-this-world hot. And built. That face. Those lips.

The scars, too. That made her think of Naldo's thin, scrawny chest. His scars. His tormented eyes.

His bloody handprint on her knee.

Then it hit her, all at once. She kept her crying quiet, so as not to disturb Luke, and felt around for a tissue box. Nothing on this side of the bed. She needed to mop herself up, but Luke was still tightly clutching her other hand.

She gave a gentle tug. His fingers did not release her, and yet, paradoxically, she could tell that he was genuinely out. She could always tell if a person was fake-sleeping or really sleeping. Or dying. Like Naldo.

She was so grateful that Luke was not dying and leaving her all alone in the middle of nowhere.

Runny nose or not, she was in no hurry to let go of his big, warm hand.

CHAPTER 10

She was so damn beautiful.

Luke lay in a state of amazed contemplation and watched her sleep.

Air was going so much deeper into his lungs now. Muscles relaxing. That clench of constant, agonizing tension had released. Looking at her made him feel softer, more flexible. His muscles, his chest, his face.

Just not his dick. That part of him stayed stone hard.

This was sloppy and dangerous. He'd actually fallen asleep for a couple of hours, to his astonishment. Real, actual human sleep, not sentinel sleep. He hadn't succeeded at that since his capture over a year ago. He'd tried so hard to achieve it, out of sheer boredom and desperation during those long empty hours alone in Braxton's cage. He had craved unconsciousness like water in the desert. But he never got that relief.

Not until now. Dani's gift to him. The latest of many. And he'd only known her for a few hours.

She was slouched against the headboard fast asleep, her long, graceful legs folded up. She'd washed her hair. Her ringlets were bouncy and wild. Floating upward. Gravity didn't seem to even touch them.

He needed to direct all of his energy at healing his wounds as fast as possible. Fueling his body would help, but that was too complicated right now.

Staring at Dani triggered a power surge to his sex drive. She looked super sexy and utterly feminine wearing his boxers and T-shirt. And imagining her under the shower, naked and wet—wow. Pure octane.

Her face was different when she was asleep. Defenses down, minus the brisk, don't-argue-with-me attitude. Her mouth looked soft and full and pink. Sweet, pillowy lips that made him want to lean down and taste her with the tip of his tongue.

His cock ached as he took in the sight of her round, high tits beneath the lightweight T-shirt. His gaze moved down over her rounded thighs. The baggy boxers didn't hide much. It turned him on that his own clothing was on her warm, fragrant body.

So his sex drive hadn't been blasted out by torture and isolation. Just sidelined.

He wanted so badly to touch her but instinct made him hesitate. He rested his outstretched hand on the sheet instead. Dani woke with a start, her eyes wide and panicked.

He stayed very still. All too aware that waking up in a strange place—next to someone you barely knew—was fucking weird.

"Don't be scared," he said gently.

She laughed. Sort of. "Right. I hate to be the one to tell you this, Luke, but you are flat-out terrifying as all shit."

"I'm not dangerous," he insisted.

She sniffed. "Tell that to the dead people all over my house."

He dismissed her comment with a shrug. "They were trying to kill you."

"Uh-huh." She was examining his bandages without touching them, murmuring to herself. "Good. Looks like the bleeding's stopped. I'll change those in a bit."

Then Dani looked straight into his eyes. Her searching gaze was so intense, he almost blinked first.

It occurred to him that until he met her, he hadn't looked anyone directly in the eyes since...well, since before. That great, blank space in his mind. Before.

He struggled to just hold her gaze. Like a normal person, not a burned-out freak.

"How did you know they were going to come after me?" she demanded. "And why did you want to be a hero?"

The silence was heavy between them. She held up her hand with a short, harsh sigh. "Right," she said. "Later, huh? I'm getting a little tired of the word."

"No," he said. "Not later. Now?"

Her eyes widened. "For real?"

"Yeah. I owe you an explanation."

Dani straightened up. "Then start with the thing that came out of Naldo's chest."

"Yes," he said. "Let me get a laptop. I'll pull up the schematics."

"Lucky me. I can hardly wait." She made a face at him. "But it sounds like I'm going to. Again."

He wished he could just pull her close to him, but it would scare her to death. "I just want you to know that you can relax here," he offered carefully. "You're safe."

She rolled her eyes. "Safe, my ass," she muttered. "I'll never feel safe again."

You damn well will. The thought took hold in his head.

He needed a mission. Making Dani feel safe would do just fine. It was something important, and it went beyond just chasing the memories of his former life like a dog chasing a fucking car.

"Up here, you are," he said. "Want to see outside?"

"Sure."

He got up and went to the window, barely limping anymore. The rapid-healing that had been vectored into his genes had done its thing. Being a bioengineered freak had its occasional upsides.

He looked around the edge of the blind before raising it. Nothing out of the ordinary out there. Same trees, same mountains. A sliver of morning sunlight warmed the side of his face. "Come here," he said.

"You should stay in bed." She swung her legs over the side of the bed, frowning anxiously at his bandaged side. "That could be infected."

"I seriously doubt it." He wished he could put her mind at ease and get that worried look out of her eyes, but this was definitely not the time to explain about his turbocharged immunity to pathogens, toxins, and radiation.

She got up and joined him at the window. "I really can't state this strongly enough," she said. "You should get yourself checked out at a hospital, Luke. Just to be safe. That wound was deep." She reached out and touched his forehead.

Her touch felt so damn good, he felt his face heat, which was going to give her the wrong idea. "I'm fine," he assured her. "No internal bleeding. No inflammation." He did a quick body scan with ASP to make sure he wasn't lying, but it was all true.

She looked disapproving. "No way you can know that for sure."

"I'm sure." He reached down to the bandage, dug his nails under the tape and ripped it off.

Dani looked alarmed. "Luke! What the hell?"

"It really is OK," he assured her. "Look. All closed up." He turned that side toward the light pouring in the window. She leaned down to take a look—and went still.

Damn. His intention had been to reassure her, not to creep her out even more. Nurses knew how long it could take for a wound to heal. And his had healed completely in just a few hours.

She stared at it, utterly shocked. "That...that's not possible," she whispered.

He pulled the other bandage off his shoulder where the bullet wound was, because what the hell, at this point. "This one too," he said. "All good."

She straightened up to examine the former hole in his shoulder, now a well-knitted scar. A mystified frown between her straight black eyebrows. "I don't understand," she said. "How on earth..." Her voice trailed off.

"I just heal really fast." He figured he'd wait on the details of Braxton's original gene cocktail, the one for enhanced muscle fiber, toughened bones, pain resistance.

That and fast healing was what got him through all the cutting and sawing the researchers had done.

"Luke," she said. "That's not fast healing. That's not...human."

He shrugged, flexing and stretching the arm. "It's just how I roll. I promise, I'm human. Mostly."

Her eyes narrowed. "Mostly? What do you mean?"

"What do you think I mean?" A cheap evasion, but he was still fishing for a good place to start, and too many impossible truths at once might make her run away screaming.

He'd hoped that the impossible truths could wait until after she'd eaten, and maybe had some coffee. One thing at a time.

"How about we start with the demon Porsche," she said. "It was you driving, right? You drove that thing yourself, eyes closed, half-conscious and not moving a goddamn muscle. Is that what you mean by mostly human?"

She had him pinned with that accusing look. "I can explain," he told her.

"You'd better. And include the following bullet points. Who are you, how do you do this science fiction stuff, what do you have to do with Naldo, and what the fuck do you want with me?"

He took a moment. "OK," he said carefully. "Point one. I'm Luke, like I told you. The quick healing and the remote driving are just—"

"Don't get ahead of yourself. Luke who? From where? Who does what with his time? This 'Just Luke' bullshit won't cut it."

He hesitated. "Can we save that part for last?"

The question clearly infuriated her.

"Do not jerk me around, J.L.," she warned. "Just answer the goddamn question!"

He lifted his hands, and let them drop. "I can't," he admitted. "Because I don't know."

Dani's eyes were full of angry confusion. "What the hell's that supposed to mean?"

He shook his head. "Literally, exactly what I said. I don't know who I am. Or where I'm from. Or what I did there."

"So…you've got some kind of amnesia? Is that what you're telling me?"

"Something like that."

"OK," she murmured thoughtfully. "Then…never mind. Just tell me how Naldo was mixed up in it."

He exhaled slowly, organizing his thoughts. "Naldo and I have something in common," he said. "You saw the scars on his chest."

She nodded. "Like yours. Except that you seem to have more."

"Right. When I was a teenager, I lived on the streets. I got swept up into an illegal research program funded by Obsidian, a super-secret international organization. They wanted to create supersoldiers, and evade government regulations on scientific experiments. So they did human testing in secret. Quick and dirty. Runaways like me got lured in. No one was looking for us and Obsidian was cool with that."

Dani's face was unreadable. "Go on," she said.

"They did all kinds of stuff to me. Gene splicing, brain stimulation, implants that ramped up my sensory and data processing capacities, you name it. Combat, technokinesis—"

"What's that?"

"When you can interface directly with a machine. Brain to computer."

"Like the car."

"Yeah, among other things. Anyhow, one of the researchers who worked on me—Braxton—was a total psycho. Eventually, even Obsidian decided he was a liability and sidelined him. At which point, he started a rival supersoldier lab in Asia. Called it Manticore."

Her eyes flashed. "Naldo mentioned something called Manticore. He said to watch out for them."

"Fill me in. Was Naldo an orphan? Nobody to look for him if he disappeared?"

"No one but me," she said.

"Was he bright?"

"Brilliant," she said. "Smartest kid I ever met."

"So he was perfect for Braxton," Luke said. "The guy was like a shark. Always cruising for smart, angry orphans and runaways. Naldo got caught in Braxton's net, just like me, and got turned into a Manticore operative."

She bit her full lower lip, her gaze intent. "How did you escape?"

"I don't know," Luke said. "I know that I was out of there for several years, but I don't remember where I was, or with who. All that stuff is gone. Then I got recaptured, but I don't remember how. And Braxton found me again. I was imprisoned for over a year."

"Were you abused? Beaten?" Her eyes traveled slowly over his face and down over his chest, taking stock of various scars, new and old.

The blunt question didn't bother him. She worked in a hospital, she saw plenty of evil shit. "Yeah. But I brain blocked myself. I had lots of time to set it up. I was real specific."

"Brain blocked?" Her eyebrows went up. "What's that?"

"Braxton was going to peel me open," he explained. "Force me to reveal my people. Whoever and wherever they are. I no longer know."

"Got it. So you blocked out specific memories of these people to protect them. And now you can't get those memories back."

"Pretty much," he said. "Braxton used selective memory block techniques to make his slave soldiers obedient. That was what gave me the idea. Took me a while, but I figured out how to use it against him. I blocked access to essentially everything in my life that I gave a shit about. They could drug or torture me, and I couldn't tell. I no longer knew."

"Hmmm," she murmured. "I see. And yeah, that happens. But I never heard it described like that."

Was she just humoring him? Hard to tell. Luke said a silent *fuck it* and kept talking. It was a relief to finally say this stuff to someone. So what if she thought he was crazy. He knew he wasn't. At least, not yet.

"Go on," she urged. "How did you do it?"

"I built virtual walls, then ran a lot of energy through them, like an electric fence," he explained. "I targeted memories with a particular emotional charge. Anything intimate, I just walled it off. It's hard to explain if you've never done deep stim. Does that make sense to you?"

Dani was silent for a moment, and then seemed to shake herself out of a trance. "Yes, actually," she said. "I'm beginning to think it's happening to me. Where are we, anyhow? What is this place?"

"You're about thirty miles out of a place called Barrett," he said. "You're still in California."

"And this place is yours?"

"Rented," he said.

"With all those junker cars parked out front?"

"They belong to my landlord. His dad died a couple months ago, left him the property and the junkers. I didn't care. I just needed a place, fast."

"Because you were on the run," she murmured. "Like Naldo. Now tell me about that thing in his chest."

He fished the metal capsule out of his pocket. "This has Manticore info on it about a shipment of hardware to augment their newest generation of supersoldiers. Naldo was a courier for them. I tried to intercept his run, but he was fighting his programming. He cut loose of them before I got to him, and ran right to you. That's hard to do. Almost impossible. Your friend was seriously bad-ass to have made it as far as he did. A slave soldier pays with everything he's got when he resists those motherfuckers and what they did to him."

Pain flashed across her face. "Sounds like Naldo."

"I'm not sure why he came to you," Luke went on. "Judging from the kind of people who attacked you at your house, the buyer Naldo was scheduled to meet must have been an Obsidian agent. They want to shut Manticore down, of course. They don't tolerate any competition."

"Tell me how you know this." Her voice was low, but it still had a challenging ring. "Since you say you were locked up all that time."

"I did some data-diving in Braxton's archives," Luke said. "I know everything he knew. Or at least everything that he documented online."

Dani reached for the metal capsule. Luke let her twitch it out of his fingers but he kept his eyes locked on it. She examined it, frowning. "Why do you want this?"

He hesitated, embarrassed. His plan was going to sound farfetched and unrealistic. More wishful thinking than anything else. But it was the only plan he had.

He owed her the truth. He gently took the capsule back, gripping it in his fist.

"The shipment includes an instrument to remove memory blocks," he said. "It's a type of probe that jacks into a slave soldier's cranial ports and then emits a certain frequency that dissolves the blocks."

Dani kept waiting, like she thought there should be more, so he kept talking.

"I want to use it on myself," he said. "I want to get my life back."

She nodded. "Fair enough. So why take me with you?"

"You're the only contact point Obsidian has," he said. "They don't have data on me, just you. They would have questioned you hard and then just killed you."

"What do you care?" she asked. "You didn't know me. You still don't. What's a little more blood in this great big sea of blood?"

"I won't let them hurt you," he said. "I like the world better with you in it."

His declaration rang in the silence between them. Her eyes were big.

"What?" he demanded. "Why the scared look? What's so terrible about that?"

She shrugged. "I'm not sure I want a genetically amped up cyborg dude who can drive cars with his mind to be so interested in me."

"I'm not dangerous, Dani."

"I've never met anyone more dangerous in my life," she informed him. "Including those freaks in my house. You flattened every last one of them."

"You helped," he said. "Stabbing that knife into the guy's hand, jumping on the woman's back—I'd be dead if you hadn't—"

"Shut up, Luke. Don't even try. We both know who did all the work last night."

"I'm not one of the bad guys, Dani!"

"Really?" Her voice was oddly soft. "How would you know?"

The question stopped him in his tracks. "I just do," he finally said.

She let out a laugh. "Great. Here I am, in the ass-end of nowhere, miles from civilization, in your bedroom wearing nothing but underwear—"

"My underwear," he specified, softly.

"So what? Don't interrupt. Where was I?"

"In my bedroom. In my underwear," he said, ever helpful.

She jabbed an accusing finger at him. "Right. Where I was fool enough to fall asleep. You say you don't remember anything about your life, right? How do I know you're not a homicidal maniac? You have all the skills."

He forced himself to wait before quietly answering. "I'd know if I was. I'm not."

"Not comforted," she said. "Not one little bit."

His data scroll was analyzing every painful detail of her stress reaction. Heart racing, adrenaline and cortisol elevated, blood pressure up, palms clammy and cold.

The best thing he could think of was to give her space. Not what he wanted, but what she needed. He stepped back.

"I'm grabbing a shower," he said. "Please relax, Dani. I'm not a monster, I swear to God."

Once in the shower, he filtered out the hiss of the water to monitor her rapid heartbeat through the bathroom wall. Just in case. Reading all her dizzying signals made him hot and confused.

Shit. What a fucking charmer he was. He really had the touch.

Luke stared grimly at his battered, dripping face in the reflection of the shower door, wondering what he looked like to Dani. Buzzed-off hair, deep hollows under his cheekbones, the weird scars, the crazed eyes, burning with lustful intensity. He must look like a total nut job in her eyes. And the massive, waving hard-on wasn't going to help convince her of his good intentions.

He couldn't leave the bathroom until he got that damn thing to stand down.

CHAPTER 11

What in freaking *hell* had she gotten herself into?

Dani paced back and forth in the bedroom. She couldn't handle any more of this crazy crap. She didn't have room for it, couldn't process it, couldn't even begin to figure it out.

Nothing made sense. The demon car she couldn't control, Naldo's death, the capsule, the attackers. Luke himself.

She had no idea if he was who he said he was. She desperately wanted to believe that he was honest and sane. But she fucking hated his story. She didn't want it to be true.

He'd blasted into her life on a wave of bloody violence. Dragged her forcibly into some strange new world where she didn't want to be.

Not even with him.

She wished she didn't want him so much. He was so powerful and skilled and tough, to say nothing of freaking gorgeous. He had saved her bacon, and yes, she craved his protection. Intensely. He was so seductive. Begging her to trust him. So big and beautiful and strong and gentle. An amazing kisser. And so intensely focused on her.

That rang all her bells like nobody's business. His skills and his physical power would be seductive even if he weren't so fucking fine. Sauntering around with the burning eyes and the sensuous lips and the steely-muscled, mouthwatering ripped torso on blatant display. Crazy or not, he sent bolts of heat through her body. It messed her head all up.

No pelvic decisions here, LaSalle. Keep it cool.

Part of her was ready to believe his story. Wild as it was, the world was wilder, and she'd seen some seriously weird shit in her life, both as a nurse and before. The scars that he and Naldo shared made a compelling case for the story just as he told it.

But please. Believe all of it? Everything he said? The science-fiction shit? Fuck no. She just couldn't.

There were other possibilities. Dangerous ones. Number one on the list was her own altered perception of reality. Trauma messed people up. It changed how they saw things. Made them vulnerable. Easy to manipulate. She wasn't going to let herself be fooled like that. She'd seen female patients in the ER who'd gotten themselves into a world of hurt after being rescued by a "hero." Some men smelled blood and moved in fast. *Help you change that tire, honey? Are these assholes bothering you?*

Who knew, maybe Luke had somehow manipulated her instincts the way he'd manipulated his own car. Maybe he'd isolated her out here, far from help, no phone, no map, to tear down her defenses. It was a classic mind control technique. Tried and true.

She couldn't risk it. She couldn't trust herself right now, and she sure as shit didn't dare trust him, no matter how badly she wanted to.

No matter how freaking out-of-this-world delicious he might be.

So get the fuck out of here. Now. Any way you can.

She searched the room, feverishly. Found her blood-stiffened sweat shorts and put them back on. Her flip-flops were still chalky with plaster dust and spotted with dried blood, but they were all she had, so on they went.

Luke's pistol still lay on the floor by the bed. It surprised her that he just left it there. She scooped it up and moved quickly through the kitchen, looking around for car keys for the Porsche. Maybe they were still in the ignition. The car had been running when she got into it last night at her house. Back in the real world, which seemed very long ago and far away.

She sneaked out into the garage, peering into the gleaming SUV. No keys. It was all locked up tight, and so was the garage door. No remote control for that, either.

Now she was crying. *Shit.* Tears streaming silently down her face. Shaking like a baby.

She picked her way back to the bedroom, steeling herself. She had to deal with him. The water had stopped hissing. Then came the squeaky scrape of the shower door.

She barely breathed in the moments that followed until the bathroom door opened.

The sight of him hit her hard, along with the waft of warm, scented steam. His big, gorgeous body, backlit by light and fog, like some over-the-top rock video. He stepped into the light. His dark eyes were fierce with interest, like she was a puzzle he needed to solve. He looked only at her face. He didn't seem to notice the gun clutched in her hands.

As if it didn't matter. As if it couldn't hurt him.

"I am not afraid to use this," she told him.

"I don't think you're afraid of anything," he said.

Hah. She wished. That voice. So deep, so fucking *calm.* It was weird.

"Give me the car keys," she said. "I'm out of here."

"You're not my prisoner, Dani," he said gently. "You never were."

"Then give me the keys and I'll just disappear. I'll leave your car someplace where you can retrieve it. Just tell me where. And I won't tell anybody about you ever. I owe you big for what you did for me at my house, but I decide where and how I do things, understand? Always. My choice."

"Of course," he said. "I wouldn't have it any other way. I love that about you."

"Just stop it," she snapped. "Where are the keys?"

"Don't have any," he said.

She gaped at him. "Huh?"

"Keys. I don't have any. They're superfluous. For me, anyhow. I start the car with my brain implant." He took a step toward her.

"Get back," she warned. "Get away from me."

"Dani," he said. "Put the gun down. I swear on my life that I would never hurt you. For any reason."

"Really? What if I stood between you and that…that thing that was in Naldo's chest? What would you do then?"

His eyes were hypnotically intent as he took another step toward her. "I would move you gently to one side," he said. "Without hurting a single hair on your head."

She edged away from him. "Back off," she warned.

"No. I have to do this." A blur of whip-swift movement made her yelp. Suddenly, the gun was in his hand, and she was in his grip.

Dani exploded in a panic, slapping and shoving. Luke placed the gun on the dresser and just held her, barely seeming to notice the scratches or blows.

Somehow she just ended up getting closer and closer to him, clamped to his broad, steely chest. Overwhelmed by his nearness. Just like in the laundry closet.

His breath was minty. He'd brushed his teeth while in the bathroom.

That incongruous little detail made her shake with silent, hysterical laughter.

"What?" he asked. "What's so funny?"

"Nothing. Let go of me."

But in her twisting and struggling, she'd knocked loose the towel he'd wound around his waist. It dropped to the floor. Suddenly she was in the arms of a stark naked guy with an erection the likes of which she had never seen.

Her gasp choked off, and she redoubled her struggles. "Oh, for the love of God, Luke! Seriously?"

"Damn," Luke said. "Sorry. I didn't mean to wave my dick at you. For the record, you knocked off my towel, not me. I didn't do this on purpose."

"So put your damn thing away, already! Stop slapping me with it!"

He held firm while she wiggled and flopped. "I can't let go of you while you're freaking out on me," he said. "I might get hurt."

"Right. Like I could ever get the drop on you. Not in a million years."

"I'm not risking it. You were holding a gun on me a minute ago. Sorry about the boner. You're super hot, and I'm all worked up from combat stress. But you're safe with me."

"Safe? Like I was in the closet with you?"

"You survived the closet." His voice was a growling rasp. "You did just fine."

"You bastard." She struggled in his arms as his thick, hard cock swung against her thigh. It felt as hot as a brand to her shivering skin. Broad and blunt. It made her breath short and her heart pound madly. She was crazily furious. So angry, she felt almost drunk.

She stared into his intense eyes, feeling the power in him. Craving it.

He burned with it. Wildfire hot. Their faces were so close now. She smelled that minty breath again. He leaned over her, like he was inhaling her scent. A flush of hot arousal stained his cheekbones.

"Don't you rub your dick on me, you pervert," she hissed.

"You're the one who's moving. I'm just trying not to get punched and slapped."

"You are so full of shit," she said. "Just shut the fuck up."

"Make me," he said.

And out of nowhere, she was kissing him.

The instant his hungry mouth made contact with hers, she was spellbound. Desperately struggling to get closer to him, fear swept aside in favor of the hot, wet writhing *now* of his warm, seeking lips, his probing tongue, his sweet-salt taste. Every frantic kiss kindled a wild craving for more.

Her legs wound around him, pressing that yearning ache at her crotch against his heat, his strength. He hoisted her up easily, and she was no lightweight. She was tall, big-boned, with muscles, curves, heft, but he was so insanely strong it just didn't matter.

God, she loved it.

Her back hit the wall. His fingers wound into her hair, her arms around his neck. Kissing, moaning, tasting, opening. Tongues dancing. A tender, desperate devouring.

Luke shifted her body over his, positioning her hips so her clit rocked tenderly against the shaft of his cock. He pulsed her slowly, sensuously against himself, his big hand holding the small of her back, pulling her ass up tight with each squeeze of her thighs, except that this time he was naked, and that was awesome. This time she could feel all his scorching heat, the texture of his skin, the rasp of his chest hair. No thick, stiff body armor blocking her from all the good sexy hot stuff.

Her whimpering moans were lost against his wild kisses. She made sounds she couldn't control with each foaming wave of energy that crashed through her.

A rush of pleasure overwhelmed her.

His arms kept her from falling. Bright sensations rippled deeply, sweetly, through her entire being. They spread out into infinity as she came…and came again …

When the pulsations had eased down to a steady glow of warmth, he was still holding her. Rock steady. His huge, stiff cock stood at attention, pressed against her belly.

He kept right on melting her with sensual kisses as he let her slide down his thighs. When her toes and then her feet touched the floor, he rested his forehead against hers, their eyes still locked, brushing her cheekbone and her jaw, with his scratched, scabbed-up knuckles.

"Holy fuck," he whispered. "That was amazing."

A quick peek down ascertained that he was still…oh, yes he was.

She actually blushed at the sight of his stiff cock, high and hopeful against her belly, swathed in the folds of the baggy T-shirt she wore. Ready and eager for action.

"Are you, uh…OK?" he asked.

She almost laughed from sheer nervous energy and shyness and excitement, but that would sound weird so she gulped it back. "Um, yeah. I'm OK. How about you?"

"I'm great," he said. "I just felt you come. Best thing that ever happened to me." He paused for a moment. "That I know of."

"But you're still…up."

He grinned. "You're so hot. What do you expect?"

Oh man, that grin just did her in. She could have controlled herself if he'd stuck to the sternly smoldering vibe. But those cute dimples, that flash of teeth, the grooves in his cheeks, the smile lines creasing around his eyes, transformed his chiseled male beauty into something utterly irresistible.

She smiled back like a starry-eyed idiot. Then compounded her mistake by grabbing his cock, squeezing and stroking. She'd lie awake nights for the rest of her life wondering what she'd missed if she didn't find out what he felt like in her hand.

For starters, hot and hard. So broad, with that heavy pulse of heartbeat against her palm, and she loved the shocked spasm of pleasure that went through him at the caress.

It made her feel strong. Dangerous, even. A femme fatale who drove men wild with helpless desire. Yeah.

She needed so badly to feel strong right now.

"Oh, God. Dani." His voice was uneven as she pumped his hot, velvet-skinned cock with her hand. Soft, smooth skin sliding over the steel-hard, swollen shaft. The throb in her hand was incredibly exciting.

"What?" she asked.

He covered her hand with his own, jerking it roughly. "You're killing me."

"Well, don't die," she said. "I need you alive and kicking, my man."

He grinned. "OK. I'll stay on the planet. If it pleases you."

"Oh, yes. You do please me."

"Thank God." He slid his hand down between her thighs, caressing her until his fingers were sliding over the thin cotton of his boxers covering her pussy. He made a low, growling noise of satisfaction as he felt her warmth, then slid his fingers beneath the fabric. She cried out at the shock of intimate contact.

He went still. "OK?"

"Don't stop," she whispered.

Luke blew out a sigh of relief, laughing under his breath as he caressed her. It felt wonderful. He had the touch, releasing—and stoking—exquisite sexual tension from her clit with every skillful flicking stroke. Just…right. Oh yes…*yes*. She moaned with excitement.

"You're so slick and tight and hot. I want to taste you. Can I go down on you?"

She pushed his chest, a sharp burst of restless anger charged with sex. "No."

He stumbled back, startled. "What the hell? What did I do wrong?"

"Shut up." She tried the same move, but he'd recovered himself now. This time it was like shoving a big tree with deep roots. He didn't budge.

"I didn't mean to piss you off," he said cautiously.

"You didn't. Stop talking." She whipped off the T-shirt, flinging it away.

He sucked in air, stunned by her tits. And why not. Tight dark nipples, a sexy bounce. Luke looked like he'd been sucker-punched.

Time for the knock-out blow.

She hooked her thumbs into the waistband of the boxer shorts and shimmied them down over her hips. She stepped out of them when they fell and advanced on him.

He reached for her. "Dani—"

"Don't. Talk." She slapped his hand down and shoved him once again, in the direction of the bed. "Just lie down."

He walked warily backward. "Whoa," he murmured. "Tough."

"You better believe it." She waited while he reclined on the rumpled bed, and climbed onto him, straddling him. She took a moment to strike a sex-goddess pose, glad to have done some self-indulgent grooming lately, trimming up her muff as if she had a lover to impress. He looked…well, impressed barely began to cover it.

She feasted her eyes on the spectacle of Luke's big, stunning naked body stretched out in all its male perfection, his eyes blazing up at her, fascinated.

His huge flushed cock, stiff and eager, rising from the thatch of dark hair.

He held it up for her, stroking it roughly as he devoured her with his gaze. "I stand ready to serve," he said. "My God, you're hot."

"Yeah. Prepare to burn." She shimmied up to position herself. He gripped her thighs as she reached for him, caressing his cock, spreading that slippery precome around. Slick—and so thick and blunt and smooth in her hand.

"Let me lick you first," he said. "I don't want to hurt you."

"That's my call," she said, swaying over him. Nudging his cock head inside her and shivering with excitement as she took it inch by inch. Slow, slick. Sinking down over him. "I want your cock. I say when. I say where. And I say *now*."

He choked off a breath as she took him deeper, rocking and surging. Relaxing around that thick club of flesh, until she'd bathed him all over with her body's slick sex juice. Up…and down…in a tight, caressing slide. Taking him in so deep.

He filled her completely. She clenched and shivered around him, charged with intense pleasure and emotion. Her body felt sensitized. The plunging sensuous strokes got even deeper, stimulating every single one of her inside hot spots. Her whole body was a universe of intense, tingling sensation. She thrummed with excitement.

He reached up to touch her breasts. She slapped his hands away.

He looked startled. "Why not? Let me—"

"No," she gasped out, rising up to take him in still deeper. "Can't. Goddamn it. Goddamn you, Luke." Out of nowhere a feeling was coming over her, like she was cracking open.

And God only knew what would emerge from in there, all naked and shivering.

She grabbed his big hands and clamped them down against his huge chest, letting her nails dig into him. He could have easily wrenched them free, but he stayed right there, bracing her, as she clutched him, rode him wildly. Yelling out the rage and the confusion as the power rose up and claimed her. Taking her all the way to a violent climax.

She found herself slumped over him after, shaking with silent sobs. Her face was wet. So was his shoulder. She didn't dare look up.

Luke tried to lift her head, but she wouldn't let him. "Don't," she said savagely. "Just…don't."

He was silent for a moment, then slid his arms around her. "No." He rolled her over on the bed, pinning her down. Cock still wedged inside her, deep and throbbing.

"What the hell?" She wiggled beneath him in a spasm of startled panic. "I didn't say you could do that!"

"I didn't ask your permission," he said. "Know that about me right up front. I can only be a good obedient boy for so long before I push back hard. Blame it on my weird upbringing. I'm not big on following orders."

She bucked and writhed, but his steely weight kept her there. He gazed down into her wet eyes. Her desperate movements only heightened the intense sensations of being so wet and slick and melting, quivering around his thick, stiff cock.

"Are you mad at me?" he demanded. "What the hell is with you? Talk, Dani."

Her throat shook. She had to stop and swallow a few times before she could speak. "I'm pissed at everything," she said. "You included."

He ignored the jab. "Is this about Naldo? Those Obsidian goons coming to your house?"

She glared up at him. "I guess. It must be."

"We won that round," he said forcefully. "Remember that. Between the two of us, we pounded those shitheads into the ground. We won, Dani. We're alive, and free, and angry as hell. Those punk assholes will think twice before taking us on again."

"Get real," she said. "Punk assholes or not, I had nothing to do with pounding them. That was all your work and you know it."

"Bullshit. You are the hottest, fightingest damn thing I have ever seen in action. And I'm going to crush those shitheads for messing with you. But first, I am going to make you come again. So hard, it blows your mind."

She wanted to laugh, but the weight of his hot body wouldn't let her. His mouth descended, kissing her breathless while he scooped her legs up over his arms, spreading her out wide. It made her feel so open to him, intensely vulnerable, but the fear wasn't big enough to withstand the pleasure. Everywhere he touched her melted and merged with him in erotic surrender. In seconds, she was arched back, offering herself, hips lifting again and again to meet each deep stroke.

It got wilder, hotter, faster. She couldn't think, no breath to cry out, just clutching and writhing as the pleasure rose to a wild crescendo.

She floated, soft as a cloud, mindless and exhausted. Luke lay next to her, playing with her hair. She turned to him, still aglow.

"You may not remember much about yourself, but just know this, buddy," she said lazily. "You're a total god in bed."

He grinned. "It's you," he said. "All you."

She harrumphed. As if. But fine. Let him give her all the credit if he felt like it.

She trailed her hand down his belly, and encountered his cock, as stiff and erect as before. "Hey. Didn't you come?"

"No condoms," he said. "Sex hasn't been on my radar for a very long time. And we hadn't talked about it. It happened so fast."

She propped herself up on her elbow, startled. And amazed that he'd been able to control himself in that wild, hot frenzy of fucking. "Yeah, but…"

"I'm good," he said. "Don't sweat it. Blue balls never killed a guy yet, and it's a worthy cause. I fucking *love* making you come. I could do it all day."

But she was already sliding down his body, inhaling the hot sexy smell, seizing his cock in her hand. Stroking and circling, licking his cockhead.

"Hey," he said. "You don't have to—"

"Shhhh." She lifted her head, waving her finger at him with a secret little smile. "Not another word. It's a matter of personal honor."

He caught his breath. "Oh. Well, if you put it that way…Oh God, Dani." His words broke into a moan as she pulled him slowly into her mouth.

Not an easy task, but she got into the groove, relaxing and adjusting around his big, gorgeous cock. It was so arousing, the hot scent and his big body, the pulse of his heart against her tongue. Pleasure racking him. She loved his skin. So smooth and taut with that tracery of veins, tasting of salty drops of precome. His shudder and groan as she flicked and rolled her tongue over it, and then swept it around his cockhead…and around. Gripping him at the root with both hands, pumping, suckling, pulling him deep.

His hands wound into her hair. His cries were thick and incoherent, body shaking when the pulsing jets of hot liquid spurted into her mouth. A few moments of gasping for breath, wiping her mouth.

Luke's face was turned away, eyes hidden behind his hand.

She dropped a tender kiss against his thigh, feeling shy.

When he finally turned to her, the look on his face was so raw and unguarded, she had to look down herself, or else start to cry again.

"That was…" He stopped. Cleared his throat. "So fine. I never felt—"

"Don't say it." She headed him off at the pass, just in time. "You can't say that, Luke. You're an amnesiac. How would you know?"

"Even so." His voice was low and stubborn.

"Am I the first woman you've been with since you lost your memory?"

"Yeah."

"Well?" She shrugged. "So you don't know. It's OK. I still appreciate the sweet talk. You're a real honey, Luke. Keep it coming."

He looked irritated. "You're a pain in the ass, Dani."

"Tell me something I don't know. No, wait. I take that back. I've learned enough. I'll stick with what I know so far. That's enough to deal with at the moment."

He grunted, and swung his legs over the side of the bed. Then he grabbed jeans from the pile of clothes on his dresser and pulled them on. He fished around in a plastic box on the desk and took out Naldo's metal capsule.

All the feelings and terrors that Luke had pushed away came crashing back at the sight of it, all the harder for having been displaced. She saw Naldo's sunken, tormented eyes, the trauma inflicted on his bleeding chest. His bloody handprint on her leg. The waxy paleness of his face. The moment when she realized that her friend was dying.

The blade, slicing into her hand. She closed her fist convulsively around the reddened cut at the base of her thumb until it stung and throbbed nastily.

The metal capsule looked seamless, but Luke peered at it for a moment, and with a twist of his strong fingers, snapped it open. He removed what looked like a minuscule computer chip, then paced silently on bare feet out into the other room.

Dani took a moment to throw her T-shirt on, and went out to find Luke on a stool at a worktable, under a powerful hanging light, surrounded by blinking electronic stuff.

He was in all-out work mode now.

She watched him type with mind-boggling, rattling swiftness on a computer keyboard. "Luke?"

He didn't seem to hear her. His face was expressionless.

"Luke!" She waved her hand in front of his face. "You in there?"

He blinked and focused on her, as if he were forcibly reeling his mind back with a very long cable from some far place. "Huh? You need me?"

"Talk to me. About that." She pointed at Naldo's capsule. "Is it what you expected it to be? Does it have what you need?"

"No," he said flatly. "At least not in a way I can use."

She was dismayed. "No? What's the problem?"

"The drop-off info is encrypted."

"Oh. Well, shit. Can you crack it?"

"Maybe. Eventually. But Braxton encrypted it with people like me in mind. It'll take a while, and by the time I crack it, Manticore will have switched everything up again. So there's hardly any point."

"So it was all for nothing," she said. "Naldo dying. You, risking your life to fight those Obsidian types."

"Nah. I did that for you." His fingers rested on the keyboard edge for a moment and he looked around, meeting her eyes "Nothing about that was wasted."

Huh. It was a nice thought for him to express, but please. She'd never been the sentimental type even before the hardest of her hard knocks.

"Did Naldo say anything about a key?" he asked.

She closed her eyes and tried to remember, but it was all just a horrible blur of blood and desperation. "Not exactly. He did say something weird. About how juvie would show me the key."

"Juvie?"

"Yeah. Where we met. In a juvenile detention facility. And he mentioned some girl I don't remember. Ivy. Said I was supposed to help her. And then he managed to tell me to watch out for Manticore. That was it. He was close to dying when he got to my house."

"Yeah." He gazed up at her. His eyes were penetrating. Pulling the moments out of her mind, even though she didn't want to remember them.

"I could barely make out what he said," she said. "And to tell the truth, I wasn't paying much attention. I was just trying to keep him alive, not understand his babble. But he mentioned juvie more than once."

"What did he say about it?"

"Not much," she said. "He could barely speak."

Luke looked thoughtful. "Juvenile detention? What did you do to get put in there?"

"I put my mom's no-good lying drug dealer boyfriend in the hospital with a broken skull," she replied. "I was fifteen. My mom took a fall for him. He'd stored his stash at our house. She got eight to ten. And while she sat in prison for him, he started patting my ass. So I clocked him with a cast iron skillet."

His eyes widened in admiration. "Good work."

She shrugged. "Anyhow, Naldo said I was supposed to stop them from hurting people."

"Ivy," he murmured thoughtfully. "But no explanation. Nothing about the encrypted data. Or where the key is."

"Nope," she said. "Nothing that I understood. If juvie was supposed to show me the key, it failed."

He turned back toward the data on the screen. Lifted up his fists, and crashed them down on the tabletop, making all the equipment rattle and shake. "Fuck."

Dani took a cautious step back.

He shot her an embarrassed glance. "Sorry," he said gruffly. "Tantrum."

Huh. She'd seen much worse from other guys, and with far less provocation. "How did you know all this stuff about Manticore if you were locked in a cage?" she asked.

"Braxton liked to brag, and I was a captive audience. Besides, he meant to break me down for parts. No reason for him to hold back."

"Got it," she said.

"He went on for hours about his techniques, his brain stim designs. The money he was making. How smart he was at investing it. I data-dived into his files before I left. Got into every last fucking thing he had. I'm renting this place and got that car and all the weapons and the other stuff with money I siphoned out of Braxton's offshore accounts. And there's plenty more where that came from."

"I see." She sort of did. Offshore accounts weren't her area of expertise.

"I learned a lot from him," he said. "Particularly about brain blocks. I even blocked my own hearing at the end so he wouldn't be able to stun code me. That was how I escaped. By making myself deaf." He shook his head. "I was so fucking glad when that one finally wore off. Scared myself."

"Wait." She held up her hand, dread growing inside her at where this was going. "Slow down. Stun code? Tell me about that."

"That was part of my original Obsidian security programming. It was embedded so deep, I couldn't scrub it out. My control codes. Three-word sequences. Three of them in all. There's a stun code which blocks my movement, a release code which undoes the stun code. And then there's the kill code. That one stops my heart."

Dani glanced away so he wouldn't see her eyes. There he went again, veering right back toward crazytown. Control codes, stun codes, kill codes. It all belonged in the paranoid fantasy category, along with hostile alien telepathy and tinfoil hats.

It was infuriating. This guy was awesome. Beautiful, brave, smart, stellar in bed. He was all kinds of amazing things. She was into him in every way.

But he could be mentally ill. Sometimes heroes were. That could be part of what it took to be one. She told herself to stop. He could make her delusional, too.

She had to grit her teeth and face that.

She kept her voice low and neutral. "That sounds terrible."

"Yeah, it sucked," he said absently, still typing. "But the auditory block worked. He tried to stun code me in the end when he was loading me up for transport, and I didn't hear him. It gave me my chance. I took a few bullets. Here, and here." He pointed at the shiny scars on his forearm, his shoulder. "But I got away. I was deaf for about a week until that block wore off. It didn't go as deep as the memory blocks. I built it faster, and it had less of a charge. But I pumped a massive charge into the memory blocks. I welded those motherfuckers shut like nobody's business."

"So how do you know you even have a family?"

It took him a while to answer. "I don't know for sure," he admitted. "I feel the shape of them in my mind. Like shadows in the space where they were. And something in me reaching for them. There must be something reaching back."

Tears sprang into her eyes. Being mentally ill didn't make his grief and loneliness any less painful or real. On the contrary. She brushed the tears away before he saw them.

"Good luck with that," she said. "I hope that they really are out there for you."

Luke turned to look at her, frowning. "You sound like you doubt it."

"It's not for me to doubt," she said carefully. "But we all have that ache, I think. For something we lost, or something we never had but should have had. I feel it, too. For a long time I thought it was for Naldo. He's the only person from my past that would reach back for me. But now he's gone, and guess what? I still have the ache. I'm always going to have it. Even if there's nobody left to reach back."

Luke's eyes blazed as he grabbed her hand. "There is now."

She tore her hand away. "Don't say that! You just met me. Just getting laid is no basis for stupid pronouncements like that."

"It's not stupid," he said calmly. "There aren't many things I know for sure about myself, but the way I feel about you is one of them. I like knowing it. Feels right."

"Stop," she said stonily. "Hold it right there."

"Dani—"

"Not one more goddamn word!"

He stopped. Swallowed, and looked away. "OK," he said evenly. "I'll save it. But it's still just sitting there. Waiting for you."

"Let it wait. Because I've got no place to put it."

He let out a sigh. "Aw, shit. Now you're angry."

"Yes. You're spouting bullshit. Just don't."

He was silent for a moment. "Sorry. I forget what's appropriate to say or not to say. You lose your social skills when you're locked in a cage."

She waved that away, too. "Let it go, OK? Just let the whole thing rest."

The look in his eyes still made her nervous. Time for a radical change of subject. Like the data glowing on the screen. She gestured at it. "So? Do you have a plan?"

"I'm getting there," he said. "One, decrypt the data on this chip. Failing that, two, hack into Manticore again and intercept another delivery. But they're careful and paranoid, and they don't make many. And after what just happened, it's going to be even harder."

"Got it."

"And protecting you," he said.

"Um…I see." Dani folded her arms over her chest. "Luke, you do know that I can't just stay up here with you indefinitely, right?"

His frown came back. "Sure you can," he said. "This is the safest place for you right now. You can't go back to Munro Valley. You wouldn't last a day. Those assholes know where you live. Where you work."

"But I have a job." Her voice was forceful. "I have a life, Luke. I had today off, thank God, but I'm due at the hospital tomorrow morning early, and I cover the free clinic in the evening. And we're short-staffed, so there's nobody to cover for me. I have to get back, talk to the police, figure out a plan for getting on with my life. I can't hide up here and play house with you. Much as I appreciate what you've done for me."

"You saw what came for you last night." His voice was harsh. "I'm the only one who can protect you from them. I'm the only one who can see them coming because I used to be exactly like them. You get me, Dani?"

She shook her head. "Keeping me safe isn't a one-man job, Luke. I also need to borrow your phone, so I can call my supervisor and tell her about what—"

"No, you don't. And you can't. You can't tell anyone anything. Any calls you make will be monitored. They'll watch and listen to everyone you're in contact with. Colleagues, friends, neighbors, everyone. You'll put yourself in the crosshairs again."

She gazed at him, appalled. "But…Luke, get real. I can't just disappear on my colleagues. It would be so unprofessional. You just don't do that."

"It's not safe for you out there!" He put vicious emphasis on each word. "Get it through your head! I'm not being controlling or paranoid. I'm just trying to keep you alive."

Dani bit her lip and stared at the floor. Shit had just gotten real.

Classic male attitude, for him to conclude that he was the only one in the world who could keep her safe. And he was so heroic about it. So fucking noble and sincere.

But he wasn't going to let her go home. Not willingly. Nor would he let her use his phone. And now he thought he loved her? Oh man.

She was in for it now. Right up to her neck. She fled toward the bedroom.

"Where are you going?" he demanded.

"I need another shower."

"Me, too." His voice was challenging. He sensed her doubts. Wanted to hover.

Luke followed her into the bathroom and stood behind her, meeting her eyes in the bathroom mirror. The harsh light over the sink threw all his ripped muscles and his rough scars into strong relief. His huge cock pressed prominently against his jeans.

The contact with his eyes, the sight of his half-naked body made her weak and stupid. She needed to get away from him, back to civilization, but right now, all she wanted in the whole world was one more fiery taste of what he had going on. The sweet oblivion that only he could give. Only Luke could drive away the sickening, sinking fear and replace it with hot excitement. And wild pleasure. Her breath came faster, her lips parted, her nipples tightened. Her pussy was still hot and soft from their last bout.

She turned around to face him, and he put his fingers up to touch her lips, caressing the shape of them with slow, reverent gentleness.

He caught his breath as she sucked his fingers into her mouth. She reached down one-handed, wrenched open the buttons of his jeans. Put her hand in, seizing that thick, hot shaft. Squeezing it.

"Oh, holy fuck…" His voice broke off at her deft, pumping strokes as she sucked his fingers more deeply into her mouth. Her eyes closed. Lost in it already.

"I gotta get us some condoms," he said roughly. "This is driving me nuts."

Her eyes opened, and on impulse, she blurted it out. "I'm covered. I have a contraceptive implant. And I don't have any diseases. I've been tested since the last time I got involved with anybody. You?"

"I'm clean," he said simply. "No diseases."

She stared into his eyes, trying to read him. He just looked right back, holding her gaze fearlessly. Like a man with nothing to hide.

Fine. He passed the test, and a good thing, too, because she could not resist this. Her last chance. She had to have him. Right…*now.*

Luke pulled his hand out and spun her around to face the mirror again, placing both her hands on the porcelain sink bowl.

"Bend over," he said. "And hang on."

She did just as he asked, bending deep, arching her ass, opening her legs. Offering herself. Never breaking eye contact. He pushed the T-shirt up, high on her back so he could see the whole length of her spine, running his big, warm hands hungrily all over her skin, over her ribs, while he shoved his jeans down. She didn't want to break this spell. Let it last as long as it could last, because she knew what waited for her on the other side.

Not yet. Let her just have this. Let her feel it. One more time.

She rocked back against him with a gasp when he nudged her with his cockhead, sliding the broad, blunt tip tenderly against her pussy lips. Then pressing slowly inside her tight, juicy inner flesh with the swollen bulb of his big cock.

When he was shoved deep inside and rocking, he stopped, gripping her ass cheeks.

"I will protect you from them," he said. "I promise, Dani."

Oh no, no, no. Don't ruin it. Please.

"Not now, goddamnit," she gasped out. "Please. Just do it. Just fuck me."

CHAPTER 12

S o…incredibly…*good.* Being inside her, skin to skin. The heat. The slickness. Luke threw his head back, eyes squeezed shut. Hung on to himself. *Nonononot yet.* Could not come yet. She had to have one of those mind-bending orgasms first.

Dani was perfect. Luscious and soft. Beautiful tits swinging below her with each thrust. That sexy rounded ass and the wet hot heaven between her legs.

She offered herself to him like a goddess bestowing her favors. But she was a hungry, prickly, dangerous, red-hot goddess and he had watch himself. Stay on his toes.

Yeah. He fucking loved that.

She let out a whimper with each hard, urgent thrust. Her cheeks had a dewy flush and her eyes glowed, dazed with pleasure. Locked on his.

He had to check, just in case. "Am I hurting you? Is it too hard?"

"I like it that way," she said, breathless. "Shut up and give it to me."

He felt a strange, unfamiliar shaking in his chest, and was startled to realize that it was laughter. He'd forgotten what laughter felt like.

Everything about her drove him to a frenzy. The look in her eyes, the sensual arch of her long, smooth back. The sensational feeling in his cock as he pistoned in and out of her hot depths. The globes of her ass jiggling with each hard thrust. The sounds she made.

He felt the tremors long before, building in momentum. Her orgasm and his, bound together somehow as if their energies had merged. The deep clenching pulses from her pussy milked him, pulling him, demanding—

He exploded inside her. Gripping her hips as his orgasm tore through him.

He sagged over her back, caressing her, when his senses returned. She wouldn't meet his eyes in the mirror any longer. Her head hung down, avoiding his gaze. Their breathing was still loud. Rasping pants.

The light seemed harsh, now. The shadows too sharp. They sliced like knives.

Dani was scared. The feeling vibrated through his inside senses. He felt it. She wouldn't look at him. She'd wanted him to fuck her to distract her from the way she felt, but it only worked until she came. Then her emotions surfaced again—and crashed down on her even harder than before.

He splayed his hands over her ass, a possessive caress. "I'll keep you safe."

She swayed away from him. "I need a shower."

"Are you OK?"

She rolled her eyes at him. "Sure. Other than being, you know. Shattered."

"Shattered about what?"

"Don't want to talk about it," she muttered.

He followed her into the shower stall. Dani shot him a wary look. "You want to do this with me? There's a whole lot of you and not much room, Luke." She glanced down at his still-hard penis. "Your dick alone will cramp my style."

"I'll make it worth your while," he promised.

And he did. Seeing Dani naked and wet under pounding hot water was exactly as stimulating as he'd expected it to be. He got busy with the shower soap, and made it his business to soap and rinse and finger every sensitive secret curve and hollow and fold of her. He spent a long, slippery time with her breasts. Almost as long memorizing the curves and hollows of her waist and hips, the swell of her belly, the dimples at the top of her ass. By the time he got down between her legs, the flowerlike pussy lips and the tight, thrumming bud of her clit, the hot glow was in her eyes again. She leaned back willingly, lifting her leg and draping it over his arm to give him access for a long, slow and deliciously skillful fingerfuck.

She was the one who slapped his hand away and reached for his cock. They groaned with delight together as he hoisted her up and sank his full length into her.

This time it was lazy and unhurried. Punctuated by wet, luxurious tongue kissing. A deep, slow swivel and slide, going for all the hot spots. He was going to drive away the fear she felt for as long as he could and this was the only tool he had to do it.

Fine with him. He could do this forever. Fuck yeah. Sign him up for that.

He didn't chart the time. There were better things to fixate on. Her half-lidded eyes, long curly lashes tangled with water, wild ringlets decked with water drops. Her full pink lips exploring his. Her sweet taste. Those amazing green eyes gazing into his.

Finally she arched and moaned and gave it up, fingernails digging into his chest as she came deeply and violently. Then and only then did Luke let his own climax take him, spurting into her hot depths for what seemed like forever.

Fear pounced on her right away. Like it had been lying in wait. Nothing changed on her face, but he still felt it vibrating in the air.

They dried themselves off silently in the foggy bathroom. He wanted to say something, but there was too much to say. She wrestled her T-shirt back on, not meeting his eyes.

He followed her back to the bedroom. "I'm starving," he said. "But I don't have anything worth eating in the fridge. So here's the plan. At the bottom of the mountain there's a strip mall, with a pretty decent steak house. Prime rib, baked potatoes, Caesar salad. Good pie."

The flash in her eyes and her stomach's audible growl was his response.

"I can't go out dressed like this," she said. "Go without me and get some take-out. If you could buy pants and sneakers for me somewhere, that would be great."

"I don't want to leave you alone," he said.

"You said I was safe here, right?"

She had a point, but he still hated it. "Come with me anyway," he urged. "Stay in the car. I'll buy clothes, and you can change in the store. Or the restaurant bathroom."

She closed her eyes, lips tight. "No, Luke. Just go, and do your food run, and give me a chance to breathe, OK?"

He felt stung. "Didn't mean to crowd you."

She held up a hand. "You're great and awesome, but you're pretty damn overwhelming. This whole thing overwhelms me. I could use some down time."

Luke felt his face heat. He got dressed quickly and grabbed his jacket off the hook by the door.

"Stay inside," he told her. "If you leave the house, I'll know."

He'd meant the words as a reassurance, but his tone and the way they came out made them sound angry and menacing. *Shit.*

Her eyebrow tilted up. "You carry a monitor with you everywhere you go?"

"No. There's one inside my eye. Projected onto my retina."

"Ah." She nodded. "Of course."

"So. Just stay inside. I'll get food and pick up new clothes for you."

"Fine, that would be great. Thanks."

Luke activated the full mosaic on his screen as soon as he got into his car. He had enough juice to watch all the vantage points at once, but the only one he currently gave a shit about was the one that showed Dani making herself a pot of coffee.

He watched her doing that for the time it took for the SUV to bounce down the rutted driveway and onto the ridge crest road, watching her pour water, spoon ground coffee into the filter. She rummaged around in the fridge and the cupboards while it brewed, probably looking for sugar and milk. She found none.

She poured a cup. Took a cautious sip, grimacing.

As if she felt his thought, her gaze flicked directly up to the camera mounted in the corner over the door. Her bright green eyes narrowed thoughtfully as she sipped coffee.

She flipped him the bird. "Spying is creepy, Luke," she called. "Not cool."

Luke's face turned red, as if she could see him. He turned his attention to the other camera feeds.

Caught in the act. Like an asshole.

Dani moved around Luke's lair, intensely aware that he could watch her by some freaky means, even if it wasn't in the science-fiction way that he'd described.

She had to play it cool. She imagined talking to him, oh-so-casually. *Say, Luke. Are those beater cars outside, like, normal? Or are they souped-up demon vehicles like the one I knew I wasn't driving?* She checked her innocent expression in the reflection of the kitchen window over the sink as she sipped her coffee.

Good enough. Possibly even convincing. She put the cup in the sink and studied the sad assortment of cars and trucks decaying in the tall, shaggy meadow grass outside.

It was drive or walk. And it would be a very long walk down that mountain, in flip flops, at high altitude. In weather that was rapidly getting worse.

She searched through the place room by room for car keys and anything else that might be useful. Luke's stuff was easy to spot, being newer, a lot less dusty and piled in the foreground. The grimy clutter behind it was older, more random. Like the drawers in the kitchen which had years worth of rubber bands, twist ties, paper clips and yellowed coupons shoved into them. A swift search through those yielded no keys.

But a back door off the kitchen led to a mudroom packed with junk, and by the screen door was a big pegboard with hooks on it. Her heart thumped as she spotted key fobs dangling from them. Four different sets. And she'd seen cans of gasoline stacked against the garage wall. She pushed aside the cobwebby curtains of the mudroom window to check out the cars and trucks once again.

She had to be swift and decisive. No false moves. But it scared her to death.

It also made her feel guilty as fuck.

The danger out there was real. Who knew what Naldo had gotten himself mixed up in. Or what info was actually stored inside that capsule. But it wasn't the coordinates for picking up an altered superman. It was something shady and bad and tragically normal, involving illicit drugs or guns or human trafficking or terrorism. Something like that.

Something real. Something that made sense. Luke's bizarre, futuristic tale of high-tech victimization and woe just didn't. No fucking way.

Still, Luke's selfless heroism was absolutely real. He'd saved her life several times over. He was going to feel betrayed and fucked over if she ran. It just crushed her heart to imagine it. Which meant he'd already gotten inside her head. And she'd let him in.

Guilt assailed her. Having sex with him? Genius way to confuse and disorient the guy still further. Jerk him around, hurt his feelings, piss him off. *Brilliant, LaSalle. Just brilliant.*

Luke didn't deserve to be treated that way.

She'd come on to the guy. No one forced her, but it hadn't felt like a choice. The attraction was...huge. Overwhelming. And if she saw him again, it would happen again.

Just looking at the man made her wet. She'd never felt so drawn to anyone.

She rummaged again through the clothes on the dresser in the bedroom. Picked out a thick hooded gray sweatshirt. The shoulders lapped down to her elbows, the hem sagged halfway down her bare thighs, and the sleeves hung way past her hands, but she just folded and rolled until she found her fingers again.

So? Get some gas into one of those vehicles and scram. She who hesitates is screwed. *Move it, LaSalle. Like right now.*

But her vision blurred as she plucked all the key fobs—she had no idea which vehicle would actually start—from the pegboard in the mudroom and darted into the garage. She grabbed a can of gasoline, and started to cry when she shoved the door open and ran, leaving the alarm box mounted on the door flashing an angry red.

She ran through a field of dead grass, gulping back tears. Gas can thumping painfully against her leg. Flip-flops flopping. One of them came apart and left her limping on the bare foot, the broken sole flapping loose as she picked her way around boulders and piles of beer bottles, old tires, cinder blocks.

She reached the ancient Toyota pickup. Got the right key inserted in the door.

Gasoline first. She unscrewed the cap, upended the can and let fuel glug in, hoping the tank was intact. Hell, just hoping there was a gas tank in there at all. Who knew? She could be pouring fuel right down onto the ground. A glance at the tires showed them to be both bald and low but not completely flat.

She'd just cross her fingers and hope for the best. No other option.

The truck cab opened with a creak and a puff of dust. She heard a frantic rustling as she slid into the seat. Little creatures who'd decided to call the place home were abruptly reconsidering their decision. Snakes, mice, beetles, scorpions? The odor of dust and mold, rotting plastic and rodent shit made her nose wrinkle.

She turned the key in the ignition, closing her eyes and praying the dashboard would light up. If it didn't, both she and the battery were screwed.

She opened her eyes. Holy cow. The dials and displays gave a steady greenish light. Someone must have started up this engine fairly recently. She turned the key all the way. The motor turned over, then died. She tried again.

It coughed and roared to life...and stayed running. The gas gauge quivered, and rose a couple of notches above empty. She shoved down the clutch and muscled the thing into gear, yelping as a huge spider scuttled across her lap.

The truck was angled downhill, so gravity was on her side. She thudded over the lumps and bumps in the grassy field, barely able to see through the filthy windshield.

Dani cursed under her breath, using the sleeve of the enormous sweatshirt to angrily wipe away the tears that just kept coming.

She'd never had much luck with love or sex. She gave it a try now and again, when she got the chance or the urge, but somehow it never panned out. Now Fate was dangling this beautiful guy in front of her. Tough, sweet, brave, smart. Amazing in bed. But Fate just jerked him right back like a cat toy. Whoopsy-daisy, and the joke was on her.

That beautiful guy was so far out of his right mind, he didn't even know his own goddamn last name.

Luke waited grimly, stuck on line at the big clothing store. The food was already in the car. He'd picked up several burner phones for Dani, a money belt for documents and cash that she could wear under her clothes, and the stuff he needed to program a key fob for her, so she could drive his car. She'd have a chance to bolt, even if someone wasted him. Some clothes and shoes and she'd be covered, at least for now.

But this was taking for-fucking-ever. Twelve minutes and counting, while the one available cashier dealt with a sour old lady who wanted to return a sweat suit that already sported a large coffee stain. The manager was called. Accusations were made about when the coffee had been spilled. Voices were raised. And the whole thing went to shit.

When they finally worked it out, he dumped his items onto the belt. The girl at the register gave him an owl-eyed look as she swiped barcodes and filled a big plastic bag. He barely noticed her, being too busy monitoring thirty camera feeds in real time while also trying not to be creepy and spy on Dani.

One of the door alarms went red. He zeroed in on it.

He saw Dani running out of the house, carrying a gasoline can. Car keys sticking out of her hands. She was bolting. Panic exploded inside him.

"That'll be three hundred and eighteen dollars!" the girl said.

Luke flung some bills at her, grabbed the shopping bag and ran.

"Sir? Sir? Your receipt! You gave me, like, four hundred bucks! Hey! I gotta give you your change! Hold on!"

His own goddamn fault for being a self-indulgent asshole, telling Dani too much. He'd freaked her out. Scared her off. It'd be on him if she walked right back into Obsidian's wide open crocodile mouth. *Fuck.*

If she'd been in the Porsche, he would have been able to stop her in a heartbeat, but he didn't have any hold on that fucking Toyota. There was no computer system in that antique thing for him to hack.

She was speeding to her doom. If the truck itself didn't fall to zombie pieces right under her on the highway.

And she had a thirty-five-minute lead on him.

CHAPTER 13

Dani parked on the shoulder of the highway, pointing downhill in case the battery conked out. If she could roll, maybe she could restart the engine.

Getting out, she took the time to pour the rest of the gas into the tank. Fingers crossed it got her all the way back to Munro Valley.

She had to reconnect with the world right now. Get the cops on board. There could still be corpses in her living room for all she knew. She was grateful that she wasn't due at the hospital for a shift today, so she didn't have to call her supervisor at the hospital. Not yet, at least.

The clerk inside was a young guy with a struggling beard. She glanced quickly his name-tag. Richie.

She gave him a big smile. "Hey. Maybe you can help me. My boyfriend ran out on me with my purse in his car. I took his truck, but it keeps stalling and I'm going to need a tow. Could I use your phone?"

Richie gave her a dull, clouded look, eyes lingering on her tits. She arched her back a little to make the most of them.

"I'm just so scared to walk by the highway dressed like this, you know?" she said. "Anything could happen."

"OK. I guess." He picked up a grubby smartphone, tapped to unlock it, and slid it across the counter to her. The touchscreen was blurry with finger grease.

She quickly looked up the number for the Munro Valley police and placed the call, moving away from the clerk and turning her back. Fortunately a delivery guy showed up right then, hauling a hand truck in the door backward to bring in some boxes. That distracted the clerk as the call went through.

"Hi, I'm Dani LaSalle and I need to get in touch with Detective Willis," she said. "I have information about one of his cases. It's urgent."

Put on hold, she kept herself busy trying to force the loose toe plug of her flip-flop to stay put. Nothing doing. The rip in the rubber sole was too big. If there was duct tape in the truck, she could manage a fix.

"Willis here."

The detective's voice was brisk. She forced hers to stay calm. "This is Dani LaSalle. We spoke when I was leaving the ER."

"Yes, I remember."

She hesitated. Might as well get to the point. "I was attacked last night. When I got home from the hospital."

"Are you injured? Do you need an ambulance?"

"No, I'm OK. I'm not in Munro Valley at the moment."

"Oh. Can you tell me who attacked you?"

"I don't know," she said. "There were five of them. But there was, um...a guy at my house. He defended me. He killed a couple of them."

"A guy. Is he still with you?"

"Not any longer, no," she admitted. She hated the way all of this must sound to him. It had *crazy* spray-painted all over it.

"Who was it that helped you?" Willis asked.

"Well—I don't know his name." Pretty much true. Luke himself didn't know his own name. His last name, at least.

"And you just left with him," Willis said slowly. "A man whose name you don't know. Who killed people in your house. Right in front of you."

"He was defending me," she explained. "Look, I know this must sound strange, but he convinced me that more attackers were on the way."

The detective didn't answer right away. Thinking it over, maybe. Or putting her on speaker so others could hear. Or recording the conversation. "Do you know why you were attacked, Ms. LaSalle?" he asked finally.

"No. I don't."

"Let's back up. You said you're not at home. Then where are you? Do you feel you're in danger now?"

Dani was silent, suddenly struck by the thought that Luke might already be on law enforcement radar for reasons she didn't know.

The detective persisted. "Can I call you at this number?"

"This isn't my phone," she said.

"I see."

"Look, I'm heading back now. I just wanted you to know that my house is a blood bath," she went on.

"We're aware of that," Willis said. "Your neighbor Millicent Blum called us this morning. From your house."

Dani gasped, horrified. "Oh, no! Was she, ah..."

"Not injured. Upset, yes. Extremely so. Which is understandable."

"Did Millie see the bodies?"

"There were no bodies, Ms. LaSalle. Just a great deal of blood. Where are you now?"

She had to tell him something. She glanced over at the clerk. "Excuse me. Where am I? What's the nearest town?"

"Goforth is the closest," Richie said. "Coupla miles down this road."

"I'm near Goforth," she told Willis.

"Do you have any idea who might have moved these alleged bodies?"

Alleged? "Ah, no. I don't," she said.

"Hmm. Then think about it. Come in as soon as possible."

"The minute I'm back," she assured him.

She ended the call and saw the clerk staring at her again. She gave him another dazzling smile. "One more call, please? To my aunt? She's eighty, and she'll be so worried about me. Do you mind?"

"OK. But just a sec. I wanna check my texts first."

He did, and then let his puffy fingers drag damply across her hand as he gave the phone back. She dialed Millie's number, which she knew by heart.

"Hello?" Millie's cracked, anxious voice came on the line.

"Millie, it's Dani."

"Oh, my goodness, girl! I thought you'd been killed! Or kidnapped! When I saw all that blood, I just—well, never mind. You're alive. What's going on?"

"I don't really know yet. I was attacked at my house, but I'm OK. A guy came to my rescue, and then took me with him after. He said more attackers would be coming."

Millie cleared her throat. "Honey, are you mixed up in something bad?"

"Not by my choice. I keep my nose squeaky clean, Millie. Always."

"But why—Dani, running off when your house is all trashed and bloody does not look good."

"I know," Dani said resolutely. "That's why I'm coming back. I'm on my way."

"And this man who helped you? Is he with you?"

"Not exactly," Dani hedged. "He, um, didn't come with me. Actually I sort of skipped out on him. And sort of…borrowed one of his cars."

"You stole a car?" Millie's voice rose to a squeak of outrage.

"Borrowed, Millie," Dani repeated patiently. "I'll make sure he gets it back. Anyhow, it's a rustbucket Toyota pickup, not worth a dime. We had a difference of opinion about my safety, and I didn't want to argue with him. He wanted me to stay in hiding. And he was very intense about it. Protective."

Millie harrumphed. "Oh, I like that in a man. It's nice when they care. Except for those serial killers that start out all friendly at first and then—"

"Right," she broke in. Millie watched every forensic show there was on cable TV. Not a possibility that Dani wanted to dwell on right now. "I just wanted you to know I'm OK. You know, now might be a good time for you to visit Reggie down in Tucson."

"Do you think I'm in danger?" Millie's voice went hushed.

"Oh, no," Dani said carefully. "But this—this happened so close to you. And I bet Reggie would love it if you stayed at his place. Just until the investigation is over."

"Well, I don't know," Millie murmured. "I wouldn't want to bother them."

"Please. Just call Reggie," Dani urged. "Tell him what happened. I'm sure he'll agree that it's a good idea. Amy too. I know they'll both want you out of harm's way."

It took a few more minutes of coaxing and urging and reassuring, but she made progress in convincing Millie to visit her son before she hung up, or hoped that she did. She kept her back turned and made one last call to her fellow volunteer at the free clinic, and left a voicemail outlining the bizarre situation in the simplest possible terms.

"I can't guarantee I'll be back for my shift, Colleen," she concluded. "You have to find someone to cover. I'll call again as soon as I can."

"Here you go." Richie looked disappointed when she handed the phone back.

Tough. She had zero energy left to maintain the protective force field needed for coping with a leering convenience store clerk. Even if she had led him on a little.

"Thanks. I appreciate it," she added. He had helped her.

"If you wanna wait til the end of my shift, I'll give you a ride," the clerk offered. "I'll even throw in a coupla corn dogs. I was s'posed to fry some up fresh a couple hours ago, but I didn't. So you can just have these. If you want 'em."

Dani eyed the cracked, greasy dogs, deep fried to a shiny cockroach brown. "Nah. Thanks anyway."

Richie leaned over the counter. Oh so close. Much too close. She hadn't noticed so many unattractive details when she was sweet-talking him. "I got the whole day off tomorrow, so uh…" He waggled a dandruffy monobrow at her. "I'm all yours."

"In your dreams, Richie. Have a nice life."

He muttered something about her being a bitch as she slammed her way outside, where it had started to rain. She ran for the battered Toyota, clutching her broken flip-flop, moving in an awkward trip-hop-skip.

Praying for the engine to start again.

Dani had been here. Luke's ASP made him as aware of her far-scent as a bloodhound. Not something he chose to do often, because no one could handle a massive overload of olfactory detail about the world and its more or less fragrant inhabitants for long. That got old real fast.

But tonight, he opened wide and took it all in. The whiff of shower soap, the scent of her hair, the blood on her flip-flops. The mold and rotten upholstery of the pickup's car seat. The exhaust emitted from its corroded muffler.

The bell jingled as he pushed inside. Sure enough, her sweet smell lingered in there too, competing with other odors. Unwashed male armpits, motor oil, farts, stale coffee, ancient frying grease and a dirty bathroom.

The guy behind the counter reeked predominantly of cigarettes and stale scalp oil.

"Did a woman just come in here?" Luke asked. "Pretty, green eyes, curly dark hair?"

The guy's face froze. "She ain't been here. Nobody's been through in a while."

Obviously lying. And the guilty look on his face when he slid his smartphone into his shirt triggered a disastrous thought. Dani had no money for gas or food. The only reason she had to stop at this dump would be to find a phone and make some calls.

And Obsidian would have been listening.

So they were on to her. And they were on their way. That big hammer was on the downswing, with Dani right under it.

No point trying to get anything else out of the clerk. Guy was useless. Luke activated the SUV. It lit up, roaring with eagerness as it skidded across the wet parking lot and slid sideways to the door. The engine revved loudly. Driverless.

The clerk stared, mouth agape as Luke sprinted for it, and already had his smartphone to his ear as Luke pulled out on the road.

Fuckhead had called the cops. Could be a high-speed highway chase in Luke's future. And there would be security cameras inside and out, retaining hard video evidence of both him and the crazy antics of his demon Porsche, as Dani called it.

Fucking brilliant. If Dani hadn't already sealed their doom, he'd finished the job himself.

CHAPTER 14

R-48 hesitated before initiating the rise from her data-dive.

Fourteen hours. She'd gone so deep and far, she might have been able to float away this time. Just let the thread holding her to her body thin out until it vanished.

No one was zapping her sensors to pull her back into her body. They seemed to have forgotten her. This was the best chance to cut loose that she was ever likely to get.

Something held her back, though. Not the stim, though her programming yammered ceaselessly, urging her to serve, serve, serve.

No, it was the shadowy flicker of memories behind her brain blocks that stopped her. If she floated away, she'd never know what was locked in there.

Blasts of punishing head pain throbbed through her skull. She was already clenched at the prospect of Hale's groping hands and foul breath, and Metzer was just as bad. A double turd helping, and she was the only female in this current squad. Their permanent piece. So fucking convenient whenever the urge struck them.

She used her implant to input the codes to lift to the surface. The tank opened like a clamshell and she kept her eyes shut against the light as she dragged herself up out of the warm liquid and broke the seal of the oxygen mask. She was still alone in the room. No staring eyes to watch her dry off with a towel from the stack and squeeze the water out of her hair.

She hurried into her clothes, and was zipping up her jacket right as Hale and Metzer entered. They both looked disappointed to find her dressed.

A rush of feverish heat disoriented her and she struggled to maintain her poker face. The less they noticed, the better. Reporting symptoms never resulted in anything good.

"So?" Hale demanded. "What did you find on your dive?"

"Daniela LaSalle just made three phone calls to people on the list of her associates."

"The one you compiled last night?"

"Yes," she replied. "I've been monitoring their phones. The calls originated from a smartphone in a Kwik Stop gas station convenience store two point six miles north of the town of Goforth, California, population 487. The phone belongs to Richard Ballard, the Kwik Stop clerk. I highlighted the location on the table monitor map, along with probable routes she'll take to come back."

The men turned to the map. "You're sure of her destination?" Hale asked.

"She stated in the phone conversation that she's headed to Munro Valley." R-48 downloaded the data to the glowing table monitor. Theoretically she could have transferred it directly to both Hale and Metzer's brain implants, but direct data-dumping was forbidden toward higher-ups. Cyber-diddling was for equals or underlings.

"The first call was to Detective Willis of the Munro Valley Police Department," R-48 told them. "The second was to her neighbor, Millicent Blum. And the third was a voicemail left for Colleen Morris. She supervises the free clinic where LaSalle works as a volunteer."

She set the first conversation to play. Hale and Metzer listened to it.

Metzer's mouth twisted in a thin smile when it was finished. "Sounded like Willis didn't believe her."

"Speaking of the police, there's those blood samples the criminologists took from LaSalle's house," Hale lectured. "They have to disappear."

"Of course," Metzer said. "I'm on it. Trust me."

"Do you want to hear the second recording, sir?" R-48 asked.

"Don't ask stupid questions," Hale snapped.

R-48 set it to play, trying not to listen herself. The old woman's quavering voice disturbed her. It triggered something like dread, making the uneasy rustling behind her brain blocks even more intense.

The woman's voice prodded at the shadow of a lost memory. And it hurt.

Hale listened to the entire recording and then turned to her. "I assume you've already dispatched the drone to monitor LaSalle's position?"

"Yes. I have a live visual on the truck. A 1979 Toyota 4X4 southbound on Cardinal Ridge highway. I can visually confirm that Daniela LaSalle is driving. She's alone."

"She can't be allowed to reach the interstate. Analyze the best interception point. We have to block traffic at both ends. Move fast." Hale gave her a suspicious look. "Jesus, R-48, what the hell is the matter with you?"

She wiped off the sweat on her forehead, trying to control the fiery flush. "No problem, sir. Just a mild temperature readjustment. Normal after an extended submerged data-dive."

That was a lie, but she barely felt the sting and emotional discomfort that lying to a commanding officer usually provoked. She already felt so hot and sick and jittery, the extra chemical torture the brain stim inflicted was barely noticeable.

"Should we get rid of Millicent Blum?" Metzer mused. "She might have seen the cleanup. Easy enough, considering her age. Heart attack, fall, stroke."

"The Blum woman should be eliminated immediately, sir," R-48 blurted loudly. "Leaving her alive is a serious risk for our—"

"I didn't ask for your recommendation." Hale's voice was chilly. "And I have serious doubts about your judgment. Now is not the time to offer unsolicited opinion."

"Yes, sir. My apologies." She looked down, subdued.

"Leave Blum alone for now," Hale said. "But monitor her."

"Yes, sir." Something deep inside her relaxed. The old lady was not in immediate danger. With luck, Hale might even forget about her. But luck was nothing to count on.

At the same time, R-48 felt the muscles around her temples and her eyeballs tighten ferociously, a deep sickening throb of pain. She paid a high price whenever she tried to manipulate a command level modified with reverse psychology. But they made it so easy with their fucking swollen egos. Who could resist?

But oh, it was bad this time. Nausea heaved inside her.

"Assemble a team," Hale said. "Metzer, take the rest of the Level Twenties. Except for you, R-48. I'm keeping my eye on you. You stay right here with me."

"On it," Metzer said. "I got a bone to pick with that LaSalle bitch."

"Don't destroy LaSalle," Hale growled as they left the room. "I want a chance to talk to her, too."

"No problem," Metzer assured him. "There are ways to make her very sorry that leave plenty for you to play with."

R-48 sagged against the wall as soon as the door fell shut. Maybe she'd get lucky and LaSalle would distract them. At least for one night. Just a short reprieve.

But the woman wasn't going to last very long. Not with those two.

The gas gauge was on empty. The only reason the pickup was still moving was because of the long, steady downhill slope. If she could just make it to another town, maybe she could find someone to help her.

Everything was closing on her. The attackers and their mystery agenda on one side. Luke with his crazy tales and macho pride and hurt feelings on the other. And she didn't even have Naldo's capsule to give them now.

According to Willis, someone had cleared away the bloody corpses of her attackers last night. She didn't want to meet whoever had done that. She had nothing to bargain with.

Then again. Bargain, her ass. Those bastards would kill her if they got their hands on her whether she had Naldo's capsule or not.

She almost wished she could just chicken out and disappear right now. But with no money, no clothes, no fake ID—how? After her childhood, her fantasy had been to live aboveground in the bright sun, in full view of everyone. Nothing to hide here, folks. What you see is what you get. No scary toxic secrets, no madness, no drug caches or hidden guns or fat stacks of cash hidden in the walls.

She'd managed it for a while, but behold, here she was again. Banged up and half-naked. Driving a stolen truck that was almost out of gas. On the run from danger, heading straight for more danger. Going out of her fucking mind.

She rounded a blind curve and braked in a panic when she saw a huge, shiny gray van blocking the road. The pickup's bald tires fishtailed on the wet asphalt.

She came to a shuddering halt just inches from it.

Her insides went cold. One...two...no, three giants all bulked up in body armor appeared from behind it, smoothly flanking her pickup. Enormous dudes, armed to the teeth. Lantern jaws. Big swollen muscles. Military style crew cuts. Flat mouths. Dead eyes.

And big handguns. All aimed at her face.

Dani stayed put. She glimpsed a steep drop-off to her left, but not what was at the bottom of it. To her right was a rugged slope studded with trees. Blasting past these fuckers was not an option. Bullets could sure as hell move faster than this old heap.

Nothing left for her to do now except to give those bastards as much attitude as she could dish out for as long as she could dish it.

She got a flash in her mind's eye. Naldo grinning. As if to say, *Don't worry, Dani. It's not so bad over here on the other side.*

Good to know, little brother. Miss you. See you soon. Wish me strong.

The thought of what they were going to do to her made her guts turn to ice water. But it was just pain, and at some point, it would end. So fuck them all.

She fought to roll down the window. It was stuck in place. Then the whole thing came loose and thudded heavily down inside the door.

She gave them a big, sweet, fake smile as chilly wind swirled into the truck's cab. "Hey," she said. "What's the problem?"

Not a muscle twitched on their faces. Then a fourth man strolled around the van and joined them. Blue Eyes.

A wave of cold, sick darkness threatened to make her pass out. She fought it.

The asshole's face was battered and scabbed and bruised. He'd taken one hell of a beating from Luke the other night, the nasty sadist prick. *Good.*

"You again," she said. "Can't say it's a pleasure. I hoped you were dead."

"I don't kill easy. I've been looking forward to this, Daniela. Get out of the car."

She hesitated. He turned to the nearest thug. "Shoot her in the thigh," he ordered.

"No, don't bother. I'll get out." Dani got out of the car, shivering in the raw wind, and crossed her arms over her chest. "So?" she said. "What the fuck do you want from me this time? I don't have the capsule."

"No? Who does?"

Her throat seized up like a small, brutal claw was clutching it. "I don't know his name," she said. "Just that he's just one big scary son of a bitch, and you don't want to mess with him. You saw how he could fight. You guys outnumbered him four to one, and he handed your asses right to you. All of you."

The boss guy lost his big fake smile and gave her the look of death. "What were you doing with him last night?"

"Well, after he was done pounding you guys all to shit, he took the capsule, threw me in the trunk of his car and drove off."

"For what? Why did he take you with him?"

She laughed out loud right in his face. "Oh, boy! What on earth could he have possibly wanted from little ol' me? Three guesses, Einstein!"

He backhanded her, a hard, head-rocking slap. "Watch your mouth, cunt. Where is he now? Answer me!"

His saliva spattered her stinging, reddened face. "Up around Winthrop Springs," she lied. "He's got a cabin in the woods up there. He did what he needed to do with me and then he got hungry. And I managed to untie myself. I stole this pickup when he went out for food. It's a piece of shit, but it runs, sort of. So I skipped out."

"Leaving the capsule behind."

She rolled her eyes. "He took it with him when he left."

"She's lying about something, sir," one of the big guys muttered. "Her heat signature indicates—"

"Any idiot can see that she's lying," Blue Eyes said. "Don't interrupt me."

The guns were unwavering, but Dani looked around at the three guys, noticing a weird, luminous flash in the eyes of the guy who had spoken up. There was hardware embedded in his corneas. And circuitry tattooed into the shaven parts of his scalp and neck. "You guys are Obsidian, right?"

The boss studied her, his eyes cold. "What do you know about Obsidian?"

No point being coy. She was going to tell him all of it anyway sooner or later.

"The basics," she said. "It's like, Hell Incorporated, am I right? A bunch of rich assholes looking to get richer by reinventing slavery."

"Something like that." Blue Eyes had that eerily calm look on his face which meant he was about to inflict extreme pain, she knew that much.

She steeled herself for it. "Not *like*," she said. "It *is* that. You kidnap runaway kids, steal their brains, and turn them into killing machines. Like these guys here. I bet that's their sad story, too. Am I right?"

She looked at the three thugs with him, one after the other. Their stolid faces did not change at all. Not that she had expected them to. They weren't idiots.

"Let's stay on topic," Blue Eyes said softly.

Dani glared at him. "How dead will I be if I don't?"

"Very dead," he told her. "Slowly. But surely." He studied her for several seconds. "So answer me."

She swallowed. "OK. So the info for a Manticore shipment was on the capsule, but he never managed to decrypt it while I was there. That's all I know."

"Do you have the key?" he demanded.

Key? Naldo had mentioned a key. Luke had asked for one too. Now this guy wanted it. The key was important. Whatever the hell it was.

They were going to press her for it. Hard. That unhappy thought made her shudder. She shook her head. "I got nothing," she said tightly. "Nobody gave me any key."

"You had no physical contact with the courier?"

"If you mean Naldo, I did try to stop him from bleeding to death, if that's what you're talking about."

"Enough of your shit. Get her inside," he snarled. "Let's get the fuck on with this."

Two of the big guys seized her under the armpits. She exploded, twisting desperately in their iron grasp. Born to fight back, win or lose, but these dudes barely noticed. What had Luke called them? Slave soldiers. Not just ordinary grunts, either. More like slave soldier special forces.

Inside the van, they muscled her down onto a gurney between cargo walls loaded with electronic gear. The windows were covered with a dark film, and a blindingly bright multi-eyed LED hung over the gurney. Rough hands stripped away her sweatshirt, her T-shirt.

She was naked, except for her shorts.

Two of the slave soldiers held her down on the gurney while Blue Eyes stepped inside and looked her over, clearly enjoying the view. The slave soldiers didn't notice her bare body, or if they did, they hid it well. Their wooden expressions never changed no matter how she struggled.

Blue Eyes whacked her on the temple with his knuckles, an explosion of pain. "Stop wiggling, bitch."

But she couldn't. She was in total freak-out mode, heaving and straining in their relentless grip as they passed a long, cold metal wand with blinking sensors over the surface of her bare body. At one point, she almost managed to knock the wand out of the bastard's hand with her knee, earning herself another ringing slap and a savage pinch to her nipple.

"I said hold her down, you stupid fucking freaks!" Blue Eyes bellowed.

She screamed as the grip of the slave soldiers on her body went from acutely painful to bone-grinding agony.

The light switched off, replaced by a purple glow from a bar on the wand. Ultraviolet light. He swept it over her body, and grabbed her thigh. "There it is."

Dani lunged up as far as the guy shoving her shoulders down would let her, craning her neck to look. Something shone on her skin in the UV light, right above her knee. A pale glowing pattern, like a mandala.

A matrix barcode. Right on her body. *How...?*

"You had the key all along. You lying cunt." Blue Eyes's voice was soft and menacing. "I'll take it back now. I'm going to skin you alive."

"I didn't know that was there!" She tried to control her shaking voice. "I...I remember now that Naldo grabbed my leg. He must have slapped it on me then. I didn't even notice. And he could barely speak. He was dying. I washed off the bloody handprint afterward. I never even knew it was there."

"She's telling the truth, sir." Another slave soldier, speaking in a monotone. "Her energy sig colors compared to her baseline suggest that—"

"Shut up. Unless you want a full-on, ball-breaking reconditioning just to teach you some fucking manners. Understood?"

"Yes, sir." The slave soldier obeyed, staring into space at nothing.

"Hold her." Blue Eyes pulled a knife from his belt. "I'll cut the key off her right now. Hold the bitch still."

The minute he set that cold steel blade against her thigh, a banshee wail ripped out of her throat.

"Gag her!" Blue Eyes yelled.

She bit the hands that tried to follow the order, drawing blood. Shrieked again as he cut deeper. Hot blood trickled down under her knee.

Big bodies all leaning over her, holding her down, a huge callused hand over her nose and mouth, blocking light, air. The knife was slicing into her again...ah *shit*—

Boom. The van rocked. Glass shattered, a side window in the front. Gunshots. Everyone froze, listening.

Boom. The van rocked again, vibrating.

Luke? She turned her head from the smothering hand, just far enough to break the seal over her mouth and drag in air before she passed out. *Oh, Luke. If it's you. I'm so sorry. Hell, even if it's not you I'm sorry.*

"It's coming from the ridge to the northeast," a slave soldier said.

"T-55, hunt him down," Blue Eyes rapped. "S-52, cover him. G-97, drive!"

The agony ceased as the men released their death grip and leaped to follow orders, rocked by gun blasts right outside.

She heard the slam of the driver's door up front, the engine firing up.

Boom. Glass shattered in the front of the vehicle.

"G-97!" Blue Eyes bellowed, holding a gun to her head. "Report!"

No answer. He slid the blackout shade up over the window to the front. Dani twisted desperately, struggling to see.

There was nothing but red. Blood splatter covered the glass.

The van lurched suddenly forward, leaving the two slave soldiers behind it exposed. The unlatched back doors swung open.

Boom. One of the slave soldiers tottered and hit the ground. The other dove to the ground behind the van, which braked to a lurching stop, sending the gurney crashing against Blue Eyes. He grunted, startled, as the vehicle went into reverse.

The slave soldier lying on the ground behind it tried to scramble free.

Too late. The van rolled over him, *thud-thud.* It braked, and jerked forward once again. *Thud-thud.*

"What the fuck?" Blue Eyes shrieked. "What the fuck is going on? Who's driving this fucking thing?"

No answer. The van was moving again. Backing toward the drop off. Picking up speed.

"Fuck!" he bellowed.

He wasn't holding the gun on her now. Dani rolled off the gurney and clutched something heavy bolted to the side wall.

Just in time. The van skidded to a halt, slewing to the side. The doors swung out wide over a vast nothingness, and the gurney sped out on its rattling wheels, suspended in the air ...

It crashed on the rocks far below.

Her tormentor scrambled out the back, eyes bugged out with alarm. He aimed his gun up the hill, shooting wildly. Then he saw something in the sky and waved his arms and the gun in the air, as if beckoning to it.

Dani let go of her handhold and crawled along the floor, peering out to see what he was waving at.

A drone floated toward them. Getting lower, faster, closer. It flashed past.

His hoarse shouting cut off. Dani leaned out as far as she could, slipping around in her own blood. The doors swung, banging in the gusty wind.

The first thing she saw was his gun on the ground, spinning on the crumbling edge of the drop off. Then she saw him. Or what was left of him.

The flying drone had sliced through his skull, right above the jaw. She barely made out a mess of red, broken lower teeth, and then a lurid smear of pinkish red. What was left of his brain was spread over the road with the drone wreckage.

His legs still jittered and twitched.

Dani nearly tumbled out of the van as it lurched into forward motion. It bumped violently over the body of the slave soldier again and turned around with swift and savagely efficient maneuvers on the narrow road, tires screeching.

Then it set off at a furious speed, leaving scattered bodies and the aging, rusted-out pickup truck behind it. The open back doors still banged to and fro as the van raced wildly around the hairpin curves.

About a mile further on, it slowed down and shuddered to a halt.

Dani was hanging on so tight, her muscles were cramped. She couldn't let go. She was sticky with blood from the ugly cut on top of her thigh. Blood ran from her nose, too, she realized. It was trickling down her neck.

She heard an engine approaching. The heavy *thunk* of a car door closing.

Boots on the asphalt. Coming right at her. Fast, like the pointed nose of that drone that went right into the screaming mouth of that guy. Not that she would shed any tears for him, but it was another blow, smacking her into some alternate dimension of reality.

One where she did not want to be.

The footsteps got closer. Something blocked the light from the open doors. A huge silhouette. "Dani?"

Luke's voice. His darkness against the bright white sky radiated an even darker fury. "Dani? Are you OK? Are you hurt? Shot?"

She couldn't answer. Her throat was locked, along with the rest of her body.

She shook, lips working. No breath to make a sound.

Then he saw the blood. "Holy shit. Did that asshole cut you?"

"I...I..." Her voice stuttered off to nothing as he leaped inside.

He picked her up like she was feather-light and jumped from the back of the van to the road, surefooted as a big cat.

"Luke," she whispered.

"Hold on. First let me get rid of this piece of shit."

The nightmare van roared to life. She wound her fingers into Luke's shirt and watched as it sped down the road toward another sharp curve with only emptiness beyond it. It drove off the edge, sailing into the air.

Two or three seconds passed before they heard the first crash. Then more, each crash fainter than the one before until the thing finally came to rest at the bottom of the canyon.

Luke loped to his own car, setting her gently on her feet as he pulled the Porsche's passenger side door open. He got her settled inside. She was shaking violently, but warmed by the blaze of fury in his eyes.

He jumped into the car and took off with a burst of speed.

"What did that fuckhead do to you?" he demanded.

She inhaled, trying to power her voice. It took several tries to make it just barely audible. "You saw it. He cut me. He wasn't going to stop. He didn't, until you started shooting. And did that thing you do with cars. It's magic."

Funny how that was growing on her. She'd never appreciated the true advantages of being able to mentally hijack machines until right now.

"Were any of them people that you saw at your house?" he asked.

"Yeah, the main guy was the same. He had three new henchmen, though. Slave soldiers. He didn't use names for them. He called them by numbers."

"Yeah. Technokinetics, like me," Luke said. "One tried to block me from taking control of the van, but I was faster. Then I shot him in the head. What did they want?"

"Same as before," she whispered. "The capsule. The key. And, uh…you."

He blew out a furious breath, and shook his head grimly. "Fuck."

"That drone," she said. "Did you—"

"What? Put that drone through that motherfucker's brain stem? Yeah, that was me. Wish I'd put it through his balls, but my fucking processer always defaults to the brain stem. The sure kill. Efficiency over style, every damn time."

"Oh," she whispered.

"Probably just as well." He talked on, restlessly, like he needed to unload his energy somehow. "You don't want to get too imaginative when it comes to killing, or you morph into a psycho-freak on top of all the rest of it. That's all I need."

She was racked by a shudder. Luke noticed, of course, and looked her up and down, cursing under his breath.

He took his hands off the wheel and his feet off the pedals and twisted himself over the central console, rummaging in boxes in the back seat while the car hurtled swiftly onward without him appearing to drive it, screeching around hairpin turns at ninety miles an hour.

Dani stared out at the road, eyes wide. Afraid to breathe.

Luke twisted back around after a couple of minutes, holding another big T-shirt, a packet of sterile gauze pads and a thick woolen blanket.

"Get something on," he said gruffly. "And get yourself warmed up."

He tried to tuck the blanket around her, but she pulled it from his hands. "Um, Luke," she said. "I know you can drive cars with just your naked mind, but it scares me to death when you take your hands off the wheel on a cliff road. Just saying."

"I'm just taking care of you. Deal with it."

She huddled further down under the blanket. "Ah. OK," she whispered. "Fine. Sure. Can deal."

Luke drove the car for several miles without saying a word, but she felt the pressure building inside him every second that passed. So she was braced for what was coming when the dam finally broke. Sort of.

"Jesus, Dani," he exploded. "Why the escape? What the fuck were you thinking?"

She waited a thoughtful moment before she answered. "Is that a real question?" she asked. "Do you want a real answer?"

"Fucked if I know. This is a disaster. Now they know what they're dealing with, and probably who. They know more about me than I know about myself. All because I couldn't just let you go. I couldn't let them destroy you. I fucked myself completely."

"I appreciate that," she said. "I'm grateful that you came for me. And I'm sorry."

"Yeah? So why did you run? I told you that you weren't a prisoner. I told you who those people are. What they're capable of."

"Yes, you did."

He wasn't finished. "You'd seen enough strange shit to know I was for real! You saw how I fought! You saw Naldo's capsule. His scars, my scars. How I healed so fast, the thing with me and the car. You knew I was for real and you chose not to believe it because it scared you. That was fucking lazy of you, Dani. And cowardly."

She took a moment before she tried speaking. "Yes, I know. And you're right. But it was just too much all at once. I couldn't let it in. It was…too much like Jimmy."

"Yeah? Who the fuck is Jimmy?"

"A guy my mom was with for a while when I was a kid," she said. "He's been dead for years now. I liked him. He was a sweet guy. When he was taking his meds."

"Oh. Oh, fuck." Luke put his fingers to his forehead. "I see where this is going."

They slowed as they reached the roadblock and the detour sign that Blue Eyes and his goons must have put there. Luke scanned the area in every direction and answered the question in her eyes. "Don't see any sign of them," he said. "Maybe the drone I crashed was the only one monitoring us. We might shake them off. With luck."

Dani's guts lurched. "We might? Wow. That's great."

"With luck," Luke repeated. He maneuvered around the roadblock on the shoulder and picked up speed on the slightly larger two-lane highway. At least this one had guardrails.

"Go on," he said. "You were talking about Jimmy."

"Yeah, well," she murmured. "So when Jimmy went off his meds, things got weird in Chez LaSalle. Aliens would come. Bad guys who wanted to take over the world. Thought control rays that could only be blocked by the bathtub. He'd lock himself in there for hours at a time, hiding from aliens in the tub. And there was the poison gas from the fridge that would turn us into mindless drones. So, your story…it pushed all my buttons."

"It's not a fucking story," he burst out savagely. "It's the truth."

"I get that," she said. "I believe you now. Swear to God. It's just that some of the details, the world domination and the secret experiments and the genetic modifications, it was just so Jimmy, you know? I couldn't make room for it in my mind."

"I see." He put on a burst of speed to pass a logging truck. "Is there room now?"

"Oh, God, yes," she said fervently. "Plenty. Being abducted and tortured is mind-expanding."

"Trust me, I know," he said harshly. "From personal experience."

His tone made her cringe. She was trying not to get defensive, but it went against every instinct she had to just shut up. Let silence sit heavily between them.

She had no business yapping at him. Not right after he just saved her ass. Again.

"So you thought I was a psycho head case," he said. "While fucking me."

She winced. "Well, no. Not only that. I also thought you were brave and selfless and amazing. And I thought it was a cruel joke that I finally found a guy who rang all my bells, but there was just one little bitty problem—he happened to be a paranoid schizophrenic."

"I'm not a—"

"I know you're not!" she yelled. "I believe you now, OK? I'm just trying to explain my reasoning."

"So what was your game?"

"Game?" She shot him an incredulous look. "I don't have a game! I got nothing, Luke! I'm hanging on by my fingernails! Right now, my game is, let's see…how about, save me from the villains! Take me to your alternate universe and fuck me all night long!"

"I was just trying to keep you alive," he ground out. "That's all."

"I know that now," she said. "Please calm down."

"I can't," he said. "My ASP is all out of whack. I'm pumped full of stress juice with nowhere to put it. So I'm liable to be in a shitty mood for a while. Be warned."

"OK," she whispered.

They drove for a while in silence. "One thing you should know," he said finally. "If the aliens ever came for us, you wouldn't find me hiding in the bathtub. I'd be out there armed to the teeth, kicking their wrinkly gray asses."

A startled laugh jolted her chest. "Are you trying to be funny, Luke?"

"Not at all," he said. "I'm not a funny guy. I am dead serious."

She blew out a sigh. "God help me."

Luke shook his head. "Joking aside, if that's what I was doing, you're in this now, Dani. Your choices are simple."

She shot him a startled look. "Are they? For real?"

"Yeah," he said. "If you believe me, then stay and fight with me. If not, go back out there and take your chances. Just let me know where you want me to let you out. I have some cash with me, a few thousand bucks. You can have all of it. Go it alone if you want to. But that's it for me. I hate it, but I'm done. I won't come back to save your skin again. This is the last time I slow down for you."

"Oh, Luke, don't—"

"Just be aware. They will come for you. They will never get tired of looking."

"I understand. And I—"

"So decide, because I need to haul ass and regroup. I screwed myself left right and sideways by coming back for you. And for nothing."

"Is that so," she said quietly.

He made an impatient sound. "I didn't mean that your life was worth nothing," he said gruffly. "I'm pissed, yeah. But I'm sorry they hurt you."

"Thanks," she said. "You're sweet."

"Hardly," he scoffed.

"You came to save me when there was nothing in it for you," she said stubbornly. "That makes you a good guy."

"No, actually." His voice was sour. "I think technically, that makes me an idiot."

"Oh, shut up. You know I'm right. And if there's going to be a battle, I want to be on the right side of it. With you."

He refused to look at her. "Don't do me any fucking favors."

"Listen to me, Luke," she said. "I think…I might actually have something that you can use."

He looked at her, which freaked her out again, since at that exact moment, the car was swerving around another hundred and eighty degree turn, and way too damn fast.

"What might that be?" he demanded, eyes locked on hers as the car speeded around the hairpin bend.

"The key. I think…I have the key to decrypt Naldo's chip. I had it all along. But I didn't know."

"Had it?" He looked suspicious. "Had it where?"

"In my skin," she said simply. "Naldo must have slapped it on me when I got down on the floor next to him, in my kitchen." Her voice caught, remembering the blood pouring out of her friend's chest. "He put his hand on my leg. A transparent film, I guess, with a code hidden in it. I never had a clue. And he tried so hard to tell me."

"Tell you what? Tell you how?"

"How to read it," she said. "Those Obsidian guys found it. Right here." She pointed to the wad of gauze over her leg. "That's why he was cutting me. He was going to flay that piece of skin right off me."

"I'm not following you," he said harshly. "I didn't see anything on your leg."

"Me neither. I thought it was strange that Naldo kept talking about juvie," she said. "But he was dying, and I was panicked, so I wasn't really listening. But now I get it. He wasn't saying 'juvie' at all."

"What the fuck was he saying?" he demanded. "What the fuck are *you* saying?"

"Ultraviolet," she said. "Naldo was saying 'UV.'"

CHAPTER 15

Zade swept his mind over his army of trawler bots as he stood on his terrace, gazing out over the Puget Sound and the Seattle skyline. He'd programmed them to constantly, ceaselessly search through databases for clues that could lead to Luke.

No hits. Not in the last forty seconds, anyhow.

"How're you doing out there with the carne asada?" Hannah called from the kitchen.

Zade dragged his attention back to the big chunk of marinated steak sizzling on the barbecue. Another three seconds, and it would have been on the far side of perfect.

Hannah had been tracking those seconds. She liked it rare.

"Ready," he called. "It just needs to rest for a couple minutes."

He forked the meat up onto a platter and carried it into the kitchen, where he stopped in his tracks. Hannah was chasing Simone around with an unmarked spray can.

Simone was laughing. "Get real! Do you have to bedazzle me before dinner? I have tortillas on the griddle already and they're going to burn!"

"What the hell is that?" he demanded.

"It's a thing Sisko and I cooked up," Hannah said. "Hair and body glitter. Specialized spray, not the dollar store stuff. I was trying to zap Simone with it before you saw. You know, for a surprise." She made a face at Simone. "So much for that."

"Glitter? Sisko?" Zade raised an eyebrow. "Since when?"

"He cuts loose sometimes," Hannah assured him. "The spray has traceable nanoparticles. The idea is, you decorate your girlfriend with it, go to a dance club, and then trace her whereabouts if she gets nabbed by nefarious villains when you're not looking."

"Nabbed by who?"

Hannah shrugged. "Obsidian agents, maybe."

Zade grunted thoughtfully. "Could be useful. Sure it's not toxic?"

Hannah rolled her eyes. "Dude. You know I have the equivalent of three advanced degrees in chemistry stored in my data processors. Yes, this amazing new product has passed every test."

"Really." Zade looked from her to Simone. "So? Let's see how this stuff works. But step away from the table. Let's not get it on the food."

"For the record, there's an edible version," Hannah said. "Just not for tacos."

"Oh, whatever. Do your worst." Simone held her nose and squeezed her eyes shut as Hannah sprayed a cloud of the stuff over her, then sprayed her again.

"Whoa!" Zade said. "That's enough."

Simone opened her eyes and turned her arms and hands, admiring the luminous shimmer. "Pretty," she said. "How long does it last?"

"It varies, depending on how hot the weather is and how much you sweat," Hannah said. "Sisko and I tested it. I went out clubbing all glittered up and he followed me using the monitor. Worked great, technically speaking. Aesthetically, too, if I do say so myself. I got all kinds of attention with my sparkly cleavage."

"Hot. Right." Zade couldn't take his eyes off Simone. She was so fucking pretty like that. "You look like you fell out of a star or something. Mmmm. Stuff works for me."

Hannah made a derisive sound, and Zade flapped his hand at her. "Look away. You're too young to witness this." He grabbed Simone and kissed her. A long kiss that promised an erotic night ahead.

Simone fought her way out of it after a moment, pink cheeked, and shot an embarrassed glance at Hannah, who watched with arms crossed over her chest, beer bottle dangling from her fingers, tapping her foot. "You guys done?" Hannah asked dryly.

"Yes. And I'm starving," Simone said. "Oh shit! The tortillas!"

She dove for the kitchen to rescue them from the grill and piled them on a plate. Only slightly overdone, he was glad to see. Dark brown spots instead of gold. Still good.

Hannah took a sip of her beer, her whiskey colored eyes boring into him. "So," she said slowly. "Distracted much?"

He stared back, sensing a trap. "Not at all. The meat's done to perfection."

"I'm not talking about the meat. I'm talking about your diving."

Zade brought the steak to the table and started slicing it. Hannah had been happily giving him hell ever since he'd met her, a scrappy, smart-mouthed nine year old, trapped with him and Luke in the Midlands program. Modified like them by the Obsidian researchers, along with her brother Noah, who was the leader of their rebel group.

Hannah was the closest thing to a sister that he had, and she took the role seriously. She considered it her sacred duty to harass him.

"You're just aching to mess with me, so get it over with," he said.

"You're diving too much," she announced. "Ten, twelve hours at a time. And you were checking your bots out there on the terrace, weren't you? I felt you. You never stop."

He set the sliced steak aside and covered it. "Don't spy on me, electronically or otherwise."

"Hannah wasn't spying," Simone said. "I asked her to talk to you."

"She's worried about you," Hannah pointed out. "And she's right to worry. Remember what happened to Pushnell's group, back at Midlands? Pushnell put those poor bastards under for days at a time with an IV and a catheter and pee bag. Every single one of them got brain burn and went to the shredder. Remember Malachi? And Aaron?"

"Yes," he said savagely. "Nothing wrong with my memory."

"Aaron tried to claw his own face off in the cafeteria, remember that?"

Simone tried, unsuccessfully, to hide her flinch.

"Goddamnit, Hannah," he flared. "There's no reason to dig up grisly shit from our past. It's all behind us now. And I'm not like Aaron."

"I hope not." Hannah wouldn't back down. Her eyes had that pinpoint laser focus she got when she was using her implants, manipulating or blocking wavelengths.

In fact, when he reached out to sweep the trawler bots, he hit dead air. Not a wave to be found, at least not any wavelengths useful for his purposes.

"You're shielding," he growled. "Quit that right now. This is my house and I own these waves. Stop throwing your weight around or else get the fuck out of here."

Hannah shrugged. The interference deadening his wi-fi winked out and connectivity hummed around them once again.

"I was just wondering how often the obsessive bot-checking was going on," Hannah said. "My conservative estimate is once a minute. My fear is that it's three or four times a minute. Which means that you have a problem."

"I am *fine*," he said savagely.

Simone put the tortillas on the table. "I invited a family member over for carne asada and beer, not a brawl," she said. "Be polite. Both of you."

He gave Simone a betrayed look. "You sicced her on me? On purpose?"

"Somebody had to come down on you," Hannah said. "Simone's too sweet on you to be effective. You need a stronger hand. Usually Noah keeps you on the straight and narrow, but God forbid we bother him on the art geek honeymoon for the ages."

"He deserves a break." He was startled to hear himself defend Noah. The guy was a royal pain in the ass who'd made Zade's life complicated for years. Still, Noah had masterminded the escape from Midlands. Noah would also lay down his life for any one of them. He owed Noah big. He owed all of them.

"Maybe, but things are weird without him," Hannah said, frowning. "I can't wait for him to get home and zap your ass back into line. Because you are scaring us, Zade."

Zade looked from Hannah's angry eyes to Simone's worried face. Simone's mouth had that tight-lipped, determined look he had come to know too well.

He let out a long, controlled breath. "I'm sorry if I scared you," he said evenly to Simone. "I'm just being focused. I swear. I'm OK."

"Too focused," Hannah said.

"I'm not talking to you," Zade said without looking at her.

"I suggest we eat before this food gets cold," Simone said.

Hannah flounced back to the kitchen to grab the salad and the silverware.

They'd just gotten well into it, and he was savoring a blend of savory meat, sour cream, salsa and guac when he felt it. Clear as a knock on the door inside his head.

A trawler bot signaling a hit.

He and Hannah stopped chewing, eyes locked.

Zade swallowed the food in his mouth, and wiped his fingers. "You feel that, spy girl?"

"Sure did," Hannah said, her eyes keen with excitement. "Felt the bump."

"What bump?" Simone asked. "Damn it, you guys. That's not fair."

"Sorry. I got a hit with one of my bots. One second while I check it out." Zade found the flagged file and ran it through his processor. Then he ran it again.

"Stop staring into space, Zade," Hannah said. "You're killing me. For God's sake, put it onto something with a screen. Is it good?"

"Yeah. It's good. Hang on." He transferred the data to a tablet that lay on the bar and grabbed the thing, thumbing the app open. "A police report. A guy came into a Kwik Stop convenience store on the Cardinal Ridge Highway today, near Goforth, California. Wanted information on some girl who'd been through there. Then a black Porsche Cayenne approached the store with no driver inside. The man got in and drove away at high speed."

The silence at the table was absolute.

Zade got up. "I'm out." He looked at Simone. "Sorry, baby. I have to go see if that place has video footage."

"I'll go with you," Simone said.

"No," he said. "Not a good use of your time. I love your company, but you're better off here, working out the sequences for Luke's code scrub."

Simone looked hurt. "Don't dive while you're driving," she said. "Not even a shallow dive. Swear it on your life."

Zade sighed. "Simone, we've been through this—"

"I don't give a shit how big your monster processor is or how good you are at multi-tasking. If you're speeding on an interstate in the dead of night, don't dive."

"Fine," he said. "I promise."

Hannah snorted under her breath. "Good luck keeping that promise. Bot junkie."

Zade ignored her, moving quickly to the weapons safe. He buckled on a shoulder holster for his Glock and an ankle holster for the Ruger six-shot and shrugged on his jacket, buzzing inside. Excitement and fear. Bright side, if this panned out, Luke was alive, ambulatory, functioning. There was no way to know if he was in his right mind, but hey, that kind of judgment call changed with the fucking weather.

But on the dark side, what the fuck? Why hadn't Luke called them? What was he running from? And this kidnapped girl? And the police, looking for a killer?

The dark side just kept getting darker.

It was weird that Luke had revealed his abilities to a convenience store clerk. He must have known the guy would yammer about it. Luke had always been super careful about secrecy. And he never lost control or showed fear. He'd always considered it his job to make everyone else feel safe. Just not himself.

Simone's eyes stopped him at the door.

"Don't look at me like that," he begged. "You know I have to go. Work on the scrub program while I'm gone. I'll be back as soon as I can."

"Of course," she said. "And I'll be ready. Just go find him."

He seized her and held her so tight, she squeaked. Then followed up with a fierce kiss, which had the unfortunate effect of making him hard and jacking his ASP all the way up to the stratosphere.

Now he was jittery and buzzed. A fine way to start a long road trip at night.

He backed away into the freight elevator that opened off his apartment, Hannah's laughter in his ears. Simone's smile made him melt. He wanted to grab her again.

"Look at you. Mr. Bedazzled," she said, pointing. "All ready for the prom."

Aw, shit. He stared down at his sparkling coat and sweater as the elevator doors closed, punching the button for the ground floor. The reflection of the glitter glow lit up the battered steel walls as the elevator ground noisily down.

Hannah needed to invent a goddamn cloak of invisibility to go with it.

Luke hated leaving Dani alone, even for the few minutes it took to go into the housewares store and buy a UV light. Then a run into the drugstore for some more gauze and disinfectant, and a faster run back to the car where Dani waited, wrapped up in her blanket. He'd been scouring travel databases for a hotel that fit all his security criteria and finally found one, but they had to drive farther than he liked to get to it.

He wanted Dani tucked up in a quality bed with clean sheets under a pile of blankets. Preferably sipping something hot. Safe and warm and protected.

That last-minute rescue had turned him into a churning black hole of rage. The sight of her crouched in the back of that van, half-naked and bloodied and terrified...*fuck.*

He wanted to bring that piece of shit back to life and kill him again. At closer range this time.

He didn't know what to do with all this wild energy. He'd lost the knack for dealing with powerful emotions. Maybe he'd never had it. Who the fuck knew.

That burned his ass, too. Not knowing. He was sick of it.

They got to the hotel, the Larsen Pines Lodge, and claimed their small cabin way out in the back. He parked the car under a thick stand of pine trees that were sure to drip sticky pitch all over his SUV, but it was worth it to have cover against satellites or drones or whatever else those pricks might have in their arsenal.

The cabin was simple. Bedroom, kitchenette and bathroom. He carried Dani inside, setting her gently on her feet by the bed.

He got an eloquent eye-roll when he tried to help her sit down. "I'm OK, Luke."

"Good. Going to grab the stuff from the car," he said gruffly. "Be right back."

He came back loaded up with bags. The UV light, the stuff from the pharmacy to patch up her cut, the long-forgotten food from the steakhouse, her new clothes, her burner phones. He immediately pried one out of its packaging and put it to charge.

She looked puzzled. "What's with the phone? I thought you said I shouldn't—"

"Yeah, I did say that. And yes, it's still a shitty idea to use this for anything but a dire life or death emergency. Use it once, dump it, get the hell away from it. That's the rule."

She nodded. "Speaking of which. I have to call Dorothy, my supervisor at the hospital, and tell her that I'm—"

"No, you don't." He snarled the words out before he could control himself.

She sighed. "Luke. Please. All I want to do is to let them know that I'm not—"

"You still don't get it," he said. "You can't call anyone, Dani. Not anymore. Not ever. From this day onward. Understand?"

"But...but can't I at least explain to Dorothy what—"

"How the fuck do you think Obsidian found you today?" His tone made her flinch, but he was too wound up to soften it. "You made calls with that dumbass store clerk's smartphone, right? And you told people where you were?"

"Ah...yes," she said, tentatively. "I called the police detective, and my neighbor Millie to tell her that I was all right, and I left a voicemail for Colleen, who handles the staffing at the clinic, but I..." Her voice trailed off. A look of horror came over her face. "But they had no reason to be monitoring Richie the Kwik-Stop clerk's phone!"

"They weren't," Luke said grimly. "They were monitoring the detective's phone. And Millie's. And Colleen's. And everyone else you fucking know. Everyone, Dani."

"But...but how could they—"

"You say the shit I can do is science fiction. Well, they've made hundreds of me. Thousands, maybe. They've got a fucking army of bioengineered freaks and there's nothing they can't track or monitor. In the blink of an eye."

"But I can't just disappear," she whispered. "That's so awful."

"That's exactly what you have to do," he said. "I'm sorry. But get it through your head. Your life as you knew it is over. You can't go back. You can't contact those people again. If you do, you're putting them in danger. Do you want Obsidian to focus down on Dorothy? Or Colleen, or your neighbor lady? Or anyone else you give a shit about?"

"No. No, I don't." She waved her hand at him. "I get it, Luke. You've convinced me. No need to keep lecturing. But...why buy the phones at all?"

"That's in case they get me. In case you have to make a run for it on your own."

"Oh, fuck's sake." She shook her head, closing her eyes. "Later for this."

Shit. "Come on," he growled. "Let's get into the bathroom and dress that cut."

Dani sat down on the edge of the tub and let him sponge the blood off with a wet hotel washrag. Her attacker had made one long, straight cut. Not as deep as he'd feared. By now the bleeding had slowed to a coagulating ooze.

"Looks pretty clean," Dani said as he sprayed on the disinfectant. "I don't think it needs any stitching or staples. It should be fine."

"I'm the one who heals quickly, not you," he said. "I wish I had some antibiotics for you. I don't ever need them, so they're not in my stash."

"It's a superficial cut," she said. "Just the skin. That's all he wanted."

He applied an adhesive wound-closing device that pulled the edges of the cut closed with transparent surgical-grade tape, sealing it. Then he laid a nonstick bandage pad over the closed wound, and ripped open the nonstick paper tape.

"Wait." She put her hand over his. "Don't cover it up yet. Don't you want to look at the barcode matrix first?"

"No. I can wait a little longer. Lie down. Warm up. I don't want you going into shock."

"Didn't happen, won't happen. Come on, Luke, I can't stand the suspense. I went through hell for this thing and I want some goddamn satisfaction."

Her soft, luscious lips curved into that persuasive smile. Her eyes were so luminous, even shadowed with exhaustion. The light in them blew his fucking mind.

"Luke?" she prompted softly. So on to him. Fully aware of her power. "Hello? Anybody home in there?"

"Yeah, sure," he muttered. "OK. Whatever. We'll tape it down after."

She took the pad off and followed him out of the bathroom, sitting down on the bed while she waited for him to pull the UV light out of its plastic and plug it in. He pulled down the blackout shades, turned off the lights, and switched on the UV light.

The complex symbol glowed brightly on her leg, barely dimmed by the transparent tape that covered it. Luke knelt down in front of her and studied it.

"Take a picture," she said.

"I already did," Luke said. "With my processor. It links to a site that has a password. I'm entering it now, and I…here we go. Oh, yeah. *Yeah*. It's all here."

A deluge of data poured in on him. Streams of files downloading into his databanks. His brain lit up like a pinball arcade. ASP flashing and scrolling wildly.

"Can you put the files onto a regular computer so I can look at them too?"

"You sure, Dani? Once you know this stuff, you can't unknow it. You've seen what those evil pricks are like. You really want to know their business?"

"Would you rather I didn't?" she asked. "Don't you trust me?"

"It's not a question of trust. The key is yours. You paid for it in blood." Luke opened the laptop, copied and dumped the files. "Look through it, if you're interested."

"OK then." They gazed at each other in sudden silence.

"I have to start processing these files," he told her. "I'm going to dive. Just so you know, I'll look like I'm stoned but I'm not. I'm awake and aware, just grinding through data."

"Cool."

"And I'll still be monitoring us every second," he assured her. "In every direction."

"Luke, saying stuff like that creeps me out more," she teased gently. "Just don't divert any fighter jets or helicopters, or mess around with the space shuttle, or redirect any intercontinental ballistic missiles. Promise?"

"Sure," he said, distracted. "Sure, yeah. I'll keep it real simple. Real focused."

She laughed, to his bewilderment, and then leaned over and kissed him. A hot, soft, lingering kiss.

The contact sent a bolt of frantic heat stabbing into him. It cracked him wide open. His dick swelled to stone-hard readiness and his body thrummed. *Now, now, now.*

"Don't," he said harshly. "Back off, Dani."

Dani shrank back, startled. "Sorry," she murmured.

"It's cold. Get some clothes on. Some blankets. Warm yourself up."

She looked down his long, limp black T-shirt. "Well. I would, but—"

"I got clothes for you. When I went down the hill to the steak house, remember? I was paying for them when I saw you leave. They're in the plastic bags by the door. And the food's in the brown paper bag on the desk, when you feel like eating something. There's a microwave in here. We can heat stuff up if you want."

Dani went to the door and hefted the two shopping bags he'd brought inside. "Wow," she murmured. "That's a lot of clothes."

"Wasn't sure about your size," he said curtly. "Use what you like. Dump the rest."

He wished he hadn't got that lacy lingerie. *Gimme gimme gimme please.*

Too late to take the stuff out of the bag now. He had to just shine it on.

"I'm diving now," he said. "Going down. Talk to you later."

He turned away so she wouldn't see the flush that was burned into his face.

CHAPTER 16

Dani fled to the bathroom just in time.

Pull it together, LaSalle. After everything the guy had done for her, he didn't need to see her fall to pieces. And just because he was being so sweet to her.

To her credit, she didn't make a sound while coming apart. She sat on the edge of the tub and hid her face. Cried. A lot.

When the tears stopped flowing, she found herself staring down at the bags of clothing at her feet. Clothes. What a novel concept. She'd been in scanty house rags or borrowed mismatched scraps for this entire bloody nightmarish adventure. Ever since Naldo showed up at the back door. It was like a classic anxiety dream, never being able to get dressed. Always exposed, shivering, barefoot, vulnerable.

She blew her nose, dabbing at her face with tissue. The closed wound on her leg throbbed nastily. At least it wasn't oozing. She and everyone else needed to keep their remaining blood inside their bodies for a while. Enough was enough.

She turned on the faucets, and ran herself a bath. Not too deep, so she could keep her knee dry. The hot water felt wonderful. It calmed her down. Slightly.

After she dried off, the contents of those shopping bags was a revelation. Luke had guessed right on the bra and underwear sizing, and the shoes were right, too, but he obviously liked women to wear tight, sexy stuff. Underwear that left her butt cheeks on display. Brightly colored, silky bras that propped her tits up. Low cut, V-necked tops. Clinging, low-rise stretch jeans. Pastel pajamas with cartoon kittens on them.

Kittens? Like, what the fuck?

Two stretch lace outfits, one a hot hooker red, the other in demure and bride-like ivory. Hmm. Some interesting internal conflict there. She could have fun with that.

She hoped. Talk about mixed messages. He'd been so cold and off-putting when she tried to kiss him. Practically shoving her away. Then again, he was still mad, and he had reason to be. She couldn't just snap her fingers and make his mad go away. That never worked.

However…she could definitely accelerate the process.

The room had one queen-sized bed. If he was lying next to her on it, no way was she leaving that guy alone. Not even after violent trauma and the wound still throbbing painfully on her thigh. Crazy, but so what. She was alive and kicking and in one piece, thanks to him.

She wanted to feel something good and true and excellent. Luke fit the bill.

Bye-bye, cartoon kittens. They could wait for a Netflix and popcorn and sex-with-socks-on night. She was going with the hot red stretch lace. Just as she was. Unretouched.

And in the mood for some intense sexual healing.

Dani wriggled into the outfit. Hoisted her boobs up for maximum lift. Hiked the panties up extra high. She pushed the door open, stepped out and struck a pose.

For nothing. Luke was in a digital trance. One hand manipulated a tablet, the other was tapping madly over the laptop's keyboard. He'd looped his devices into a chain and his brain was the connector. No attention to spare for sexy lingerie.

But she wasn't giving up. By no means. "How's it going?"

"So far so good," he said. "I've pinpointed the location of the second shipment, and the combination for retrieving it. All the backup equipment needed to activate the slave soldier and make it function. Coordinates for the pickup of the wetware are included."

She tugged at the lacy shoulder strap, adjusting it. Luke still hadn't noticed what she was wearing. "What the hell is wetware?"

"It's a Manticore term. It refers to the slave soldier. He could be dormant, possibly suspended in fluid. There's a file on him. I89VY262. I haven't gone through that one yet. C drive on the laptop, if you're interested."

"I am interested," she said. "But later."

"The equipment is in a self-storage unit at an E-Z-U-Store in Serrati Flats, California," he said. "About a hundred and fifty miles north of here."

"I suppose you want to get going right away?"

"No, we'll wait."

She was startled. "Why? Aren't we in a hurry?"

"You went through hell today. You need a decent night's sleep. In a real bed."

Well, bless his heart. How sweet. The bed part he'd gotten right.

She walked toward him slowly. Swaying her hips. Still nothing. He was locked and loaded in data processing mode. His eyes reflected squares of blue from the screen. A stream of files rolled constantly down it. Like she was peering directly into the data churn in his brain.

He was about to get forcibly reminded that he was not a robot.

She stepped between him and the desk and sat down on his lap.

Luke went rigid. "Holy fuck, Dani."

She leaned in so her tits were right below the level of his nose. Nipples on red alert from being so close to him. She put her arms around his neck, running her fingers slowly through his hair. Inhaling his hot male scent.

"I like the red outfit the best," she said, her voice low and husky. "Do you?"

Luke put his hands around her waist, fingers splayed wide. Holding her as if she were made of blown glass. "You don't have to do this. That stuff I bought for you—I just thought it would look hot on you. You owe me nothing."

She gazed down at him, taken aback. "I never thought I did," she said coolly. "That's not what this is about."

"No? So this isn't another mercy fuck for the psycho who's gone off his meds?"

She recoiled. "You *asshole!*" She smacked him, not hard. Just a stinging little tap to the cheek. He could have blocked it easily, but he didn't.

He was silent for a few moments. "You get a free pass today, after what happened," he said evenly. "But don't do that to me ever again."

"Then don't put words in my mouth. I never said that, never thought that about you," she told him.

He was silent. Reading her. Which she found infuriating. She could beat him at the silence, though. Because his dick definitely wanted to talk. She moved slightly, sliding over his muscular thighs. Up, down. Down, up. *Hello, dick.*

"Understood," he said.

"OK. Well, then. Where does that leave us?" She settled herself deeply onto his lap again. He was so thick and hard and hot, with a stellar erection pressing against her ass. His heat melted into her, sending a deep, hot pull of raw craving through her body. "Do you want to start this conversation again from the top?" she asked.

His face was still unreadable, but a muscle pulsed in his jaw. "Yeah, I'd give this conversation another shot," he said slowly. "If you're offering a do-over."

"I am," she said. "Choose your words carefully. Don't fuck it up."

He was silent again, for several minutes this time, studying her face. His scrutiny was hard to bear. She felt like she was missing a protective layer. Hell with it. She wanted this *bad.* She shifted on his lap so that the pulsing ache between her legs was positioned strategically right over his cock, and gave him some bedroom eyes. Threw in a little teasing, lip-licking action to get a sexy glisten going. Because she felt like it. Because no lip gloss.

"I need to be sure of you," he said slowly.

"Huh?" She was baffled. "Sure of what?"

"Exactly what you want from me."

She laughed. "Are you still confused? I'm wiggling around on top of your hot cock, Luke. How clear do I need to be?"

"Tell me exactly what you want," he said. "I am making zero assumptions, after everything that just happened."

She rolled her eyes with a sigh. "Could you just relax?"

"No," he said. "I can't. You saw what I did out there. I'm wound up like a spring. Relaxing is not an option for me. And I do not want to fuck this up."

"Honestly, Luke, I don't think you could," she told him.

"Indulge me anyway." His voice was adamant.

She didn't know where to begin. She kept her chin up, her eyes locked boldly on his. Pulling him in. *Come to me now.*

"I will indulge anything you want, buddy," she said. "Tell me your fantasy about how you'd like to get this going, and I'll tell you if it jives with mine. Show me yours and I'll show you mine."

"You too chicken to go first?"

She gave him a smoky, mysterious smile. "What do you see yourself doing with me when you close your eyes? Tell me. That would really turn me on."

He slid his hand down over her back, the rough spots on his hand snagging on the delicate fabric. "I want to go down on you," he said. "I want you to open up your pussy lips until your clit pops out, and lick it and suck on it until your juice is all over my face and I'm all wet too. I want you slippery and soft, legs splayed out. Squirming and begging. Coming against my face. I want you to be wet and soft and ready, because it's going to be a long hot night. And I am in one hell of a goddamn mood."

Her face was hot now, her breath choppy and uneven. She fought to keep her voice light and teasing. "Sounds interesting."

"Does it? How exactly? Be specific."

"OK. How about...hot. Sexy. Wet and dirty and incredibly fabulous."

"That's much better," he said. "Does it jive with your fantasies?"

"It's a perfect fit." She was squirming on his lap. Trying to play it cool. "And it works with the lingerie."

"Yeah? I had a hell of a time picking the colors." He studied her body, his hands sliding over her, cupping her breasts. Making her tremble. "There was a black one, and a purple one, and a peach colored one. A brown one, and a sort of bronze color. They all would've looked awesome on you."

"You chose right," she assured him.

"I should've gotten them all," he said dreamily, caressing her hip.

Her laughter was cut off by his fierce kiss. She froze for just a second, startled, but his ardor melted her instantly. Heat pulsed through her. Wave upon wave of hungry yearning.

He pulled away, his breath uneven. "Whoa. You make me so hot. I feel like I haven't had sex in years, every time."

"Me too," she told him. "Except for me, it actually is years. Before you, I mean."

His eyes widened. "No way. But you're so fucking hot."

She gave him a secret smile. "I'm picky. So it's been...wow. Almost two years."

"Huh," he muttered. "What happened? What did he do to piss you off?"

"I found out he had a girlfriend and a three year old son in another city."

"That's bad," Luke said. "Lying prick."

"He sure was." She slid her fingers into his hair. "But I shouldn't judge him. Who knows? I might be screwing a married man right now and I don't even know it."

He looked alarmed. "No way. I'm sure I would know if I—"

"Yeah? Really? Would you? What makes you so goddamn sure?"

He scowled. "I'd feel it," he said. "Like a voice in my head. Telling me to take out the trash and pick up my socks."

"Hah. You don't know," Dani said. "You have no clue. Most men have no clue even without the excuse of amnesia. And let me tell you something else, buddy. Guys who look like you? They have to beat the ladies away with a great big stick. You have women in your past. I'd bet you body parts. So don't shoot your mouth off until you know for sure."

"Oh." He looked dubious. "So, ah. Does this mean that we have to stop?"

"No," she whispered. "I'll cross that bridge when I come to it. For now, let's live the moment. Birth control's covered, and my bloodwork is good. So go for it."

He dug his fingers into her hair, nuzzling the side of her face hungrily. "I'm immune to everything, with my genetic mods," he told her.

She nodded. "OK."

"Is it?" he asked. "It's only OK if you believe my story one hundred percent. What a choice. Either I'm a psycho maniac or else you're fucking a genetically modified freak. What'll it be?"

She shoved at his chest. "Oh, shut up. I believe you, OK? Amnesia and all. I believe every last goddamn word you ever told me. I think you are absolutely for real."

His eyes were fiercely intent. "You trust me, then?"

"With my life," she said. "You've saved it twice. You didn't have to."

The kiss sucked them in again, a vortex of uncontrollable need, and suddenly she was clinging to him, twining and gasping. "Oh, God," she whispered. "Oh, Luke."

He lifted his mouth from hers, kissing her cheekbones, eyelids. The bright blossoming heat of those kisses sent delight rippling through her body.

"So?" he murmured. "Lead the way."

"Me?" She blinked, disoriented. "You just told me what you wanted! I'm all for it. Do it! Proceed!"

"Tell me," he said. "Every move. Spell it out. Word by word."

"What the hell? Are you playing power games?"

"Call it whatever you want. If you want something from me, reach out and take it."

She gave him a narrow look. "Come on, Luke. Are you punishing me?"

"I don't know. Let's get on with it. Later, you can tell me how punished you feel when I'm swirling my tongue real slow around your clit. While I find that secret place inside your pussy and stroke it with my fingers or my cock. God, I love that. I can't wait to tongue-fuck you into a screaming orgasm."

"You bastard," she whispered. "Not fair."

"I don't give a shit about fair," he said. "I just want to make you come."

"You are very bad." She slid off his lap, and grabbed his hand, pulling him up off the chair and toward the bed. "And I'm not even sure where to start."

His lips curved, in a slow, taunting smile. "So I'll just wait around until you figure it out," he said softly. "I'm not going anywhere. Neither is my boner."

She thudded on the edge of the bed, struggling to recover her dignity. Giggling or joking around did not fit with the commanding goddess persona that he seemed to require of her tonight. She kept her face stern as she leaned back onto her elbows.

"Take off your clothes," she ordered him.

His grin flashed. "That's better."

"No backtalk from you. Keep your mind on what you're doing."

"Yes, ma'am." He grinned as he kicked off his shoes.

It didn't take him long to get naked, and when he did, her main challenge was not to gape at how freaking fine his beautiful body was. So massive and ripped. Not an ounce of extra fat. So lean and lithe and cut, and every muscle looked like it had a job it was supremely ready to perform.

He seemed still, but his tension was betrayed by his taut jaw, his fists clenching and flexing. His burning eyes and his big, stiff cock, dripping precome. Oh, yes.

He deserved a little teasing, so she stood up, unhurried, dragging her fingernails down over his chest. Savoring the coarse scrape of his chest hair, the complex texture of the scars that covered him, and the velvety patches of unmarred skin between them. She moved on to his tight nipples, the muscles of his pecs. His taut abs. The treasure trail leading down to the dark thatch of pubic hair, and the thick phallus jutting from it.

She squeezed his cock, milking it. Clasping her thighs together as he arched and groaned in helpless response. "Now," she said throatily. "Take off my panties."

He dropped to his knees, dragging the skimpy red lace thing down slowly and flinging it away. Then he just waited there for her next move. Not giving an inch.

Staring at her, bare-assed, ladybits on display, and she had to run everything.

She sank down onto the edge of the bed, and gracefully opened her legs, showing him her pussy lips. Opening herself, dipping her fingertips into her slick, sensitive well. Looking at him made her wet. The hunger in his eyes could make her come then and there.

She petted herself, showing off her clit.

"You're so fucking beautiful," he said.

"Thank you," she whispered.

He looked like he was an inch from losing it. Which was fine with her. Either she made him suffer and writhe in agonized anticipation, or she made him snap and lose control.

It was all crazy hot. It all worked.

She thrust her fingers inside herself. Made them glisten. Pulling her mound up so her clit protruded. Working it delicately with her fingers.

"My pussy is totally slick from thinking about you," she told him.

"I see that," he said. "My mouth is watering."

"Good." She gave him a slow, dangerous smile. "So lick it."

He did, and so much for her tough talk and her domineering routine. The second he put his mouth to her, it all dissolved. It was too good, that warm luscious glow, the licking and sucking, the tender flutter of erotic pleasure…and oh *yes* …

He held her open and licked and lapped. Keeping her still was a challenge with all her frantic writhing, but Luke was equal to it. She couldn't stay still with that screaming intensity building, rising...until the energy burst, shattering her.

She came back to her senses cradled in his arms. He was tucking her into bed. Then sliding in himself, covering her with his hard body. The sheets against her back were chilly but the hot, sensual weight of him pinning her to the bed made up for it.

He kissed her. Demanding, devouring kisses. Her legs wrapped around him eagerly. The sheets tangled, the blankets fell as he pushed his cock inside her, sinking so slow. Impossibly deep and thick, the heavy sliding strokes. Arms braced, eyes locked.

She was wide open to his body, each deep, heavy thrust a sliding caress. Each stroke of his cock ignited a desperate need for the next one. Her body felt charged and full, glowing with light, thrumming with awareness. The waves of sensation built and broke and then built again, bigger every time.

Finally he reared up onto his knees, fucking her with long slick strokes while he worked her clit tenderly with his thumb.

"One more," he said thickly. "Give me one more and I'll come with you this time."

As if she could help it. As if she could choose. She was high on the crest, and the wave broke over her, an endless pulsing surge.

He shouted as his own pleasure exploded, collapsing over her.

They stayed that way, locked together, sweat-soaked and panting. His back heaved. She could barely breathe, but her legs would not release their hold on his hips.

She wanted to keep him right where he was. Way down deep.

Luke finally rolled to his side, pressing the small of her back to keep his cock still inside her. She still felt the hot blood pulsing in his cock, deep inside her. He stroked the damp curls at her hairline and tugged one ringlet, letting it spring back into place.

"Even your hair has attitude," he said.

"Yeah, that's me," she murmured lazily. "Attitude everywhere you look."

"I love that about you," he said. "I want that. I want you."

"You have me," she told him.

But she was getting self-conscious. He was pulling her closer, peering right into her shook-up soul. The look on his face was making her heart hurt. That raw wonder, like he was looking at something miraculous. It made her nervous.

"Stop," she murmured. "You're too close."

"Can't," he said. "Sorry. Get used to it."

"I meant what I said, Luke." She hid her face against his chest. "You're so intense. Cool it already."

"She burns me alive, then she tells me to cool it. That's my Dani."

Their arms tightened around each other for a long hug, so tight and desperate they both shook with the effort. Then he released his grip, rolling away from her.

"We have a pack of cyborg assholes trying to pull our plugs and here I am rolling around in bed," he said. "This is bullshit. I can't indulge myself like this. I gotta get back to work." He gave her a swift, hard kiss, and rolled up into a sitting position.

She rolled up onto her elbow. "For real? Right now?"

He looked around, gazing at her body hungrily. "Yeah, right now. We have a long drive ahead. Plus I need to generate believable ID for you before we go any further."

"ID? Tonight?"

"Hell yeah. If anything happens to me, you need to be able to drop out of sight. For that you need ID and cash strapped to your body twenty-four seven. Sit up for a second."

She did so, then squawked in alarm as he lifted a camera then and there. "Hey! What the hell are you doing? I'm naked!"

"I'm just photographing you from the neck up," he assured her.

"But I look like hell, and I don't—"

"Nah. You look great." He took a bunch of quick shots, and came to the bed, leaning over to show the results. "See? I think you look pretty."

And amazingly, she almost did. She definitely needed some cover-up, but her color was high and her eyes were bright. She looked intensely switched on.

"This will work." Luke set down the camera and pulled his jeans back on, all business. From red-hot lover boy mode into super-geek robot mode, in the blink of an eye.

Disorienting, but hey, the guy had a plan, and he got shit done. She admired that in a person. It was hot. And a trip and a half to watch in action.

She padded off into the bathroom and peeled off the little red number, which had suffered somewhat from its erotic adventure. A shame, but well worth it.

She washed up and rummaged through the bags again, once again gazing at the kitten pajamas. They looked soft and warm. Just right for cuddling up in front of a fire with a plaid blanket and hot cocoa. Not tonight. She'd rather sleep in jeans and a sweater.

And shoes. Oh how she loved having herself some shoes.

She pulled on jeans, a black velour top. Good enough. Possibly even respectable.

Luke glanced over when she came out. "Why are you dressed? I got sleepwear."

"I'm not sleepy. And I want to be ready to roll. I'll nap in my clothes. Can I look at the Manticore files on your laptop?"

"Have at."

The first few files she saw were pretty much what she expected. Fawning congratulations to the proud new owner of a Manticore operative, one who had just joined an exclusive club of the most discerning elite who were the only ones truly capable and indeed, worthy of pulling the strings that moved the world, blah, blah, blah. A truckload of ass-licking promo bullshit.

Then came the endless disclaimers and a long list of horrible scenarios that Manticore would under no circumstances be held responsible for. Then the anonymous testimonials, designed to showcase the vast range to which the products could be put.

Then a reminder that the product recently purchased was designed for maximum super-connectivity, not combat. It was capable of manipulating enormous quantities of data at high speed. Hacking power grids, satellites, nuclear reactors, financial institutions. Mostly incomprehensible techno-gobbledy-gook, but even she could tell it was a product marketed to the high-tech criminal underworld.

Dani chose a file at random. *Modalities Of Use.* It covered the physical limitations of the slave soldiers' human bodies, particularly those of this particular product, destined specifically for tech interface. The buyer was invited to consider a number of caveats, and the recommendations made a cold lump settle in her stomach.

... for extended periods of time, when utilizing full immersion deep cyber-connectivity, certain malfunctions may occur. The operative is unlikely to survive extended continuous use for more than a four to six week time period, even when provided with intravenous nourishment and hydration. If a longer range of use is desired, shorter intervals of active work must be scheduled, including enough recovery time to slow the physical degeneration ...

That was so fucking cold. It chilled her to the bone.

Her eyes fell on Luke's powerful naked back, cross-hatched by scars of every size and shape. Luke knew all about being bought and sold and used, but his heart was still alive. Strong and beautiful. Their cruelty had scarred him, but it hadn't broken him.

She dragged her gaze away and it fell on a folder entitled "Wetware." The word made her cringe. It stank of hatefulness.

She clicked it. A sub-file, I89VY262. The one Luke had mentioned.

A jpeg opened on the screen, and the world stopped. So did her breathing.

Luke's head turned. "What is it?"

She tried to speak, but she still couldn't inhale.

"Your heart rate just spiked," Luke said. "What happened?"

"Luke," she said, her voice tight. "Did you look at the slave solder's file?"

"Not yet. It's downloaded, but I haven't worked it all through the processor. I figured I'd get into that data set on the drive up to Serrati Flats. Why do you ask?"

"Come look," she said. "She's...there's a photo. Look."

In two swift strides he was there, leaning over her shoulder.

I89VY262 was a little girl, shriveled and thin. Sallow skin, short black hair that looked wet in the photo. Dark brown eyes with luminescent points around the iris and pupil. Ocular enhancement.

That first photo was a head shot. There were other pictures as well. Full body shots that showed her, naked and tiny and pitifully thin, patches of her head shaved to show gleaming metal data ports, various wires and plugs inserted into them.

"She can't be more than five," Dani whispered.

"Eight," Luke said. She could almost hear the data humming in his mind. "Stunted, though. Her birthdate's in the metadata. She turned eight a couple weeks ago. In a coma, hooked up to tubes and wires. In a coffin in a container ship on the Pacific. Sick motherfuckers. They need to die screaming. By fire."

"Yes." She swallowed hard. "Yes. Exactly."

"Hold on a second. Let me dive," he muttered. "Maybe there's more on her somewhere."

Dani waited for him to dive, barely breathing. She couldn't look away from the little girl's image. Those huge brown eyes. The short hair around the shaved patches on her scalp were black and spiky. Her mouth was flattened, colorless. Like she was in pain and trying not to cry.

Well. Of course.

Dani caught the moment that the blank, faraway look on Luke's face shifted back to its normal laser sharpness.

"What did you find?" she asked.

"Nothing good," he said. "They've had her three years. They bought her. From an agency. She's one of a set of six. From what I could see in a fast dive, the agency's job is to comb orphanages all over the world for kids younger than nine who score high on certain cognitive tests. It's an experimental new program designed to 'take full advantage of the neuroplasticity of developing young brains.' That's how they put it in the literature."

Dani bit her lip, tightening against a clench of nausea. "Was there a name for her anywhere?"

"No." Luke's voice was bleak. "They know better than to use a name."

"I have to call her something," Dani said, studying the file.

"So pick one out for her," Luke said. "Something pretty. It'll be the nicest thing anybody's done for the poor kid so far. In her whole goddamn life."

Dani stared into the computer screen. Something was eluding her. A faint memory, flashing across her mind, prodding her to remember something. Something important.

She stared at the file name, fishing for it. Opening herself to it. I89VY262. Like a prisoner's number.

It hit her all at once. So hard she was lucky she was already sitting down.

"Oh, my God," she whispered.

"What?" Luke's gaze whipped around. "What is it?"

"Another thing Naldo said, on my kitchen floor. He mentioned a girl, remember? I told you. A name I didn't know. Help Ivy, he said. But I never knew anyone named Ivy, so I put it out of my mind."

"Yeah? So?" He looked back at the screen.

"Yeah! Look at the file number. I89VY262. I...V...Y. This is Naldo's Ivy. He broke away from Manticore, and fought the brain stim, and died...for her. For Ivy."

Luke didn't answer. He just stood there, a raw look blazing in his eyes.

"Oh, shit," she whispered, wiping tears angrily away with the back of her hand. "That's so Naldo. All the way. Even back when we were kids, it always burned his ass when the bullies went after the weak ones or the weird ones or the little ones. He got his ass kicked regularly, jumping in. Trying to save them."

He reached out, grabbing her hand. "He kept on doing it," he said. "To the very end."

She took a moment to mop up her face and straightened up. "We're helping Ivy," she told him, a ring of challenge in her voice. "For Naldo's sake."

"Fuck yeah," Luke said. "I'm shutting those fuckers down. I'm going to find everyone who participated in this and I am ripping them apart. Piece by fucking piece."

"Me too," she blurted out.

She caught his wary glance and shrugged, slightly defensive. "I don't know exactly how I'll help yet, but I'll think of something. I'm totally on board for the ripping."

"Uh…thanks, I guess."

Their hands tightened on each other, to a grip that was almost painful. But the hot, relentless look in his eyes fed her soul. Gave her strength. She needed it. All of it.

Because this evil, horrible shit had to stop. Nothing in the world was more important to her right now.

"The info on her location is in the storage container at Serrati Flats," Luke said. Dani was the first one to break the charged silence.

"So?" she said. "Put your goddamn shirt on, Luke. Let's hit the road."

CHAPTER 17

Jada? Jada? Where are you? Jada!
       The voices faded in and out. Flashing lights sliced through a fog, disorienting her. *Jada, here! Over here!* She stumbled toward the voice… and ran head-on into a rock solid barrier—

"…goddamn you! R-48! Wake up! That's an order! How long has she been like this?" Hale's voice, blaring in her ear, impossibly loud.

"Only a minute, sir." It was E-677's voice, a Level Fifteen from another combat team. "She might have accidentally detached in the deep-dive. I'll try to drag her back—"

"She cannot fucking detach! She's my last Level Twenty! Give me that pain wand. Goddamn fucking insubordinate *bitch.*"

"Sir, the wand isn't recommended during data-dives. It creates conflict in the—"

Buzzzzzz. A grunting gasp, and E-677 hit the floor, engulfed in a seizure.

Then R-48 felt the prods of the pain wand against her chest.

Agony. It filled her whole self. One long, blinding, endless shriek of it.

It ended, at some point. The pipes on the ceiling came into focus…hanging above something ugly. Hale's face hung over her. He stuck the wand back into his belt. His lips were purplish, wet with anger spit. Jowls quivering with rage.

"There you are," he snarled. "Finally. Had a nice nap, bitch? Were you thinking of checking out permanently? Was that the fucking plan all along?"

"No, sir." The whispered croak of words had no air behind them.

She struggled up into a sitting position. So cold. She hadn't felt pain like this since the gene therapy flu back at the beginning. She was hot and cold all at once. Her lungs were on fire. Her bowels churned.

Hale ripped the adhesive sensors off and yanked the probes out of her cranial ports. She sat naked and dripping, staring straight ahead. He was too angry to notice.

"You understand how badly you fucked up out there?" he demanded.

"I reviewed the drone recording, yes," she said. "And the data we downloaded from Metzer's implant."

"You did, huh? Up to the point where you drove the drone through Metzer's head?"

"That was not me," she said mechanically. "That guy hijacked the drone. Just like he hijacked the van from G-97."

"Who is also dead. Because of you! All of them are dead because of you!"

There was no point trying to defend herself. He was going to pin this on her and her alone, and there was nothing she could do. She'd be slapped and zapped and reconditioned. Up the ass and back down again.

"Can you do what he did?" Hale demanded.

R-48 blinked the haze out of her eyes, taken aback by the question. "Theoretically yes, but it would take time to develop that kind of technique. He hijacked the van, piloted the drone and sniped us, all simultaneously."

"We need defense strategies against this new threat," Hale said. "All operatives must learn to match his speed. Evolve or die. Show me what you found on your dive."

"Downloading now."

Hale turned away to watch the video. She took advantage of his distraction to dry off, and looked longingly at her clothes, which hung across the room. Her teeth were starting to chatter.

The video she had retrieved was from security footage of a housewares store in a strip mall, about fifty miles from their location at the High Mesa facility. The rogue operative walked into the camera frame and had a brief conversation with a girl at the counter. There was no audio, but they could read his lips. *I need a UV blacklight.*

The girl's back was turned as she responded, but she spun toward the security cam and beckoned him to follow her up the aisle. *Having a party?* The girl simpered at him hopefully. *I got lipstick that glows in blacklight. Can I come?*

No party. He didn't crack a smile, or even look at the girl.

The salesgirl pulled a box from the shelf. The rogue operative studied the specs listed on the box and walked away with it, apparently satisfied.

Asshole, the girl mouthed as she flounced off-screen, pouting.

"He didn't know about the key before. You handed it right to him, R-48. Have you identified the operative yet?"

Pain flared violently in her head. Her vision blotted out. The girl's voice. *Jada!*

A head-rocking slap from Hale jolted her back. "Don't space out! Answer me."

She opened her mouth to obey—and heard the sound only in her mind. *Crack.*

And something broke inside her like an iceberg shattering. A wave of pain and loss flowed into the breach, so intense, she sucked in a loud, shocked gasp.

"Goddamn it, R-48, what the fuck is wrong with you?"

"Ah...sorry, sir. I'm fine." She tossed her hair back, striking a pose that would draw attention to her chest. Arched back. Boobs out. Diversion.

Not easy to look sexy while sodden, shivering and wrenched by stomach cramps, but it worked. Hale's eyes dropped to her chest and stuck there.

She was seeing faces. A girl with shining dark hair, eyes streaming with tears.

Zoe. The girl's name was Zoe. And then she saw the guy she fought in LaSalle's house. The teenaged boy he had been when she saw him last, at…at Midlands.

"Did you get a hit on the rogue operative's face?" Hale demanded.

She blinked back tears. "No," she said. *Luke.* That was his name. The girl was Zoe. And her own name was Jada. She had a fucking *name.* It electrified her.

Hale reached to his belt and pulled out the punishment wand. "You're lying."

"No, sir," she croaked.

"Just don't piss yourself, OK? I hate it when you freaks short out and do that."

Hale pressed the thing against her face. She tried to brace herself.

Pain. The world disappeared into a grinding buzz of pure agony.

When she could see again, she was on the ground. Hale looked down on her, nudging her breast with the punishment wand. "Tell me what you know about the rogue."

She realized now why she'd resisted. Those faces had been behind her memory block. They belonged to Before, and the block had hidden it from her, but it had also kept it safe and pure, her hidden treasure, locked away and safe. Maybe she didn't have the key to open it, but it was still hers and hers alone.

Now Hale had broken it open. He wanted to stick his slimy, grunting self into it. To paw around in there, soiling it. Fuck it. No. She'd rather die.

She opened her mouth to answer with the part of her brain still obedient to Hale.

But the part that generated sound just stopped. She was mute.

Hale pointed the wand at her head. "You dumb cunt," he hissed.

More blinding light…and abruptly, she was out of her body. Somewhere else.

A dream landscape of huge, tumbled rocks. A mass of dark gray storm clouds hung low and swollen, dimming the light. She scrambled and leaped, moving closer to what she soon saw was an unimaginably high cliff.

She got closer to the edge, staring over. A long, soaring flight to freedom.

Jada lifted her hot face to the blustery wind, letting it lift her damp hair off her neck. Her muscles bunched, preparing to run, to leap—

Someone appeared right in in front of her. She tripped, stumbled to her knees.

Her eyes fell on slender bare feet. Traveled up long golden legs. A white dress. Dark hair, lifted by the wind. Long dark eyes. High cheekbones, like an Aztec princess.

"Zoe," she whispered. "Am I dead? Is this real?"

"What's real?" Zoe asked. "Who cares? Be wherever you are. If it's real to you, it's real enough."

"Easy for you to say," Jada said. "You got away. You're free."

Zoe's eyes were bleak. "Sorry, baby sister. They hid you from me. I tried so hard to find you. And you can't be free when your heart's locked in a cage."

"Now it's my turn to escape," Jada said. "Get out of my way. This is my chance."

"No," Zoe said. "You're not done. I won't let you."

"You're not even here. You're just a ghost, so leave me alone. Let me go."

"I can't," Zoe insisted. "It's not your time."

"You don't control when I live or die!" Jada yelled in frustration. "If I go back, they'll make me tell them about you and Luke and the others! They knocked a hole in my memory block and they'll pry it out of me. No one had images of you after the fire, but I have them! All of you! In my head!"

"So give them up," Zoe said. "Do whatever you have to do. But live."

The vision swirled into a shriek of agony again. Pain, with no beginning or end.

An eternity later, she bobbed up to the surface, seeing Hale's face. He was bellowing questions. She was answering them, like a robot. No choice.

She identified the man who had been in Daniela LaSalle's apartment as D-14. One of Braxton's primary group. A leader of the Midland Rebellion. One of the rebels who torched that research facility and slaughtered almost all of the researchers before vanishing without a trace.

With positive ID, they could match D-14 to the verbal control codes Braxton had established for him years ago, and he could be safely neutralized.

When she was done spilling her guts, Hale was no longer angry. He was in a festive mood, which was almost worse.

"Excellent!" he said, chortling. "With control codes, I can move on the rogue without approval from the Committee. Weren't you at Midlands for a while yourself?"

"Briefly," she said. "I was brought in to Midlands initially, but I got transferred after a few weeks to Urness Island. They had training groups for younger kids."

"Yes, yes, I see." He barely heard her answer, he was so swept away by fantasies of his own bright future. "Well. This has been an expensive operation, and I don't know what the fuck I'm going to say to George Metzer about his dead son, but if I bag a newly minted Manticore operative plus a Level Twenty-five Braxton operative from the Midlands Rebellion, that's a fucking coup. That should give me immunity from retaliation from Metzer. You have a drone locked onto D-14?"

"I used the satellite to track him until a drone was in place," she said. "He drove to a motel. Stayed for a couple of hours. They're driving north on the interstate right now."

"We need to take him down somewhere remote. No witnesses. I want the Level Fifteen squad ready to move on the double. Where's E-677?"

"Still unconscious, sir. You pain-wanded him."

Hale looked at E-677's body, sprawled by the tank. "Oh. Fuck. Well, what are you waiting for? Wake him up and tell him to mobilize his crew. Control codes or no control codes, I'm not taking any chances with this sneaky son of a bitch. And I'm sure that Metzer's going to want his son's assassin in one piece. To play with."

"I'll prepare the team myself, sir—"

"No. You stay here. You're too unpredictable right now. But I do want you to prepare the Committee presentation. A Manticore operative and a Midlander rogue." Hale grinned nastily. "What a sacrificial offering that'll be. This has to go just exactly right."

Jada's stomach lurched. She clapped her hand to her mouth, but Hale didn't notice. "Put in a request for twelve more Level Twenties from the Committee. We need to plan for some important visitors, R-48. This is going to be huge. Absolutely huge."

"Yes, sir."

He chuckled. "And when you're done, get a bottle of chilled champagne, put on something sexy and come to my quarters. We'll celebrate together. I'll get a head start on reconditioning you. By hand." He laughed unpleasantly. "You'll be very good when I'm done with you. Hey! You're spacing out again. Did you even hear me, R-48?"

"Every word, sir."

"Yeah? What will you do after you requisition the Level Twenties?"

"I'll get a bottle of champagne and bring it to your room," she said.

"And what will you wear?"

She hesitated for a fraction of a second before forcing the words out. "Something sexy."

CHAPTER 18

They found Unit 67 of the E-Z-U-Store halfway down a seemingly endless double row of storage units in the sprawling outdoor complex. Luke stopped the SUV, and they both just stared at it for a moment before they got out. He entered the combination he'd found in Naldo's chip. Amazingly, it worked. He raised the roll-up door with one long rattling shove.

The two of them gazed in at the large metal cases, grouped in a precise cube in the middle of the dingy unit. They gleamed with unearthly brightness against the stained concrete floor.

The place was deserted and eerily quiet. Just the desolate whine of the wind. There had been no one in the prefab structure near the entrance, no big surprise at six AM. The gate had been easy to open. The alarm needed only the barest nudge from his implant to deactivate. They had driven right into the place. As if they were expected.

Luke's senses were amped way up, but he picked up nothing that suggested a threat. Birds, bugs. An occasional truck on the nearby highway. A distant train whistle.

"I don't understand." Dani's voice was hushed. "How can it be this easy?"

He shook his head. "Don't worry. They'll make up for it later."

She was in no mood for snark. "How come no one intercepted this shipment?" she demanded. "And why is it just sitting here unclaimed when Obsidian wants it so badly? Why aren't we in the middle of a firefight right now?"

Luke took a careful step into the unit. "Maybe Manticore's security actually is like they advertise it. Once the package ships and the courier's on his way, no one can force Manticore to say where they shipped the goods. They don't know and they have no way to find out."

"The courier would know, right?"

Luke shrugged. "If he survived. I think Naldo was done and Manticore was just using him up. But he got 'em a good one, in the end. Right where it hurt. Thanks to you."

Dani tugged her new jacket more closely around herself. "So how did Obsidian manage to chase Naldo down with all these safeguards?"

"I'm betting they squeezed Manticore for Naldo's tracer data," Luke said. "But there are no traces on this equipment. At least not any my sensors can detect. We might be the only ones who know it's here. Other than whoever delivered it."

Dani spun around, looking unnerved. "Something's off," she whispered.

His eyes flicked over to meet hers. "It could be a trap," he said.

"Let's load up and get the hell out of here," she said.

"Agreed."

Luke shifted his own gear around in the back of the SUV make room. They loaded the cases up quickly and drove out of the place. Just like that. No explosions, no scream of challenge, no sniper fire.

It almost creeped him out. Sneaky fuckers. Playing with him. Biding their time.

His systems were on high alert, but as wigged out as he was, he didn't trust his own perceptions. He'd probably be hyper-vigilant until the day he died.

Dani didn't say much as they drove through the depressed looking town of Serrati Flats, but she looked anxious and tight-lipped. "What now?" she asked as they got onto the highway. "Shall I find us a room? So we can look through the shipment?"

"I rented a place already."

"When? I never saw you do that!"

"On the way up," he admitted. "In my head. I browsed local vacation rental places online. Sent the emails, did the bank transfer, got the security code for the gate and door. Grab the laptop. Take a look at the confirmation email, if you're curious."

Dani opened the email and scrolled through the pictures. Her jaw dropped. "Good God! This place is huge! And super-luxurious."

"So? I liked the looks of it. We'll have it all to ourselves."

"But…but eight bedrooms and twelve baths? A game room, a dedicated movie theater and an indoor swimming pool? Holy freaking shit! Seriously?"

"I liked the lake," he said defensively. "And the trees. And the security system."

"A one room cabin would have done the job. How much did it cost?"

"Doesn't matter," he told her. "Braxton's paying."

She looked alarmed. "But can't they trace you if you use his money?"

"Nope. I covered my tracks a thousand times over. Don't worry."

She didn't look reassured. Truth to tell, he'd chosen the outsize accommodations solely because of the bedsteads on view in the virtual tour. He'd seen one bed made of thick wrought-iron. Strong enough to hold the shackles for his wakey-wand session.

In case he became dangerous.

They wouldn't hold indefinitely, but if worst came to worst, they would buy Dani the time she'd need to get the hell away from him. Maybe. But he'd explain that later.

He wasn't looking forward to that conversation.

Luke couldn't shake the feeling that he was putting Dani in greater danger by keeping her close to him. But on the other hand, she was already on their radar and in their files. Until he could figure out a better plan for her, the safest place in the world for her was behind his body.

The fact that he fucking loved having her there was entirely coincidental.

Right. He'd just keep telling himself that.

They arrived at the gated driveway on the lakeside road in early afternoon. The security code opened it, and they wended their way through a park-like, fairy-tale forest.

And there it was. A huge, rustic chalet with big windows on all three floors offering views of manicured woods, lake and hills. He entered another security code and led her inside, into an enormous front room with a wall of windows two stories high.

They had the place completely to themselves, as he'd specified a preference for absolute privacy. But a fire had been lit for them and was crackling in a huge fireplace in the main room. Cushy couches were grouped around it.

Too bad they weren't actually here to play. It would have been fun.

He got to work, hauling all the new equipment up to the bedroom with the wrought iron bed while Dani trailed behind him. She had very little to say as he rearranged the furniture, arranging the various devices around the bed.

"I take it you have a plan?" she asked finally.

"A general plan," he replied. "I have to go through all the files. And, uh…a lot of it hinges on you."

"Me? In what way?"

"You're a nurse. I was hoping you'd help use this equipment."

"What? I've never seen anything like it. I don't know what you think I can do."

"To start, run the imager," he said. "And then thread the probe into my data port and get it through the traces to where it needs to be inside my brain. Operate the direct brain stimulation wand. I can't do it myself. The placement of my implants and ports is going to be different from the Manticore implants in the literature. So we'll have to improvise. To a certain extent."

She crossed her arms over her chest, frowning. "Yeah? How? You obviously have no idea what you're doing. What's liable to happen?"

He shrugged. "My hope is that I get my memory back. Best case scenario."

"And worst case scenario?"

He hesitated a little too long before replying. "Hard to say. Too many unknowns." He pulled out the shackles.

Dani's heart rate and stress hormones spiked. "What do you intend to do with those?" she demanded.

"They're not for sex," he said. "If that's what you're thinking."

"No. But what are they for? And where did you get them?"

"A nasty corner of the deep web," he said. "And they're for me. For when you pulse the wand."

Her eyes went from uncomprehending to wide with horrified dismay. "Wait," she said. "Back up. Back way the fuck up. You've been misrepresenting this."

"Of course, there's risk involved," he said. "We're talking Braxton, after all. Criminally insane, but brilliant. So anything he devised is bound to have a very high risk to reward ratio."

"Don't try to snow me, Luke. Are you asking what I think you are? To risk hurting you? Or even…killing you?"

Luke lifted his hands, helpless. "Yeah, I guess I am. But I might not die."

Dani closed her eyes. "Oh," she whispered. "So, would it make you a howling madman? Comatose? Put you into a persistent vegetative state?"

"It might do nothing at all," he said. "We don't know until we try it."

"Don't bullshit me," she said harshly. "Spill it."

He sighed. "I'll have seizures," he admitted. "And it could trigger a recurrence of stim sickness. That's what happens when you fight their deep brain programming. Pain, high fever, anxiety. Sometimes psychosis."

"Huh," she muttered. "You don't happen to have a crash cart in the back of that Porsche, do you?"

"That's why I have shackles," he explained. "They'd give you time to get away."

Dani sank down onto the bed, and dug her fingers into her hair. "Great. You thought of everything."

"Dani," he said softly. "Please."

"I know you want your memory back," she said shakily. "Of course you do. But what if this fails? You could die on me. That's not allowed, you fucker. I don't like it when patients die on my shift."

He shook his head. "I don't want to die."

"Stay as you are, then! Maybe time will give you your memory back. Maybe you just need to wait a little longer. Isn't your life still worth it?"

It took a minute for him to answer. "Two days ago, I would have said no," he admitted. "But I can't say that anymore."

"Um…I'm confused."

He cleared his throat. "I had nothing to lose, before. I genuinely gave no fucks whatsoever if this went bad on me. But you ruined that for me, Dani. That's all over now."

"Don't get carried away," she said tartly. "We just met."

"True. But I was carried away in the first five minutes."

She harrumphed. "Don't change the subject."

"I'm being honest," he said. "I don't know much about myself, but I do know how I feel about you."

"Let me head you off right there, and propose something totally nuts," she said.

"I'm listening," he said warily.

"Let's run away together," she said. "Leave all this behind us. Whoever you were before, say goodbye to him unless he comes back to you naturally. Make a clean break. Mexico, Argentina, anywhere is fine. Fuck Manticore, fuck Obsidian. Fuck all of it."

Luke allowed himself the luxury of picturing it, for just a minute. Rolling around on the beaches on the Yucatan with Dani, rubbing coconut scented cream over her fabulous curves. Turquoise ripples over glittering white sand. Yeah.

"What about Ivy?" he asked.

"I was thinking about her, believe me. You're not the center of the universe. We grab her somehow and we run like hell." Dani's mouth tightened. "I don't want to have to do that alone. If this memory recovery thing of yours goes sideways."

"This is the thing about Obsidian," Luke said. "They never give up. And now they're hyper-focused on you. I'll protect you, but I'm just one guy, and if they take me down—"

"Don't say that!"

"If they take me down, you need backup," he persisted. "You need people to turn to. Family. Safe haven. You and Ivy both, if we manage to rescue her. I can't protect you alone. We need my people for that."

"If they exist," Dani reminded him. "You're just guessing. Hoping."

"They do," he said stubbornly. "I'm sure of it."

"How about your girlfriend or fiancée or wife? Any of them likely to show up? Wouldn't that be a hoot."

He flinched. "Not relevant."

"Hmm." She shot him an ironic look. "I've heard that song before."

"Do not lump me in with the losers from your past," he said.

"Don't worry, Luke," she said quietly. "They pale in comparison to you."

An awkward silence fell. She wouldn't look at him. He just got more and more anxious as the seconds ticked by.

"So?" he prompted. "Will you help me?"

Dani shot him an anguished look. "Luke, my job is to help people, not hurt them. Particularly not someone that I…care about."

"It's on me, not you," he said. "And it'll happen whether you help or not. The only question is whether you'll help me do it, or let me do it myself."

"But…" She waved at the shackles on the bed. "Like this? Really?"

"In case I turn violent," he said. "Yes. It's absolutely necessary."

"And what if you do? What the fuck do I do? How do I help you?"

"You don't. Walk away. Call 911. At that point, I'll be past help and no longer your problem. Obsidian will probably get to me before the police do anyhow."

"Walk away?" She looked shocked. "Not an option."

"You have to," he said. "If it all goes to shit, it's the only—"

"Listen, Luke," she said. "I don't 'have to' do anything. You can't control me. Certainly not if you're shackled and out of your mind."

"You have a point," he admitted. "So where does that leave us?"

"In a really uncomfortable place," she said. "But yeah, I'll try to help you. Goddamn you all to hell, you crazy-ass son of a bitch."

"I want to protect you," Luke said. "Nothing is more important to me than that."

Luke turned back to the heap of stuff he'd hauled up from the car and pulled a folder and a small remote out of a knapsack. He held them out to her. "For you."

She took the items and looked at them, puzzled. "What's this?"

"The remote will start the SUV," he said. "I programmed it last night, just in case. The folder has your new identity. You're Jessica Mass, Arizona resident. Birth certificate, Arizona driver's license. You went to UCLA, by the way. Got good grades, too. As good as Dani LaSalle's grades. Identical, actually."

"Oh," she murmured. "Wow. Really? Yay, me."

"She took the MCATS, just like you, by the way. Got the same high score."

Dani looked startled. "How do you know about me and the MCATS?"

He gave her an are-you-fucking-kidding-me look. "You could go to med school, with scores like that."

"Right." She laughed. "With what money?"

"The money in this folder." He didn't miss a beat. "There's a big wad of cash, clean and untraceable, and some bank accounts in Jessica Mass's name that hold about eight million bucks, give or take. And contact info for people who can hook you up with a new passport. Fucking expensive, but you have what you need."

She looked dumbfounded. "So if this procedure goes wrong, I'm supposed to just…run away from you? Into hiding? Alone?"

"Alive," Luke said harshly. "The operative word here is 'alive.' "

Pain jarred Jada out of her stupor. She lay on the narrow cot in her tiny room, chest burning. So damn hot. Her head pounded. The overhead light blazed down into her watering eyes.

Hale was silhouetted against it, brandishing the punishment wand in her face.

She focused on the processor feed, and caught her breath. *Shit.* She was late.

It was scarcely possible for her to be late. Forty minutes ago she should have come out of a brief restorative sentinel sleep in time to follow all of Hale's orders, dress as he'd directed and fetch that bottle of champagne.

But the system hadn't automatically roused her. What the *fuck?*

She cringed as he made another move with the wand. "Did you forget the time, R-48?"

"Sorry, sir." She struggled up into a sitting position. "I'm having functional issues. A fever and abdominal cramping. I seem to have gotten some kind of food poisoning."

"Bullshit. You're immune to everything!"

"Ah, actually, a few pathogens can get past our defenses and cause infection in pre-Carelton era operatives," she said. "It's rare, but it happens. The Carelton edit wiped that issue out, but those of us who were modded before—"

He backhanded her across the face, knocking her off the cot and onto the floor. "No excuses, bitch."

Jada crawled up onto her knees. Hale stared down at her, slack-mouthed, the toxic haze of his lust still tainting the air. He put his hand to his belt buckle.

Her guts convulsed. She lunged for the wastebasket by her desk console, reaching it just in time.

Hale recoiled as she vomited up her guts. "Christ, R-48. Never do that in front of me again."

"Sorry, sir." She sagged over the wastebasket, face clammy with sweat.

"For fuck's sake, get yourself to sickbay and get some drugs. You need to hold it together for the next forty-eight hours, at least until my reinforcements arrive from Oakline. Two squads of Level Fourteens were the best I could get, even after I told them about the Level Twenty-five Midland rogue. Power-tripping fuckstick assholes."

"Yes, sir."

"But the new squads won't be here for twenty-eight hours, which leaves only you as my top-level operative. I need you to prepare High Mesa to secure a Level Twenty-five and a Manticore cyber-operative, and organize to welcome the Committee at the same time. You can't break down on me now. You better than anyone know how dangerous that rogue is, control codes or no control codes."

"Yes, sir," she said faintly. "I'll get right on it."

"E-677's squad is ready to back me up for the pick-up, but there's just one more thing. Remember the telephone call from the Kwik-Stop? The monitor you put on the place's security vidcam caught this about an hour ago. Look at it."

He downloaded a file to her head. It consisted of grainy security footage inside a featureless convenience store.

A greasy-haired young man picked his nose and played with a smartphone behind the counter. The bell over the door dinged. A man walked in. The vidcam's vantage point revealed only his broad back, long coat, and buzzed dark hair until he turned his head and looked around.

Jada's senses jangled at the resemblance to the man she had fought in Daniela LaSalle's kitchen. This was the younger brother. She remembered him. Teasing her, clowning for her, making her and the younger kids laugh. A superhuman feat in Midlands.

His number: D-13. His name: *Zade.*

He looked different now. Bigger, taller, bulkier. A glinting earring, a tattoo on his neck. More tattoos on wrists and hands. Dangerous intensity in his keen dark eyes.

She knew him. She had no way to hide it now. She couldn't protect either man. Hale had forced open the doors in her mind. He would pick the info out of her brain, and she'd watch him feed all her old friends back into Obsidian's jaws one by one. Once they'd cross-referenced D-13's number with his control codes, he'd be fucked.

The clerk's eyes went wide when he looked up from his phone. He stumbled back, knocking over a calculator, a can of soda and a wire stand that held tourist brochures and roadmaps. "I'm calling the cops," he yelped.

"No need." The man's voice was low and even. "Do I remind you of someone?"

The guy blinked rapidly. "Wait," he said. "Hold on. No. You're someone different. That other guy didn't have the tats. But he looked like you. You got a twin?"

The man ignored that. "Did you see which direction he went?"

"I ain't telling you nothing. Talk to the cops if you're curious."

The clerk's gaze darted to the parking lot and back.

"Maybe I will." The tall man strode out of the camera's field and was gone. The clip ended.

Hale swam back to the forefront of her vision in front of the blank screen. "Recognize him?" he demanded.

She took a deep breath, fishing desperately for a way to stall. "I...I—"

"Skip it. I can see from your reaction that he's another rogue agent from the Midlands rebellion. And I know that you recognize him. What's his number?"

She swallowed over a burning coal in her throat. "D-13," she whispered. "He is...he *was* D-13."

Hale turned to her computer and entered his security codes to access Obsidian archives. "Yes," he muttered. "Fucking *yes*. His codes are right here. Biological brother of D-14. Another Braxton boy. Hot damn, a matched pair. This is a game-changer. Get the fuck back to work, R-48."

The thump of Hale's boots faded down the corridor. He'd been too preoccupied to grab her ass or pinch her breast as he left. She should be grateful for small mercies. But she just lunged for the wastebasket again.

She imagined his face at the bottom, and let go.

CHAPTER 19

Usually, tackling a complicated task would ease Dani's anxiety. When she was concentrating hard and doing something that took all of her attention, there just wasn't room for it.

This was different. She couldn't keep her hands from shaking, or control the sensation that she was falling right through the floor, never hitting bottom, just an endless, sickening plummet downward.

It made her heart hurt. He was doing this for her. And there was nothing she could say that would make him change his mind.

She was haunted by the thought of finding herself alone with Luke's lifeless body, Obsidian wolves circling, licking their chops. He thought she could help him, but she wasn't so sure. She had to set aside her ethical concerns to even attempt the memory recapture. If it didn't succeed, she could be charged with medical malfeasance. Or worse.

As for herself…well, hell, even with the money he'd thrown at her, plus the car and the new identity, it took relentless energy to run and hide, and a super high-level of organization, not to mention mental clarity. Where was she going to find that if her worst nightmare came true?

They studied the equipment for tedious hours, poring through computer files and PDFs with fine-print instructions, warnings and explanations for the info they needed. Luke's super-fast data processing capacity was a godsend. He could flip with blinding speed through the irrelevant stuff and glean the exact information they needed to put together their plan. If it could even be called that.

At one point, she opened a case and found a transparent cap. The rubbery material it was made of held a tangle of colored wires, circuits and sensors. Luke's face contracted with revulsion when he saw it.

"Seen those before," he said. "Braxton used one on me. It hooks up to…yeah. This thing here, the 3D brain imager. So you can see where in my brain the probe is going."

"Great," Dani muttered. "Amateur brain surgery. I love a challenge."

"Good." Luke's voice had the same joking-not-joking tone. "Because this is challenging. But it's not surgery. You thread the probe through the data ports and through the correct turns so it gets to the right terminus. No cuts, no stitches. It's just an access point."

"Right," she said flatly. "Access to your vulnerable brain tissue. Everything you are now, or were once, or could be in the future. No big deal, right? Shut up, Luke. There is no way to make me think that this is OK. You only make it worse when you try."

Luke was smart enough to zip his lip, but she was getting ever closer to a state of screaming panic. And those shackles just skeeved her out. Any procedure that required steel restraints had to be a seriously terrible idea.

"You could still stop this," she told him. "We rescue Ivy, just the two of us, and run away with her, someplace safe where she can heal. Maybe you won't have your past, but we might still have a future. As much as anyone can hope for."

But she could see from Luke's face that she was wasting her breath.

He stripped off his shirt and stalked off into the big en suite bathroom. Ultra clean, to Dani's relief. Just not sterile. Stark black and white tile, gold-toned fixtures. He opened a cabinet and found guest toiletries in a classy package, helping himself to a razor and some shaving cream.

She followed him in. "What are you up to now?"

"My scalp has to be smooth," he told her.

She watched for a moment, and came to a silent conclusion. "Wait."

"For what?" he growled. "I want to get on with this."

"Just wait for me." She hurried back into the bedroom and grabbed the stool in front of the vanity, setting it down in front of the bathroom sink. "Sit," she said.

He did, setting the razor and shaving cream by the sink. Dani pulled off her own shirt, displaying a peach-colored bra.

He liked it, judging from the pole-axed look on his face. "Dani? What the hell?"

"What? Is something wrong?" She fizzed a fluffy cloud of shaving cream into her hand, and slapped and slathered it onto his jaw. "Don't move. I'm busy."

She took her time. In fact, she stalled shamelessly, turning the interlude into a long, slow seduction with every stroke of the razor. Bending over him, letting her tits spill halfway out of the peachy bra right in his face. She was sorry to take off all his hair, but it was so short, it would probably be as long again in a few weeks anyhow, and what the hell, it was a great opportunity to memorize every detail of him. The shape of his forehead, the bold slash of dark eyebrows, the chiseled angles of jaw and cheekbone. Ridiculously gorgeous. The lines around his mouth and eyes spoke of toughness and endurance and never giving up.

They just did something to her heart. Squeezed it so hard, it hurt.

Shaving him revealed all the data ports, too. He was going to need a knit hat to cover up all his cyborg mods once they were out in the world again.

If he made it out into the world again.

Dani pushed that thought right back down into the dark. She was living the moment. To the last possible second.

When she'd gone over his jaw and scalp for the umpteenth time, she soaked a washcloth in hot water and slowly wiped off all the goo.

Shaved, the effect was striking, throwing his male beauty into sharp relief. Made it outsized, extreme. He looked insanely sexy that way. Oh surprise, surprise.

He glanced at the mirror, lips twitching in a rueful smile. "I look like an android."

She shook her head. "Not at all. You're the hot futuristic fantasy man. Ready to fulfill my wildest sexual fantasies. In zero gravity. So you can spin me around any way you like."

The look in his dark eyes heated. "Oh yeah. Got any other unfulfilled fantasies, Dani?"

"I do," she said. "Plenty."

They gazed at each other in silence for an achingly long time, hearing only the slow drip of the faucet into the sink.

"Give me my memories back," he said. "And I'll fulfill any fantasy you want. Until the end of time. I will be at your service. One hundred percent."

His eyes glittered as she slid her fingers over the velvet smooth skin of his scalp, sliding down his neck, and into the thick, bunched muscles and tendons of his shoulders. His hands rose up, fastening around her waist.

"Dani," he murmured. "We don't have time."

"You started it," she said.

"Because you took your shirt off. I think you're gonna have to own this one."

"OK." Dani reached behind herself to undo the clasp on the bra. She tossed it away. "Owning it."

"Oh fuck," he whispered. "Not fair."

"But you get me." She shucked her jeans and panties, kicking them away. "That is, if you want me."

He rose to his feet, shoving down his jeans and kicking off his shoes, but Dani pushed him back down onto the stool.

"Stay there," she said. "We're not going to that bed." She meant it. If this was the last time they made love—and it really could be the last time—she didn't want to even think about shackles or data ports or the incredible danger of what he wanted her to do.

Luke pulled her down onto his lap. She straddled his hard, muscular thighs. He burned her deliciously with his life-giving heat. The fierce energy of his kiss sparked something defiant and hungry inside her and she kissed him back aggressively, demanding more. Pulling him closer. One big hand clamped her to his body, the thick hot club of his cock against her belly. He lifted her up, pressing his mouth hungrily to her breasts.

Erotic pleasure shocked a cry from her mouth, and her whole body was taken over by the throb and thrum of intense awareness. He made tender relentless love to her breasts, his hand between her legs caressing her clit and plunging deep inside her pussy.

She writhed, craving more. All of it. Forever.

He held her so easily. She lifted her damp face from his shoulders. Licked her lips and tried to speak. "Luke." Her voice cracked. "Please."

He lifted her up and positioned her right over his cock. Forcing himself to slowly glide his thick, hot cock inside her quivering pussy folds. So good.

Her breath caught on a soft whimper. She loved that deep, slow shove inside her. So deep now. Pulsing himself inside her. Rocking her on his hard, massive thighs.

"Too much?" he asked.

She laughed at him. "Oh no," she whispered. "Fill me up. All the way. And rock me just like that."

He did so, staring up into her face as he moved her body skillfully over his cock. After a few minutes of slick, pulsing bliss, he stood up suddenly, cupping her ass.

"Luke? What the hell?"

"Keep your legs wrapped around me." He gave her a kiss that blotted out everything with sensual sweetness.

Then she gasped at the shock of cool wall tiles against her back, her legs draped over his arms, her ass supported by his big hands. Wide open to the heavy strokes of his cock. Calculated to drive her into a hot frenzy of mindless delight.

She abandoned herself to it. Nothing else to do, here at the edge of doom, the brink of the fucking abyss. She would take what she could, and beg for more.

She came, hard. So did he, seconds later, letting go with a shout and exploding into her.

Silence, broken by rasping pants for air.

She didn't look at his eyes, aware that the ecstasy was over. It was replaced by growing dread.

Maybe this was the last time. So be it. There was nothing left to do now but see this nightmare through. All the way to the end.

Luke dragged his cock reluctantly out of her and set her down carefully on her feet. They showered briefly. Separately this time. Then dried off and pulled their clothes back on, not talking.

Dani watched him sit down on the bed barefoot, in only his jeans. "Aren't you going to put on a shirt before we do it?" she asked. "It's cold in here. You'll get chilled."

He shook his head. "I'm expecting some stim sickness," he said. "I'll have a high fever. Don't freak if I do."

"How high? Your standards are different from mine."

"I don't know. A hundred and seven, a hundred and eight?"

"But that's lethal!"

"I told you." His voice was weary. "I'm resistant to temperature extremes, which includes internal ones. Trust me. It's not the fever that'll get me."

"Oh? So what will?"

Luke carefully avoided her gaze. "Try to relax, Dani. The procedure is—"

"We can stop calling it a goddamn procedure. It's an assault on your brain."

He reached for a small case that he'd set aside and showed her the contents. A jumble of syringes, still sealed in their sterile packaging, and vials of medication.

"I have fever reducers," he said. "And anticonvulsants. Don't know if they'll work. They're standard meds, not designed for modifieds, but they're all I could get my hands on. And it might be tough to stick me with a needle once my muscles are tense, but you can try."

"I'll do my best."

He reached out and grabbed her hand. "So," he said. "We're clear on the plan?"

"I thread the probe, following the brain-tube map you made for me using the 3D imager until I reach the implant in the zone you specified. Then it's three quick pulses, keeping the dial at 95. At that point, I reassess. Are you bleeding out your eyes? Or just dead?"

"Dani," he said quietly. "Please."

"Yes, yes. I know. We've been through it, there's no other way, your mind is made up, blah blah di-fucking-blah." She held up the probe. "I just don't understand how this can penetrate a living brain—your brain—without running the risk of massive infection."

"There are flexible seals at the end of each tube to prevent contamination," he explained "Braxton's invention. Functional, but totally illegal. Which is why you never heard of it."

Luke put on the flexible cap, positioning it so that the reinforced holes in the latex corresponded with his data ports, and then reached for the shackles.

Dani put up her hand. "Wait."

"No more stalling," Luke said, his voice tight. "Please. This is killing me."

"I'm not stalling. This is necessary." Dani rummaged in the kit for some rolls of gauze. "Hold out your wrists."

Luke made an impatient sound. "That's not essential. We're wasting time."

"I'm the nurse here, and I don't like the looks of those shackles."

He humored her, grumbling, as she wrapped a protective barrier of gauze around each wrist and each ankle. Then Luke stretched his long body out on the bed, his head propped up on a foam cushion while she fastened the shackles.

She stepped back when it was done, unnerved by the sight of him spread-eagled on the bed. "You really think those shackles are necessary?"

"Yes," he said. "If this goes south, take the ID and the bank account info and the car and get far away. Fast. Promise me."

"And just leave you here," she said, angry again. And scared. "Alone, at death's door. Right."

"Once you're a hundred miles away, call 911 from a pay phone." Luke's voice was maddeningly calm and matter-of-fact. "Tell them the address and then disappear."

"Yeah? And what happens to you?"

"Whatever the outcome, I accept full responsibility. You need to be far away when the authorities or Obsidian find me." He gave her a coaxing smile, way too weird coming from a guy chained to a bed. "But it won't come to that. I'll be fine. I have a good feeling about this."

She scowled. "That makes one of us."

After that, there was nothing else to say. Just essential details. The placement of the machines, the adjustments to the cap, the visual of Luke's disembodied brain generated by the 3D imager. The handling of the thin probe and its almost invisible wire, which she had to thread slowly through the branching tubes inserted into his brain.

It was a slow, incredibly precise task, but Luke was calm and emotionless, talking her through it as if he'd done it himself hundreds of times before.

The imager enlarged the brain visual, making all the implants and trace tubes fully visible. Someone had put that crap into his skull against his will for evil, selfish purposes.

She wanted to find those monsters and crush them out of existence for hurting and using him. For putting her into a position where she had to hurt him, too.

Fuck them all sideways. This was so wrong. She was really angry now. When she most needed to be cool.

She knew how to work fast and hard without getting rattled. She'd worked in big city hospital emergency rooms, she'd dealt with gunshot wounds, car accidents, stab wounds, amputations, burns, violent trauma of all kinds. She knew how to stay calm in a life-or-death crisis.

But this was Luke. This was personal.

It took forever to get the probe where it needed to be. She showed Luke the image with a hand mirror. He peered at it for a moment, and confirmed that it was as close as his trace tubes could get.

"Go for it," he said. "For fuck's sake. Get it over with."

"Don't rush me."

Stay cool, she told herself. *Act, don't react. His life is in your hands.*

"This isn't goodbye." He was reading her mind. And he had that raw, naked look in his eyes that made her heart twist and ache.

She took hold of the wand, swallowing hard, and studied the probe's position on the imager one last time.

"Dani," he said. "I have to say it. Just in case. You know it already, but I—"

"Stop," she said abruptly. "Don't, Luke. Tell me after."

His brow furrowed. "But what if I—"

"Then nothing. Having heard you say it before would only make it worse. Don't you dare say it. I'll kick your ass. And you're shackled, so you won't be able to stop me."

He let out a sigh. "OK. I'll say it after. Every day, all day. For the rest of my life."

"You sneaky bastard." Her voice had gone thick. "Always getting around the rules somehow."

"Always." His dimples flashed. "Do it. It's not going to get easier if you wait."

"Three short taps," she repeated, her finger hovering over the button.

The tendons stood out on Luke's neck. His jaw was clenched. "Hit me," he said.

She hit the button. Held her breath. *Tap, tap, tap.*

There was no noise. She felt a faint vibration in the wand, and saw holographic explosions of light on the imager. Wild activity.

Luke's eyes went wide and frozen. He no longer saw her.

She couldn't seem to exhale. Or even blink, as she watched him. Just waiting.

Then the convulsions began.

CHAPTER 20

He was floating away from the storm and the noise. On some level, he registered shock waves convulsing his body, but his consciousness was jolted loose, as if someone else was suffering a soaring fever and brutal spasms. Chains jerked and rattled. The bed shook and danced on the floor.

Worst of all, Dani had to see him like this.

Then the thought dissolved into pure pain and he was sucked into a vortex, whipped violently through a vast, unknown inner space. Images, faces, places. Broken pieces of himself flashing by, whirling into blackness—

He landed someplace solid. He felt it, smelled it. He was in a dark hallway, but it seemed huge to him. The ceiling was so high. The floor very cold beneath his bare feet.

He looked down at his feet. Small feet. He was small. In Superman pajamas.

A loud, piercing noise sounded in his ears. Penetrating and desperate.

The place smelled. Old cigarette butts, unwashed laundry. He picked his way across the dirty linoleum of the kitchen floor. Unwashed dishes stank in the sink.

The piercing sound came from the bedroom behind him at the end of the hall. A baby crying. He made his way into the living room where the grownups were stretched out on the couches and the floor. He picked his way around the needles on the carpet to where Mom lay, curled up next to the coffee table. He shook her shoulder, calling her.

She wouldn't wake up.

Then he clambered over sprawled bodies of other people, who he mostly didn't know, until he got to Dad, who was sprawled on one of the couches.

"Dad? Dad? Wake up. The baby—"

Dad's backhand swipe knocked him backward and he fell, sprawling across the sleeping bodies and hitting the coffee table. Rattling the burnt spoons and foil and other stuff that covered the coffee table when the grownups did their long naps.

"Fuck off," Dad muttered thickly. "Go to bed."

He got himself up and went back to the kitchen. There was a diaper bag by the door. He searched through it, pulling out the plastic bags of powder until he found a spare baby bottle stored in there. He dragged a kitchen chair over to clamber up on the counter, trying to find a place for his feet in the jumble of dirty dishes and straining up to reach the jar Mom used to mix up the baby's bottle. He sniffed suspiciously when he pried off the lid. There was a lot of white powder around the house. He didn't want to give the baby the wrong one. This smelled right, though. Sweet and milky. It tasted right.

He didn't see any of the special water Mom used for the baby, so he just filled the bottle with tap water and poured in some powder. He closed and shook it the way Mom did, and made his way back through the hall to the back bedroom.

The wails had gotten louder.

In the bedroom, the baby had pulled himself up with the crib slats, chubby face looking over the top rail wet with tears, mottled and dark with the hard work of screaming. He wore just a diaper. It was cold. He shrieked even louder when Luke came in.

Luke clambered up onto the side of the crib and climbed into it, plunking himself down cross-legged on the mattress, and stuck the rubber nipple into the baby's mouth.

Instant silence. Fierce, rhythmic sucking. The baby's huge dark eyes, circled all around with long wet lashes, stared up at him, like it was look or die.

Luke fished around between the crib slats and the mattress until he found a blanket. Everything smelled like pee and the blanket was stiff with it, but it was dry, so he wrapped it around the baby's shoulders and pulled him onto his lap. The diaper was soggy and hot.

But the gurgling sound the baby made was good. Little grubby wet hands clutching his Superman pajama top for dear life, that was good. Even with a heavy wet pee-pee diaper on his lap, this was the best place in the house to be.

Luke hung onto the long-ago feeling as memory fragments broke and whirled around him. His little brother's eyes, locked on him like a lifeline. His brother had been alone on the day he'd come home from school and found their parents dead. Killed by rival drug dealers.

Luke had stayed late at school that day for basketball practice. He'd seen his little brother from across the big gym when he showed up at the door.

His eyes had been like big holes burned into his face.

Luke had known in a heartbeat. The coach bellowed at him for missing the shot, but he let the ball roll and ran to his brother, and they went back home to face it together.

Mom and Dad had been duct-taped to the kitchen chairs. Clubbed to death and they hadn't died quick.

Disjointed flashes of the time on the streets afterward. Selling Mom and Dad's private emergency drug stash for money and food kept them going for a while, sleeping on park benches, in bus stations, eating fast food, dumpster diving. A fat guy in a tailored suit had once offered Luke forty bucks for an hour with his little brother. He could still see the hunger squirming in that guy's beady eyes. His pink, shiny lips.

Luke had beaten the man to a pulp and left him gasping for air on the ground.

He remembered the day Braxton spotted them in a bus station. He'd offered cheeseburgers as he tried to recruit them for what he said was a scientific experiment. The plan had been to score some free grub, get the perv's wallet, blast outta there and fuck you, too.

Next thing they knew, they woke up in a cell under a blazing white light, tied down. Realizing too late that this guy was so much worse than the perv or pimp that they'd taken him for. This guy was a monster from the deepest fucking pits of hell.

Faces, names. Floating and disembodied. Familiar voices blared, faded again. His brother. Other kids, restrained, hooked up to big white helmets. Screaming. A girl's voice, shrieking over and over again. *Jada!*

White-coated researchers were pulling a tiny girl with dark eyes and long black hair away from an older girl who was fighting furiously with a group of white-jacketed guys. Holding her own, too, until one of them stabbed a needle into her throat.

He still heard the high-pitched, reedy voice of the little girl yelling for the older one, her voice receding as they dragged her away. *Zoe! Zoe!*

He saw a battle. Blood, noise, fire. Midlands. Reliving it, remembering the death blows he'd inflicted. Muscle tissue tearing open, bones splintering, hot blood spurting. Their eyes as they died, wide and scared and baffled. Blood and fire, smoke and death.

Too many memories all at once. Not one following another, but all of them together, rolling over him like a landslide. He was engulfed.

An eternity later, he heard a sound in the darkness. A bird chirping. A sweet warbling trill.

His acoustic ASP program flickered into functionality, identifying sounds, frequencies, tonal intervals, volume, distance, the direction from which the sound came. Then the ASP trawled the remaining intact file archives for the bird itself. Western Meadowlark. *Sturnella neglecta.* He saw pictures in the database. Black, white and yellow. Long beak.

Pretty bird. Pretty song.

He just listened, not paying any attention to the data. Just enjoying the tune. A mental jolt started his ASP clock again with a startled flicker. It was 6:48 AM. The bird's seven note melodic warble was a crystalline rise and fall of sound.

ASP worked. His ears worked. The archives worked, at least this one. His other senses were coming back online more slowly. Suddenly he could smell again. His own fear sweat. Blood. Disinfectant spray. Chemical compounds. His ASP started to automatically analyze and catalog them, identifying them as the drugs he told Dani to use for fever and convulsions. From the smell of it, not much had gotten inside him.

Dani. Warm and sweet. Shower soap and shaving cream and stress hormones.

The thought of Dani hit him like a shot of adrenaline, kicking his faculties into high gear. He came back into his body. Arms and legs still splayed. Muscles exhausted and sore from the cramping, the convulsions. Ankles and wrists bloody and inflamed from fighting the shackles. His head hurt, his jaw hurt, his eyes hurt.

Everything hurt like a bastard. As if he'd been thrashed.

One half of his body was warm, the other half was cool. A soft curl of hair tickled his nose. Dani had cuddled up to him on the bed, and she was fast asleep. Dark bruised marks of exhaustion shadowed her eyes.

His processor went wild at the sight of her. It frantically sorted and sifted Dani data to make sure she was OK. Temperature, heart rate, blood sugar. He'd scared her half to death. He gazed hungrily at her face, the pen strokes of her elegant eyebrows, her curling lashes, the freckles on her nose, the mole on her temple. The sexy folded indentation in the center of her pillowy lower lip. Not as pink as it should be.

God, so beautiful. He wanted her so bad. It was a crazy idea, and no favor to her. But there was nothing he could do. There was no way to stop this feeling.

Her eyes fluttered open at the intensity of his scrutiny. Comprehension dawned.

"Luke!" She propped herself up onto her elbow, eyes wide. "Oh my God. I can't believe it. You're alive. I didn't think you'd make it."

I'm so sorry. He tried to say it, but his vocal cords were swollen and dry. He coughed. It hurt his chest. "Sorry," he forced out.

"You? *You're* sorry?" She peered into his eyes. "So are you still…"

"Still me?" he responded, thickly. "Yeah. Think so."

"I didn't doubt that," she said. "Who else could you be? I just wondered, you know." She sat up, murmuring in dismay at the bloodstains on the loosened gauze beneath the shackles. "Let's get these off of you. I hate these things."

She fussed over his wrists and ankles as each shackle came off, but he wasn't concerned about it. They would heal in a matter of hours. By tomorrow there would barely be a mark. He tried to sit up, but sagged back down, wincing. Hurting.

"Rest," she said. "I don't know how you survived. The fever alone was high enough to kill you."

"My genetic mods—"

"Yeah, yeah, resistance to temperature extremes. But the convulsions. I thought your heart was going to explode. And it went on for hours. The meds were useless. It was hell. The fighting, the screaming. And look at you. You open your eyes and ta da! You son of a bitch. You scared the living shit out of me, you know that? All night long."

"Sorry," he rasped again.

"Stop apologizing."

He reached out to touch her hand, noting that his hand was streaked with blood from his wrist. "You didn't do what I told you to do," he said. "You were supposed to take the car and escape if I went nuts."

She harrumphed. "I don't do as I'm told. You should know that about me by now. Like I could walk away and leave you writhing in agony. Stupid thing to ask. Unrealistic."

"I know." He coughed. "I was desperate. I used you. I know it wasn't fair." He pulled her hand close, raising her knuckles to his lips and kissed them. "I'm sorry."

She yanked her hand away. "Stop it. You're being manipulative."

"Nah," he said. "I'm not the devious type."

"How would you know?" she demanded, and suddenly her eyes went big. "Oh, wait. Ah…do you know? More about yourself, I mean? Did it work?"

He thought about it, but his brain was too exhausted to make any sense of the garbage heap of cracked up pieces in there. Later for that.

"I guess," he said. "Maybe. In a sense. The memory blocks are all broken up, that's for sure. But everything else is broken, too. It's all in there, but there's so fucking much of it and it's all out of sequence. Plus I no longer have hard data to cross-reference my memories and pin them down by date and time. So it's just a pile of disconnected crap in there."

"Ah. Well." She gave him a smile that was both exhausted and faintly amused. "Welcome to the real world, buddy. That's what it's like for us normal folks."

"Yeah?" He shook his head. "Jesus. What a fucking mess."

"Yeah, I think that pretty much sums it up. But do you know anything about yourself and your people now?"

He couldn't stop touching her. He flicked his finger around at that sweet ringlet tumbling over her forehead, enjoying the way it sprang back into place once released. "I haven't sorted through it yet," he said softly. "But there's one thing I know for sure."

"Yeah? And what's that?" Her eyes were bright, expectant.

"I love you," he said.

CHAPTER 21

Dani froze.

It was too damn much. After being jerked around, torn apart and scared out of her wits, the sex god woke up and pledged his love.

She was too battered and bruised to let herself believe it. It couldn't be this easy. He had put her through pure hell and now he was messing with her head.

"What are you saying?" she yelled. "You can't say that!"

Luke's calm gaze had that direct quality that always flustered her. Breaking his memory block hadn't changed that aspect of his personality one bit.

"Why not?" he asked. "Anything else would be a lie."

She scrambled off the bed and stood there, her hands clenched. "But you can't say it now. After what you just put me through? It's like saying you love me when you're stoned. It doesn't even count!"

"I hear you," he said. "My folks were junkies and their word was for shit. But I'm not stoned or crazy, Dani. I'm in my right mind. Like never before."

"I just watched you have screaming convulsions for hours straight! After you deliberately brain damaged yourself, for the second time in two months. What you made me do last night tore me apart. Damn you, Luke." She wiped away hot, angry tears. "Aw, crap. This again."

He pushed himself up so he was sitting on the edge of the bed, and reached out to her. "Dani—"

She slapped his hand down. "Don't. I hate when I cry. Makes me look like shit."

"I think you look beautiful."

"Nix the sappy compliments, too," she snapped.

Luke's mouth twisted. "You wouldn't let me say it before you zapped me last night and I got my memories back. I lived through it, and my blocks are gone, but I'm still not qualified? At what point am I going to be in good enough shape to make a big declaration to you?"

"Oh, I have no fucking idea." She rummaged for a tissue from the fancy marble box on the antique dresser and blew her nose noisily. "Maybe when things have calmed down a little. When things are more, I don't know. Normal."

"Shit." Luke looked discouraged. "Is that your goal? Normal? Good luck with that."

She stared down at the floor for a while, working on making the tears stop. Now was not the time for blubbering. She had to keep it together.

"OK," Luke said gently. "Don't freak. I'll wait. We'll work toward normal together. I'll put the romantic declarations on ice. But stay with me. Stand by me."

Dani straightened her shoulders. "I'll consider it."

Oh man. That smile. His clear dark eyes read her so easily. He knew how she felt about him. How crushed out and turned on and upside down he made her feel.

But he wasn't rubbing her nose in it. He was a classy guy. For all his faults.

"Thank you," he said seriously. Like she'd made this big concession, which was such a load of crap. They couldn't pry her away from this guy with a crowbar and a blowtorch and he damn well knew it. She'd never been particularly good at hiding the way she felt. In fact, she absolutely sucked at that.

"Tell me one thing," she said. "Since you have your memories back, fish for this one. Are you married? Engaged? Involved?"

She held her breath. He closed his eyes, brows knitted. It was an intense physical and mental effort for him, and he was beyond exhausted, but she didn't relent. They had to know.

After a few minutes, he opened his eyes. They were full of relief. "No," he said.

"Just…just no?" She was too suspicious to let herself relax. "A guy like you?"

"Like me?" He frowned. "What the hell is that supposed to mean?"

She rolled her eyes. "Skip the fake modesty. I mean the drop-dead gorgeous guy who's huge and tall and ripped, with the dimples and the great teeth? The one who has the big beautiful cock and knows exactly just what to do with it?"

His eyes brightened. "I do?"

"Don't get distracted. Yeah, that guy. The one who can't walk through a bar without getting cocktail napkins with phone numbers on them handed to him right and left. How are you still single? What's your fatal flaw?"

"I don't know. Maybe it has something to do with being a cyborg freak."

She waved that triviality away. "Apart from that."

He pondered it for a while. "I saw women, from time to time. Around the time I was abducted, I was seeing this girl named Bea. A grad student at the University of Chicago. Real casual. We hung out, had sex. She was a great cook. But I think I freaked her out. She knew somehow there was something off about me. It made her nervous."

"You didn't tell her? You know, about…all of it?"

"About my mods and Obsidian? Fuck no. None of us ever…" His face froze, in wonder. "Oh, man. I almost…oh, shit."

"What?" She braced herself. Here it came. And he was the type who'd keep his promises even if they hurt him. "You remembered someone?"

"Family. My people. I just got a big rush of them, images and stuff. But I can't hold onto anything solid. This is driving me nuts."

"Give it time," she said. "Don't rush. Back to the burning question. About Bea. So, uh…no romantic declarations to Bea? No pronouncements or promises?"

"Nah. She was polyamorous. You know, into multi-humping. No guilt. We agreed that it was fine."

"Oh." She cleared her throat. You, too? No. Forget I asked."

"Nope. Not into that anymore. Too much trouble. And the scheduling is tricky." He grinned at her.

"Is it?" she asked. "I wouldn't know."

He beckoned her to him, grabbing her hand and tugging until she slowly consented to sit down on the bed next to him. "You have absolutely nothing to worry about," he said. "I'm not fooling around. You want me, I'm yours. For as long as you want me."

"Got it," she whispered around the lump in her throat.

"I remember the day I realized I was freaking her out," he mused. "She saw us sparring. She'd come to meet me at the dojo, and I was sparring with my brother and we…" His voice broke off.

Dani could hardly breathe. She reached out and put her hand gently on his forearm. "Your brother," she repeated. "What's his name?"

Luke cleared his throat. "Zade," he said roughly. "His name is Zade. Oh God." He hunched over, and hid his face in his hands. His bare shoulders shook.

"Luke," she whispered.

"Give me a minute. I just need a minute."

It took ten. Dani slid closer. Thigh to thigh. She put her arm around him and hid her face against his vibrating shoulder. Feeling his harsh breathing. Sternly refusing to cry. Too much emotion would create a feedback loop, and that wasn't fair to him.

Finally he lifted his head. "I'm OK now," he said, his voice colorless.

She wiped her face. Tears. So what. Just a few. "So. Zade, then. Last name?"

"Ryan," he said. "Ryan was the name we took. Noah told us it was dangerous to share a last name when we created our new identities, but Zade was my goddamn brother, and I just wasn't giving that up. I don't know why it was so important to me."

"So you're Luke Ryan," she said. "That's a nice name. I like it."

The raw emotion in his eyes touched her heart. She tried to think of something to distract them both before they lost it again. "And, ah…you mentioned someone named Noah? Who's that guy?"

"Noah Gallagher." Luke still had that tone of astonished discovery. "The leader of our group. That was the name he took after rebellion day. When we escaped Midlands."

"And Midlands is…?"

"It was the facility where they modified us. A group of us escaped on rebellion day. A lot more died. We killed the researchers. Burned the place to the ground.

Laid low for a long time. Used fake identities, but we built lives on top of them. As real as anybody else's life, I guess."

"And your real life?"

"High level tech security. I worked for a retail tycoon. Long story short, I was set up with a son-of-a-bitch named Mark Olund who stun coded me, killed my client and stuck me in a hidden cage beneath his house. That's where I stayed for a fucking year. Mark stopped coming, and the food and water stopped with him. I thought I was done for. Then Braxton showed up, and things really went to hell. Deeper into hell, I mean. Starving to death would have been better than him."

"Back up. Who's Mark Olund?"

"Another Midlander. One of our rebel escapees, but Mark went bad. He liked hurting people, and he got riled up when we told him to cut that shit out, so he left. We hadn't seen him in almost ten years, but there he was, with my control codes. He murdered my client right in front of me. A guy I'd promised to protect."

"It wasn't your fault," Dani said.

Luke shook his head. "I had no business selling myself as a security expert with a weak spot like that."

"Come on. What were the odds that you'd run into someone with your stun code?"

"It doesn't matter," Luke said. "Whatever the odds were, I lost that hand, and so did my client. And his widow, and two little girls. Eight and ten years old." He paused. "Nine and eleven now."

"So more is coming back to you now?"

"It's pouring in on me, yeah. I remember them all now. There's Noah, and his little sister Hannah. And Sisko, and Zoe—oh, sweet holy fuck. *Zoe.*"

Dani winced inwardly. Was this a more recent girlfriend he was only just now remembering? "And Zoe is?"

"Another rebel. Part of our group. Damn, I saw her sister!" Luke turned to her, his eyes alight. "That woman who attacked you at your house, remember? When we saw each other, we both choked for a fraction of a second. Because we recognized each other. That was Jada! She was only eight years old when I saw her last. She's Zoe's little sister and she's still alive!"

"She recognized you?" Dani was bewildered. "But...I saw her try to kill you!"

"Of course," Luke said, as if it were obvious. "She had to fight. She's all stimmed up. She'd start bleeding out of her eyes if she didn't. She probably paid in blood for that split-second delay. Zoe's going to freak when she finds out her baby sister is still alive."

Huh. It took heavy-duty mental adjustment to recast the terrifying she-demon from her kitchen into the role of somebody's victimized baby sister. She'd work on that some other time. "So if Obsidian finds you and identifies you, they can use that code on you?"

"Yes," Luke said. "Zade and I are the last ones left alive who got the verbal control codes. It was a limited experiment, back in the beginning. It went along with the most extreme gene cocktail. Braxton got off on using the control codes on us. It was a big sexual thrill for him."

She tried not to picture it. "So you guys were based in Chicago?"

"No, I was only in Chicago for that job. I have a condo in Seattle. And a cabin on a lake a couple hours north of the city. Long drive, but always worth it. Before I blocked my memories, I used to imagine the cabin and the lake for hours at a time in that cage, just to keep myself sane. A whole group of us settled in Seattle. Including my brother."

"I like Seattle," she said.

His eyes had that flash as he looked at her. "Good."

She was embarrassed to feel her face heat.

"There are fourteen of us in my extended family," Luke said. "Zoe, the sister of the woman who attacked you, is near San Francisco. There are more on the East Coast, a few in Europe and Asia. A couple in Africa, too, ex-Special Forces. They run a mercenary army."

She smiled, shaking her head. "Of course they do."

"Noah was our leader. Zade and I were the shock troops, but Noah was the brains of the rebellion," he said. "He has a biotech company now. Hannah is his sister. She's a piece of work. You'll love her. And they'll love you."

"Hey." She held up her hand. "Give them time. Give all of us time."

"All the time you need. But they will. Why wouldn't they? You're beautiful and smart and tough and brave and honest and you take no shit from anybody. That's what they like. Damn, that's what I like."

"Stop it, Luke."

He rolled his eyes. "Yeah, right, no passionate declarations until you're sure I'm not still out of my fucking gourd. I know the rules."

Dani looked away. "So. What now?"

"I contact them. I have to find them first. I have no data. Phone numbers, email addresses, I wiped all that stuff from my files so that Braxton couldn't get it. And I don't have a functioning retrieval system. It's like a big garbage dump in there. I've never fished for data and come up empty, not since I was modded. It sucks."

"I can imagine." Dani tried not to smile. "Sounds like me every time I lose my smartphone. Poor baby. How about social media?"

"We don't use it. Too risky. Too much facial recognition software out there. Secretly picking up data unbeknownst to the entire fucking world."

"OK. What does your brother do professionally?"

"He has a consulting business. Wait…let me see if I can find …" Luke closed his eyes for a few seconds.

When he turned back to her, he was beaming. "He changed the header on his business website. It has a line written in Midlander encrypted code that lists everyone's contact info and positioning coordinates. Noah's company has it on their masthead too…and Kane…and Devon, and Hannah…all of them have it. Only a Midlander would notice it. But it's there. Like a beacon for me."

Dani smiled at him, holding back another rush of tears by sheer force of will. "So this whole time they've been calling you, just like you said," she said softly. "And you sensed it. You had faith. Good for you."

Luke turned his face away. "Oh hell," he whispered. "Dani. Don't."

She leaned against him, taking his hand and twining her fingers through his. "I'm here."

Luke looked at her, glowering. "I am not crying," he said stiffly.

She suppressed a smile. "It's OK if you do."

He made a disgusted sound, but didn't protest when she got up, sat down on his lap and wrapped her arms around his neck.

They hugged each other like they'd never let go.

CHAPTER 22

Luke studied his inner screen, focusing on the code that decorated the logo of the Angel Industries home page. Links to geotags constantly updated everyone's geographical position. An insane security risk on their part to put their coordinates out there, encrypted or not. If Obsidian got him, he'd betray everyone. He wouldn't have time to re-establish a memory block like the one he'd created before. That had required a complicated analog-build that took weeks of intense concentration.

Through the constant flow of data, he saw Dani's worried gaze on him. The exhausted look in her eyes. He'd done that to her. He needed to fix it. He had to persuade her somehow that he was capable of keeping a deathless promise.

It was a done deal on his side, signed and sealed and date-stamped. He just had to get her to trust him somehow. Hell of a job, after what he'd put her through.

He pinned the shifting coordinates onto a mental map. Devon was driving northbound on I-95 from Philadelphia to New York. Kane was in New York City. Zoe was in San Francisco, Sisko was in Seattle, and Noah was in Vienna, of all places. Maybe there was some big biotech conference there. It felt great to think of their names. Connect the names to faces, places, memories. Then he checked on Zade.

Holy shit. His brother was less than two hundred miles away. Right here in California. Less than three hours driving, if he pushed it. Which Zade always did.

He had to put his head down between his knees for a second. "My brother is really close," he said. "He must have heard about my car driving itself. He's near Goforth."

Dani held out a smartphone from the electronics box. "He raced down from Seattle to talk to some glue-sniffing butthead in Goforth just on the off chance that the guy might have seen you? He'd follow any lead, even a stupid one. I love him for that. Call him."

"Yeah." Luke took the phone, but his fingers shook, and his eyes blurred as he stared at the touchscreen. He had to enter the number twice. It rang only once before the line opened up.

"Yeah?" Zade's voice, tense and wary. "Who's this?"

Luke tried to speak but his voice failed him. He let out a rasping croak.

"Don't fuck with me," Zade growled. "Who are you? Is this...?"

"Yeah." Luke coughed the words out. "Yeah. It's me."

For a few seconds, he couldn't hear at all. His ASP was nuts. His heartbeat roared in his ears. Waves of hot and cold, waves of random data scrolling frantically down his processor feed. He pushed it away, desperate to hear his brother's voice.

"... fuck have you been since you got away from Braxton?"

"I lost you." Luke's voice broke. "I lost you guys. I blocked you out so Braxton couldn't get at you. When I escaped, I couldn't get back in. Just did tonight, finally. Saw your message. Picked up the contact info. So you're in California?"

"Yeah. I happened to see a police report about some numbnuts remote-driving a Porsche Cayenne. That's you, right? Made a real big impression on that dumbass convenience store clerk. Jesus, Luke. You're being sloppier 'n all shit."

"My bad. Sorry I couldn't call you. It was just, you know. Brain damage. You know how it is."

"Yeah, whatever." Zade understood. "Crazy ass son of a bitch."

"I know, I know. Good to hear your voice."

"Yeah. You too."

The silence that followed was heavy with emotion. Zade finally broke it. "So, uh, what's your deal? Are you well? Hurt? In trouble?"

"On the run," Luke admitted. "I intercepted a Manticore shipment. Turns out Obsidian placed the order."

"OK. They on your tail? You need backup?"

"Backup would not suck," Luke said. "And I want to see you."

"Fuck yeah. Give me the coordinates. How did you get your memory back?"

"Manticore gear," Luke said. "Threaded one of Braxton's probes into one of the holes in my head and zapped myself to hell and gone. But it worked. I remembered you."

"*What?* Jesus, Luke, you could've killed yourself!"

"I know. I had help." His eyes flicked to Dani. "She saved my life."

"Who?"

"Dani. This woman I met. The Manticore courier, Naldo, he was a friend of hers. He broke free somehow and ran to her instead of going to the meeting with the buyer. That's how I met her."

"Ah. OK. Is she, like..." Zade's voice trailed off suggestively. "Are you...?"

"Yeah, we are. She's incredible. Gorgeous. Brilliant."

"Oh, shut up," Dani snapped under her breath.

"Moving on. Is the group OK?" Luke asked. "Everyone still under the radar?"

"Pretty much. We've had some incidents," Zade said. "We got into a brawl with Mark a couple months ago, but he's dead now. Guess you must have figured that out when he stopped coming down to feed you at that fucking hell-hive of his in Wyoming."

"Yeah, that was bad," Luke admitted.

"We finally tracked you all the way there and ran into Braxton. Must have been right after you bolted. Maybe only a day or two later, no more."

"Braxton? How the fuck did you not get coded if he saw you?"

"I did get coded," Zade said. "Simone saved me."

Luke sucked in a startled breath. "So what's up with Simone?"

"Everything. She's my bride. She's amazing. You'll like her."

"Bride?" Luke's mouth sagged. "Holy fucking shit. *You?*"

"I know, right? But it's not just me. Noah got married, too. Off on a honeymoon in Europe that just won't quit."

"I saw on the map that he was in Austria," Luke said. "Seemed weird."

"Yeah. His new wife, Caro, she's heavy into art so they're doing this art extravaganza wedding trip. He's crazy in love. You wouldn't recognize him. All starry-eyed. But Caro's cool. She has nerve. We approve."

"Wild," Luke said. "How about you? Where did you go on your honeymoon?"

Zade laughed. "Nowhere yet. I couldn't go lie on a beach while you were still lost. But now maybe I can. After we get you someplace safe and catch up for a while. Holy shit, Luke. Holy shit. You're fucking found, for real. I can't believe it."

"Same here," Luke said. "But listen. I've got business to finish up and I could use help with it before you and Simone hit that beach."

"Anything you need, brother. Where are you?"

Luke gave their position, and quickly explained about the Manticore slave soldier Obsidian had ordered. The tiny girl in a hibernation tank in a container in San Francisco.

"Dani and I have to pick up Ivy before anything else," he said.

"Ivy? She has a name?"

"Her file number is I89VY262. Dani's friend Naldo called her Ivy."

"Got it. Standing by for your orders."

"Cool. Oh, and tell Zoe when you call them that I saw Jada."

Zade was startled into silence for a few seconds. "No shit," he said quietly. "Was she…OK?"

"Hard to say. She almost killed me. But she choked for a fraction of a second when she looked me in the eye, so I think she recognized me. On some level."

"Fuck," Zade muttered. "That's gonna blow Zoe's mind, and she's hard enough to deal with as it is. Sit tight until we can get to you. The others can drive down in less than a day. I'll call everyone and they'll gather up some gear and get rolling right away. We'll all go pick up Ivy together. I can be at your location in about three hours. Maybe less."

"Got you. We'll catch up then."

A few more gruff and inadequate words and Luke closed the call, his throat too tight to speak.

Dani put her hand on his shoulder. "You good?"

"I want to take a shower," he muttered.

He went in, got started, and stood there for a very long time with the hot water pounding down on his face.

"What's that I smell? Bacon?"

Dani turned to see Luke slouched against the kitchen entrance wearing nothing but his jeans, just as she put the platter of sizzling, thick-cut hickory smoked bacon on the huge table next to the tower of buttered toast slices.

A glance at his face showed that he still felt shaky and raw and guarded, but sheer hunger had drawn him out of his hiding place. The smell of frying bacon was a potent lure. It had been a long time since those raggedy prime rib sandwiches she'd cobbled together during their drive up to Serrati Flats. So much had happened since then.

"Sit down," she told him. "Get going on some bacon while I do your eggs. How many do you want?"

"How many do you have?"

She was nonplussed. "Ah...a dozen, I guess."

"Give me whatever you don't want."

"For real? You can eat ten eggs?"

"If that's all there are, yeah," he said around his first mouthful of bacon and toast.

She'd never seen anything like the way he ate. He devoured everything she'd cooked, and then toasted up more slices from the second loaf of bread, and then ate the berries, bananas and pears. A healthy appetite was always a good sign, but holy flipping crap.

Dani sipped her coffee as he polished off a tub of yogurt, admiring the broad flare of his shoulders, the thick ropy muscles in his forearms.

"Are you ever going to put a shirt on again?" she asked. "Not that I'm complaining."

"It smells bad," he said ruefully. "Combat sweat. I gotta buy fresh clothes or do some laundry. But that's not happening anytime soon, the way our lives are going."

"True enough."

Their eyes locked, and heat leaped between them. It made her blush. Her gaze fell.

"We have time before my brother gets here," Luke's voice was a seductive rumble. "Let's go upstairs. Lie down for a while."

"Hmmm." She studied him carefully. "Are you coming on to me, buddy?"

He gave her an innocent smile. "Just to chill. After all the drama."

Sounded sensible. It also sounded fabulous. "There's a bedroom I like at the other end of the house," she told him. "The one with the lake view. I'm not going anywhere near the evil shackles and the brain-zapper."

They gulped the last of their coffee. Luke seized her hand and led her through the big, dim chalet, all the way up to the bedroom Dani had indicated, a light, peach-toned room. A soft mohair throw covered the bed, which had a lacy wicker headboard. The big window showed mist rising off the mirror-glass of the lake.

Luke shucked his jeans and stood there, buck-naked. That gorgeous, teasing smile on his face. He was being actually playful, after a night like that. The guy was so strange and unexpected. Chock full of complicated issues, but screw it. She loved him that way.

Loved him.

Yeah, she had to admit it. It wasn't a crush. It wasn't just her hormones. It wasn't because he'd rescued her so many times. The look in his eyes made her heart melt into hot syrupy goop, and her brain wasn't far behind. Total slop. Then tears.

Shit. Nonononono. She wasn't doing that right now. No more tears.

She drew in an uneven breath at the sight of his outsized erect cock, and lunged for the en suite bathroom. "Hold that thought," she mumbled. "Grabbing a shower."

Maybe the pounding hot water could wash off the lingering fear. The dread and the guilt and the grief. It clung to her like a stain.

Goddamn it. She should be glad. They'd come through the darkness and back out into the light. She'd lived, against all odds, and Luke was reuniting with his family. That was cause for celebration.

But part of her didn't dare relax, not even for a second. Didn't dare congratulate herself. It was tempting the gods.

She didn't bother to dress again as she dried off. She just laid her clothes on the wicker chair. Luke seemed fast asleep, and she slid naked into the crisp sheets next to him. The fog was so ghostly outside, wisps of vapor tangling in the dark pine boughs.

She cuddled up to the huge cloud of heat his body threw off. She felt warmed by it and she wasn't even touching him. She examined the sores around his wrists. They were scabbed over as if they'd already been healing up for a week. Wow. Her magic man.

She just couldn't stop staring at his stark male beauty. That rugged face plus a sexy hint of dark beard shadow did her in.

His eyes opened, as if he could feel her gaze. The look on his face was too much for her lacerated nerves to bear. "Don't," she whispered. "Please."

He frowned. "Don't what?"

"The lovey-dovey look. I can't take it."

"It's your own fault for rocking my world. Don't blame me."

She rolled her eyes. "Oh, Luke."

"Get used to it," he advised her solemnly. "A lot of things I can control, but the look on my face when I stare at you? Not so much."

She bit her lip, trying to think of something smart-assed to say.

"It scares me," she blurted. Lame comeback, she thought, but it was true.

He nodded gravely. "Yeah. Me too. So let's be brave."

She laughed, breaking off into a gasp as he pulled her close to him. It felt amazing, yielding to the gentleness of a man who was fully in control of his own strength. The delicious sensation of relaxing into his sensual heat. Feeling it ripple through her whole body. She smiled in spite of herself as she opened up to tender, exploring kisses. So sweet.

His hands on her body, between her legs, made her whimper. His fingers probed and stroked her, slipping inside her with a slow, pulsing rhythm that made her gasp and clench around him.

A rush of cold air, and suddenly his heat shifted, sliding down her body, exposing her to the chill. The he moved her and himself, settling between her parted legs, about to taste her. Kissing and licking and lapping, thrusting his tongue inside.

His way of doing it. Insisting on making her come before he would give her that gorgeous cock. As if at least one glorious oral orgasm was his entry fee.

Come on in.

Her pleasure intensified as he licked and suckled with intuitive skill, sliding his fingers inside her pussy as he fluttered his tongue across her clit. Dani suddenly couldn't think at all. Her body shuddered as she lifted herself against his face, pleading, then demanding that he…oh *yes* …

Erotic bliss reverberated through her whole being.

Her eyes opened as he shifted, climbing up over her body, lifting her legs up high. Gazing down at her body beneath him, soft and yielding and open. He caressed her clit as he nudged his thick, blunt cockhead against her slick pussy lips.

They groaned at the sweet perfection of joining. She moved against him, taking him deep.

She grabbed his upper arms, but she couldn't get much of a grip on him, his muscles were so steely thick.

He responded with swiveling moves that made her clench and writhe against him. "I could keep fucking you forever," he said roughly. "It's so good. You're so sweet and hot and tight. I love to watch my cock going into you. I love watching your face, your mouth, your eyes. Your tits shaking."

She braced her hands against his chest, feeling the rough texture of his scarring, his chest hair. Digging in her nails as he pumped his cock into her. No words, just breathless, heaving pants as the pace quickened. Hard and frantic, driven by raw need.

The storm broke, shattering them both.

The afterglow was intense. Astonished joy, and all around it, sheer fear.

His arms tightened around her. "Got you right where I want you," he murmured in her ear. "Safe."

"Am I?" she asked dreamily.

"Yeah. With me. And the rest of us now, too."

"Oh, right."

"Zade's on the way, and the rest of my people. Once they're here, we'll come up with a good, solid plan. And do what needs doing before we move on."

"To what?"

"A real life. With everything you want in it."

"What I want?" She grinned. "You mean, besides you?"

He kissed her again, with an ardor that left her breathless, and smoothly finished his thought. "Like med school."

She was taken aback. "Seriously?"

"Damn straight. If that's what you want to do."

"I've thought about it," she admitted.

"Good. Glad to hear it. All of us Midlanders found ways to do stuff we like. My brother makes bank on his consulting business. Noah has a hot biotech company. Zoe's a researcher with multiple degrees in chemistry and pharmacology. We've all got a thing. None of that is fake. And the new names are nothing new for us. You just compensate by being the hands-down fucking best in your field. Which would be no big deal for you."

She felt bewildered. "Whoa. You don't know me that well."

"I intend to."

"Luke…"

"Let it sit. It's not for right now. But you'll have a life. I'll bet my own life on it."

She sat up, alarmed. "Do not bet your life on anything, Luke Ryan!"

He let go of her and slid out of bed. "Whatever you say. Time's up. Zade should be here soon. I gotta pack the gear. We'll need it for Ivy."

Dani got up, put on fresh clothes and headed downstairs. She felt restless and for some reason, uneasy. She got herself more coffee before sliding open a massive glass door, then stepped out onto a huge terrace furnished with outdoor stuff, benches, a barbecue.

Overlooking the lake, every vantage point was beautiful. She was surrounded by the grandeur of nature but her feet never even had to touch any dirt. Weird.

She looked up as the shadow of a bird sliced across the white sky.

It left her field of vision quickly but she replayed the image in her mind. Maybe not a bird. Too smooth. No swooping or fluttering or flapping of wings.

Fear seized her, deep and cold. "Luke!" she called in a strangled whisper.

Seconds later he'd stepped out onto the patio, gun in hand. "What?"

"Drone." She indicated the direction she'd seen it disappear. "Very low."

"Shit," he muttered. "I hear it now. Stealth drone. Sneaky motherfuckers. Get inside."

"Luke—"

"Get inside!"

The tone of his voice jolted her into movement.

Everything happened at once. The drone appeared, floating like a huge buzzing insect around the corner of the house. Luke swung up his gun to take aim just as a loud, amplified voice spoke.

"Calliope! Banner! Ibex!"

Luke was frozen in place, gun hand held high, his suddenly halted motion leaving him off center.

A moment of shocked disbelief. His eyes met hers, full of mute desperation. Then he fell. Hard.

CHAPTER 23

Couldn't…see. Fuck. Luke fought to breathe. Eyes straining to take in more. He'd fallen on his side, in the exact position he'd been in when the control code blared out of that fucking drone. His ASP was nuts, churning useless data across his screen, but he was powerless to act on any of it.

Dani was bent over him, yelling something as she felt for his pulse, but he couldn't focus on her words over the roar in his head. The shiny black cover of the fallen barbecue reflected the scene behind him. Operatives were boiling out of the woods. They'd stayed far enough away to not trip his sensors and they wore thermal shield gear, so they were fucking invisible, heat-wise. He wouldn't have seen their body warmth even if he had been looking. Which he hadn't been. Like an asshole.

He was so angry at himself. Dickhead moron. That assault on his brain last night had made him soft. Rolling around in bed fucking while they should have been on the road speeding toward safety. Jesus. He almost deserved this for being so sloppy.

"Lift him up," someone ordered. "Let me have a look at him."

Where was Dani?

He was seized on both sides and hauled upright, still in that goddamn position, like an action figure or a plastic toy soldier frozen into place. Chin up, gun up, taking aim. Only his eyes could move, and his lungs. Somewhat. Not well. He could barely drag enough air into them to stay conscious.

The smirking guy in front of him was no one Luke had ever seen before. A beefy, thick-necked, red-faced bull of a man with buzzed hair, cold eyes and flat, pale lips. He looked pleased with himself. In charge. Convinced of his own superiority because he'd designed and engineered it himself. Prick.

Whereas the guys holding him were modded slave soldier grunts, as he had been. They had the tight facial mask he remembered from his own younger face, and still felt in his stress flashbacks. From the bad old days, back when every thought or feeling had to stay small and secret, huddled in the dark to avoid punishment or discovery.

"Hello, D-14," the bull asshole said. "My name is Hale. Interesting that your control code still works so well after…how long has it been? Before my time, that's for sure. The powers that be can't wait to know about your life. Where you've been, what you've done. Where your friends are located."

Luke let his mind detach. Months of torture, first with Mark, then with Braxton, had trained him. His body could be pounded into jelly, but he could simply float away.

But when they started pumping their drugs into him, they would all be fucked.

Maybe he could reinstate the memory block. How fucking ironic. Hours after he'd shattered it, he needed it again. It took immense concentration to construct and activate.

Maybe a second time it would go more quickly. Or, more probably, the strain would rupture his brain. Which was a solution in itself. If it came to that, he could just plant an analog bomb in his mind and detonate it.

If he survived at all, he'd be a drooling vegetable. Interrogate that, fuckheads. *But Dani.*

The slave soldiers clapped an oxygen mask over his nose before trying, violently, to cram him into the travel pod. It was painful, being forced into a container meant for a slave soldier when he was lying like a marble effigy, arms down, legs straight.

Coded in action, Luke didn't fit.

"Stop it," Hale sounded disgusted. "There's no point. You'll just break his bones." The guy leaned over him. "Listen to me carefully," he said. "Four of my operatives will hold you to the ground. When I say your release code, you will straighten your arms and legs. If you resist, one of my operatives instantly fires a bullet into the head of your woman friend. We have no use for her otherwise." He looked up at his slave soldiers. "Hold him down now."

Four huge guys practically sat on him. From the corner of his eye, he saw the one holding the gun under Dani's chin.

"Jaguar. Lava. Talon," Hale said loudly.

Luke's contracted muscles released. He straightened out, as the man had ordered.

"Good," Hale said. "I see you can be reasonable. Calliope! Banner! Ibex!"

Frozen again. This time they heaved him up and tossed him into the pod like a mannequin. They were dragging Dani away. He felt the vibrations of her kicking and thrashing. Blows, thudding into flesh. Dani, puffing out air. Trying not to cry out. *Bastards.*

"Settle down, you dumb bitch." Hale was speaking, but Luke could no longer see outside the pod, except for a rectangle of gray sky. "Cuff her and put her in the van. Give her a shot. I don't want to be bothered with her until we're back at High Mesa."

Luke followed the ragged sound of Dani's breathing for as long as he could.

Hale crouched over his pod, peering down at him. "Would've been a shame to break your arms when the lid came down," he said. "Not that I care, but the big boys are coming to see you in all your glory, and they reserved the pleasure of breaking you for themselves. That prick Metzer gets to go first. He's hot for revenge since you drone-decapitated his son the other day. Something tells me he's going to enjoy hurting you a lot."

He grinned widely at Luke as the lid came down.

Zade felt heaviness in the air the instant he got out of his car at the mountain chalet. The gate had hung wide open, which was strange in itself, and the silence was dead flat. No buzz of activity, heartbeats, footsteps, voices, vibrations. The subtle hum of sound that his enhanced sensors were reaching for just wasn't there. Only quiet emptiness.

It made him sick with dread. Luke wouldn't have left here when he knew Zade was coming. No way. And the black Porsche Cayenne parked there was the same one the Goforth clerk had reported seeing. That was Luke's car.

Something bad had gone down. He felt its bitter residue in the air. A large vehicle had pumped out exhaust here recently. He put his hand on the hood of the Porsche.

Stone cold. Not this one. He fought down a primal howl of frustration.

Zade thumbed his phone to the app for today's group chat. The others were almost here. After his phone call, Hannah had bullied her brother Asa into flying the Seattle gang down to the closest local airport in Asa's own private plane. Too many people for Luke to deal with all at once, in Zade's opinion, but there was no stopping Hannah. She was too excited to see Luke again, like a little kid. Not like he could blame her.

Their group policy was to hide in plain sight, and their online chats were no different. Today's venue was the comment thread of Chrissy Honeywell's vlog. Chrissy was a reality TV star building her brand with videos of her day-to-day adventures. Currently live-streaming, Chrissy's pussy wax at The Dare To Bare Salon. From what he could hear, Chrissy was not enjoying the process. There were already 532 comments on the thread, ranging from fawning muff divers to run-of-the-mill trolls.

He swiftly filtered to pinpoint the Midlanders handles. Hannah popped up first. She'd chosen the tasteful handle 'FackToy78.' FackToy78 had written *hey chrissy u done pullin weedz in the ladygarden? Stop squeakin like a little bitch and show us ur landing strip.* Hannah was impatient for news, and she liked to play the troll.

Zade tapped in a comment from HungHenry69. *dont let the h8trs get u down chrissy they're not worth it cuz nobody's home in there, the dumb f*cks. Stay smooth chrissy u r so BAD!*

Let them chew on that. 'Nobody home' and 'BAD!' was enough to put the group on their guard even if something should stop him from messaging again.

He walked slowly toward the house, his senses reaching out in all directions. The front door was locked, but a stroll around the place brought him to a terrace overlooking the lake, where a huge picture window had been left wide open.

He stared around himself, guts sinking ever deeper. There had been a struggle. Lawn furniture overturned, a barbecue on its side. A coffee mug, handle snapped off, lay on the wooden planks around a splatter of spilled coffee.

He crouched down to touch it. The splatter was still wet. It smelled of cream. Luke took his coffee black. The new girlfriend's coffee, then. So they had taken her, too.

He moved silently into the house and crept from room to room, gun in hand, piecing together his brother's morning from visual and olfactory clues. They had eaten over an hour ago, judging from the lingering bacon and coffee odors, the residual heat of the stovetop. He smelled sweat, fear hormones, metabolized drugs.

He walked up the stairs. Found a bedroom with a rumpled bed, steel shackles on the bedframe and the familiar smell of stim sickness. Short hairs clung to the side of the bathroom sink from when Luke shaved his head. Scratch marks on the wrought iron from the shackles. Blood, smeared on the bedclothes, the pillows.

Down the hall was another bedroom, another rumpled bed that smelled like sex.

Maybe Luke's phone call had tipped Obsidian off somehow. Rage and grief were building up inside Zade. Too fucking much. Obsidian had snatched his brother less than a half hour ago.

Then he heard it. The whirr of a lightweight stealth drone, approaching fast.

He pulled out his gun, crouching, back to the wall—

"Gargoyle! Magpie! Vortex!" a staticky male voice blared out of a speaker.

Holy shit. That was *his* damn stun code. He doubled over, gasping at the sharp pain—and straightened up again, making a swift decision.

His stun code had been deactivated after Simone's scrub treatments. Being coded gave him a stomach-turning cramp, but it passed. If he were running, he might trip but probably wouldn't fall. Same with the kill code. His heart hiccupped, and then found its rhythm again.

But Obsidian didn't know that. They thought they had him cold. It was a weak spot in their armor. Probably the only one he'd ever find.

They'd be all over him any moment now. He wished there was time to text something to Simone. *So sorry. Didn't mean to do this to you. I love you.*

But his thumbs were already tapping out a swift comment to the thread from HungHenry69 to warn the gang off:

u shriveled-d*ck pr*cks u lv poor sore chrissy alone cuz if u c me comin u btr RUN RUN RUN cuz its DOOMSDAY4U GAMEOVER gdbye s*ckrs

He pried open the phone, pulled out the SIM card. Tossed it into a vase of dried flowers that sat on the vanity and sent the phone skittering under the rumpled, unmade bed.

Just in time. He froze into a statue just as the drone drifted in front of the window and hovered there, observing him through its tiny, unfriendly red eye.

"Hello, D-13," the blaring speaker said. "So glad you decided to join us." That same voice that had coded him.

Oh man. He was gonna hate the butthead who owned that voice so hard.

CHAPTER 24

Asa studied the group of Midlanders huddled in the space between his parked Lexus LX and Zoe's black Jag in their strip mall rendezvous point, just a few miles from the address Zade had sent them. All scowling down at Zade's apocalyptic message on their phones.

As usual with this crowd, he felt six steps removed. They fascinated him, but to them he was just a clueless unmod, incapable of understanding their big fat fucking issues.

Too damn bad that all those Midlander modifieds tended toward self-importance, his big brother Noah included. Even though Asa had saved their collective asses a couple months ago in the fight against their archenemy, Mark Olund, he still wasn't a veteran of their famous rebellion day, he wasn't in their inner secret circle, he hadn't gone through the terrible ring of fire, blah blah blah. And they never let him forget it.

But there was Hannah, his baby sister. He'd lost her to Obsidian's secret research program when she was ten. She and his older brother Noah had been sucked into that black hole together. It took Asa over a decade of searching to find them again.

They were all still getting to know each other again. Slow, prickly work, but Hannah was his baby sister and he was sticking with it. Which meant that her problems were his problems.

This was evidently a big motherfucking problem, judging by the way Hannah's freckles stood out. Asa had flown her, Sisko and Simone down to California in one of his planes right after they got the call from Zade, arranging for someone to meet them with an SUV to save time. All because Hannah was so desperate to see the famous Luke.

Great. Another modified Midlander brother for Asa to love.

True to form for this crowd, it had all gone to shit. No more happy reunion. And now Zade had been abducted too. Asa liked the guy, but for fuck's sake, seriously? Zade should've been more careful. He'd always thought the guy had a few screws loose.

Sucked for Simone, though. She thought the sun rose and set on Zade, and they had only been married for a few weeks. Simone hadn't even spoken since Zade's warning showed up on the vlog thread. She just stared down at her phone's screen, looking more or less like she'd just been found frozen solid in a snowbank. He felt bad for her.

She needed to get warmed up. Have something with some sugar in it, maybe.

"I don't suppose we could go to that coffee place on the corner, and talk about this over something hot," Asa suggested, without much hope. "It's fucking cold in this wind."

Zoe spun around to face him. For some reason, that woman had it in for him, which was a shame because she was ridiculously beautiful. Strong, curvy body, flawless golden skin, tilted dark cat eyes, luscious red lips. She looked like a hot and deadly assassin in her black leather coat and black jeans and high heeled boots, her long, glossy black hair whipping in the wind.

She hated his guts, for some reason. And yet he went rock hard whenever he caught her eye. Which admittedly was not often. She disdained him. He wasn't worthy of so much as a glance from up there on her lofty high horse. Maybe he had some kinky masochistic thing happening in his brain that made him switch on for that.

If so, he didn't really want to know more. Some things were better left unobserved.

"Maybe you don't understand." Zoe enunciated like she was speaking to someone who was cognitively impaired. "Didn't you read what he said? And you're whining about the cold? You want to, what? Grab a fucking pumpkin chai and a scone?"

"I wouldn't mind," he said evenly. "No matter what happened to your people, we still have to eat and stay caffeinated."

Zoe made a sound of disgust and turned her back on him, providing an ideal opportunity to ogle her ass. With some effort, he tuned back into the general conversation.

"...the doomsday plan," Hannah was saying. "I'm just not ready to think it's come to that. Not yet. We can't just leave them and run."

"If they've both been taken, you know what comes next." Sisko's voice was bleak.

"Wait, wait. Hold on," Asa said. "What's this about running?"

Sisko turned to look at him. "Zade said 'run,' and 'doomsday.' Obsidian has them both, and they'll extract every detail about us. Noah worked out a contingency plan for this. If anyone gets retaken, the others scatter. We have secret passports and a hiding place not known by the rest of the group, so names and locations can't be drugged or tortured out of us."

For fuck's sake. He'd had enough of this tormented, apocalyptic crap. Asa turned to his sister. "You're not flying off to the ends of the earth without telling me where."

"I agree," Hannah said. "I won't do it."

"If one of us is taken, we run," Sisko repeated.

"Luke's been gone for a year, and you guys didn't dissolve your group," Asa said.

"We weren't sure it was Obsidian," Sisko said. "We didn't want to throw away our homes and livelihoods for nothing. This time, we know for sure that it's them. We put the doomsday mechanism in place years ago and Zade just pulled the switch."

"Fuck the switch," Zoe said rebelliously. "I'm not going anywhere."

"Don't be an idiot," Sisko said harshly. "It's a trap, and Zade just dove in."

"So go," Zoe said. "All of you. Go. Scatter. Do the doomsday plan, but just write me out of it. If they've got Zade and Luke already, what does it matter if I walk into Obsidian's open mouth? They won't find anything different about you in my memory archives than what they already have. And I have a kill pill, like the one Zade wears. I can stick it right onto my back molar. I can make it all stop whenever I need to."

"Used to wear." Simone's voice was hollow. "He stopped wearing it. For me."

"Oh. Did he now." Zoe looked at Simone's pale face, started to speak, and stopped herself. "Whatever. The house might have clues. Something that could lead me to them."

"Obsidian will lead you to them," Sisko said. "In chains. It's a fucking trap."

"So let me fall into it! Maybe I could see her, once I'm inside. Maybe I'll have a chance to talk to her. Besides, it's a done deal. Nothing changes for anyone if I go in, too."

"Like hell," Sisko growled. "It changes for you. It changes for all of us."

"Wait. You lost me." Asa held up his hand. "See who? Talk to who? What are you guys talking about?"

"Zoe's little sister," Sisko said. "She's still inside Obsidian. She never escaped."

"She was younger," Hannah said. "Even younger than me, so they sorted her into a junior group and sent her to another facility before the rebellion. She was nine."

"Not quite," Zoe said. "She had a couple of months to go. And she had a name."

"Jada," Hannah said softly. "We remember it."

"Hold on," Asa said. "I thought we were looking for Luke and Zade."

"We are, but Luke saw Jada, when he was fighting with them and he told Zade about it," Sisko said. "So Zoe's been in full blown freak-out mode ever since she heard."

Zoe made an impatient sound and stalked away, staring out onto the busy road that fronted the strip mall.

Asa grunted. "I wonder if there's anything left of her sister in the thing Luke saw."

Sisko grunted. "Don't let Zoe hear you say that."

"Too late," Zoe called. "I have augmented hearing. Fuck you both."

Zoe was posed against the roiling sky, hair flying like a banner. Wow. She was something else. He wondered if that glossy hair was as satiny as it looked. He wanted to wind some of it around his fist and find out.

Her attitude bugged the shit out of him. Her pain and tragedy and loss were all real, but life was never fair. It didn't care how much you suffered.

"The sister's not part of the equation," he said. "Keep it simple. This is about Luke and Zade. Never mind this Jada."

"Listen up, asshole," Zoe said. "She's my sister. And I'm going in."

"No," Sisko said. "You're following the doomsday plan like the others."

Zoe gave him an unbelieving look. "What? You mean we run for cover and just let them kill three of ours?"

"No," Sisko said quietly. "I'm just saying if anyone is going to walk into the trap, it should be me. Not you."

The rest of the group was shocked into a brief silence.

"Why?" Zoe asked. "Why you? What's the reasoning?"

"If Noah were here, he'd do the same," Sisko said. "It should be me. I'm the oldest."

"Bullshit," Zoe said. "We're all adults now. That's not relevant anymore."

"Zade's getting farther away from us while you argue." Simone's voice was tense.

"Listen, guys," Hannah said urgently. "Face it. The doomsday plan sucks. We never liked it. It was Noah's idea and Noah's a genius, but we can't do it to save our lives. Literally. We'll warn the out-of-towners so they have time to cover, but the present company stands together."

"OK, that's inspiring," Asa murmured. "So what's the new plan?"

Zoe turned her cold gaze on him again. "Step one, you go back home."

He looked at her calmly. "Nah. I'll stay and help."

"You can't help us," Zoe said. "You're an unmod. You're a liability."

"Zoe!" Hannah sounded scandalized. "That's not true."

Asa shrugged. "I'm less helpless than I appear."

"He saved our asses when Mark and his slave soldiers came after us," Sisko said. "You weren't there. You didn't see him fight. He can handle himself."

"And Brenner would be dead if not for him," Hannah said. "We would never have found Luke or known about Jada at all. So back the fuck off. You're way out of line."

Awww. How cute. Asa shot a fond glance at his little sister. He wished he could rake his hand through that tousled mane of blazing fake-red curls, but he figured he might lose that hand.

"You don't have to defend me," he told her.

"Actually, she will," Zoe said. "That's precisely the problem. She'll be distracted. Compromised. It could get us all killed."

"This may shock you, but some unmods can handle themselves in a crisis."

"Guess what, tough guy," Zoe said coolly. "Our yardsticks are different. You just don't measure up."

"Whoa." Asa refused to let himself smile. "Harsh."

"Don't be a cranky bitch, Zoe," Sisko growled.

"There's no time to be nice. We can't carry dead weight into battle."

"You don't have to," Asa said blandly. "My helicopter is currently on its way to the airport where we flew in. It'll be standing by for eventual emergency extractions. Brenner's piloting the copter. He's the rogue Obsidian operative who's alive because of me. In case you forgot that detail."

"Helicopter?" Zoe turned to Sisko. "Is he shitting me?"

"Nope," Sisko said evenly. "He has three. This one's the newest."

"And the biggest," Asa told her.

"OK. I get it. My cue to shut the fuck up," Zoe muttered.

"About fucking time," Simone snarled. "Zade posted the comment just a few minutes ago. He might still be nearby." She pressed against her eyes with the back of her hands. "Shit," she whispered to herself. "I do not want my last words to him to be so damn stupid. Busting his balls about being ready for the prom."

"The prom?" Sisko gave her and then Hannah a questioning look.

"Before Zade left," Hannah explained. "Product testing, remember? He bedazzled Simone and then got it on his jacket when he…oh. Simone, the glitter spray!"

Simone's eyes went wide with terrified hope. "You think…but it was only second hand. We didn't spray him directly. Would it register?"

"He double-dosed you and then he dragged you into a crotch-grinding face-sucking bear hug, so maybe. It's short range, but…Sisko, hurry! Get the laptop!"

Hannah and Sisko scrambled for the back of the Lexus. They started digging through their gear.

Asa watched, impressed in spite of himself. Had to hand it to them. Those Midlanders always had something else up their sleeves.

Curiosity eventually got the better of him. He peered over their hunched shoulders. From this angle, he barely saw a faint flickering blip on the screen. It came and went.

"There's a signal." Hannah's voice shook with excitement. "Faint. Heading south. Fifteen, maybe. Another mile and we'd have lost it. Come on! Move!"

"I'll drive with you," Asa told Zoe. "You shouldn't travel alone."

Yowza. If looks could kill he'd be gasping on the ground, choking his last.

"I prefer to drive alone." She turned to her Jag with a toss of her glossy hair.

Hannah shot him a warning look as he got into the driver's seat of the Lexus.

"Asa," she said. "About Zoe. It's a lost cause. And even if you won? That is trouble you don't need."

"Trouble pulls me," Asa said. "Why else do you think I hang out with you losers?"

Hannah propped the laptop on her knees, shaking her head. "Don't say I didn't warn you," she muttered. "Floor it."

CHAPTER 25

Light assaulted his eyes. Slicing in through his eyelids like a blade that jabbed his brain...and twisted. *Fuck.* Hurt so bad. Drug headache.

He forced himself to let more light in, peering through slitted eyes. He was pressed against a heavy wooden wall, with thick plastic bands over his body keeping him upright. He was poised on the edges of his feet, off balance. His muscles cramped and burned.

The auditorium was huge, dim and mostly empty. White spotlights blazed down right where he stood, illuminating a dais surrounded by chairs.

Zade was fastened to a wall at his right, apparently still unconscious, and just barely in his field of vision. He stared hungrily at his brother. Holy fuck, Zade had buzzcut hair. Unreal. They looked so alike now that Zade had sheared off his mane.

A big, heavy chair like a throne was positioned at his left. A bunch of white-coated types bent over a metal hibernation pod beside it, now open. All of the equipment he'd retrieved from Serrati Falls was arrayed around it.

They'd collected Ivy, too. Those fuckers moved fast.

Dani lay crumpled and forgotten on the floor, an afterthought. He ran the data on her that he could catch from where he was through his ASP. Low blood pressure, low temperature. She could have a concussion, hypothermia, shock. She needed medical attention, and he could not move a fucking muscle. Jesus, it had only been a few weeks and he'd already half-forgotten how it messed with his head to be stun coded. The soul shriveling, crushing frustration and humiliation of it.

And burning, killing rage. His temperature was rising.

Do something. Hack this place. Find a way.

He sensed the electromagnetic radiation in the air, the place hummed with it. But whatever drug they'd pumped into him screwed up his brain's ability to connect to his implants. He felt them buzzing in there, all powered up and ready, but the bridge just wasn't there. The connection had been severed somehow.

He heard footsteps and then a low, oily chuckle. He shifted his gaze to look at his captor, who now stood directly in front of him.

Luke dragged the name out of his disordered memory banks. Hale. That was what this prick had called himself.

"Trying to cyber-connect?" Hale asked. "I recognize the look on your face. My operatives get it too. But you blow them all out of the water." He shook his head in mock surprise. "We've never seen anyone so skilled. You're going to teach us how. Before we flush you."

Luke gazed around the room, looking everywhere but at the smirking scumbag in front of him. Fuck that guy.

Jada worked alongside the white-coated tech types. A swift ASP scan ascertained that of the people present in the room right now, only Hale and Jada were significantly enhanced. The others were just unmod grunts.

Hale followed his gaze and more or less read his mind. "You won't get a chance to fight. You and your brother are both stun-coded and drug-blocked. We're using a Braxton formula that disables the technokinetic connection. How's it working for ya? Wearing off yet?"

Hale blinked for a moment, as if waiting for Luke to answer.

"Guess I have my answer, D-14," he went on smoothly. "You'll be drugged even more during the interrogation, since you're the starring act in my big floor show. You and your brother are going to make my career."

Not if I can help it, ass face. He ached to spit the words out.

He focused in on Ivy's pod. The techs were pulling her out now. A puddle of hibernation fluid had formed around the pod. The little girl was limp and unconscious as they hauled her up onto a rolling table, threaded the probes and attached the sensors, arguing about what they were doing and how best to do it. He could only see her feet. Small and bluish. Ankles, shins, all skeletally thin. Fluid dripped steadily from the table to the floor.

"…dead?" One of them was asking another in a low, hushed voice.

"Don't tell me she's dead." Hale's voice got nastier. "Unless you want to join her in that state."

"No, sir. Just getting vital readings, that's all."

"Wake her up," Hale said. "The committee members arrive in an hour and I need her conscious. Zap her now. Make her presentable. That's an order."

"Yes, sir."

Luke fought for breath. He needed to damp down all non-essential functions so he could stay conscious on less oxygen. The trick was to not let himself panic. If he did, he passed out. Not an option. Not with his brother, the woman he loved and a victimized little kid laid out on the altar, waiting for him to think of something.

A shriek and then shocked, bewildered whimpering from Ivy hurt him inside. He knew exactly how that brain-zap felt.

A tech propped her up to swab the fluid off her body. The little girl was shivering. Her eyes looked bruised and shocked, uncomprehending. She didn't seem to see anything that was in front of her.

Then Jada appeared in his field of vision with a fleece-lined man's jacket and draped it over the little girl's shoulders.

"What the hell are you doing?" Hale snarled.

"Her temperature's falling, sir." Jada's voice was lower than Zoe's, and husky, as if she'd been coughing. "She could go into shock."

Hale scowled. "Only until the committee gets here. Then take it off."

"Of course, sir."

Dani was stirring. Moaning inaudibly. Luke strained to see her face, but the way he was positioned made it impossible to see above her waist.

"R-48!" Hale bawled out. "Get over here!"

Jada turned with a barely perceptible delay. When she approached, Luke was struck by her resemblance to Zoe. Similar haunting dark beauty. Her braided black hair revealed a geometric design on the skin of her neck. Looked like some kind of circuitry.

Her face was blank except for her trapped, burning eyes. She would not look at him. She had no expression on her face at all, yet she exuded misery.

"Yes, sir?"

Hale gestured at Dani. "Hold her up for me. I want to take a look."

Jada did as she was told, hoisting Dani's limp body up by the armpits. Hale tilted up her chin, then let her head drop as his hand wandered. And squeezed.

"Nice tits." He looked over at Luke with a grin. "And best of all, she's not an operative so I don't even have to be careful. With this bitch, I can let loose. Anything goes, because nobody cares."

Luke's ears were roaring. The data scroll was a frantic double-sided white stripe, a cascade of info on the quickest, ugliest ways to kill this sadistic motherfucker. Shoving his nose into his brain, reducing his trachea to jelly and watching his throat swell closed, smashing his ribcage and pulling out his lungs. Disemboweling him. Tearing his head off. It all worked. If he could use it. Which he couldn't.

"Take her to my rooms," Hale said to Jada. "Restrain her. Wrists to the bedposts. Then get into uniform and get down here. I want the new squads set up in formation behind the chairs. There's not much time."

"Yes, sir."

"Get a move on. Your reaction times are slowing and it's pissing me off."

"Apologies, sir," she said woodenly. "With your permission."

"Yeah. Go."

Luke tried to catch Jada's eye as she heaved Dani up over her shoulder with an ease that surprised even him.

She still refused to look at him as she carried Dani away.

Dani's head swung and bumped strangely. Blood pounded painfully in her head. She was staring down at somebody's upside down, gray-clad ass, and the moving heels of somebody's black boots. *Click, click, click.* It was so hard to breathe. Pressure on her belly. Something was squishing it.

She opened her eyes wider. Noticed the smooth black braid against her cheek. She was slung over someone's shoulder. Couldn't...*breathe.* She tried shifting, and the grip on her legs tightened painfully.

A pause, then a pivot, and the light brightened. They had gone through a door.

Swift movement left her dumped on her ass, pain shuddering through her sore joints, which hurt worse when those black boots kicked her into a kneeling position. The woman in gray who'd carried her reached down and pulled her hands up.

Click. Dani was shackled to a metal ring in the wall.

Hanging like that, twisting her upper body was agony, but she had to see the room. Just a narrow cot, a metal locker, a computer console. A chest of drawers. A cabinet, open, full of neatly folded clothing, towels and linens.

The woman was throwing open cabinets, pulling off her jacket. She changed her undershirt, put on deodorant, pulled a neatly ironed uniform out of the closet, laying it on her cot. Black, with green and blue piping.

Dani tried to make eye contact. Just in case she was dealing with a human being.

The woman just ignored her as she buttoned the uniform coat over her undershirt. She turned to a mirror framed with bright bulbs. She pulled makeup out of a drawer loaded with brushes, sponges, tubes and pencils, bottles, puffs and pats.

Dani hung there in captive misery. Forced to watch this crazy hellbitch fix her face while Luke was probably being tortured to death.

The woman applied a crimson lip stain, then opened another drawer, rummaging for nail polish and scissors. She shook a tiny bottle. Unscrewed the cap.

The sickly sweet smell of nail polish hit Dani like a brick, making her head throb and her stomach flop.

A plastic-lined container appeared under her face just in time. She emptied her guts into it. It went on and on. Her head felt like it would split with every heave. Finally, she just hung there from her ring, spitting bitter slime from her mouth. Eyes streaming.

The woman briskly mopped Dani's nose and mouth with a handful of tissues, dropped them into the container and tied the noxious mess off inside the plastic bag.

Maybe she was human.

The woman looked down at herself, turning her arms to inspect her sleeve. A careful glance in the mirror, turning to this side, then to that. Making sure she didn't have any vomit splatter on her nice uniform.

Dani focused closely on her face for the first time. Sweat shone on the woman's forehead. Her eyes were staring, her face so tense and taut.

Years as a nurse had sharpened her perceptions. She could tell when patients were exaggerating minor ailments to get attention, and she could tell when the proud ones were suffering the agonies of the damned but hiding it so as not to upset anyone.

This woman was suffering the agonies of the damned.

Suddenly she remembered Luke's phone conversation with his brother. *I saw Jada...she choked when she looked me in the eye, so I think she recognized me. On some level.*

Dani took a deep breath. "Jada," she whispered. "Help me."

The woman's reaction was sudden and violent. She recoiled with a gasp as if she'd been struck. "Shut up," she hissed.

"Jada, I'm with your old friends. They've been looking for you."

"No." Her voice was rising. "Shut up. No!"

"Luke and Zade? You remember them, right? From Midlands."

"I said to shut...*up!*" Jada whacked her across the face, hard enough to make her ears ring. "Not one more fucking word! Or I knock you out!"

Dani's head reeled. Her eyes swam as she watched Jada take a gleaming black helmet out of the cabinet. She fastened the chin guard, tucked hair wisps inside.

Then she pulled out a heavy belt, with a baton, pistols, an electric stun baton. Her red lips were tight, jaw taut as if she were fighting pain. Color had drained from behind her makeup, leaving a mask of paint. Her vibe seemed...familiar.

Dani understood. Stim sickness. Like Luke.

One last time. "Please listen," she begged. "Your friends—"

Her voice broke off into a gasping shriek of agony as the electric shock baton jolted electricity through her. Shattering, white-hot pain ...

It stopped and Dani sagged, hanging limply from the shackles. They cut into her wrists.

"I warned you." Jada's voice sounded dead.

She released Dani from the tethering ring, hoisted her up and tossed her over her shoulder once again.

Dani tried to remember the way. The turns, the stairs. Two flights of stairs and another long corridor. Jada paused, and she heard the click of a door lock.

From what Dani could see, dangling upside down, this room was very different, more like a luxury hotel suite. Jada carried her through a big living room and into a large bedroom, with a picture window that overlooked a river canyon. The sun was sinking, and the sky was streaked with lurid red-orange clouds.

She tossed Dani down onto a big four-poster bed, and brandished the stun baton, grim faced. Her forehead was shiny with sweat. Her mascara was running. Her eyes were wet. With tears.

"One word and I zap you." Her voice sounded hoarse and thick.

She grabbed Dani's wrist and jerked it up, twisting a thick zip tie around it.

Dani had learned to fight dirty very young. She'd perfected the skill in juvie and refined it at the Riplinger foster home. She had nothing to lose.

She looked up at Jade. "Zoe loves you," she said.

Jada froze, mouth agape. She stared at Dani, her face full of panicked confusion.

Dani wrenched her arm free, lashing the loose zip tie across Jada's eyes like a whip. She wrenched the stun baton from Jada's hand and jabbed it at her chest.

The long, buzzing zap blended with her own horrified shriek.

Jada arched back, choking—and slid heavily off the bed to the ground.

Dani stood there, disoriented. Her ears rang, her legs shook. *Move or die.* She moved, forming a plan out of nothing. Out of thin air and no alternatives.

Jada's boots. Too small but fuck it. She jammed them on. Dani ripped open the straps that fastened the armored vest, unbuttoned the uniform jacket with cold and clumsy fingers and yanked it off Jada's powerfully muscled shoulders. Pants next, a very tight squeeze. Weapons belt, fast adjustment.

Jada's eyes fluttered. Maybe she was cold. Nothing left on her but military-style underwear. Panic exploded in Dani's chest. She lunged with the baton and gave Jada another long zap, feeling fucking awful. This was not what she wanted to do or be.

She took one of the zip ties and threaded it through the bedframe, fastening Jada's wrists together and ratcheting the thing as tight as she had the stomach to pull it.

Then she stared down, her eyes watering. Jada's face was hot with fever and her eyes were glazed and unfocused. Her braid had come loose and was unraveling in ripples over her shoulders. She was muttering.

If she lived through the stim sickness, she was going to suffer for what Dani had done. But that wasn't Dani's fault. She hadn't started this fight.

But she was going to finish it. Or try like hell to.

The black armored vest barely closed. The rest of the outfit was way tight on her and the boots were pure, screaming hell but fuck it. No whining. *Go go go.*

She put Jada's helmet on but didn't fasten the strap. She looked down at the raised design on Jada's neck. Same as the one on the helmet. Silver, black, red. The slave soldier guys who helped capture her on the highway all had similar tattoos.

She was going to have to fake that part of the getup somehow. She glanced at herself in the big mirror that faced the bed. God, she looked like crap. Ashy skin, reddened eyes, colorless lips. She would fool no one looking like this.

She had to primp like Jada if she wanted to masquerade as one of them.

Jada was stirring and moaning under her breath. Some crazy impulse compelled her to kneel down next to the woman. It was sentimental, idiotic and dangerous, but screw it. This was who she was. It was all she had to work with.

"Jada," she whispered. "I'm so sorry. Know this. It's true that Zoe loves you. She never forgot you. She never stopped looking for you." She bent lower and kissed Jada on her damp forehead. "That's from Zoe."

She stumbled to her feet and backed away, trying not to cry. She'd expected Jada to headbutt her, smash her nose, bite her face. She'd expected to get sliced and diced in a lightning-fast scissor move between Jada's powerful legs. But she hadn't been.

Jada just stared up at Dani, a confused, vulnerable look in her fever-dazed eyes.

Dani fled, blinking away tears, and pounded toward the stairwell.

Two flights down, if she remembered right. Yes, here was the long corridor with the black speckled tiles and the fluorescent lights, but there were lots of unmarked doors. Not locked, thank God, but they were all dormitory cells, each identical to the next.

Dani looked for the room with a wastebasket by the door that held a tied-off plastic bag of vomit. She found it on the fourth try. Eureka. Her guiding star.

She dug through Jada's makeup drawer with feverish haste. The foundation was the wrong shade, but eyebrow pencil, liner, mascara and some bronzer blush helped. So did that crimson lip stain. Wow, potent stuff. Almost too attention-getting for her current situation. She didn't want to stop men in their tracks. She wanted their eyes to slide over her and keep on going.

Too late to fix it. This whole thing was a long shot, anyway. She'd take a run at it and hope for the best. She yanked open the nail polish drawer and rattled around until she found the colors she needed. Red, silver and black.

She stared at the helmet in the mirror and carefully tried to reproduce the pattern on her neck with nail polish. She had to swab off a few false tries with the nail polish remover, but the stuff went on in a thin line and dried fast, and she had a steady hand. It wasn't perfect, but it wasn't half bad, considering.

She used the hair dryer mounted on the wall to dry it and headed for the stairwell, wondering what in holy hell her next move could possibly be.

To start, she had to imitate the walk and talk of a woman who could break a guy in half with the greatest of ease. It was all about attitude. She summoned up some 'a that and kept going.

Fake it til you make it. She'd done it all her life.

She stopped in front of the elevator...and it slid abruptly open.

CHAPTER 26

"Goddamn it, Sisko, hurry," Zoe muttered.

"He is hurrying," Hannah said, an edge in her voice. "Leave him alone. He dives faster and farther than any of us do, so just shut up and wait already."

Sisko didn't respond, or even appear to hear them. He sat there in the back of the Lexus, laptop on his knees, eyes wide and completely blank. Deep in a data-dive for info on the building complex to which Zade's nano sparkles had led them. Public archives listed it as a research facility owned by Antares Tech, a company based in Southern California.

Asa never ceased to be startled by the shit this crowd could do. Hacking without hardware. Or rather, the hardware was already in their skulls, interfacing with their naked neurons. It creeped him out, but they seemed used to it.

Hannah had survived it, and so had Noah. Having siblings with superpowers complicated the family power dynamics, but fuck it, he liked a challenge. And he always held his own.

They were parked about twelve miles away from the place on a remote country road. Brenner was on his way with the helicopter. Zoe had parked her sleek Jag a ways back and joined them. Currently, they were huddled inside the SUV pondering their next move.

Finally Sisko's eyes opened. "Security is tight," he muttered. "Didn't get much."

"What did you find?" Zoe asked.

Sisko closed his eyes for a moment and nodded toward the tablet Zoe held. "Have at, people," he said. "Done and downloaded on all implants and linked devices. Building plans filed fourteen years ago. Building completed ten years ago. No idea if they're accurate."

Zoe, Simone and Hannah hunched over their various devices. Asa looked Sisko over critically. "I've seen you look less tired than this after battle," he commented.

Sisko grunted. "Battle's more fun," he said sourly. "At least you get the buzz. This is more like a disembodied mind-fuck. Playing ten games of 3-D chess at once. And the stakes are your best friends' lives."

Asa nodded, trying not to gawk at Zoe's elegant profile. No point. She stared fiercely down into her laptop. She was convinced that he was an unmod deadweight. Plus, she could probably snap him like a twig if he pissed her off. Which he would, of course. It was a mathematical certainty. He pissed her off just by breathing and existing.

Imagine what he could do if he applied himself.

He wrenched his gaze away from her. "You got a visual? In real time?"

"Satellite feed," Sisko replied. "Take a look." He held out the laptop.

"You can hack satellites with your mind? It's that easy?" Asa felt almost offended.

"Watch who you're calling easy. Hey, you guys." He looked up at Zoe, Hannah and Simone. "Take a look at this live feed."

Asa took the laptop. Sisko enlarged the image until it filled the screen and all of them bent over to peer at it.

"The place is swarming with people," Asa commented. "Looks like a convention."

"Of course," Zoe said grimly. "They've come to see the show."

"Three main entrances," Hannah murmured. "The front lobby, this one next to the dining hall, and around back where all these trucks are."

"Bet that's a shipment of weapons for the slave soldier reinforcements," Sisko said.

Asa studied the image. Each new batch of operatives had its own dedicated equipment coded specifically for their implants, and after the recent battle with Mark, Asa had ended up fielding a whole truckload of high-tech Obsidian weapons that psycho fuckhead had left behind. But since the gear only responded to Brenner, the Obsidian slave soldier they'd rescued and salvaged from that battle, the weapons were completely useless to the rest of them except for research purposes. They took up a crapton of storage space, but whatever. You didn't haul shit like that to the municipal dump.

"Could be weapons," Asa conceded. "Could be frozen broccoli florets, chicken tenders and hash browns for the cafeteria. Sometimes things are random and boring."

Zoe rolled her eyes at Hannah. "Is your brother always this annoying?"

"He's usually much worse," Hannah told her. "This is as good it gets with him."

Asa tuned them out and turned his full attention to the satellite image of the building complex. He manipulated the touch screen, zooming it out and catching a subtle flash of movement that quickly vanished. He zoomed in tighter.

"Look," he said, pointing to a steep, meandering canyon. The Antares Tech facility was built on a high plain which abruptly cracked into the canyon. The river running through it gradually widened out to a silted-up delta.

"What?" Hannah demanded. "What are you looking at?"

"You guys didn't see that truck moving, about four seconds ago?" He pointed to the canyon upriver. "See that line? That's an asphalt road. It was there. Going west, down into the canyon."

Sisko frowned. "Wait," he murmured, and his eyes went blank, inwardly focused.

Asa knew from his experience with Noah, Hannah, Zade and Brenner that Sisko was replaying a clip archived in his memory banks, stopping now and then to examine every pixel, metaphorically speaking. From the looks on their faces, Hannah and Zoe were doing exactly the same thing.

He and Simone exchanged rueful glances. The only two schlubs here with no cranial implants. Sometimes it felt lucky. Sometimes it didn't.

"I see it now," Sisko said. "The truck went in but it didn't come out."

"Any record in the blueprints of an elevator or stairway leading down to the lower canyon level?" he asked.

"Nope," Hannah said. "Not a thing."

"Look. There goes another one." Simone pointed.

The vehicle disappeared beneath the cliff overhang. They waited, but after several long moments, it still didn't reappear.

"There's an entrance there," Asa said. "Maybe it leads to a bolt hole, or a storage space, or an underground testing facility. A place to do unspeakable research where no one can hear you scream."

The Midlanders frowned at him.

"Is that supposed to be funny?" Zoe asked coldly.

"Nah, just thinking out loud," Asa said. "I vote for the canyon. There won't be as many people down there because of the circus upstairs. And they'd see us coming for miles away from all the other approaches. Plus, there's a place out here for the helicopter to land. Trees and bushes by the riverbed for cover."

A brief silence. "OK," Zoe said. "We go in at the canyon entrance. Hannah tries to communicate the plan to Zade and Luke. Brenner and Simone stand ready to extract. Everyone on board?"

Nods all around.

"Suit up," Sisko said. "Brenner will be here any minute. He's got the rest of the gear. Thermal camo for everyone." He looked at Hannah. "You ready to start messaging?"

"I need to get closer before I start jiggling the signal," Hannah said.

"Tell you what. You get as close as you need to be, and just stay right there with Zoe and Simone," Asa said. "Sisko and I will go in."

"Fuck that," Hannah said stonily. "Zoe and I both need to go in with you. Obsidian has their kill codes and Luke hasn't been scrubbed. The chances he comes through this thing without being coded are zero. We need Zoe there to help if his heart's stopped."

Asa looked around, lost. "What the fuck?" he asked Zoe. "Starting his heart? Are you a cardiologist, or a trauma surgeon, or something? I thought you were a chemist."

"I am," Zoe said.

Asa waited, but more was not forthcoming. "So? What's the deal?"

"She's a healer," Hannah said.

There was an uncomfortable pause. Zoe would not meet his or anyone's eyes.

"Healer," Asa repeated. "What, you mean, like...faith healer?"

"I don't have any faith," Zoe muttered. "I just sometimes...help people who are hurt or sick. I don't know how it happens. I can't explain it, and it's not reliable or controllable. Not at all. So don't ask. Because I genuinely don't know."

"She's a healer," Hannah said forcefully. "She doesn't want to be, but she is."

Zoe looked rebellious. "Whatever. I'm going in. My little sister's in there. You're the one who should stay back. You're an unmod. It's insane."

Asa nodded in Hannah's direction. "I have a little sister, too. She goes, I go."

"They'll rip you to shreds!"

He gave her a thin smile. "Bring it," he said.

Shit. Dani put on her best robot face. No time to retreat as a skinny guy pushing a big rolling luggage cart piled with identical silver travel cases shoved his way out into the corridor.

The second guy stepped out, face turned away, still complaining. "...their fucking beauty cases up to their rooms for them? Just because The Great Dickbreath himself wants them all in fucking formation in the auditorium to look good for the committee! So now we have to haul about two tons of their personalized weapons down to the cave from this level? Like, fucking *fuck,* man. If they'd just come in through the canyon road to begin with, we could have rolled it right into the cave with no trouble, but now we have to make sixty fucking separate trips with a fork lift to haul all their fucking shit down into the—"

"Stu," the other guy said, eyeing Dani. "Shut up. Company."

The guy stopped short and turned to stare at her. Big dude, double chin.

She gazed back. Her heart thumped so hard, those guys must be able to hear it.

"What the hell are you doing up here?" Stu asked. "You're a new one, right? I thought all you soldiers were supposed to be downstairs."

"Under orders. Prisoner transport." She kept her voice flat and clipped. "Hale wanted her confined in his room."

Stu laughed unpleasantly and exchanged a knowing glance with the skinny guy. "Yeah, he likes to school those bitches up close and personal."

"Good for him." The skinny guy heaved the rolling cart into the corridor and began tossing the metallic cases off haphazardly. "I'm leaving these bags right here. I don't do door-to-door baggage service for fucking cyborgs. They should be doing it for us."

He muscled the cart back into the freight elevator. The doors started to close, but Stu held them open, giving her a questioning look. "Coming?"

She gazed at him, panicking inwardly. "Ah..."

"I heard he wants you new ones all in the auditorium."

"Right." She wished she knew how operatives talked. Probably they didn't, unless questioned. And she hadn't counted on elevator scrutiny from interested men checking out her ass. Probably wondering why it wasn't more tight and toned.

"Jeez." The skinny one looked her over as the door slid shut. "Does he pick out you girls online somewhere or what?"

She was terrified of giving a wrong answer. "Huh?"

"Hale, I mean," he specified. "You girls are all so hot. He switches it up every time, you know? He got that black-haired one who looks Polynesian or something. Before that was the tall blonde with the big rack. Before that the redhead."

"Redhead didn't last long," Stu said. "Sam said he loaded her into the incinerator a few months ago. Couldn't tell what killed her, though."

"Guy's a goddamn pervert, if you ask me," the skinny guy muttered.

"Nobody asked you, Bailey," Stu said, eyeing her crotch. "But you girls don't mind, right? I mean, like, the operatives are programmed to just do what he wants, right? You're sexbots. You don't care. Do they program you to like it?"

"Shut the fuck up, Stu," the other guy muttered. "You're not supposed to—"

"Just asking." Stu waited for an answer, eyes hot with interest.

Wow. There were so many ways she could answer his question, and now was not the time to indulge in any of them. No matter how desperately this dude needed a lesson.

Dani gave Stu a secret smile. "Not exactly," she said throatily. "We're just programmed to kill, Stu. In fun, different, creative ways. The more blood, the better. The more pain, the better. And yes. We are programmed to like that. A lot."

"Ah." Stu blinked rapidly. "Yeah. Right."

The elevator opened onto an active loading dock. People shouting orders, pushing stacks of crates and cases. Bailey shoved out his rolling cart and another guy made straight for the elevator with a loaded forklift.

"Gotta get these down to the cave," the guy said. "Hold the door."

"One second," Stu said. "I'm taking her to the auditorium level. Be right back."

"Goddamn it, Stu! We don't have time—"

The elevator shut in his face. Just her and Stu, with the probing eyes and the dirty mind. Gross, but it hardly registered on the scale of her problems right now. The elevator labored downward.

"Better make sure they issue you a key card for the elevators right away," Stu advised her. "You'll need it for the doors, too. And if they send you down to get something in the cave and you can't use the elevator, it's, like, eight flights down that spiral staircase, and it's slippery down there in the cave. Floods all the time. Big pain in the ass."

"Got it," she said. "Thank you."

The doors slid open, and she stepped out into an echoing hallway that seemed empty. But someone could turn a corner any second and start asking smarter questions than these bozos. She needed to move fast.

She looked at Stu. "Which way to the auditorium?"

"Don't they download blueprints right into your head and shit like that?"

"Not yet," she said. "I'm a last minute reassignment."

Stu shrugged and pointed to the right. "All the way down and make a left. Then go through the double doors and you're there. Follow the noise. Big crowd today."

The elevator closed on his puzzled face, and Dani took off running.

CHAPTER 27

Something loud was going on outside of the protected space in Luke's mind where he was doing the analog build. Noise, agitation, movement. He needed to come to the surface and pay attention to it.

But he wasn't done. The analog had to be perfect. It was all he had.

Five more minutes would do it. *Rivers of lava. Trees burning like torches. Pits of fire. Volcanos exploding. Buildings ablaze.*

His body temperature was soaring. He wasn't trying to spike a fever, just fire up the furnace to metabolize the cyber-blocker faster than Hale anticipated. To grasp connectivity again. No clue what he'd do with it once he got it, but one thing at a time.

Hale's floorshow was about to begin and Luke was the starring act. Sensory info was starting to filter in. Something had been fastened around his head. Voices, talking. He heard Hale bellowing from far away. Felt blows, faintly. His face was being smacked.

One …more…goddamn…*minute.* Just one.

He charged the images with all the emotional energy he could summon, old and new. Ivy. They were putting a helpless child up naked on the block. Dani, shackled to that asshole's bed. Zade, who risked everything to come help him. *Baby brother.* Lightning bolts, jabbing deep, making the fire burn hotter.

A sting in his throat burned, like a wasp had gotten him. A stimulant drug. Fuckheads. It didn't seem to be affecting the accelerated metabolization of the cyber drug, but it was pulling him back up to the surface.

He opened his eyes to Hale's red face and screaming mouth and was weirdly happy to have pissed that prick off so much. Something was squeezing his head, heavier on one side than the other. Cool metal, sticky sensors. An elastic band around his scalp.

"…son of a bitch!" A head-rocking slap. Hale panted, hairy nostrils flaring, eyes wild with angry excitement.

"Calm down, Lewis," said a soft, cooing female voice. "The committee members are out there taking their seats and they can hear you through the curtain."

Luke's eyes finally focused enough to see the source of that voice. He was in a dim space behind a heavy curtain, but still strapped to the wall. Behind the curtain, he felt the energy and heard the low muttering and murmuring of a large crowd. A straining eye roll showed him that Zade was still next to him, in the same condition. Their eyes met.

The emotion from the contact sent energy searing through his analog. Many memories funneled into one crushing, overwhelming moment, like when Dani used the probe. He saw it all; his brother's eyes in the crib as he sucked on his bottle, his eyes from across the gym at basketball practice on the day their parents had been executed. His eyes at the Midlands lab when he was strapped down to the table.

"Just look at that, Oscar." The female voice again. "All that brain activity showing up on the monitor. You'd think he was playing a Bach fugue, solving calculus equations and engaging in pitched battle all at the same time."

"The stun code doesn't appear to slow down his mental function." A male voice.

"It might enhance it," the woman murmured. "And feel that, Oscar. He's radiating heat, as if he were running a marathon. I wish I could run some tests right now."

The woman next to Hale was maybe in her late forties, but she had that tight, stretched facial perfection that suggested that she was older than she seemed and carefully kept up, bony and sharp. Blood red lipstick, slicked-back blond bun, glittering eyes. Diamonds glinted in her ears. She wore a tailored black dress. Cold, angular beauty.

But the look in her eyes as she raked his body up and down was anything but cold.

He'd been lustfully checked out by women and men ever since he was eleven years old, but it was mega-disgusting while stun coded. Her long silver fingernails raked over his throat and chest.

"You're the one experiencing the heat wave, Sondra," the man chided. He was a guy in his fifties, with a narrow, fox-like face and rimless glasses. "Stop fondling him, please. It's inappropriate."

"Don't be a sanctimonious prig, Oscar. I was just assessing which of the subdermal implants he'd managed to remove himself. Quite a few. Impressive."

"We'll figure that out during the autopsy."

"Where's the fun in that? Don't tell me you wouldn't like to fondle him, too." Her hungry eyes drifted over his chest and belly, and lingered at his crotch. "You know what they say about Braxton's earliest batches. These two are the last of them."

"Yes, yes," the man said impatiently. "We've all heard the legends."

"And we have two of them." She shot her companion a teasing look and glanced in Zade's direction. "One for each of us. And we don't even have to share."

"Don't be ridiculous," Oscar muttered back. "They're too dangerous to play with. Put it out of your head and be good."

She sniffed. "You think I've advanced Obsidian's research and development by leaps and bound the past eight years by being good?"

"Where is that murdering sonofabitch?" A new voice, from the side, male and furiously angry. The man shoved Hale out of the way and leaned into Luke, bristling. "Is this the worthless piece of shit that killed my son?"

"This is the rogue operative D-14," Hale said stiffly. "And yes, he was involved in that event. I'm very sorry about what happened, Mr. Metzer. Rob was an exceptional—"

"Shut the fuck up. I am not in the mood for platitudes."

This guy was older, with heavy square features and curly gray hair. He looked ashy and unshaven and wild-eyed. He grabbed Luke's chin, his fingers digging in with crushing force. Nails slicing into his skin. "I'm going to tear you apart," he hissed.

Take a number, asswipe. Luke wished so hard to say it but he could only stare.

"Hush, Gerard," Sondra said. "I'm sorry for your loss, but control yourself. Do not mark him."

"Why? Because you want to fuck him, Sondra? I won't stand for it. No treats. This one is not going to become one of your kinky lab pets. This one dies screaming."

"He dies, certainly," Oscar said sternly. "But no one here indulges their baser instincts today. Do not make me raise my voice."

Oscar must have clout, since both Gerard and Sondra subsided. Sondra looked miffed and sulky. Gerard Metzer released his pincer grip but his mouth shook with rage. His reddened eyes rolled in his head. He stank of old alcohol.

Hale pushed his way back to the fore, rather clumsy in the narrow space. He appeared both nervous and self-important. "Mr. Mittwoch, Dr. Laera and Mr. Metzer," he said. "I'm honored to have you all back here, but I would have preferred to meet after my presentation, in a private room where we can take our time and talk more freely. My idea was to present the captured operatives to the committee first."

"Yes, we noticed that," Laera said. "I understand you wanting to make a fuss and show off, but we must assess them first. Do you have the control codes?"

"Of course," Hale said. "As requested."

"Very well," Mittwoch said. "Go ahead and proceed with your dog and pony show. But we would have preferred to be contacted privately before you organized it."

"But I—but the rogues are—"

"It's too late now, of course," Mittwoch said impatiently. "Go out, give them the sideshow they're expecting. And we'll take it from there afterward."

Hale blinked at him. "Take it from…you mean…you want to take—"

"The rogues? Yes, of course we do." Oscar Mittwoch gave Hale a thin, toothy smile. "From here on we'll do the heavy lifting. We'll eliminate one of them immediately. We'll sever the spinal column of the other one, debrief him here and kill him, too."

"But…but that's a waste! Mr. Mittwoch, please reconsider. I've initiated a plan to debrief them myself!" Hale's gaze darted frantically from Laera to Mittwoch and back again. "I have the experience to do it. And the new Manticore operative—"

"The little girl, yes. We'll take her as well," Mittwoch said. "I've already assembled a team for her. The labs at Urness Island are far better equipped to deal with her than you are here."

"In the meantime, for God's sake get some clothes on the poor little thing," Laera said. "She's no use to us if she dies of shock and hypothermia. And Lewis. Be reasonable. Two Level Twenty-fives? Please. You were never equipped to contain them here."

Hale's chest puffed up. "Our ranks got shredded from combat with the rogues!"

"No one is blaming anyone," Oscar Mittwoch said.

"I am," Metzer said harshly. "You got my son killed, you fucking moron."

"High-level agents tend to die quickly and often in your facility, Lewis," Mittwoch lectured. "You simply go through them too fast. Don't think we haven't noticed."

"But that's finished now! I just got two new squads of Level Fourteens today. They're out there standing in formation in the auditorium, at the ready, so you damn well don't need to question my ability to secure—"

"Fourteens aren't up to the task of securing those two rogues," Mittwoch said. "We'll have them reassigned. The operatives you've lost in just the past few days are worth hundreds of millions, Lewis. Do you expect a pat on the head?"

"I bagged two Midland rebels and a Manticore!" Hale's eyes bugged in outrage. "You got an excellent return on your investment!"

Laera's eyes rolled. "Yes, Oscar. He actually does expect a pat on the head."

Luke looked at Hale until the force of his gaze drew the man's attention.

Take that, you fuckstick loser. Right up the ass. Mods won't help you if you're a pea-brained asshole to start with. From Hale's face, he could see that the guy received the silent message. His face was beet red.

Luke channeled concentrated fury into the analog. It was starting to work. Burning away the fog that obscured his connectivity. He couldn't quite dig in and connect yet—but at least he could feel the waves around him.

Then he felt them stutter and cut out. The signal wasn't steady.

Luke exchanged glances with Zade. His brother's eyes were shouting, too, but Luke could not decode the message. Only feel the desperate, mortal urgency of it.

The signal stuttered again. And again. And again. In the same way. A rhythmic riff. He ran it through his ASP, analyzing the pattern.

It was one of the Midlanders' own codes. An upside down and inside out Morse code. The dot and dash sequences, but with a reordered alphabet.

He decrypted the message swiftly. **sw door...river canyon...230 feet down.**

The same message, repeated over and over. His people were outside, risking capture and death to help. Jesus. The stakes got higher every fucking second.

He looked at Zade, and hazarded using his eyelids, since their captors were so self-absorbed. Braxton had left out eyelids from the paralyzed muscle groups for the stun code, being reluctant to let multi-million dollar eye enhancements dry out. Communicating with them was noticeable and obvious, but it was all he had.

can u hear wifi

yes, Zade blinked back. **crazy freaks gtta luv em**
hang in there he blinked.
The look Zade gave him blazed with irony. **or what**
His baby brother. Smart-ass to the bitter end.
"Oscar, it's not strictly necessary to kill them now," Laera wheedled.
Mittwoch scowled. "Have you seen the videos? We're not prepared to contain these two, Sondra. For God's sake, am I the only fucking adult in this entire group?"
"It's not about that. It's just a shocking waste. The range of his abilities is astonishing. If we could just study—"
"We can't," Mittwoch said harshly. "Not safely. He's uncontrollable, Sondra. Even with his spinal column severed, it will be a risk to interrogate him. And two of them can pool their abilities and multiply the risk. Under no circumstances will I authorize it."
An aggressive sigh from Sondra. A vicious finger snap of frustration. "I'm fucking sick of playing it safe!"
"Remember what happened to Braxton," Mittwoch said.
"Braxton was a psychotic freak, Oscar. And this kind of passive, reactive thinking will drive Obsidian into the dirt!"
"But not off a cliff," Mittwoch said. "That's my goal, Sondra. Avoiding cliffs."
She snorted. "We'll debrief them, I hope? At least? We do want to locate all the other rebels, don't we? Or are we too afraid of them?"
"Watch yourself," Mittwoch said coldly. "You may debrief one. As agreed."
"But they're cyber-inhibited!" she protested. "We have their control codes! We can put them into pods for the debrief! We have the upper hand, Oscar, many times over!"
"So did Phillip and Jordan Holt. Who are now both dead."
"They were idiots!" she hissed. "And this is a tragic waste of resources. These Midlanders actually have the gene mutation that makes Braxton's extreme gene cocktail potentially viable again. They're worth whatever research and development will cost. They need to be thoroughly studied."
"We can study their corpses." Mittwoch turned to Hale. "Get on with it. The committee wants a show, and the slave soldiers can always use a reminder about what happens to rebels. Kill-code one of them during your presentation and we'll dissolve the other one's spinal column and debrief him immediately afterward. Are the meds ready, Sondra?"
"Yes." She was still sulking. "Which one do you want to kill first?"
Mittwoch shrugged. "It's all the same to me."
Metzer came closer, staring up into Luke's face. "Leave this one alive," he said. "I want quality time with him before you shred all his nerve endings." He leaned closer to Luke. "My son had a closed casket funeral because of you," he growled. "You're going to learn all about pain before we sever your spine."
"Stop it, Gerard," Mittwoch scolded. "We need his mind clear for the debrief, and his body intact for study. Watching his brother die and having the nerve toxin dissolve his spine will have to be enough punishment for you. Content yourself with that."

Metzer shook his head, muttering under his breath.

Mittwoch looked expectantly at Hale. "Well? Go on. Proceed."

Laera let out a petulant sigh and came up in front of Luke, loosening the band that held the monitor and sensors on his head. Her hands lingered on his face as she did so.

"Such a goddamn waste," she murmured, running her hand down his cheek, then petting his chest.

Then Metzer, Mittwoch and Laera sidled away behind the curtain to the wings, where they watched as Hale leaned close.

"This is for fucking with me and my operatives," he whispered to Luke. "You get to watch me kill code your brother and sever your spine. Consider yourself spanked, dickwad."

No no no no no. Not Zade. Fuck.

His brain flailed at its bonds. The fire inside him burned hotter and hotter. Lights blazed in his face as the curtain was pulled away to the swelling murmur of the crowd.

CHAPTER 28

Dani skidded to a halt when she reached the lobby outside the closed doors of the auditorium. She tried to walk normally through the double doors, struggling to catch her breath. This place would be full of people capable of hearing her heartbeat and measuring her blood pressure at a glance, for fuck's sake. All she could do was hope like hell they'd all be concentrating real hard on something else.

Except that the something else was most likely to be Luke, Ivy or Zade.

She saw security guards posted at the far end of the large lobby, underneath a vaulted ceiling and sky-lit dome. She'd emerged inside of the security perimeter, evidently.

Lucky. She'd take luck wherever she found it.

She slipped inside the doors, letting her eyes adjust to the darkness. The space was packed full of people. Spotlights blazed down over a raised platform, and Hale stood on it, in front of a hanging curtain, his harsh voice blaring into the microphone.

Ranks of soldiers stood behind the seating, dressed just like she was except that their uniforms fit perfectly. Hale was droning on about how proud he was to be the one to revolutionize the next wave of exploratory research, paving the way for future yada yada.

She moved forward and took a spot next to a soldier in the back row, a tall black guy. He gave her a swift, penetrating look. The frown of perplexity that appeared on his brow scared the shit out of her. The guy had her number in one single freaking glance. So much for her disguise.

"Lock in," he whispered.

Dani looked up at him, all innocence. "What?"

"Lock in," he repeated. "I can't access your data. I can't reach you at all."

"Oh," she whispered. "Ah, yeah. That. I'm having connectivity issues."

His eyes widened. "You're fucking nuts," he hissed. "They catch you out here in service without connectivity, they'll recondition you right up the ass!"

"It's OK," she whispered. "Hale told me to come out anyway, just to help fill out the audience. He knows about it."

The slave soldier's puzzled frown deepened. "What's your ID number? I'll try to boost you in remotely before anyone notices."

"Thanks, but I'm authorized. I'm covered. Really. It's cool."

His gaze dropped to the symbol on her neck, and she pivoted swiftly away to hide it. She gave him a grateful smile and slithered back behind the line of uniformed soldiers. Some swiveled their heads to follow her progress.

Whoa. Close call. Nice of him to try to help, though. Kindness was a problem she hadn't anticipated.

"…ladies and gentlemen, I present two Midland Rebels from the flagship Braxton study group!" Hale paused for effect. "*And* a live and fully functional Manticore operative!"

The curtains parted behind him, and the murmur of the crowd swelled as the prisoners were revealed.

Zade and Luke stood rigidly, naked to the waist and held against a white wall with thick black straps across their chests to keep them vertical. Ivy was slumped in a big chair, her skinny shoulders and spine painfully obvious, wires coming out of the ports and shaved patches of her scalp.

Dani took her place at the other end of the line. This time, the young soldier next to her didn't notice her at all, just watched as if he was frozen. Except for a twitching muscle in his jaw.

It suddenly occurred to her what this spectacle meant for the soldiers. The Midland Rebels were legends for these poor guys. A fantasy of escape and freedom, crushed before their eyes. They were watching the public destruction their most secret dream.

Which was why none of them noticed her edging slowly forward.

All the way to the front ranks. She couldn't take her eyes off Luke. The pain in his face burned her inside. She was afraid to breathe. The release code she had overheard Hale say to get Luke into that coffin-like transport container was all she had. That, and her own nerve. Her guts churned. Her heart pounded wildly.

Hale's speech blared out of the speakers, drilling into her ears. "…terrible loss to the Obsidian community. Junior Squad Leader Robert Metzer's leadership potential and dedication was evident at an early age. We are devastated by his loss—but justice will be done. We have captured the operative responsible for Robert Metzer's death."

The smattering of applause grew louder as Hale savored it.

"Not his first atrocity," he continued, lowering his voice dramatically. "Both of these rogue agents participated in the Midlands Rebellion, the darkest moment in Obsidian's history. Thirty-four researchers and administrators died in the massacre and the firestorm that followed."

Hale paused for a moment as the crowd's murmur swelled excitedly.

"What I am about to do may seem shocking, and may be difficult to watch," he went on. "But we at Obsidian are accustomed to facing harsh realities and difficult truths. With great power comes great responsibility. Therefore, for the savage crimes committed against Obsidian staff so long ago, and for the murder of Junior Squad

Leader Robert Metzer, Obsidian declares that these rogue agents will be put to death. One dies now, the other immediately after interrogation. Their deaths will be swift and painless, because Obsidian always seeks to uphold the highest values of rational civilization…truth, justice and mercy."

The fuck it does, you violent asshole. The crap he was spouting was obscene. And in front of a bunch of slave soldiers, too. How could he not choke on his own words?

Hale's face was solemn as he stopped in front of Zade, but Dani was just close enough to see the gloating triumph in his eyes and the desperation in Luke's. *Now.* She inhaled to scream out Luke's control code—

And was jerked backward, a hand clamped over her mouth with savage strength.

"May God have mercy on your soul!" Hale bawled. "Mustang! Cameo! Stamen!"

Zade's eyes rolled up. The tension in his body released.

He sagged forward against the straps that held him to the wall, head drooping.

Oh no no no. Dani struggled wildly against the arms that were clamped around her, tears streaming from her eyes. This couldn't be happening. It couldn't be over just like that. Luke's beloved brother, slaughtered just for spite. *No.*

"Shut up, you dumb bitch or you'll get us all shredded," a slave soldier hissed into Dani's ear. "He's meat. It's done. Get your shit together or I'll flag you myself."

Hale turned back to his audience. "We will now administer two injections to the remaining operative," he boomed out. "The first is a nerve toxin that will dissolve neural connections in the cervical spine. The other will prepare him for interrogation. Afterward, he will be kill coded. D-14, for the sake of your conscience, I hope the gift of your body to science will in some small way atone for your sins." He gestured to the side of the stage. "I now invite Committee Chairman Oscar Mittwoch and Dr. Sondra Laera of Research and Development to do the honors. Chairman? Doctor? Would you come forward please?"

After a brief pause, a skinny blonde with a peeled onion hairdo, wearing a little black dress and spike heels sashayed out onto the stage with a brightly lipsticked smile on her face. She lifted a tray with two syringes on it.

The blonde set down the tray and took a syringe. She gave the other to an older man who'd followed her out.

The two of them advanced on Luke. Predators circling their prey.

Kill kill kill kill kill.

The ASP battle imperative raged unchecked as Luke stared down at Zade's lifeless body. No breath, no heartbeat. His brother was dead.

The heat inside him surged. He would rip them to shreds. All of them. Starting with his brother's murderer and ending with the sadistic assholes enjoying the show.

The firestorm analog in his mind no longer needed to be stoked. It raged on its own with terrifying force.

His cyber-connectivity was back. Moments too late to help Zade, but he was going to death-hack the living shit out of every brain here with a cerebral implant. Fuck them up hard.

He barely heard Hale's blathering, his mind furiously busy finding and exploiting security weaknesses in every device in his range. Mittwoch and Laera both flanked him now, holding up their needles.

"I suppose I should ask if you have any final words, but I'm not about to release you to let you say them," Mittwoch murmured. "Not until you're a quadriplegic. Dr. Laera, proceed with the nerve toxin. Let's get this over with. I find this spectacle distasteful."

Laera leaned close so he could smell her acid sweat and stifling perfume, see the red lipstick bleeding through the tiny lines at the edges of her collagen plumped lips and the mascara clumped on her lashes.

She whispered in his ear, her breath hot against his neck. "I can see how proud you are. How strong. I admire that. You're a magnificent specimen. I bet I can guess what your last words would be. You'd say, fuck you. So I'll just imagine you saying it tonight…while I'm touching myself. Bye-bye, D-14."

The needle came up, resting against his spine, barely pricking his skin.

Dani's voice screamed out something. Three words. He couldn't hang onto them with his conscious memory, but stun-coded muscle tension suddenly released.

He exploded into action. Burst out of the thick bands bolted to the wall. Hoisted Sondra Laera up and hurled her across the room. She landed hard, somersaulting, shrieking. Shoes flying, skirt flipped up, showing the black gartered hose on her pale, bony thighs.

Mittwoch stumbled back, hands up, eyes filled with fear. Luke grabbed him and flung him right into a dense mass of spectators. There was a commotion. Screams, wails.

His battle yell fused with a piercing electronic scream. His firestorm fueled it like a nuclear furnace, his release code had unleashed it, and now he let it blast through everyone's cerebral implants, far more powerful than the scream that broke his blocked memories open the night before. Raw fury unleashed.

A monumental electronic *fuck you.*

Pandemonium. Everyone screaming, staggering. Buckling, falling to their knees. Blood streaming from noses, ears. Committee members and slave soldiers alike. Convulsing, jittering and writhing on the ground.

A female slave soldier was running straight at him. His body snapped into instant defensive motion.

"Luke!" she yelled. *Dani.* That was her, wearing a slave soldier uniform.

He reeled, barely stopping a kick that would have snapped her neck. "Dani!" he rasped, stumbling. "I almost killed you!"

She barreled into him, clutching him. Soaked with sweat, vibrating with emotion. "But you didn't. Let's get the hell out of—"

Hale bellowed something he couldn't make out, and then—

Crack. Grunts, gasps…a snarl of rage. Luke spun around. *Zade?*

Yeah. Zade. Alive, on his feet and fighting with Hale. Zade was trying desperately to keep that motherfucker from shouting out the rest of Luke's kill code. Zade was on top right now, his hand in Hale's screaming mouth, trying to break Hale's jaw.

Somehow, Hale bit down hard. Blood poured down Zade's arm as he dragged up Hale's head, pulling against those teeth—

And smashed his head down onto the hard tiles. Again…again…again.

Zade hunched over Hale for a bare second, then staggered to his feet, cradling his bloody, mangled hand. Eyes wild. "Luke?" he asked. "You OK?"

Luke gasped for breath. "Dude. The *fuck?*"

"Later," Zade said, scanning the place.

Chaos. A female committee member in a silky dress thudded to her knees and vomited, then collapsed on the floor at their feet, shuddering and foaming at the mouth.

Slave soldiers staggered upright. Two, then a third. A fourth. Tough bastards, even with blood streaming from their noses, their ears. One took aim at Luke, but stopped when his gun jammed. Luke's electronic scream had shorted out their weapons interfaces.

A fifth joined them, wiping blood from his eyes. They flung the rifles away. Pulled out stun batons, clubs and knives. Advancing.

He shoved Dani behind him. "Get Ivy. We got this."

Almost dark. Asa hadn't put on the infrared specs yet. He was the only one who needed them, since the others had their eye implants. It was pure chance that he heard the faint rattle of sliding stone, the soft thud. He turned to look behind him.

Hannah was down. Sprawled on the rocks. What the *hell* …?

He ran back to her and pulled down the infrared goggles, peering farther into the gloom. Spotted Sisko and Zoe not far away. Both of them also flat on the ground.

He kneeled next to Hannah. Blood streamed from her nose. She was shaking violently, back arched, eyes rolled back.

"Hannah!" he called. "Hannah? Wake up! Talk to me!"

She didn't hear him. Couldn't see him. He put his fingers to her throat. Her pulse was weak, erratic. Holy shit. What *was* this?

He grabbed the comm device Sisko had given him. "Brenner! Simone! Come in, Brenner! Brenner! I got a situation here!"

There was a burst of static, and a long pause. Simone's voice, tight and tense. "Simone here. Brenner's down. Bleeding from his ears. Don't know why."

"They're all down!" he said.

"Got it. I'll take the chopper to location two, as agreed and set down there."

Still a novice pilot, but she was all they had. "You've got my location on the monitor?"

"Yes. I'll get to you as soon as possible. Brenner's starting to move again. Thank God."

Sisko rolled with difficulty onto his back, coughing. "Fuck me," he muttered.

Zoe was stirring, too. Struggling to sit upright, every movement slow and faltering.

"What just happened?" Asa demanded.

Sisko put his hand to his head, wincing. "Implants," he said. "Somebody pulsed a bad freq through our implants. Real brain-fucker."

Asa looked down at Hannah. Not moving. Still out of it. "She's not waking up," he said. "She's not moving at all."

"It was worse for her," Sisko said softly. "She has more hardware in her skull than the rest of us."

Something inside Asa went into free fall. "Is she...will she ..." His voice trailed off. He couldn't put it into words.

"Don't know," Sisko said.

Zoe crawled over to them, coughing out dust. "Oh, no," she croaked. "Hannah?"

Asa put his fingers to her throat again. "Her pulse is still weak," he said.

Zoe wiped blood from her mouth and chin with her sleeve and put both hands on either side of Hannah's head. She closed her eyes.

The utter silence that followed freaked Asa out. "Hey," he snarled. "Not now. That's not going to help her. What's the matter with you people?"

"Shut the fuck up, Asa. Let her do her thing."

The hard note in Sisko's voice was unmistakable. Asa shut up.

Agonizing seconds ticked by. Pulling him, one after the other, into a future he didn't want to face. One where he'd found his little sister after all those empty years, and then lost her again, Whoosh, gone.

After what seemed like forever, Zoe let out a long and ragged sigh. "OK."

"What do you mean?" he demanded. "She hasn't moved!"

"She'll be OK," Zoe said. "Hannah's tough. There was damage, but she'll pull through. But she won't be conscious for a while. We have to get her somewhere safe."

Asa held Hannah's limp hand as he looked around the dark, rocky canyon. "Meaning out of here."

"Ya think? Yeah, take her back to the helicopter," Sisko said. "You too, Zoe. If this mission tanks, get the hell out. And get Hannah and Zoe and Simone and Brenner to safety."

"I'm going on with you," Zoe insisted.

"No. Healing exhausts you," Sisko said. "And you got burned by the bad freq. Don't be an idiot." Sisko heaved himself to his feet. Then he stumbled, falling heavily to his knees again.

"You're both idiots," Asa growled. "You can barely walk."

Zoe looked at him. It occurred to him that this was the first time they'd made eye contact when she didn't have that guarded, hostile look.

"We can't just abandon them," she said softly.

Asa sighed and got to his feet. "I'm on it," he said grimly. "I'll find the canyon entrance. I'll keep you posted on the comm. You two get Hannah back to the chopper."

"But you're alone," Sisko said. "I can't let you—"

"Nobody 'lets' me do anything. You're wasting time. Zoe can't help Hannah back to the chopper alone. Get moving. Go!"

"Yeah." Sisko looked miserable. "I'll come back as soon as I can."

"Do that," Asa barked. "Now move!"

He waited until Zoe and Sisko lifted Hannah together and set off back the way they came. Both still staggering themselves. What a clusterfuck.

He put on the infrared specs and slunk onward through the scrubby cover of the trees. Trying not to see Hannah's deathly pale face in his mind's eye.

Typical of the Midlander crowd to pick the middle of a deadly dangerous rescue extraction to demonstrate to him the physical limitations of their invincible freak squad. Leaving him to cover for them when their heads were monumentally messed up.

While they were his wounded baby sister's only protection.

CHAPTER 29

Just like old times.

He'd died and gone to combat heaven. His brother, fighting with him back to back. Knowing each other's thoughts, moving like a single being. The way they fought on the streets before Braxton bagged them. The way they fought on rebellion day.

No time to think or reminisce. Kick and block, punch and twist, lunge and spin. Luke grabbed a baton before it bashed in Zade's head, wrenched it away and crushed someone's throat with it all in the same move. Zade blocked kicks and punches and knife thrusts, blood spraying from his bitten hand. A slave soldier leaped on Luke's back, zapped him with a stun baton and brought him to his knees. Zade charged him from the side, breaking the baton zapper's neck with a vicious twist as they hit the ground together.

And that was the last of the ones with any fight still left in them. Luke staggered to his feet, looking around the room for more opponents.

Dani. She was running toward him, Ivy in her arms. Zade brandished a knife—

"No! Not her!" Luke yelled. "That's my girlfriend!"

"Whoa," Zade lowered the knife. "Sorry."

"You stay ahead of her, I'll go behind." He herded Dani before him, wishing he could take Ivy from her arms, but not yet. He needed to stay on guard, weapons at the ready. "Zade, what the fuck?" he said as they ran toward the exit. "He kill coded you!"

"Simone fixed it," Zade led the way, stepping over sprawled bodies on the floor. "Told you she was smart."

"But your heart stopped! I listened for it!"

"New trick." Zade shoved the auditorium door open. The guards at the entrance were on the ground like the others, shocked and disoriented. "I dropped real fast down into hibernation mode the second he coded me. Slowed my heart way down, but didn't stop it. Scared ya, huh? Sorry."

"Catch up later, guys," Dani said grimly. "Let's scram."

"Right. Got a message from our people," Luke told her. "River canyon, southwest entrance, lower level—"

"I know where that is," Dani broke in. Come on!"

She took off running. Zade and Luke gave each other a startled glance, and followed her.

Ivy's gaunt face was expressionless, her eyes clouded. Blood trickled from her nose and ears.

Just live, little girl, Dani thought. *Just live. We'll take it from there.*

She held the child closer and murmured in her ear, wondering if she even spoke English. "Hey," she whispered. "Me and my friends are trying to get you away from the bad people, and you have to hang on tight. Arms around my neck. Can you do that?"

Ivy trembled when Dani stopped. Then her arms slowly reached up, encircling Dani's neck. Her thin legs wrapped around Dani's waist. Squeezing. *Yes.*

"Great job," Dani huffed out, breathless. "You're an awesome kid. So brave."

She led Luke and Zade straight back to the elevator where she'd met Bailey and Stu. The stairwell door next to it was locked. *Shit.*

The elevator light was lit up as it rose from below. "Just a second, baby," she murmured to Ivy. "Hang onto my friend here. I gotta try something." Dani pulled Ivy's arms from her neck and held her out to Luke.

The little girl looked up at him with wide, startled eyes. Luke hung the knife handle through the belt loop on his jeans and took her carefully, cradling her in his strong arms. So gentle.

Dani pulled her gaze away with difficulty as she sprinted for the elevator. No time now to get gooey, but damn. From raging warrior to real man. In a single heartbeat.

She skidded to a halt right as the door opened. A forklift emerged from it.

As luck would have it, it was Stu again. He gawked at her, surprised. His forklift stopped halfway through the elevator door, holding it open.

"Give me your keycard, Stu," she said briskly. "On the double."

He didn't do shit. Just stood there, eyes popping, mouth open. Blocking them.

She hated to be the hag from hell, but whatever. Up came the stun baton, right to his throat. A long, hard *buzzzzz.* Stu went down fast, gurgling.

She wrenched the lanyard off his neck and ran back toward Luke and Zade with her prize. "We're taking the stairs," she said breathlessly. "They all hate the stairs. Fewer people."

She swiped the keycard through the lock. It flashed green and the door popped open. A light on a sensor snapped on, revealing a rough tunnel of blasted rock and a heavy steel staircase spiraling down into the darkness below.

Dani moved to go first, but Zade held out a hand and swiftly went ahead into the dark. Luke was last. Ivy seemed even smaller huddled against his big torso. Her eyes had closed, as if she didn't have the strength to keep them open.

The descent seemed endless. Sensors flipped lights on and off as they went, a weak bubble of light following them down…and down. Water trickled over the rocks around them. The stale air was heavy with the smell of mud and mold. The silence was deadening.

The staircase ended at the jagged opening to a cave, lit only with a single bulb that sent flickering shadows moving over strange mineral formations that filled the huge cave. A huge, lumpy stalactite hung down from above, blocking the passageway further on. All Dani could see was a faint, winding path leading deeper into treacherous blackness.

At one side of the cave, a cinder block wall had been built, and in it was a huge armored door.

"I smell fresh air," Zade said. "There's another opening somewhere."

Good to know, but she didn't like the wide foot plank that descended into the water, submerged by an underground flood. The faint light from the stairway cast an ominous glimmer over the oily black water.

It was undoubtedly deeper than it looked.

Zade waded right in, all the way to the middle. Dani watched with dread. The water came up above his waist.

He turned back to them. "Pass me Ivy," he said to Luke. "You help Dani."

Luke waded in. Zade reached out for Ivy. The poor kid shrank away from him.

Dani was about to tell Luke she didn't need help when a huge dead weight hit her from above, knocking her backward. Going down, a huge splash—

"Calliope! Banner! Ibex!" Hale screamed the words out.

The water swallowed her.

CHAPTER 30

Someone dragged her up by her body armor. Dani gasped and choked, coughing up weird-tasting water. A blade stung her throat, breaking the skin. A heavy arm crushed her ribcage. No air. Lungs burning.

Hale. That bastard.

She blinked the water out of her eyes, sputtering. Luke and Zade stood, motionless. Zade had both arms wrapped around Ivy, his big hand cupping the back of her dark head. As if trying to shield her.

"Say one word of his release code and this bitch dies, you piece of defective shit," Hale said to them. "So you beat the code, huh? You thought you won? Your kill code was a dud, but what about his? Let's try it right now."

"Fuck you!" Dani yelled. "You sadist motherfucker! Shut up!"

"Trapezoid! Acorn! Albatross!" Hale screamed out Luke's kill code over Dani's bloodcurdling screech of protest, digging his knife deeper into her throat with each word.

Luke's eyes locked with hers for one timeless instant—and then he crumpled, sliding into the dark, gurgling water. It closed over his head.

"No!" She struggled wildly, heedless of the knife.

"Your turn, bitch," Hale spat out. "My operatives will put down this bad dog and take the Manticore girl. All the trouble you caused is coming right out of your skin, you stupid cunt. Since everyone else will be dead."

The huge metal door in the cave wall swung wide. They turned and saw a figure stumble forward, backlit by the fluorescent blaze of hanging lights in the warehouse space behind her.

Jada.

Barefoot, black hair hanging loose and wild. Wearing only a blood-drenched undershirt and panties. An automatic rifle with a long clip was slung over her shoulder, and she held a crossbow in her hands. Her face was streaked with blood. Nose, ears, even her eyes ran with bloody streaks like tears. The front of her shirt was soaked in red.

"R-48!" Hale yelled. "Kill him! But don't hit the Manticore!"

Jada's crossbow swung up. Dani yelled out a shriek of agony as the knife dug into her throat. Hot blood gushed down her neck, soaking into her shirt. "Jada! No!"

A wet *thunk* ...

The vise grip around her ribs loosened. Hale's knife splashed into the water.

His thick, massive body sagged heavily against hers, bearing her down into the water beneath him. Again.

Dani struggled out from under his dead weight and shot up into the air, sputtering.

Hale's body was half submerged. The bolt of a crossbow protruded from his throat.

She dove back in, right where Luke had gone down, groping around in the liquid blackness down there among the huge, tumbled rocks until she found him. It was so hard to get a grip on him. He was huge, wore no shirt, had no hair.

She got her arms beneath him finally, trying to hoist him up, but he was so damn big, and *fuck,* now she needed air...had to breathe ...

She came up gasping. Found Zade in the water with her.

"Take Ivy, quick," he said. "I'll pull him out."

Dani seized the shaking child, hugging her tightly as Zade dove into the roiling dark water. He emerged moments later with Luke's dripping body in his arms.

Zade carried his brother to the far side and laid him on the rocks, his legs still dangling in the water. Dani set down Ivy next to him and mumbled a few soothing words to the child as she and Zade started on the CPR. Compressing Luke's chest in a steady, lifesaving rhythm, doing mouth to mouth, alternating.

She swallowed back her tears as they kept at it. Pumping harder. She gave him her last breath and changed places with Zade, trying not to let herself sob.

After several minutes of that, Zade looked up at her, his eyes bleak.

"We should keep at this," he said. "But they're coming for us. I can hear them getting closer. We go now or we go never."

Her throat clutched. "Fuck," she whispered, but her hands couldn't seem to stop with the compressions. She looked back at the door to the warehouse.

Even she could hear them approaching now.

Zade was waiting for her nod. She drew in an agonized breath...and gave it.

Zade lifted Luke up, loading him over his shoulder. Dani struggled to her feet, lifting Ivy with numb arms.

They turned to Jada, still slumped on the ground in the doorway to the warehouse, dragging in harsh, raw breaths.

"Come with us," Dani said impulsively. "You can't stay here now."

Jada glanced behind herself and shook her head. "Can't walk." Her voice was hoarse and halting. "Too late...for me."

"Try," Dani urged. "I'll help you, if you can just stay on your—"

"Follow the water." Jada forced the words out. "Hurry. They're coming."

Zade shook his head and turned, heading into the blackness between the huge tumbled boulders. "Stay close to me," he said. "I can see in the dark. Let's go."

Dani hugged Ivy close as she backed away, tears still streaming from her eyes. "Jada, please," she begged. "Come with us. They want you back. They miss you."

A sad smile briefly curved Jada's mouth. She set aside her crossbow, touched her mouth and blew a kiss. "For Zoe," she whispered.

Then she swung up the automatic rifle and aimed it at the giant mineral formation hanging over the sinister dark pool.

"Run! Now!" she yelled.

Jada waited until Dani stepped further into the dark, and then emptied the clip, a long, punishing *rat-tat-tat-tat* that echoed through the cave. The big stalactite blew apart and crashed down into the pool in huge chunks. Blocking the walkway, blasting water everywhere.

They made their way through the damp, stifling blackness. Dani tried to stay close to Zade, feeling her way through jagged clefts in the stones. Ivy wound her arms tightly around Dani's neck again, and thank God for the kid's strong grip, because she kept tripping and stumbling in the utter blackness, straining to see Zade leading the way.

Ahead was the faintest bit of light, or rather, a lesser grade of darkness. Finally she could see Zade against it, hunched over. Luke's limp body loaded onto his back.

Ivy. Think about Ivy now. All you can do. One foot in front of the other.

She hugged the little girl tighter with one arm, and felt her way through the rocks like a blind woman with the other. Suddenly, fresh air. A cool breeze dried her wet eyes.

She looked up…and saw the stars above her.

Gunfire. Sharp bursts, cracking and whining against the rocks.

They scrambled for cover behind big boulders by the canyon wall. A punch to the back knocked her violently forward against a huge boulder. She'd caught a bullet with the body armor.

She braced herself on the rocks, clutching Ivy, who made no noise at all. Dani put her mouth to the little girl's ear. "Hey," she whispered. "Honey? You OK?"

A tiny whimpering noise. *Yes.* The kid was still there. Still hanging on.

"Zade! About fucking time." A low voice from across the canyon startled her.

"Who's there?" Zade hissed. "Is that Asa?"

"Yeah, it's me. Luke?"

"Kill coded. The rest of them?"

"Got fried by a bad frequency. Had to retreat. I'll tell them you're coming. Go around the bend, stay to the right. Long straight stretch on the riverbank. Where the bushes stop, stay down until the chopper comes for you. Run like hell. I'll cover for you. Go!"

They did. Gunfire hissed and whined all around them, zinging off the canyon walls. At one point Zade's stride hitched. He stumbled, limping.

"You hit?" she asked.

"Just run," he huffed out. "Go, go, go!"

They heard the rhythmic *whump-whump* of the helicopter, and then it was all a confusion of noise and wind, yelling, more gunfire.

Someone pulled Ivy from her arms. She saw the little girl's mouth open in a wail of pure panic but couldn't hear the sound over the roar of the helicopter. People hoisted her up. By her arms, under her ass. She tried to help them, but her arms and legs no longer responded. Too much screaming that didn't make sense. Couldn't make out a damn word.

Luke lay on the floor beside her. A dark woman was crouched over him, her eyes closed, face intent. Hands resting on his bare chest. She looked like Jada. *Zoe.*

Luke looked still and cold. She couldn't reach him. She was lost in the dark and the noise and the space between her and Luke was getting wider.

They were drifting farther and farther apart into the darkness.

Asa raced back after them, staying low and going on instinct, ducking the occasional bullet that whined past his cheek or over his bent head. The body armor was taking a real pounding.

But fuck it. He deserved to be shot. For pure stupidity for agreeing to this. Mostly because—*zinggg,* another near miss—he didn't want to disappoint his baby sister. Wanted to make up for abandoning her. *Zannng...*a bullet hit the rock face inches from his face, stinging him with flying fragments. He kept running, blood streaming down his face.

Like he could ever make up for that.

But he was going to punish those bastards for hurting her and Noah. One way or another, they were all going down.

The chopper was hovering, Sisko at the open door, throwing down a rope ladder. He leaped for it, stretching out, and was lifted in a long sickening swoop into the night sky.

A white-hot stab of pain at his side. Bottom of the vest. *Fuck.*

He risked a one handed hold to reach down and touch it. He pulled his hand back drenched with blood.

Shit. If he bled too much he could pass out. Fall to his death on the rocks down there. The chopper was climbing swiftly. The fall getting longer by the second.

Nah. Not happening. Not tonight.

He hung on to his perforated guts, to the ladder, to consciousness. Tried to climb, but that wasn't happening either.

Hanging on. All he could do.

Sisko was yelling down, mouth open. Confused, frustrated. Asa conserved his energy. None left for yelling back.

Good thing Sisko was a big muscular brute. Braced at the door, he hauled both Asa and the ladder up by himself, then seized Asa by the arm and pulled him inside.

"What the fuck?" he snapped. "You hurt? Shot?"

"Some," Asa gasped out. The rest of the team was all bent over Luke. "Took a round. It'll wait."

Sisko turned away and Asa crumpled into the metal framing, out cold.

Luke was in a deep well. Impossibly deep. Clinging to the sheer side.

The wet rock walls were disintegrating, chunks falling down into nothingness without a sound. He felt so heavy. So tired. His fingers shook with strain. He wouldn't be able to hang on much longer. About to fall.

No. He felt a desperate urgency. *Don't let go.* A voice, low and pleading. *Please, baby. Come back to me.*

Light burst in his head. Pain detonated in his chest and screamed though his failing body. His heart seized…and stopped …

Started.

After a while, he started to see again. There were anxious faces hanging over him. Glowing greenish from his night vision implants. Their names were out of reach, but he knew their eyes.

"Luke? Can you hear me?" The beautiful shining woman with the wild curls and the bright furious eyes. "Luke! Guys, his eyes are open!"

Luke. Yeah. His name was Luke. Right. Good to know.

"Jesus, man." Another man, leaning over him. "He kill coded you! And your heart's beating again!"

Got the idea from you, you sneaky bastard, he wanted to say to his brother, but couldn't find enough air. Hibernation mode. He'd gone into hibernation mode as soon as Hale had stun coded him. Worth a shot, to see if he could live just a little bit longer.

He had. Holy fucking shit, he *had.* He was still here.

They lifted him carefully to a semi-sitting position. Sisko wrapped a thermal blanket around his shoulders and Dani hugged him, resting her forehead on his shoulder.

He looked around, taking stock. Zade was on the other side of him, slumped in exhaustion, a bloody bandage around his thigh. Ivy was huddled between two crates of equipment, eyes huge and shocky. Crazy spikes of dark hair stuck straight up from her scalp. She'd been snugly wrapped in a thermal blanket. Even swaddled, she looked so damn small.

God only knew what shape she was in, but she was alive. It was a start.

Hannah lay on the other side of Zade, unconscious. As far as he could tell with an ASP scan, her vitals were steady, but he didn't like the waxy stillness in her face.

A guy he didn't recognize was slumped on the other side of the helicopter, head resting on a bundle of gear. ASP surged again automatically to analyze the guy's vitals, his thermal sig. A lot of blood had leaked out, pooling beneath him.

He gathered up all the energy he had to speak. "Hey," he said, glancing toward the mystery man. "That guy. He's dying."

Sisko and Zoe turned instantly to help. A flurry of activity. Good. Handled.

Luke felt Dani's hand slide into his and managed to squeeze it. Contact with her gave him energy. Enough to lift her hand to his lips and kiss it.

She leaned down, spoke right into his ear. "I thought I'd lost you. I thought you'd let go. Left me."

It took a minute to gather the energy to speak again. "I stuck around for you."

She waved her hand. "Zoe brought you back," she said. "She did…something to you. Put her hands on your chest."

He pondered that. "She pulled me out of the well," he said. "But the strength to hang on…that was from you."

She laughed through her tears. "Come on. You're the strongest dude I know."

"You gotta be strong for something. Or someone. Or it's all for nothing."

She cuddled closer. "Great," she said fiercely. "Fine. Be strong for me, if that works for you."

"It works," he whispered. "Works great."

Then she was kissing him, and that was great, too.

Hey. The fuck? Why didn't you say you were gutshot? You asshole!

Sisko's furious voice seemed to come from miles away. Asa didn't have the juice to respond. He had nothing to say for himself anyhow. *You guys were busy. Luke was dead. Zade was shot. Hannah was down. Didn't seem like the right moment.*

It was the right moment now, though. The only moment. He fought to stay conscious. Zoe hung over him, her beautiful dark eyes slicing right into his mind. Yelling orders at him. Wow, look at that. What a fucking trip. He liked getting attention from her.

I'd obey you if I could, girl. I'd be gooder than a goddamn angel. But I'm all messed up right now. Ain't happening. Sorry.

Still, he couldn't look away. The exploring pressure of her hands on his ripped up guts was burning, twisting agony. He inhaled to scream—

And the pain was gone. He stood in a strange, misty nowhere. An in-between place. Quiet, glowing.

Zoe stood there with him. Asa looked around. "Am I dead?" he asked.

"Not yet," she said.

"Where the hell are we?"

"Shhhh," she soothed, taking a step toward him. "I don't know. It's the place I always go when I do this. Don't worry about it." She reached out as if to embrace him.

He flinched back, startled. "What are you doing?"

"Don't be afraid," she said gently. "I won't hurt you."

He felt vaguely stung. "Not afraid. Just confused."

"You don't have to understand," she said. "Just…let me."

And she was right there, all around him. Like she was hugging him, but it was more than that. An incredible heat raced through him. Like they were a single column of fire.

He felt her. All of her. Merged with her. No boundaries. He saw her like he'd never seen anyone, or imagined seeing anyone.

The intimacy was unspeakable. Unbearable. It burned him.

Changed him.

Asa broke away from the contact, shocked and scared. The image dissolved, and he was back in the dark and noise and pain, guts screaming again. Zoe shouting to Sisko, her voice tight and businesslike as she pressed a folded piece of cloth to his wound.

A big chunk of her shirt was torn off. Same material, he noticed. Huh.

"He's stable now, but he needs a transfusion fast, and surgery," she was saying. "Tell Simone to head for a major trauma center with a helipad. Let them know we're coming. And think of something good for the cops. A jealous husband, maybe."

"Fuck no," Asa forced out. "I don't do married chicks."

"Is that so. All right. A drug deal gone bad, then. If you like that better." She pressed down slightly on the cloth, but wouldn't look at him.

"What the fuck just happened?"

She shrugged. "You panicked," she said. "You broke the link."

"I…I did what? What link?"

"Nothing." Her voice was impatient. "It's OK. What I did was enough. Now you just need to get patched up. We'll be at a hospital soon. Everything's under control."

"What did you do to me?" he insisted.

She sighed in frustration. "I got the bleeding to stop, obviously."

"Right. With the magic cloth from your healing shirt," he said.

Her eyes flicked down to his, and as quickly away again.

"What was that…place?" he asked.

"Nothing. You were dreaming," she said crisply. "Shhh. Don't think about it."

But she wouldn't meet his eyes.

CHAPTER 31

D ani had no idea where she was when she opened her eyes.
She lay in a comfortable bed. No one else had slept in it. On the other side, the pillow, sheets and coverlet were undisturbed.

Luke. Wherever he was resting, it wasn't in her bed. Where the hell was he? And how could she have zonked out when Luke's heart had just stopped and restarted? What the fuck was she thinking?

She dragged herself to a sitting position. *Ouch.* She was sore and bashed up every which way. Scrapes and cuts and bruises everywhere, bandages and tape wound all around her.

She wore a man's big soft sweatshirt. A pair of neatly folded yoga pants were draped over the foot of the bed. Pulling them on hurt. Ouch. She was creaky and stiff.

The room had French doors that opened onto a terrace with a panoramic view of the ocean and the hills. She pulled them open, filled her lungs with cool, sweet air.

She couldn't tell what time it was, the sky being overcast, but she smelled coffee and food, so she followed the aromas out into a corridor. From there she passed into a simply furnished living room.

In front of a big TV was a soft, fuzzy white rug with a pink fleece blanket crumpled on it. Stuffed animals were scattered around it. Probably for Ivy. This room was so tidy. The kid stuff was brand new. Any kid who'd lived here for long would have left more of a mark on the place.

Dani continued onward through the house, following the sound of voices now. A turn and a few steps down took her into a huge kitchen.

Luke, Zade and four other people were seated sitting around a large table, Ivy among them. She saw Zoe, the beautiful dark-haired girl who looked like Jada, and a pretty young woman with lots of freckles, long, wavy red hair and golden eyes. There was also a tall, muscular guy with long, tousled dirty blond hair.

Ivy sat between Luke and Zade, perched on a pillow booster tied to the kitchen chair, in purple leggings, a pink sweatshirt and bunny slippers. A fuzzy pink knit hat covered her head, the same color as the upside down stuffed cat she was hugging, although the cat was twice as fuzzy.

Her shadowy gaze fastened onto Dani, brightening when Dani blew her a kiss. She stuck up her small hand and caught the kiss. A good sign. But the plate of food in front of her looked untouched.

Luke rose to his feet. "Dani! I didn't want to wake you. You OK?"

"Fine." She smiled at him and nodded at the rest of them, feeling self-conscious. "Just wondering where you were. Had to be sure you were all right."

"I'm great," he assured her.

Dani moved closer to Ivy, who hugged her stuffed cat right side up now, her wide-open dark eyes taking it all in.

"Hey there, sweetheart," she said to the child. "I'm glad to see you. How are you doing?"

Ivy opened her mouth, and tried to speak a few times. Finally she blurted out something unintelligible, in a hoarse, scratchy voice.

Dani leaned closer. "I didn't catch that, honey."

"It's not English," Zade told her. "It's a random mix of languages. Her databases got scrambled somewhere along the line. If I understood it right, she told you that she likes her new clothes, and her cat. And her cinnamon roll."

"Oh," Dani murmured, seeing the goopy roll clutched in the girl's small hand. "Well, good for her. They do look yummy. I might have one of those myself."

Dani leaned down, and pressed a very gentle kiss onto the top of the girl's fuzzy pink hat, and almost yelped when Ivy grabbed her suddenly around the waist. Her wiry little arms shook with tension.

Dani's heart melted in a hot rush. She hugged Ivy back, her eyes fogging up.

The room got quiet. Everyone suddenly fascinated with his or her coffee.

As quickly as she'd begun, Ivy let go and almost dropped the cat. She whispered something into its plush ear. Who knew what.

Dani put a soothing hand on the little girl's back. "Where are we?" she asked the group.

"This is my house," the dark woman said. "A little north of San Francisco. I'm Zoe. This is Hannah, and this is Sisko."

"Hey." Dani smiled around at them. "I seem to remember more people in the helicopter."

"There were more," Zade said. "Asa, Hannah's brother got himself all shot up. He's in the hospital. A guy named Brenner was there, and Simone, my wife. She piloted the chopper when Brenner got zapped by Luke's freq scream. They both flew back up to Seattle this morning. To prep for Luke's treatment. And Ivy's."

"Treatment?"

"To scrub out the control codes," Zade explained. "Like she did for me."

Dani looked at Luke, wide-eyed. "Holy shit," she said. "You can do that? Is that dangerous?"

The men exchanged glances. "Do you mean, ah…more dangerous than having control codes in the first place?" Luke asked cautiously. "That's kind of hard to quantify."

Dani waved a hand at them. "Never mind," she muttered. "Dumb question. Don't answer. I just forgot for a second who I was talking to. My bad."

Luke reached out for her. Dani leaned into the embrace, pressing her ear against the warm bare skin revealed by his open flannel shirt.

The slow, heavy throb of his heart was the sweetest, most desirable sound in the world. It brought tears to her eyes, but there were too many people here to indulge in a tender moment. Luke was nuzzling the top of her head, and that was not helping one bit.

She got herself under control before she turned to the people at the table.

"Thank you all for coming to get us," she told them.

They exchanged grins. "No problem," said the blond guy that Zoe had called Sisko. "Thank you for keeping this bozo alive for us."

"Actually, it was him who kept me alive," she corrected.

"Nah," Luke said. "We took turns."

His dark hair was growing in. So was that sexy beard stubble. He couldn't seem to stop petting her back. Long gentle strokes, from shoulder to hip, like he didn't quite believe she was real and had to be constantly reminded.

"What about the other guy?" Dani asked. "The one who got shot? Is he OK?"

"Asa. My brother," the girl named Hannah said. "He'll be all right, but he's in a foul mood. He hates lying still."

"Here, sit down," Luke said, gesturing at the chair he'd occupied, next to Ivy. "I'll get you coffee. And a plate."

Dani got a few bites of omelet down and a little bit of toast, but she wasn't quite ready yet to face food. The coffee was awesome, though. Hot and strong.

She stared around the table at Luke's people as they ate together. Talking, teasing, laughing at their own inside jokes. Grateful to be alive, and to be with each other.

It came over her, all at once. The sadness she hadn't yet had the space or time to feel.

"What is it?" Luke leaned closer, concern on his face. "You OK?"

Of course, he'd notice. He saw everything that flashed across her mind.

She swallowed over the lump in her throat. "I guess I'm just…jealous all of a sudden." Her voice was halting. "Seeing you guys together. Looking out for each other. That's what Naldo was for me. Family."

He slid his hand into hers, fingers entwined. "I know. I'm sorry."

"He would have liked this." She nodded down the table at the rest. "All of this."

"I wish he were here with us," Luke said.

She rubbed her eyes fiercely. "Me, too."

Ivy spoke, another unintelligible burst. The only word Dani caught was 'Naldo.'

Dani looked wildly from Zade to Luke. "What? What did she say about him?"

"She says Naldo was her friend," Luke translated. "He was nice to the kids. Brought them candy sometimes. When no one was watching. And he turned on the TV to cartoons."

Ivy smiled and slipped down from her pillowed chair, aiming a string of words at Luke, and a questioning look.

"You bet," he replied, pointing to a TV in an alcove just outside the kitchen. The TV snapped on as she made her way over to it, tuning itself to a cartoon channel.

Dani wondered if Luke had turned it on or if Ivy herself had done so, but didn't have a chance to ask. Zoe suddenly got up and deposited her coffee cup on top of the dirty dishes in the sink. She looked over at Dani like she was bracing for pain.

"You saw the most of my sister," she said. "Tell me what you saw."

Dani's throat tightened again as she searched for words. "She was…heroic."

Zoe stared at her, expressionless. "Details. Please." Her voice was clipped and flat.

"Hale ordered her to shackle me in his quarters," Dani began.

Zoe nodded. "They told me."

"I think she was fighting stim sickness even then. Her face was flushed and she was sweating. When we got up to his room, I…I spoke your name. I think she had another…attack, I guess you'd say. With her in that condition, I was able to, ah…" Her voice trailed off. Damn. This was awkward.

"Able to what?" Zoe prompted.

"I got the stun baton away from her," Dani said uncomfortably. "I used it on her. Cuffed her wrists to the bed. Took her clothes. So I could pretend to be one of them."

Zoe nodded. "I see."

"Before I left the room, I told her that you loved her," Dani said. "I said that you never stopped looking for her. I kissed her on the forehead. I said it was from you."

Zoe turned away. Her black hair fell forward and hid her face.

"In the end, she saved us," Dani went on. "She killed Hale with her crossbow. I tried to get her to come with us. She said no. That it was too late for her."

Zoe, quietly. "Go on."

"The last thing she did for us was to blast the roof in the cave with her rifle," Dani said. "She brought down a bunch of rocks. To block the others from pursuing us. But before she did that, she blew a kiss. She said it was for you."

Zoe opened the door to a patio behind her kitchen and went outside. The door swung shut behind her.

The room was silent. Everyone's face down, or turned away.

Hannah blew her nose into her napkin and stood up. "Um…I'm making a run to the hospital," she said, hurrying past with her face averted. "Gotta check on Asa."

Zade was next. "Need to call Simone," he said as he strode past them. "See how she's doing on that treatment prep."

That left Sisko and Ivy. Sisko gulped down the last of his coffee and got to his feet.

"Ivy and I have a Netflix date," he said. "There's this show we watch, on the jumbo widescreen in the den. Unicorns and friendly dragons. Whaddaya say, Ivy?" He held out his hand to her. "Want to binge with me?"

Ivy got to her feet with a big smile, stuffing the rest of her cinnamon roll into her mouth. She took Sisko's huge hand with her small, sticky one and said something incomprehensible, but it sounded enthusiastic.

Sisko glanced at Dani. "She's totally on board with the unicorns," he translated for her. He squeezed Luke's shoulder as he passed. "Later, dude."

And they were alone.

CHAPTER 32

Luke had to break eye contact first. He just couldn't maintain it. It was too much. She was so fucking beautiful, with her curly hair flying all over the place. Those gorgeous green eyes full of light. He felt weirdly shy. Out of nowhere.

He gestured toward a door leading out onto a small side patio. Could be slightly more private. Which was to say, it lowered their probability of having every last word overheard by his Midland family from a hundred percent to maybe ninety-seven percent. But whatever.

After what they'd been through, he couldn't really see that as an actual problem.

They stepped outside. The fragrant, rain-drenched shrubbery around them created a semblance of privacy. Wind chimes hung from the porch roof tinkling and clanking with the slightest breeze. The metallic harmony got his ASP humming along with its calculations, but he stopped it cold.

All he wanted to do was look at her. Convince himself that this was real. They'd actually made it through. They were still there, and alive. Both of them.

His people, too. Miraculously alive and safe. As safe as it was possible to be.

But the look in her eyes worried him. Like she wanted to smile but wouldn't let herself. The wind ruffled her dark curls. Her eyes were bright and clear as she waited patiently for him to speak.

He took her hand, that being as good a place to start as any. "Dani."

She covered his battered knuckles with her other hand, assessing the new scrapes and slashes. The bands around his wrist from the night with the Manticore wakey-wand were now just bands of shiny pink. She traced them tenderly with her fingertip. The sensation went straight to his dick.

Not now. This was not what this conversation was about. Later for that.

"It's incredible," she murmured. "How fast you heal. I totally love that."

"Dani," he said roughly. "The last time I tried to say this you shut me down."

She opened her mouth to reply, but he hurried on. "Let me finish. You thought I was too messed up. For what I said to be real, I mean."

"Luke," she said gently.

"I know you think you can't trust what I say to stay true. But I—"

"I trust you," she said.

He stopped, reeling. "Huh?"

"I trust you now," she said again. "With my life. You're as solid as a rock. Say anything and I'll believe you. You always came through for me. Even when I didn't trust you, you came through just the same. I think you're awesome."

His mind had gone blank. No words. All he could do was feel this wild new feeling inside him. Like the sun coming up, but inside his chest. Shining out of his face.

"Damn it," he said. Confused, but in a good way. "Now I lost my thread."

Dani lifted his battered knuckles, kissing any patches she could find of unscabbed skin. "Take your time," she said softly. "I'm not going anywhere. We'll find your thread together."

"But…you saw Obsidian. You saw what's hunting us. Can you deal with that?"

Her mouth twisted in a mischievous smile. "It's a little late to ask me that," she teased. "I'm on their hit list now whether I like it or not. They saw me, they've got me on video, they can probably even get samples of my DNA if they try. And so?"

"But…but your chance of having a normal life is gone."

She shrugged. "My former normal life wasn't all that freaking fabulous anyhow. I'm going to miss Millie, and my friends, and the good people I worked with. But I hope there's some way for me not to leave them hanging, wondering where I disappeared to. I hate to do that to them. It's cruel, and rude."

"There isn't a way," Luke said. "Not until we take Obsidian out for good."

"OK," she agreed promptly. "So let's do it."

He blinked, and realized he was grinning. "Just like that."

She shrugged. "Somebody's got to."

He laughed out loud. God, he loved this woman. This kickass, badass, gorgeous woman. "Wow," he said. "Ambitious."

"That's me." Her eyes were so direct. "Evildoers, watch out. They're going down."

He nodded. "OK. So, that's the grand plan. But in the meantime, we need, you know. A life."

"I'm looking forward to that. You're fun. And hot. And incredibly fine. You know what? I can't wait to get you alone. So I can totally blow your mind."

"Oh, yeah," he groaned under his breath. "Oh, please."

"Preferably someplace where your family can't hear us," she added demurely.

"Uh…I'll think of something." *Fast.* He was already evaluating possible places.

But Dani wasn't finished. "If I have to look over my shoulder for Obsidian goons for the rest of the foreseeable future, it better be with a sexy badass supersoldier who has my back. And heats up my bed."

"Anytime," he said distractedly. "You got it. I'll do anything you want me to do. But I want to be more than that to you. I want to be your man. I want everything. I love you, Dani LaSalle."

She laughed, but her eyes were wet. "You take everything so literally. Let me spell it out for you. I love you right back, Luke Ryan. I want to be your woman, your lover, your wife. I want the whole package. All of it. You and me. For as long as we get."

There was nothing left to say now that couldn't be said better by wild kissing. So they got right to it.

If you liked *In My Skin*, keep reading for a peek at the first two Obsidian Files books, *Right Through Me* and *My Next Breath*, both available now!

If you enjoyed this book, please consider leaving a review! I would appreciate it tremendously, and it helps your fellow readers to find their next great read. Thanks!

RIGHT THROUGH ME

Stranger, speak softly . . .

Biotech tycoon Noah Gallagher has a deadly secret: his clandestine training as a super-soldier gives him abilities that go far beyond human. Yet he's very much a man. When Caro Bishop shows up at his Seattle headquarters with a dangerous secret agenda, his ordered life is thrown into chaos. Caro is a woman like no other—and her luminously sensual beauty cloaks a mystery he must solve.

Caro's lying low, evading a false charge of murder. She means to clear her name, and she'll do whatever it takes to survive—but seducing a man like Noah is more than she bargained for. His amber eyes have the strangest glow when he looks at her—she could swear he sees the secrets of her heart. The desire smoldering in Noah's eyes awakens her own secret hunger, but Caro has to resist his magnetic pull. Anyone close to her becomes a target. The only right thing to do is run, far and fast, but Caro can't outrun Noah's ferocious intensity—or deny the searing passion that explodes between them.

Nothing else matters—until a vicious enemy bent on the ultimate revenge puts his murderous plan into play. Noah and Caro must battle for their lives . . . and their love . . .

CHAPTER 1

Someone just cut the lights. What the hell?

Noah Gallagher put down his pen and looked around, startled, as drums began to thump from the hidden sound system of the penthouse conference room. Some exotic instrument joined in, throbbing and wailing.

The door to the conference room opened to a shimmery jingling sound, then a flash of fluttering purple. Everyone at the table was staring and murmuring.

Oh, Christ. Not possible. Noah rose to his feet, but the belly dancer was already halfway through the door, her hands weaving in a hypnotic pattern. Wide, light-catching green eyes laughed at him brazenly as she shimmied straight toward him, leading with one pulsing hip.

Her eyes caught him . . . and held him.

The world narrowed down. Whatever he was going to say or do stopped. Words were gone. Air was gone. Air didn't matter. Nothing moved while she moved.

She had commandeered all movement. With that smile. Those eyes.

He was sitting again, with no memory of deciding to do so. His mind had gone blank. The woman was like a walking, breathing stun code, personally keyed to him. He'd always wondered how it would feel to be one of the unlucky chosen few at Midlands who'd gotten stun and kill codes embedded in their minds. His own brain implants had been bad enough. Stun and kill codes were worse.

But this dancer wasn't a goddamn stun code. She was just a random woman, shaking her stuff. When her act was done, he'd pull it together. Exert the fucking authority he was entitled to as the CEO of Angel Enterprises.

He had exactly until the music stopped to get control of himself.

Simple enough to figure out who'd dreamed up this unwanted birthday present. His younger sister Hannah lurked by the door. The wide-angle enhancement of his sight made it possible to see the gleam in Hannah's eyes without looking away from the belly dancer for a single second.

Not that he could have looked away.

He saw his fiancée Simone's face with his peripheral vision. She'd chosen to sit at his side for this important meeting. It was painfully obvious from her tight, expectant smile that she was waiting for him to turn to her, to smile and laugh and make light of this stupid situation. Not just for her. For everyone in the room.

He couldn't do it.

Try. Do an analog dive. Grab a hook. Concentrate.

A spotlight from somewhere gilded the dancer's body, highlighting every perfect detail. Silver anklets that jingled over her small, bare feet. Golden toenails. Shapely legs flashed between purple veils that floated from a low-slung, glittering belt. The belt and top were swagged with shining chains and dangling beadwork. Still more chains, draped from an ornate headdress, dangled over her forehead and under her chin, creating a constant soft shimmer of sound.

High, full breasts quivered, lovingly presented in the spangle-studded velvet bra. She arched back, floating a purple veil edged with spangles high in the air above herself and swishing her thick fall of glossy black hair around. Had to be fake hair, falling to well below her ass. It brushed the curve of her hips. Fanned out as she twirled.

Everything he'd monitored in his peripheral vision was gone now. He no longer saw Hannah, or Simone, or anything else. His inner vision was too busy with the vivid fantasy of that woman straddling him. Imagining her bold, sensual smile as she swayed over him, teased him. Running her fingers through her hair, lifting it, tossing it. Coiling it around her waist like a slave rope.

He wanted to rip away all the filmy veils and all the goddamn beads and chains. See her bare-assed. Bare-breasted. Yeah.

The deep curve of her waist was perfectly shaped for his fingers to grip. The curves and hollows of her belly and her hips looked so soft. Touchable.

His hands shook with the urge to reach, stroke. Seize.

The rush of erotic images ramped up his advanced visual processor into screaming overdrive. Even with eyes shielded from eighty percent of the ambient light, even using a double layer of custom-designed shield specs, his AVP combat program was off and running, scrolling a thick column of data analysis past his inner eye.

And even that couldn't distract him from her show. Not for one instant.

His heightened senses reached out, so greedy for more that he found himself actually taking off the back-up shield specs. He'd have popped out the contacts, too, but his AVP was already going nuts at the lower protection level. Combine that with adrenaline, and a huge blast of sexual arousal—*fuck.*

The light level in this room could zap him into a stress flashback if he didn't protect his eyes. Not only that. The dark shield strength contact lenses hid the animal flash of amber luminosity caused by his visual implants. Outsiders couldn't be allowed to see that. The room was packed with outsiders. He wanted them gone.

Especially Simone. Which made him a total asshole. He tried hard, really hard, to feel guilty. Not so much as a twinge. His conscious mind had been almost totally hijacked by the dancer.

He wanted to throw everyone else out and lock the door. Study that woman with his naked eyes, dancing under the spotlight. But only for him. He wanted to gulp in the whole data flow. It was being filtered out in real time and lost to him forever, and it drove him . . . fucking . . . *nuts.*

And he couldn't do a thing. Not with an audience. His fists clenched in fury.

Heart racing, temperature spiking. Sweating profusely. No way to hide it. It was an AVP stress dump. A massive dose of fight-and-conquer energy, channeling straight into his dick, which strained desperately against his pants.

He struggled to grab onto the analog hooks that he'd established. His hooks were emergency mental shortcuts, activating an instant, deep withdrawal into the ice caves of his subconscious mind when the AVP got out of control. Best way he could devise to calm his stress reactions and stay on top of himself.

Not a hook to be had. Couldn't find them, couldn't feel them. Couldn't use his highly developed power of visualization at all, after years of grueling practice. All gone.

He was fully occupied imagining that woman naked and writhing beneath him.

His intense reaction to this spectacle made no sense. He'd seen belly dancing before and been unmoved. He did not have complicated fantasies or fetishes. He didn't even get the fun factor. He wasn't known for his sense of humor. In fact, he had no imagination at all, unless you counted biotech engineering designs, or plotting ways to grow his business, or scheming to keep his chosen family alive, secret, and safe.

That demanding enterprise left no bandwidth for fun and games.

He wasn't playful about sex, either. He was tireless, focused. Relentless in making sure that his partners were satisfied. To the point of exhaustion, even. Theirs, not his. They would tell him he was the hottest lover ever and then call him cold.

So? Noah didn't do emotions. Cold was safer for everyone concerned.

Not that he could explain that to whoever happened to be in bed with him.

He couldn't change his nature. He saw to it that his lovers had many orgasms to his one, to compensate for those mysterious intangibles. Whatever the fuck else they wanted from him, it just wasn't there. He didn't even know where to look for it.

The dancer's arms lifted, swayed. He inhaled the scent of her dewy skin as she spun closer. Fresh, sweet, hot. Sun on the flowers. Rain on the grass. His mouth watered.

Since what happened at Midlands, his senses were sharper than normal by many orders of magnitude. He had ways to blunt the overload, but not this time. He was catching a full data load now, shields and all. Tripping out on her undulating hand movements.

He was reading her energy signature, right through the shield lenses. A cloud of hot, brilliant colors surrounded her. Her floating purple veils blended with trailing clouds of her body's energy, to which his AVP overstimulated brain assigned all the colors of the spectrum and more besides. Colors not visible to anyone but him.

Along with it a strange sensation was growing. Tension, anticipation. Dread.

He was used to being alone in an insulated bubble. Other people's drama raged outside that protective barrier and left him completely untouched. He needed it that way to stay in control. Maintaining isolation required constant effort and vigilance.

Now, suddenly, he wasn't alone. The girl had danced through his force field. Invaded his inner space. It was messy and crowded in there now.

She took up room. Confused him with her colors, her scents. Her smile was so unforced and sensual. She was bonelessly flexible, yet still regal in her diaphanous veils.

It made him jittery to have someone so close. The intimacy felt awkward. Ticklish.

He felt hot, red. No control over his face. Stuck here, sitting among colleagues and family, right next to his fiancée. Any one of them could watch him watch her. At least the massive conference table concealed his colossal hard-on.

He had not felt this helpless since Midlands.

Her luminous green eyes met his and then flicked away, but the electric buzz of that split instant of intimacy jolted him to depths he'd never felt before.

He knew he'd never seen this woman before, and yet he recognized her.

Caro narrowly missed slamming her hip into the table. For the third time.

Look away from the guy, for God's sake. Get a grip. It's just a dance.

But her gaze kept getting sucked back to Noah Gallagher, the birthday boy. Ultra-powerful CEO of the oh-so-myserious Angel Enterprises, cutting-edge biotech firm.

The man was gorgeous. Barrel chested. A dense slab of muscle. Short hair showed off the sharp planes and angles of his face, a wide, strong jaw. He wore shaded glasses, but he'd taken them off a few seconds into her dance. It was incredibly hard to stay focused on the music and remember her moves while being examined with such blazing intensity. It wiped her mind blank. Made her lose the thread.

To say nothing of her physical balance.

Holy flipping *wow*. They said he was turning thirty-two today, but he seemed older, or maybe it was just his expression. Each time she twirled, she snagged a new yummy detail. The shape of his ears. Thick, straight dark brows. Sexy grooves framing a stern but still sensual mouth. Sharp cheekbones. His face was a taut mask of tension, as if he were suppressing strong emotion. But it was his eyes that really got to her.

His scorching laser focus made her temperature rise. She'd always been sensitive to the quality of a person's energy. Noah Gallagher's energy dominated the room. He looked like he'd tear you to pieces if you gave him any trouble, despite the elegant suit that sat just right on his huge shoulders. He didn't laugh or look embarrassed like most men did when surprised by a belly dancer. He just sat there, with the charged stillness of a predator poised to spring. Radiating danger.

Her smile faltered as she shimmied and spun. Suddenly, she was hyper-conscious of the erotic allure of the dance. His silent, very male sexual energy made it feel deadly serious. As if they were alone, and she'd been summoned for a private, uninhibited performance designed to drive him crazy.

Oh my. What a stimulating scenario.

She was actually getting aroused. For the love of God. Rising panic began to shred the sensation. Enough of this ridiculous crap. She had to get out of here, and fast.

Finish the dance. You need the cash. He's only a hot guy, not a celestial being. You're freaking yourself out. Chill. Usually she spread the wealth, bestowing flirtatious smiles on everyone. Not tonight. They weren't feeling it. Young men were usually always enthusiastic, and there were several of them here, but no one made a sound. Tension was thick in the air. No laughter, no snickering, no whistles.

Who cared. Her mind was fully occupied with the task of not gaping at Noah Gallagher's godlike hotness. Being aware of every inch of skin she displayed to him.

Her gaze bounced across the blond woman who sat next to him. A little younger, but not a colleague or an assistant. They sat too close together for that. The woman's mouth looked tight and miserable. Next to her sat a flushed, heavy older man who stared fixedly at Caro's beaded bra, nostrils flared.

Rise up, cupcake. Take back the power. This was a tough crowd, maybe, but everything was relative. The people in this room weren't trying to frame her for murder, kidnap her or kill her. And she certainly had the birthday boy's full attention.

So she'd play with it. What the fucking hell. That man needed to be humbled. To worship at the feet of her divine awesomeness. She'd dance like she'd never danced before, blow his mind, and melt away, forever nameless. Leaving him to ache and writhe.

That's right, big boy. Prepare to suffer.

But Noah Gallagher's fierce, unwavering gaze was having a strange effect on her. Ever since she'd gone into hiding, she'd had a sick, heavy lump in her belly. For months it had been sitting there, like a chunk of dirty ice that would not melt. But when she looked at him, that pinched coldness eased. It turned soft and warm and alive.

It felt amazingly good. Dancing for him, she could actually breathe again.

For as long it lasted.

The dance was ending. Caro sank to her knees, arching back in a pose of abandoned sensual ecstasy as the music reached its climax, luxurious fake hair brushing the ground in her grand finale. Dancing had never made her feel so naked before. She was stretched before him like a sacrificial virgin on an altar.

Take me.

The pose felt obscene, but only because there were other people in the room. If there hadn't been, it would have felt right. It would have felt . . . *hot.*

The sound of one person frantically clapping broke the silence. Hannah Gallagher, the girl who had hired her. Noah Gallagher's younger sister, from the looks of her.

Caro rose slowly to her feet. Noah Gallagher didn't applaud. He just stared at her, as if he wanted to leap over that table and pin her down.

Tension built like an electrical charge. The other people in the room looked up, down, anywhere but at her. Caro smiled brightly. Held her head as high as possible.

Not fair, to throw a paid performer into the middle of someone else's big fat faux pas and make her swim in it. Bastards.

"That was fabulous!" Hannah's voice was a little too high. "Thanks for a gorgeous dance, Shamira! Happy birthday, Noah! Wasn't she awesome, everyone?"

Not one yes. There was only dead silence, downcast eyes, awkward looks exchanged all around. And still, Noah Gallagher's devouring eyes.

So what. She'd stay dignified. While running for her life, fighting the powers of darkness, scrambling for money. Even if it involved putting on a scanty costume and shaking her booty for rude or indifferent strangers.

Or, in this case, one single intense, lustful, smoldering stranger.

She took a slow, deliberate bow, as if she were in front of an adoring crowd. Taking her own sweet time. Rubbing their faces in it.

Take that, you rude shitheads. Like it would kill you to clap.

She didn't need any validation from these self-important bio-tech-nerd idiots. Just her fee, which she would get whether they liked her performance or not.

Fuck 'em. She had things to do. Important things. After one more hungry peek at the mouthwatering godking. Lord, he was fine.

She flash-memorized him in one breathless instant, whipping her gaze away from his face before eye contact could start the inevitable sexual mind-melt reaction. Then she swept out of the room, chin up, shoulders back. A regal sweep of purple veils.

That was it. She would never see him again. She wasn't going to feel that hot rush of opening in her chest, ever again.

Suck it up. Ignore the lust buzz. Sport sex is reserved for normal people. Fugitives do without. And don't whine.

Hannah followed her out of the room, and slammed the door harder than was necessary. "You were gorgeous," she said fervently. "You're so talented. I'm so sorry they didn't clap or anything. I'm going to tell them all off. Noah will kill me, but I'm used to it."

"I'll rather not watch that," Caro said hastily. "I'll just be on my way."

"Oh no! Stay just a minute! You have to at least say hi to Noah. No matter what he says to me, he certainly enjoyed your dance. I'm the villain here. You're just an innocent bystander. Noah's very fair that way. And I'm sure he'll want to meet you!"

In your dreams, honey. "Let me, ah, change first," Caro said, backing away.

"You remember the way to the office? Come back after. I'll introduce you."

The door flew open. A man strode out, not the birthday boy. This one was tall, blue eyed and very built, his thick dark blond hair hanging down to his shoulders. His eyes flicked over her with controlled curiosity and then turned back to Hannah.

"What the *hell* were you thinking?" he asked.

Definitely her cue. Caro took off, hurrying back toward the nondescript office that'd served as a dressing room. She didn't even want to know what Hannah's answer might be. Not her family, not her fight.

Once inside the empty office, she could still hear them arguing from behind the door. Other people had gotten into the mix. Voices were being raised. Her heart pounded as she peeled off her costume and packed it up. She pulled on her shapeless street clothing, trying not to overhear. She had her own problems. Big nasty ones. Time to cruise discreetly away and let them get on with theirs.

Makeup pads got most of the paint off. She rolled the expensive dancing wig into its carrying bag, and put on her street wig, a thick brown bob with heavy bangs and wisps curling in around her face to conceal its shape. When she arrived, she hadn't worn the mouth prosthesis, which puffed out her cheeks and distorted her jawline. She'd figured that the coat and hat were enough weirdness for the client to swallow. But the job was done, and she hoped to God she could slink out unnoticed, so in went the mouth thing. Big tinted glasses finished the look, topped off by her hat with LED lights in the brim, ordered off the Internet to foil facial recognition software her pursuers might use to find her on social media.

Who knew if it really worked. At least the wide brim kept the Seattle drizzle off.

Her hands still shook as she pulled on her oversized black wool coat. The foam lining she'd sewn in bulked up her shoulders and hips. She looked sixty pounds heavier, and slightly humped.

At first, she'd tried changing the way she moved as part of her disguise, but after all the bodywork she'd done in college, she decided that the psychological toll of slumping and shuffling was dangerous to her soul. Inside her frumpy cocoon of foam and wool, she still had her pride and attitude. Hidden, maybe, but structurally intact.

When she exited the office, she looked like a sketch that had been blurred on purpose. Noah Gallagher would stare right through her even if she were inches away.

That thought was so depressing, she could barely stand to think it.

Chin up. She'd had her fun, turning him on. Time for the disappearing act. Eat your heart out, Laser Eyes.

But disappearing didn't feel powerful to her. It just felt flat. Empty and sad.

The route back to the elevators took her right past the conference room.

Hannah Gallagher and several others were still arguing outside it. If she kept her head down, turned the corner and cut swiftly across the open space, she'd only be in their line of vision for a few seconds. Then it was a straight shot to the elevator.

One, two . . . *go.*

When she was squarely in the danger spot, Noah Gallagher came out the door.

That was her undoing. She slowed down. Not consciously, but simply unable to resist the temptation to steal one last look at him before fleeing.

His gaze snapped onto her, like a powerful magnet coupling.

Oh, God. Oh, no. He strode through the center of the group, scattering them, and followed her. Even with her back to him, his eyes burned through her layered, ugly disguise, a focused point of heat against her concealed skin. She stabbed the elevator button. He was twenty yards away. Fifteen, and closing. Picking up speed.

He couldn't have recognized her. In this dreary get-up, she couldn't be more different from Shamira the sexy dancing girl. She barely recognized herself dressed like this. The door slid open. She lunged inside. No other riders, thank God.

"Hold the door!" Gallagher called, loping for the elevator.

Asfuckingif. She punched the close button, and the mechanism engaged.

Their eyes locked, as the doors shut in his face.

Her heart was thudding, as if she'd done something wrong and had almost gotten caught. Maybe he was just wondering who the scruffy stranger was. Dressed like that, she stuck out like a sore thumb in the muted corporate elegance of Angel Enterprises.

She hurried through the lavish front lobby. Outside, a cab was letting a passenger out. She bolted for it, waving it down.

Noah Gallagher emerged from the entrance just as her cab pulled away. His eyes locked onto hers again instantly. Even shadowed by the hat, obscured by the dark glasses, through the back window of a cab that was already a half a block away.

He started running after her. Right out onto the street. Eyes still locked. The contact felt like a wire, pulling tighter and tighter. Then the taxi turned a corner and he was lost to sight. It hurt. As if something vital had been snipped with bolt-cutters.

Her fizz of excitement died away. The cold lump of fear was back in place.

She was so sick of feeling this way. She wanted to yell at the driver to circle the block, just on the off chance of catching one last glimpse of Noah Gallagher. To feel something different than that cold, heavy ache in her core. Just for a second or two.

But she could not have this. Not even a stolen taste of it. She could not let lust trash her good judgment. She had to stay murderously sharp. Constantly on the defensive. Without rest.

Sexual frustration wouldn't kill her.

But there were other things out there that definitely could.

Keep reading for a peek of *My Next Breath*, the second installment in The Obsidian Files!

MY NEXT BREATH

Never count the cost ...

Zade Ryan. Rebel supersoldier. Nearly superhuman. On a desperate quest to rescue his missing brother Luke by any means possible. To do it, he must seduce the elusive Simone Brightman, inventor of the ingenious and deadly tech used to capture Luke and hold him prisoner, location unknown. Zade will do whatever it takes to get close to Simone. Her mysterious beauty and highly sexual allure have him at a disadvantage, but time is running out . . .

Simone is fighting battles of her own, on her own. Until Zade—six foot four of sinewy muscle and lethal combat skills—rescues her from street thugs and leaves her breathless. His smoldering black eyes and overpowering sensuality—and his seductive invitation to spend one wild, unforgettable night with him—prove too tempting to resist.

Their passionate encounter unleashes scorching desire that neither can control—leaving them vulnerable to their enemies who watch from the shadows and wait. And when they are lured into a trap by a monstrous killer hellbent on their destruction, they must fight with every weapon they have to save Luke, and each other.

Because one night together could never be enough—and they might not live to have another . . .

CHAPTER 1

That voice. Hers.

Zade isolated that sound from all the others competing to be heard: traffic, gusting wind, cold rain driving down on the black asphalt, dripping off the vinyl awning he lurked beneath.

Fading out. *Fuck.*

Zade listened hard for that free-floating sound thread, thin as a strand of spider-silk waving around out there in the humming urban buzz of Seattle.

Yeah. There she was. Coming out of the Mercer Center with some people. Adults and kids. Umbrellas whooshed open. Cars pulled up. A few taxis stopped. He heard her, talking, laughing, saying goodnight. A subtle thrill racked him as that low, husky female voice stroked delicately down his nerve endings.

Simone Brightman. He liked her voice.

His phone vibrated in his pocket. He checked the display.

cold out here wtf

He tapped back a response.

wait

Lightweights. His hired goons had been waiting hours in the rain. Boo-fucking-hoo. He was damp and chilled, too, but he wasn't bitching about it. Nor should he.

It was what he deserved for prowling around in the dark like a fucking criminal.

Whatever it took. He'd kill for information about his lost brother Luke. And what he was about to do fell way short of killing. Nobody was going to get hurt tonight. At least not physically.

Simone Brightman had to know something. And that was as far as he'd gotten. Months had crawled by without a single opportunity for a chance meeting with her. He'd plotted and schemed, increasingly frustrated. But no dice.

Mostly she stayed stubbornly locked in her house. No errands, shopping, gas stations, malls, post office, restaurants, movies. No workdays at her biomed lab, which used to be the sum-total of her life. This once-a-week math tutoring thing she did with kids was the only reason she'd gone out at all since she and Noah Gallagher broke their engagement.

She must be depressed. Fine. He could work with that. All she needed to make her misery complete was some mouth-breathing scum menacing her on a dark street.

Add terror to the mix. And himself, never on the side of the angels.

He followed a brief conversation she had with some kids on their way out of the Center. He could barely hear what they were saying, but they seemed to really like her.

"Get home safe. See you next week." There was laughter in her voice.

Finally it was just her, making her solitary way toward her car, not knowing that it had been disabled. About three blocks away now. Her rubber-soled lace-up leather boots squeaked.

Lately, for some unknown reason, she no longer bothered with her ultra-professional ice maiden look.

At first, he thought he'd miss that super-controlled vibe. It had been stimulating to watch that round, taut ass twitching purposefully along in tight pencil skirts as she went about her business, heels clicking.

Also gone: her sleek designer suits and smoothly styled hair. She'd been so tightly buttoned up it was actually kinda kinky-porno-hot. He got off on it.

Now when she got dressed, it was in battered jeans or pilled leggings, sloppy sweatshirts, full-length skirts. Black, horn-rimmed glasses so butt-ugly they passed for aggressively cool. Her curly blond hair—surprise, surprise, not smooth at all—was out of control, unless she bothered to pin it up or put it in a messy ponytail.

Her new look was as different from the old as it was possible to get. And it jazzed him just exactly as much. Go figure.

And he looked at her a lot. Getting surveillance vid-cams installed in her place had been a hell of a thing. Her home security was top of the line. He'd finally succeeded in maneuvering a few micro-drones through her front door, two while the housekeeper came in to clean, one while Simone was having groceries delivered. Completely silent, nearly impossible to see. One was perched on the kitchen light fixture. One was on a bedroom curtain rod. The last sat on one of the wall-mounted speakers in her living room.

She was always in her studio or bedroom. Always working. She slept very little, and ate so seldom it had actually started to worry him. The fuck? An adult human being couldn't live on yogurt, a slice of toast, and the occasional fucking fruit chunk. It was a miracle that she functioned at all.

Damn, now he'd lost the sound thread again. He reached for it—listening harder... *yes*. Rubber boot soles on the wet pavement. He'd know that little squeaky-squeak song anywhere. He'd memorized its exact rhythm and pitch.

Less than a block away now. He was already getting a whiff of her. Warm, female smells. He seriously dug that honeysuckle shampoo. Couldn't wait to sniff it at close range.

He stepped out of the shadow of the awning, and raised his hand to signal the men waiting down the street. One of them lifted his hand in response. They were ready. She was an easy target, parking an almost new Audi on a badly lit street like this.

His heart raced as his augmented sensory processor kicked into high gear, as if revving for combat. Which was overkill. He didn't need an ASP jolt for this. The Obsidian researchers had wired him and rewired him during the Midlands experiments on their quest to produce the ultimate, relentless war machine. The data that speed-scrolled over his field of vision whenever he was stressed was a constant reminder of how they'd changed him. Permanently.

But he ignored it. He'd stolen himself back. He and all the rest of the Midlanders. He was more than what Obsidian had tried to make of him. Fuck them all.

Tonight—for her—he needed to be funny, smart, and unthreatening, for starters. And good in bed, if he got lucky. Past experience suggested that he would. It was bad form to get cocky about it, but whatever. A guy could hope.

In fact, he quivered with hope. Watching Simone for two whole months had kept him perpetually half-hard. It wasn't like she was doing anything sexy. On the contrary. She mostly just sat there on the bed, cross-legged in a thick snarl of wires and cables, surrounded by screens, dressed in leggings and a sweatshirt. Braless. Eyes narrowed with ferocious concentration as she typed so fast and hard the detached wireless keyboard bounced against the mattress.

He loved how the mad typing made her nipples jiggle.

He could watch that for hours without losing interest. Simone Brightman's life was slit-your-wrists boring, yet watching her somehow kept him continually buzzed.

He was in a groove with surveillance monitoring. Forget sleep. Not happening, even thought he'd sworn never to inflict sentinel sleep on himself again after their escape from Obsidian's research facility at Midlands. He hated the way sentinel sleep made him feel. Constant vigilance turned even the strongest into a numb, circuit-fried robot, no matter how skillful he might be at alternating his brain hemispheres, resting one while using the other and blah-blah-di-fucking-blah.

He was good at it, yeah. And so? He was good at a metric fuckton of unspeakable things. That didn't mean he would ever do them again. He'd won his freedom back. Obsidian could go suck its own dick.

But he'd do sentinel sleep for Simone. He'd do any number of desperate, unspeakable things for a chance to find out what happened to his brother.

Besides, watching Brightman prance around in her underwear was no chore. She was so damn pretty it just turned his head around. Why sleep when he could look at that?

She was almost upon him. His ASP processor sent a fire-hose of data scrolling wildly up both sides of his field of vision. His senses sharpened to a level beyond painful. He hadn't expected this. Bullshit timing.

Her footsteps echoed in his ears, *boom-scrape-squeak.* Her soft breathing, the quick and steady drum of her heart. He smelled the warm mix of her hand lotion, her wool coat, the leather of her boots, heard the swish of her long skirt, the brush of wool tights between her thighs. He smelled the coffee she'd had not long ago and a hint of the vanilla flavored creamer she'd lightened it with. Whiffs of the perfume she used to wear back in her corporate days wafted out of her purse like little ghosts.

He also smelled the festering mouth-breathers who waited across the street.

His heart thudded loudly. In a few seconds, he'd see Simone in the flesh. The mysterious ex-fianceé of Noah Gallagher, Zade's friend and fellow Midlander rebel.

A woman who might or might not hold the key to the last possible clue that could lead him to his brother.

Or to his brother's bones.

That thought stabbed through him like a thin blade of ice just as Simone Brightman rounded the corner and hit his line of vision.

Showtime.

Of course she'd left her umbrella in the car on the one night that the rain decided to dial it up from the usual Seattle drizzle and start pelting down. At least she had the right boots for the rain these days. No more fancy designer shoes for her. She was done striving for feminine perfection. Who gave a shit?

Years of effort, down the drain. She was so done with it.

She tried to hang on to the happy buzz hanging out with her Sci-Tech team gave her. She loved those kids. Creative to the max. Going places, all of them.

They were a complicated bunch. Too smart for their own good. Builders, makers, coders, geeks, videogame nerds, hackers. She scrambled to keep their hungry, restless minds busy. They'd had a blast brainstorming tonight. Goofy, giddy fun.

Goofiness was in short supply in her life. Those kids had taught her how it felt.

There would be no more fun tonight, that was for sure. Her happy buzz was draining away and that strange roar was filling up her head again. Stabbing pains, flashing lights, and that constant, grinding noise.

It started last year after she broke up with her first fiancé, Jordan. Then, after the humiliating episode with Noah and his exotic belly dancer, the problem had gotten abruptly worse.

Stress, her family doctor said, before handing her a scribbled prescription and recommending hypnotism. *Not.* She did not want Dr. Laera's flesh-creeping hypnosis sessions, and the drugs the doctor prescribed put her into a robotic fog. She felt like crap most of the time, but she preferred misery to feeling nothing at all.

Lately, the predominant feeling had been fear. Because Mom's illness had started like this. Just exactly like this, when Simone was twelve.

You either inherited the gene mutation or you didn't. Don't anticipate the suffering. That way you suffer twice. Simone repeated that silent mantra as she turned the corner and hit the button on her key fob. The car squawked and flashed a greeting. Rain was beating down even harder now, so she made a dash for it, splashing through dirty water rushing through the gutter.

She pulled open the door and plopped down into the leather seat, shivering as she listened to the rain drumming on the roof.

Breathe. Think of nothing. Or just good things. She'd enjoyed four great hours with the Sci-Tech team. She could try to call Megan, her oldest friend ever since that first Mayburg summer internship years ago. They had shared an apartment through college and grad school. Two girl nerds against the world. The original idea had been for Megan to fly in to visit her and hold her hand while she got the test results. Then Megan's asshat boss insisted on sending her to some conference in England.

Still, evening in Seattle was morning in England. If anything could make her feel better, it would be hearing Megan's voice.

Get that heater going. She shuddered, teeth chattering, thinking of the hot tea she'd make at home. Honey and lemon, to warm her from the inside. Her hand was so cold and numb, she couldn't get the key into the ignition.

After a few stabs, it went in, but all she got when she turned it was *click, click, click.* No purr of a motor humming to life, no lights, no heater's comforting hum.

She tried again. *Click. Click.* Her car was dead. But it was an excellent car. Almost new. Recently serviced. What the hell?

She popped the hood and the trunk and got out. Rummaged through the odds and ends in the trunk until she found the flashlight, a super nerdy one that she could strap to her head like a spelunker. She grabbed a heavy wrench, just in case something needed banging back into place.

Lifting the hood, she saw the problem at once. The battery cables were ripped off the battery and cut so that they couldn't be reattached.

Someone had sabotaged her car.

Then she heard them. Men's voices, low and indistinct, but with an aggressive tone that made her skin crawl. They smelled. Armpit fug and cigarette ash.

Simone straightened and turned, shining her headlight into the reddened eyes of a beefy, thick-faced guy with patchy stubble. The man beside him was taller. Lanky and balding.

She tucked the wrench under her arm and yanked out her phone, backing away, but the first guy darted at her and knocked it out of her hand. It hit the brick wall behind her with a sharp crack and broke apart.

"Shit," he muttered. "Coulda sold that."

He followed her, his gag-inducing breath a hot cloud in her face. She waited one more moment…then whipped the pepper spray out of her pocket.

She blasted him right in the eyes.

He screamed and lurched back, pawing at his face. The taller man froze for a second, then his mouth twisted with rage. He leaped at her with a shout.

She slammed the wrench down across his forearm with all her strength.

He howled. Walloped her with his good arm across the side of the head. The wet street swung up and body-slammed her, knocking out her breath and her senses. Everything went dark.

When her hearing slowly came back, what she saw and heard made no sense.

A huge dark silhouette in violent motion. Arms, legs, moving too fast for her tear-blurred eyes to follow. Kicks and blows. Choked squeals of pain.

She focused on a huge, long-haired man in a black leather coat crouched near her, holding her second attacker, his arm clamped across the tall guy's throat. The trapped man thrashed, clawing at the powerful forearm that barely let him breathe.

"You laid your hands on her, asshole," the big guy said. "Bad call."

The guy coughed, sputtered. "But she hit me with a—oof!"

His voice cut off as the leather-clad man rose and let go suddenly. The guy stumbled, arms pinwheeling.

An enormous leather boot connected with his jaw. He yelped and hit the pavement, sprawled in a puddle.

Suddenly the leather-coat man was beside her, sliding an arm behind her back and propping her up. She realized, dazed, that she was lying in a puddle of rain.

"Hey," he said. "I saw that guy hit you. You okay? Are you hurt?"

She blinked, dumbstruck. The man before her was unbelievably handsome. Not a hallucination. She caught his scent. Leather, salt, musk. She drew it in again, greedily. "Y-yes," she stammered.

She did a swift inventory, assessing herself for damage. She was bruised and shaky. Her ear had gotten a sharp, head-ringing whack, but the sensation was fading, driven away by excitement and astonished goggle-eyed gawking.

"How's your head?" he asked. "Let me look at it. Any bleeding? A bump?"

"I'm fine," she said, meaning it. "I'm not concussed. I'm really okay." She looked around for the glasses that had been knocked off her face when she fell.

Her rescuer spotted them before she did and handed them to her. She dug around in her pockets for a tissue to dry them with. Too bad it was still raining hard. She longed to find out if sharp focus made him even more gorgeous.

A sound made them look around. The jaw-kicked attacker was dragging himself onto his knees. In the dim light from the streetlight, he ran a careful hand over his jaw. Then he spat out a bloodied tooth and stared at it in slack-mouthed disbelief.

The other man was rubbing his pepper-stung eyes. "Goddamn fucking *cunt!*" he howled, lurching toward her.

The man in black leather leaped up and blocked him with an uppercut that sent him flying backward into his companion.

The two men hit the ground together, sprawling and rolling.

"Get lost." Her rescuer's low voice was menacing. "And stay lost. Unless you want me to kick you down into the sewer. Got that?"

The men struggled hastily to their feet and broke into a shambling run. The pepper-sprayed guy banged into a street sign, bounced off, and reeled away into the darkness.

Simone stared after them, speechless. Her mind was blank.

The mysterious man crouched next to her again. Rain dripped over his starkly chiseled cheekbones and down to his jaw. He didn't seem to notice or mind.

His eyes were intent on her face. His hand came to rest on her shoulder. Through layers of cloth, the gentle contact felt like a bright electric shock, releasing a sweet shiver of goosebumps. Her spine straightened. Her chin rose.

She just stared, not caring how bedraggled she must look. Her mind was empty of such considerations. Even the scary, shocking thing that just happened had been pushed to the side. There wasn't enough space for that and this man to coexist in the same thought cycle. One thing at a time. Him first. For sure.

He waited. Patiently. A faint smile formed on his sensual lips. It suggested that he'd been through this before. Probably rescued spaced-out women from muggers all the time. He just crouched there and let her gawk, his face spotlit by the flashlight that had somehow stayed on her head.

Self-consciousness came flooding back. *Shit.* She must look crazy in that thing. She pulled it off. Her crocheted hat came off with it and she tried in vain to smooth down her hair. Her gaze darted around the empty street. Her hands had begun to shake.

"You okay?" he asked again. "I can take you to the emergency room."

"No," she said. "I'm fine. Thanks for…uh…that. What you did."

"It's nothing. I'm sorry it happened to you. Having trouble with your car?"

"Don't worry," she said hastily. "I'll take care of it."

He stepped toward the open hood. "Can I take a look?"

She tugged her hat back down over her damp hair. "No need," she told him. "I know what the problem is."

His eyebrow shot up. "Already? Really? You do your own car repairs?"

"I'm an engineer," she said. "I like knowing how machines work."

He nodded, thoughtfully. Then his gaze was caught by something on the ground gleaming wetly in the streetlight's glow. The wrench.

"Oh. That's mine," she told him.

He picked it up and looked it over. "This is what you used on that fuckhead?"

She nodded.

"I have one just like it," he said conversationally. "Engines turn me on. I like tearing them apart and putting them back together."

"You're a mechanic?"

Her incredulous tone made him grin, which carved deep, beautiful grooves into his cheeks. "What? I don't look like one?"

No. You look like a sexy movie vampire, a famous extreme athlete, a billionaire rock star. Somehow, she managed not to blurt it out.

He changed the subject. "So what's the problem with the car?"

"The, ah, battery cables were cut."

"I see," he said. "So that's that. You're not going anywhere in this car tonight."

"Nope. I need a tow truck and a taxi. But those guys trashed my phone."

His face darkened. "Use my phone. I'll make the calls for you if you want."

"Thanks, but I still want my phone. Even if it's in pieces." She tried to get up, but her legs wobbled and she thudded down into the puddle again.

"Let me help you." He rose to his feet, bearing her up with him in an effortless anti-gravity surge. She floated up and just kept on floating. At least that was how it felt. Even the waterlogged skirt that clung to her legs couldn't weigh her down.

He helped her collect the pieces of her phone. The screen was broken and the battery knocked out, but she found all the parts and slid them into her coat pocket.

Then she just stood there. Foolish, half-frozen, and tongue-tied.

"I have a suggestion," he said. "You're soaked. There's a bar down the street. Let's go in there to warm you up while we call the tow truck and the taxi. I'm Zade, by the way. Zade Ryan."

She took his hand. The zing that raced up her arm from contact with his warm palm was just like the thrill she'd felt when he touched her shoulder, but a hundred times stronger. "Ah…I'm, ah, Alison," she lied, on impulse. "Alison Wilson."

"Alison." The fake name was a velvety caress coming from his mouth. "Can I buy you a drink?"

Her voice was locked in her throat. A barrier between two warring realities.

True Fact #1: Not smart to go to a skeevy dive bar with a huge guy in black leather who appeared out of nowhere on a dark street corner in a bad neighborhood. In the driving rain. Next to her dead car. Her shattered phone. Even if he had rescued her. Not smart at all.

True Fact #2: He *had* rescued her.

True Fact #3: It was impossible to look away from him. A diamond stud earring glinted between the thick wet locks of his black hair. The effect was intensely masculine. He wore a metal pendant in the hollow of his collarbone, which caught the light, flashing like a mirror. Raindrops made their slow, loving way along the bold slash of his dark eyebrows, over his cheekbones, his hawk nose, his sensual mouth.

He stood there dripping, pulsing waves of raw sexual energy at her. What in the freaking *hell* would she do with all of that?

Which brought her around to True Fact #4: She was a repressed, workaholic nerd with no life, and this astonishing man-god seemed to be almost, well, coming on to her. At least she was about ninety-five percent certain that he was. She'd never been great at decoding nonverbal male/female interaction.

Maybe he flirted with every woman he saw. Some men didn't know any other way to relate to a woman. Maybe this was just him being nice. Could be that the whole thing was just a hopeful fantasy on her part. Maybe she was projecting all this.

Then he smiled down at her. Mmm. Maybe not.

Besides, she'd now inevitably arrived at her ultimate destination, which was True Fact #5. Nobody got out of this world alive.

Tomorrow she had an appointment with Dr. Gregory Fayette. He would give her the final word on whether she'd inherited the gene mutation that would change everything.

If the news was bad, well, rolling around with a red-hot leather-clad bad boy was a bucket-list classic.

One night. No names. No numbers.

Get *Right Through Me* here!
Or try *My Next Breath* here!

Join Shannon's newsletter mailing list to never miss a new book or a fabulous promo! http://shannonmckenna.com/connect.php.

Follow her on Bookbub to receive new release and discount alerts! https://www.bookbub.com/authors/shannon-mckenna

MEET SHANNON MCKENNA

Shannon McKenna is the NYT bestselling author of seventeen action packed, turbocharged romantic thrillers, among which are the stories of the wildly popular McCloud series and her scorching new series, The Obsidian Files—rip-roaring romantic suspense with a sci-fi twist. She loves tough and heroic alpha males, heroines with the brains and guts to match them, villains who challenge them to their utmost, adventure, scorching sensuality, and most of all, the redemptive power of true love. Since she was small she has loved abandoning herself to the magic of a good book, and her fond childhood fantasy was that writing would be just like that, but with the added benefit of being able to take credit for the story at the end. Alas, the alchemy of writing turned out to be messier than she'd ever dreamed. But what the hell, she loves it anyway, and hopes that readers enjoy the results of her alchemical experiments.

She loves to hear from her readers. Contact her at her website, http://shannonmckenna.com, like her on Facebook at https://www.facebook.com/AuthorShannonMckenna/ or join the newsletter by signing up here: http://shannonmckenna.com/connect.php.